Other Books by Robert Hinshaw

Ethnography

Panajachel: A Guatemalan Town in Thirty-Year Perspective,
1975, University of Pittsburgh Press

Memoir and Biography

Currents in Anthropology: Essays in Honor of Sol Tax
(Editor), 1979, Mouton Publishers

*Living with Nature's Extremes: The Life of Gilbert Fowler
White,* 2006, Johnson Books

Fiction

The Rape of Hope, 2008, Look Back Books (Companion
novel to *My Lake at the Center of the World*)

My Lake
at the Center
of the World

AN HISTORICAL NOVEL

ROBERT E. HINSHAW

 Look Back Books

Published by Look Back Books
    13013 State Line Rd. Suite 200
    Kansas City, MO 64145
    E-mail: lookbackbooks@sbcglobal.net

ISBN 978-0-9814752-0-2

Printed in the United States of America

Acknowledgments

I owe my greatest debt of gratitude to the countless members of the Panajachel community of Mayas and Ladinos: to neighbors during two stints of field research in the 1960s and 1980s, and to research informants and friends surrounding Lake Atitlan over forty-five years of association. I dedicate the first of these companion novels to Licenciado Juan de Dios Rosales of Panajachel, my Maya assistant during 1963-65 fieldwork. I dedicate the sequel to Sol and Gertrude Tax who introduced me to Guatemala. As my mentor at the University of Chicago, Sol generously bequeathed to me much of the data he had gathered — also with the able assistance of Juan de Dios Rosales — from a decade of fieldwork in the Midwestern highlands beginning in 1933.

Friends too numerous to list in full have critiqued one or more of the many drafts of these novels or provided counsel with their publication. With apologies to those who go unmentioned, I thank in particular David Butler, Ben Fuson, Sterling Olmsted, Mira Perrizo, Betty Randal, Herbert Smith, Ardith Tjossem, and friends with Guatemalan career involvements Richard and Betty Adams, Elizabeth Bell, Christopher Lutz, Paul and Mary McKay, and Ralph Lee Woodward, Jr. Elisabeth Nord orchestrated the graphic design. My wife Linda assisted with editing and provided the encouragement to see the endeavor through to publication, patiently enduring my many absences over the course of the past decade of writing in Guatemala.

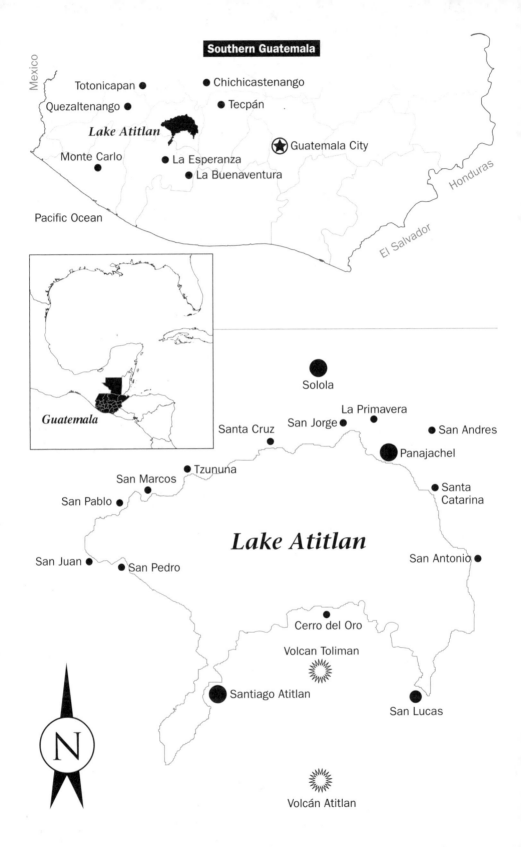

Southern Guatemala

Mexico

Totonicapan ●   ● Chichicastenango

Quezaltenango ●   ● Tecpán

Lake Atitlan

Monte Carlo   ⬟ Guatemala City
●   ● La Esperanza
      ● La Buenaventura

Pacific Ocean

Honduras

El Salvador

Guatemala

Solola ●

La Primavera
San Jorge ●   ●
Santa Cruz ●   ● San Andres

Panajachel ●

San Marcos   Tzununa
●   ●   ● Santa Catarina
San Pablo ●

Lake Atitlan

San Juan ●   San Antonio ●
      ● San Pedro

Cerro del Oro ●

Volcan Toliman
✳

Santiago Atitlan ●   San Lucas ●

N

✳
Volcán Atitlan

My Lake at the Center of the World

Principal Families

Ajcojom

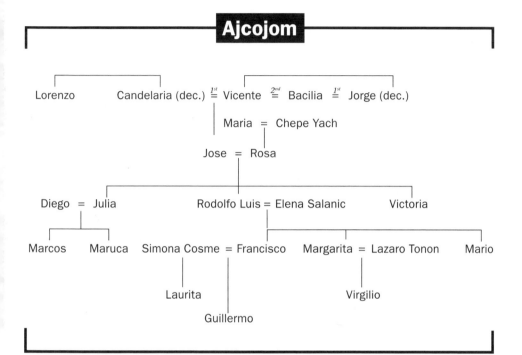

Lorenzo   Candelaria (dec.) $\overset{1^{st}}{=}$ Vicente $\overset{2^{nd}}{=}$ Bacilia $\overset{1^{st}}{=}$ Jorge (dec.)

Maria = Chepe Yach

Jose = Rosa

Diego = Julia   Rodolfo Luis = Elena Salanic   Victoria

Marcos   Maruca   Simona Cosme = Francisco   Margarita = Lazaro Tonon   Mario

Laurita   Virgilio

Guillermo

Ramirez

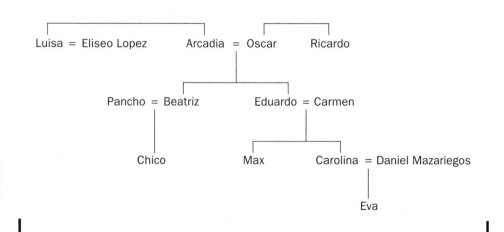

Luisa = Eliseo Lopez   Arcadia = Oscar   Ricardo

Pancho = Beatriz   Eduardo = Carmen

Chico   Max   Carolina = Daniel Mazariegos

Eva

1886-1915

I am Rodolfo Luis Ajcojom Yach. Yach for my mother's side, Ajcojom for my father's, and Rodolfo Luis for a priest from Spain who was killed in 1886, four years before I received part of his spirit. I believe that it came to me at my birth in the form of an enormous fish in Lake Atitlan here at the center of the world. Many years later I came to understand that my most helpful companion spirit is a coyote, but from whom my coyote came to me I have no idea. It might have been passed down from my grandfather, since grandparents usually do bequeath some of their spirit to grandchildren. But coyotes are lucky, both smart and clever — and according to my father, my grandfather was not born with much luck.

I had the good luck to attend three years of school, the last two in neighboring Panajachel...the first person in our town of Santa Catarina to do so. With that I learned to talk good Spanish without an accent — even to read and write a little — which is the secret to matching wits with Ladinos. Who are these Ladinos, you ask? They are the Guatemalans who aren't Mayan Indians, or who at least don't so regard themselves and can point to the European ancestry of which they are so overbearingly proud. They seldom take the time to learn any of our Mayan languages. They have run the country since the war of independence from Spain back in the time of my great-grandparents, and they are a whole lot richer than us Indians. But with more Indians than Ladinos in Guatemala, these generalizations have some exceptions. The biggest complication is that most Guatemalans have some Indian and some Spanish ancestry, resulting in most of us looking a lot alike. And Indians who learn Spanish and how to act like Ladinos sometimes manage to find Ladino acceptance, regardless of their blood.

My birth *municipio* (county) has only Indians, and all twelve towns on the shore of my lake have many more Indians than Ladinos. Panajachel has a larger proportion of Ladinos than does any other town in our *departamento* (department, or state) of Solola; this because the only good road between the nation's capital city, three days walk east of the lake, passes through Panajachel on its way to the city of Solola sitting on a promontory overlooking the lake. The lake and all the towns around it are in the *departamento* of Solola, one of Guatemala's twenty-two departments.

The *municipio* boundaries here in Solola and all across Guatemala were the decisions of the Spanish after arriving and subjugating my Indian ancestors beginning some 475 years ago. Christian saints arrived with the Spanish and have become the guardian spirits of our *municipios*, with the saints' names sometimes added to the names of our towns. Accordingly, Saint Catherine is my patron and is why we have the town name of Santa Catarina Palopo and refer to ourselves as Catarinecos — children of Saint Catherine. And our custom is to marry another child of Saint Catherine and accept her blessing of the knowledge and luck to catch the fish and crabs of our lake for our living.

Santa Catarina Palopo lies equidistant, about an hour's walk each direction, from its sister and wealthier all-Indian *municipio* of San Antonio Palopo — on the lake's northeastern shore — and from Panajachel to the west that occupies the delta of the largest river flowing into Lake Atitlan. Among the children of Saint Catherine, poorest of the lake's poor, has lived the family Ajcojom for who knows how many generations.

With the help of my fish and coyote companion spirits, we now tell you the stories of my Ajcojom family and our lake region here at the center of the world. The story we tell begins before I live and continues after...because ours is also the story of our country. But with coyote's reputation as storyteller, I should tell you that our tales — their people and the events of their lives — are true, except when they are not. When not, they very well could have been true — at times should and would have been with more assistance from other Indians' companion spirits. I speak sometimes as coyote — timeless and omniscient as my most vocal guardian spirit is wont to be — sometimes as fish with his special understanding of our lake, and sometimes as me, Rodolfo Luis. Together we tell you what we remember from those years of what I think has been my first life. As for my name, never before received in my village, I would have been given the name of my grandfather, Vicente, had it not been for this priest whom I never knew except in my sleep. From my dreaming we begin with his story.

Chapter One – 1886

The trail snaking down and around the flanks of volcanoes San Lucas Toliman and Santiago Atitlan at last came up for air. It stopped with astonishing abruptness at the base of an immense outcropping of basalt. The path was replaced by moss-slickened footholds hewn in the eroding granite that stepped gingerly up among competing vines and bromeliads through the first and middle canopies before leaving behind even the tallest cedars. At the end of a ten minute climb, and for a stone's throw along the bone-smooth igneous summit, there was none of the shade that the two men had enjoyed since sinking into the forest's dankness at daybreak.

The cleric unburdened himself altogether of his sweat-heavy wool tunic, emboldening his Indian companion to strip to the waist as well. Incongruously exposed, they headed toward comparably naked protuberances of stone conveniently located for viewing this vast panorama of southern Guatemala. And only then could they appreciate the wisdom of their steep ascent — the promontory massively bridging a deep ravine immediately below with paths striking off along its ridges descending precipitously to the southeast and southwest. Father Rodolfo Luis challenged Jorge with the launching of a small stone out over the abyss. Jorge chose a much heavier rock to ensure that he did not outdo the priest, but even its landing on the scree far below went unheard.

Rodolfo Luis collapsed against the mammoth sun-seared joint, arms and legs spread-eagle, while Jorge eased down against a companion knob of broken and blackened, sun-cauterized stone forming what everyone on the south coast knew as volcano Atitlan's 'Broken Shoulder.' "See Atitlan," advised Jorge, pointing with a swing of his long wisp of a beard toward the higher of the two peaks towering behind them. "A long time ago, before your Spanish ancestors added their saints' names of Santiago (Saint James) and San Lucas (Saint Luke), those brother volcanoes fought over which was the favorite of the Owner of the Hills. Toliman knocked off Atitlan's head to prove that he was the taller, and as it rolled down it broke off Atitlan's arm as well here at the shoulder. See that large hill down below… that's his head. And the ridge off to our left…that's the arm. Atitlan couldn't get even until the arrival of your Christian saints. In return for his name, Santiago (Saint James), being added to the Atitlan volcano, Saint James knocked off Toliman's head and made him finally the shortest. It's his head there on the shore of the lake where we left our dugout canoe early this morning."

"You mean Cerro del Oro?" asked Rodolfo Luis. Jorge nodded, already having told his priest about Mayan Tzutujil lords hiding their treasures in the vicinity of what now is called Gold Hill before Pedro Alvarado's arrival with his conquering army in 1525. "The Hills' Owner — you call him the Devil — tricked your saints and the Spanish conquerors by letting Saint James topple Toliman's head squarely on top of the Mayan treasure. Ladinos never give up searching for all that gold and silver, but the only folks who find a coin now and then are poor Indians rewarded by the Hills' Owner. A small flame coming out of the ground marks where the deserving can find it if they dig deep enough."

"Does Cerro del Oro also have a Mayan name?"

Jorge laughed his usual guarded chuckle, tongue between his teeth where he could bite down if laughing wasn't safe. "Don't think so, since as I just told you it wasn't there before your Spanish ancestors brought your saints and your language!"

Nonplussed, the priest nevertheless ruefully returned Jorge's teasing grin ...no better able now than when they'd first met to determine when Jorge was credulous and when skeptical of the history and legends he loved to relate. So Rodolfo Luis as usual held his tongue. He welcomed, frankly, his assistant's occasional impudence. By putting up with it he gleaned considerably more information about Mayan beliefs than did any of his fellow priests. Letting the conversation end, the genuinely good friends — pondering in silence their vastly differing beliefs — studied the sweep of green and distant gray to the south where lowland jungle disappeared beneath afternoon cloud banks moving in from the ocean. Above the billows, every hue of blue...other-worldly where tranquil sea met Pacific sky.

Fanning the sticky heat that rose, shimmering, from the verdant growth below, Jorge searched the horizon for buzzards that would betray the morbidity — the cruelty and unfairness — of another God-forsaken coffee plantation. "There they are," he said finally, pointing toward pepper specks circling in an eddy of roily clouds spilling into the ocean. "We'll be there before dusk if we take the shortcut down from here." Giving his weary companion no chance to object, and worried lest he had been too forward in his teasing, Jorge abruptly donned

4

his shirt and took off toward the humid humus and virgin tangle of vines and trees in search of a faintly remembered path.

Rodolfo continued to gaze down the volcano's flank. Somewhere out there lay the boundary between the counties of San Lucas and Patulul. And to think that all the land from here to there was owned by one man, Carlos Cabrera. Or so Guatemala's President Rufino Barrios barbarously had declared twelve years before, after mounting this same Broken Shoulder to survey the southern reaches of the *municipio* of San Lucas. Unannounced, Barrios had come riding up from Patulul with soldiers to pace off the boundaries of the Buenaventura (Good Fortune) plantation. Then, as he passed through the county seat of San Lucas on his way back to Guatemala City, he informed the Indian Elders of their forest land's new owner. Told them he assumed that they had no need for land so far from their homes.

Rodolfo Luis Aragon de Leon had arrived from Spain and been assigned to the parish of neighboring Patulul the following year. For ten years he had watched Indians of the region clear all but the best native trees for shading coffee, plant seedlings of coffee and the new fast-growing gravilea shade trees, and now harvest Cabrera coffee on land where they had hunted everything from squirrels to deer in their youth.

———

Jorge's shout of the path's discovery drifted up from surprisingly far below. Rodolfo Luis donned his tunic and futilely wiped his brow with the wool cloth that made absolutely no sense in this humidity, but which the bishop nonetheless insisted that his priests dutifully wear. He then donned the irreverent straw hat that he had adopted in protest of the tunic and tramped off in the direction of Jorge's flailing twangs and thuds. An exhausting half hour into the underbrush he spotted his assistant, brown-skinned in the light, loose-fitting red and white-striped pants and shirt of the native cotton that made so much sense in this climate. With Indians in some *municipios* finally having adopted the Spanish wool in men's clothing — four centuries after Europeans had introduced sheep — such foolish mimicry only demonstrated to Rodolfo Luis the subtle influence of power and authority that conquerors often unintentionally wield over sensibility.

By the time Rodolfo Luis had caught up with Jorge, busily widening with machete a path not intended for travelers as stout as the priest, they had reached the first newly-cleared terrain of the Buenaventura plantation. With only the native shade trees left standing, the swelter of the forest floor proved unbearable as they picked their way through decaying logs of felled trees, fernery, and endless rows of newly planted gravilea and coffee seedlings. Jorge paused suddenly to examine his bare foot before seeking out the well-armed trunk of a spiny palm. He cut a large thorn and sat down on a log to dig out the splinter that had worked its way into one of the deeper cracks in his leathery sole. "I'm thinking, *Padre*, that things might not go so easy at the Buenaventura."

"You have that feeling, too?" agreed Rodolfo Luis, glad for the conversation after a kilometer of nervous silence. He left the path before undoing his frock to relieve himself, watering the fronds at his feet. Then he lifted the robe's hem to again mop his crimson face and neck. "Sure you don't want me to do it alone tonight?"

"Absolutely not," Jorge replied with none of his usual deference. "In fact, I was thinking that I should hand out the papers by myself this time. I could wander in without being noticed and wait around 'til workers gather in their sleeping area. I can't read your paper to them, but at least they'd have it to take home."

His priest retreated several paces to the shade of a *ceiba* tree that threatened to eliminate the sun completely. After wiping the rivulets of sweat from his legs, and still unbuttoned from the waist down, he slumped wearily against its massive trunk and threw back the black cloth to air calves and thighs so contrastingly white that Jorge could no longer resist the staring he had controlled on the promontory. Rodolfo Luis noted his friend's embarrassment, but closed his eyes to indulge the stares rather than exert the energy to cover himself. "Kind of you to offer," he yawned, "but I'm looking forward to the excitement! Wasn't it the Buenaventura where you got into trouble?"

Jorge continued to gape at the incongruous sight of a priest's bare legs straddling the support root of a sorcerer's tree. "Un huh," he replied finally, "with the foreman. I'd like to hand him one of the leaflets myself...to see the look on his face now that he thinks I'm dead! I doubt that he would recognize me, though. I doubt that anybody there will recognize me if the workers for December still come only from San Antonio Palopo. The Buenaventura crew in January sometimes includes workers from Santa Catarina as well, though, and I'd rather not be along when we come back next —"

"No worry about next month, my friend. No worry beyond tomorrow night, I've decided. I fear for both of us if we try to continue, and I don't want to have to worry about your safety when I've left the country. After the Gloria plantation tomorrow night we'll have gotten leaflets to workers from all of the

6

counties south and east of the lake. We'll just have to hope that a few find their way to people who can read in the neighboring diocese's counties to the north-west."

Jorge adjusted his load of leaflets and provisions suspended from a leather head-strap and got slowly to his feet, sorry to be reminded that his friend would be leaving so soon. "Well, that leaves out Santa Catarina. There's only two or three men there who can read enough to make sense of your paper. My nephew's one of them, and he was teaching my son —"

"Son? I didn't know you have children!" Rodolfo Luis was less surprised than perplexed. Why, after being so close-mouthed about his past, would Jorge open up now?

Embarrassed, Jorge's lips tightened as he averted his eyes to gain compo-sure. "Bacilia gave me a boy and a girl. The girl died right away...the boy when he was ten." Jorge knew the priest would want to know more, but he still wasn't ready to talk abut his son's fall while carrying too heavy a load of maize down the mountain. He would have been in school if they hadn't been so damn poor. More because of his son's senseless death than for the reasons Jorge had given the priest, he had decided to stay in the lowlands and help Father Rodolfo Luis. Now, with the priest leaving, he'd have to decide about going home. Turning away in pre-tense of relieving himself, he offhandedly changed the subject. "That *ceiba* tree has me worried, Padre. Maybe a priest's power is stronger than any sorcerer's tree, but that's one huge *ceiba!*"

"Sorcerer's tree? I thought you told me the *ceiba* is the holy tree of the ancients —."

"Holy, indeed it is, with so much of it deep inside the Hill. That's why it's so dangerous. There's as much in roots beneath us as in all the branches overhead. Must be a basketful of the Owner's snakes that live in them roots. Here...let me help you up," and he extended a hand to pull the cleric to his feet. Then, to be sure that the talk about family had ended, "Tell me how a wind — what was that thing you read to me about in the Don Quixote book?"

"Windmill."

"That's it...windmill. Tell me how it gets water from the ground."

For the next hour of trekking through coffee trees, Rodolfo Luis tried to explain the workings of windmills to his assistant who hadn't seen even a wheel-barrow until he first came to the Buenaventura to do forced labor several years before. Not until Jorge had asked about the printing press left behind by depart-

7

ing Jesuits — the first foreign priests to be exiled — did Rodolfo Luis realize that there were no wheels of any kind used by Indians in the highlands. No axles, no pulleys — even pottery was coiled rather than thrown on a wheel. The printing press with its cogs had been a complete mystery to Jorge.

Father Rodolfo Luis had seen no way to make safe use of the printing press until Guatemala's president conveniently died and gave him the idea of telling Indian workers what their president had written about them when he introduced the hated *mandamientos,* the forced labor on coffee plantations of all able-bodied Indian men to accelerate Guatemala's involvement in the growing international coffee trade. It was providential that Rufino Barrios got himself killed when he did…before Rodolfo Luis had to go back to Spain, yet with enough time left to do something to ease the pain of being kicked out of this country that he had come to love with such passion. Without the confusion caused by Barrios's death, Rodolfo Luis wouldn't have dared take the risk. As it was, he had managed to distribute the leaflets on plantations in his own parish and on several in neighboring parishes with hardly a stir from the powerful Ladino plantation owners.

Jorge had offered to help as soon as he heard the idea. Even after Father Rodolfo had explained the risks involved, Jorge still insisted on coming along. What made Jorge so different from other Indians — outspoken and dissatisfied with his lot — Rodolfo Luis still didn't understand. Jorge refused to talk about himself. They had met when some Indians found Jorge by the road, badly beaten, and had brought him to the Patulul rectory for any help a priest could give the poor man. Rodolfo Luis had cared for him until Jorge recovered — almost six weeks — and then to his surprise Jorge had announced his decision to stay and help around the rectory. Everybody in Santa Catarina would assume by then that he was dead, and if he went home he would have to face Don Ramon again the next time he was assigned to the Buenaventura plantation. So Rodolfo had decided not to argue, not to inquire further, and for well over a year now Jorge had been his faithful companion…his 'Sancho' as they went about tilting at windmills.

It had taken Jorge about as long to understand tilting at windmills — the similarities between the legendary Spaniards, Don Quixote and Sancho Panza, and his helping Father Rodolfo Luis distribute leaflets to illiterate Indians — as it had taken Rodolfo to appreciate how difficult it was for Jorge to imagine someone creating fictional characters, in such a story, for such a purpose. Despite his thirty-seven years, there had been no fictional beings nor fictional stories in the mind of Jorge before he got to know Father Rodolfo. Since learning about a priest's world of books, Jorge's questions and their discussions had deepened immeasurably. The Spanish priest and the Maya Indian had slowly come to understand how different were the meanings each gave the beings and places they revered. The power of such beings and places — from fire and crosses to caves and stars, from sun and moon to the Hills' Owner — Jorge understood and enjoyed explaining. But that some spirits are wholly good and others only evil — the juxtaposition of God and a Devil, of a heaven and a hell — as Father Rodolfo Luis kept insisting, Jorge had not become convinced. But then, nor had he adequately conveyed to his priest the frustration and pain that had produced Indians' caution toward and accommodation to the powers that be. As Jorge liked to remind Rodolfo Luis in the little saying of his father's, "There are branches and roots of goodness and ill in everything 'round us, from Heaven to Hill."

—

By the time the workings of windmills had been explained to Jorge's satisfaction, the two men had reached the Buenaventura plantation store. It was not quite dusk, too early yet for the workers to be returning from the day's coffee picking. With time enough for a meal, Jorge ordered lemonade and a pinch of salt for the tortillas he had retrieved from his bag. "Where do the workers come from this month?" he asked the storekeeper.

"From San Antonio mostly…all but two, and they're from Santa Catarina."

"Know the names of the Catarinecos?"

"Can tell you in a moment," the storekeeper replied, eyeing the unlikely pair of travelers while thumbing through his credit book. The priest he recognized, but the overly direct Indian… he couldn't be sure. Obviously from Santa Catarina with those faded red and white clothes, but his Spanish was unusually good and lacked the usual Indian accent on final syllables. He didn't drop last syllables of Spanish words as Indians commonly did. But, carrying with the headstrap, he clearly was more Indian than Ladino. "— their names are Jose Subuyuc and Esteban Saquin."

"Don't know any Jose Subuyuc, but I know Esteban," Jorge whispered outside as they settled down on the ground against the rough-hewn wall to munch tortillas. "He's a friend of my nephew. Wouldn't want him to see me. I'll stay out of sight and watch for Don Ramon when the crowd begins to gather here after their harvest weigh-in."

9

They finished their meal, and as the first workers began to drift in for food and firewood Rodolfo Luis handed out leaflets and invited them to stick around a few minutes to hear what he had to say about their dead president Barrios.

From shadows at the rear of the store, Jorge watched the storekeeper leave. At a safe distance he followed him down the road toward the coffee's earthen drying floors until he could see that he was heading for the foreman's house. A few moments later the foreman and storekeeper left on the run for the Cabrera plantation house. "Just what I thought would happen if we came here!" he muttered. "Damn that Don Ramon!" With that proof Jorge hurried back to the store. Under a lamp in the doorway, Father Rodolfo Luis had begun to read his leaflet to workers gathered outside. At the point Jorge saw men coming down the road — running — he called, *"Padre,* there's no time! Leave the leaflets and let's head for the river."

"Barrios is dead," exclaimed Esteban, out of breath. He dropped the leaflet into Jose's hammock and plopped into his own. "Rufino Barrios — the president?" Jose lifted his feet free of the sides of the hammock to sit up.

"Yup — killed outside the country in some fighting over making all the countries around Guatemala one big one...like Mexico. Some priest was outside the store just now handing out these papers telling about it."

"Doesn't a priest know us poor *Inditos* can't read?" mocked Jose as he studied the paper. He had worked as a house boy in the home of one of San Antonio's few Ladino shopkeepers and had learned to read some of their Spanish. Because he had gotten to know Indians from there as well, he'd been among the first from Santa Catarina to be hired by the wealthier Indian landowners of San Antonio to take their place at forced labor on the Buenaventura plantation. This was his third and last trip to earn the money needed to ask for a wife. He had found a San Antonio patron willing to pay him six pesos per Buenaventura trip — three times what the plantation paid for four weeks of work and more than he could earn working for anyone in Santa Catarina. For Esteban it was his second time down with a *mandamiento* crew from San Antonio. He'd been asked to serve in the *cofradia* for Santa Catarina's patron Saint Catherine but lacked the money needed; couldn't afford even to rent a dance costume. At Jose's suggestion Esteban had pawned his wife's land bordering San Antonio to a brother of Jose's patron employer. Esteban would lose this year's harvest, but after one more trip he would have the land back.

10

Esteban enviously watched Jose's eyes more slowly back and forth across the page. "The priest started to read it to us at the store, but Don Ramon and Don Carlos showed up and chased him away. They told us to give them the papers, but I was in the back and ran off before they saw me."

"First part here tells about Barrios dying," Jose began. "Now that he's dead, the priest wants us to refuse to do this forced labor. Then it has some of the law —" He labored through the text of a letter written to governors by President Barrios a decade earlier...the letter that Father Rodolfo Luis wanted Indians to know about before he was forced to leave Guatemala.

The letter continued:

> If we abandon the Ladino plantation owners to their own resources and do not give them strong and energetic aid, they will be unable to make any progress, for all their efforts will be doomed to failure due to the deceit of the Indians. It is also apparent that the only way to improve the situation of Indians and remove them from their state of misery and abjection is to create among them needs which they will acquire by continuous contact with the Ladino class, accustoming them also to work so they can fill these needs, thereby converting this immense majority of the republic into something useful for the agriculture, commerce, and industry of the country. You should therefore see to it:
>
> First: that the Indian villages in your jurisdiction be forced to give the number of hands to the farmers that the latter ask for, even to the number of fifty or a hundred to a single farmer if his enterprise warrants this number.
>
> Second: when one set of Indians has not been able to finish the work at hand in a period of two weeks, a second should be sent to relieve the first so that the work may not be delayed —"

Jose threw down the leaflet in disgust. "Two weeks!...Shit! Nobody gets done in two weeks! We kill ourselves to get done in four. And my God!...saying that Ladinos need to show us how to work. Don Carlos hasn't worked a full day in his life! He acts like all of us owe his Cabrera family this underpaid work...two pesos for four weeks in this ungodly place. What did we ever do to deserve this?"

11

"Maybe if we complain to our mayor....He might be able to arrange with Solola authorities to send us Catarinecos to a different plantation. I've heard that the Gloria and Esperanza plantations treat their workers better," Esteban offered lamely, in hope of ending the pointless conversation that threatened to interfere with the sleep that they simply had to have to finish this *mandamiento* assignment.

"Don't you love those names?" Jose chortled "— Glory and Hope! I've got a new one for this hell hole. Since the newest coffee trees still haven't put on many berries, I'm calling the Buenaventura 'the Barren Lady,' and Don Carlos 'the Mule's Cock!'"

"Not so loud, for God's sake!" Esteban whispered "— never know who's listening around here. If one of the plantation's 'ears' heard you joking like this, it could be the end for us."

Jose bit his tongue, but couldn't contain his laughter. Down deep, however, he knew that Esteban was right. Especially after what had happened to his Uncle Jorge. His father learned only that Jorge had been arrested above Patulul. With maize so scarce at home, he had asked to pick in Buenaventura maize fields after finishing his work assignment. According to what Vicente had learned from Jorge's companions, the foreman had agreed to give Jorge as much shelled maize as he could carry home in return for harvesting five acres. But after Jorge had carried it half-way home, the foreman had ordered him stopped. Claimed Jorge had stolen it. Ladinos took him away and no one had heard of him since. Vicente stopped coming to the Buenaventura after that; said that Don Ramon might give him trouble simply because he was Jorge's brother.

Jose began coming in Vicente's stead, after Vicente bribed Santa Catarina's Ladino town secretary to enter Jose's name as Subuyuc rather than Ajcojom on the work lists. But Jose suspected that Vicente stopped coming less because of Don Ramon than because of Jorge's wife. Vicente couldn't stand the thought of leaving Bacilia, his attractive sister-in-law, alone for weeks at a time. How Jose felt about his father in love with his aunt, he hadn't decided. His mother had been dead six years, and it was time his father married again. But he felt uneasy about it being Bacilia, mostly because he hadn't given up hope that Jorge was still alive and would someday come home. He preferred to believe the rumors started by Bacilia's family: that Jorge had run away and was hiding in the low country to avoid his family duties. No question but that his uncle Jorge was restless and angry at being so poor...always thinking about how to get more land, or paddling farther around the lake to look for better fishing and crabbing. How unlike

Vicente! "We are what we can get hold of," Jorge used to remind the family, and Vicente stubbornly would reply, "But if we can't drink the water, best to let it flow!"

The sleeping area had quieted. Only the usual snoring on all sides. Most had turned in earlier than usual in hopes of finishing their work obligation the next day. "Want to try to finish tomorrow?" yawned Esteban.

"Sure do! We've still got half our maize to harvest back home, and my pa wants me married before Father Sebastian leaves the country. He's determined for me to have a priest's blessing."

"That's right! You're having trouble finding a woman that will have you, I hear..." teased Esteban.

Jose blushed, embarrassed that everybody in Santa Catarina seemed to know that the town's most respected curer had turned him down. "Yup, asking for Marcelo's daughter was a mistake. Guess we're too poor for a curer!"

"It is just as well. You'd have had nothing but trouble with old Marcelo. Rich as he is, he'd have insisted on your moving in with them. And busy as he is with his divinations and curing, you'd have become little more than a hired hand. Who are you asking for now?"

"Rosa Yach, Chepe's daughter, as soon as I get back."

"Chepe...the sacristan?" When Jose nodded, Esteban smiled, "So you've decided to settle for the saints' help in the church if you can't have for your father-in-law a cave witch in good with the Hills' Owner! Pretty smart of your pa, I'd say! Chepe will be in charge of the church and our saints after Father Sebastian leaves, I hear. He could become a pretty valuable father-in-law."

Jose shrugged. Frankly, that hadn't been a consideration. Not in his mind, at least, and he doubted that Vicente had thought about it either. Especially since he was at odds with Chepe over the town's saints: Chepe was determined to keep the saints in the church during the priest's absence, but Vicente favored moving them into private homes. The idea to approach Chepe and his wife, Maria, had been Lorenzo's, Vicente's brother-in-law, after the shaman Marcelo had so rudely turned them down. Lorenzo had felt badly to have handled the petition so badly. It had been a mistake to go so late at night, but in truth Lorenzo had been afraid and had gotten himself drunk to get up his nerve. With Rosa's parents, however, it was another matter. They were Lorenzo's *compadres* (co-godparents), and he was certain that they would give Rosa unless someone else already had asked for her. "If you believed everything you hear," mused Jose, "every eligible girl in town will be married by the time our Father Sebastian leaves. By the way, what's the name of this priest here this evening?" He retrieved the leaflet from the bushes and lit a candle in the waning light. "Rodolfo Luis Aragon de Leon. And beneath his name he has drawn a fish. Name sounds foreign. Seems strange that a priest, foreign priest at that, would go out of his way so for the likes of us. He must know that it will make the plantation owners angry. Why do you suppose he does it?" Jose secreted the paper in his woven shoulder bag before settling back in his hammock to ponder how any priest, foreign or not, could become so concerned about the plight of Indians. "Think I'll name my first son Rodolfo Luis." But Esteban already was fast asleep.

"A la gran chuchu (son of a bitch)!" whispered Esteban in disbelief.

Jose was too overcome to comment. Mesmerized by the smell and sight of more buzzards than he'd ever seen in one place, he left the cluster of homeward bound workers to attack single-handedly. Only when he was close enough to kick a few of the satiated birds resting on the perimeter did they all take flight. The shreds of clothing left no doubt as to the priest's identity. It came as no surprise. Since dawn the previous day, there had been an unusually large circle of buzzards in the direction of the river presumed taken by the priest and his assistant as they fled.

Despite the stench, Jose was too transfixed to retreat. Not until a returning vulture settled on the priest's remains and pulled at a chain still encircling his neck did Jose move. Holding his breath, he jumped into the mess to rescue the chain and its cross from such an unseemly fate. Turning to jump clear of the carnage, the bloodied red and white tatters clinging to the priest's companion were unmistakable. A Catarineco?...he puzzled, turning the head with his foot. Face to face with what remained...the recognition brought Jose to his knees. No one else in Santa Catarina let his beard grow so long...to cover such a poor excuse for a chin. It had to be his uncle Jorge! Hands on his knees, he vomited, sobbing at the core. Waving his companions on, he turned away and waited until the retching abated. Hands too bloodied to wipe the tears, he struggled blindly to his feet and turned toward the sun warming the back of his neck. His uncle had taught him how to greet the sun — just topping the horizon. Wiping the crucifix on his shirt he kissed it and extended his arms to San Bernardo. "Thank you, Father, for returning to show us the way another day...for opening the way for us to our food and drink, our shelter and labor another day. We thank you, Father, for your charity, and for letting at least some of us live another day. Forgive us our sins and our

14

faults. Father, please have mercy on us, your children, as we try to find our way another day." Then, as an afterthought, "Please let my uncle be one of your brightest stars." There was so much that he didn't understand...that Jorge still could have told him. How does a soul get from here to become a star?

"I had to do it. Their poor souls deserve some sort of blessing. I'll get rid of this stench at the river," he apologized on rejoining his companions. Of the crucifix and Jorge he said nothing, even to Esteban. Already he had misgivings about appropriating a martyred priest's crucifix. Would that he had been spared the truth about Jorge.

Chapter Two

Jose was with his father, Vicente, at their highest milpa field, beginning what he prayed would be the last day of their own maize harvest before starting on his aunt Bacilia's. It was the end of December, and every field they had passed in the hour and a half of climbing had been harvested. It wasn't so much the embarrassment of being late as it was the loss this time of year from raccoons. One, sometimes two ears of corn hung from stalks drooping and broken from marauding animals, mostly raccoons. When father and son had last hoed weeds from beans and squash and hilled soil around the maize, the proud stalks had towered several feet above their heads.

Vicente was philosophical. "Can't really blame the varmints. Why bother with gleaning harvested fields when ours sits here like a gift to every Hill creature around! Look at these ears! Haven't found one yet that doesn't have a bite out of it. But then, if the Hill creatures put in a good word for us with their Owner, I guess we can't complain. The way things have been going around here of late, the saints don't seem to pay us no mind. Might as well settle for the luck of our Hill Owner's blessing."

Jose was too weary to offer even a deferential response to his father's banter. It was looking like a three-trip day up and down the mountain, and he could only be grateful to the coons for lightening his load. He and Esteban had returned home the day before, late in the afternoon after a day and a half's walk around the lake's eastern end. Their wait of half a day in hopes of a canoe ride across the lake had been to no avail. What little sleep he'd gotten after finally reaching Santa Catarina and sharing the news of the priest's murder with his father and aunt Bacilia had been filled with imaginings about the killings and images of half-eaten bodies. He had decided to show them the crucifix, but about Jorge he couldn't bring himself to report. Vicente would think it served his brother right, and with all hope gone Bacilia would have no way of keeping his father out of her bed.

Savoring his hatred for Don Carlos and the grotesquely misnamed "Good Fortune" plantation, he mused, "Good luck for no one but its Mule's Cock of an owner..."

Vicente caught only the final word of the retort, "So you think the Hills' Owner will prevail after all?"

"No, Papa, I wasn't referring to the Owner of the Hills. I was thinking about Don Carlos calling that slave plantation of his the 'Good Fortune' and then killing the one priest who was trying to help all of us who have to do the work there....Why do you suppose the poor fellow drew a fish under his name?"

Vicente had asked himself the same question. "Could be that he has a fish in his soul...could be that all priests do. I remember my grandfather telling me about a priest who used to come to our village. Told my grandfather that he liked to come to our village because the apostle Peter he'd been named for was a fisherman. Said Jesus Christ gave fish a special blessing and chose mainly fishermen for his helpers. Jesus told them that if they gave up fishing and followed him, he'd make them fishers of men. The other fishermen who became apostles were Andrew, John, and James. Must be true, because none of the men from the towns around the lake with those saints for their patrons are fishermen anymore. It may be because those apostles and the men of their towns stopped fishing that our Saint Catherine was able to give the luck of fishing to us."

"Not much of a gift if you ask me," Jose snorted, reminded that Jorge had become convinced it was the fishing that kept their town so damn poor...money didn't like their smell! "Sure wish Saint Catherine had given us the luck of growing vegetables instead. When men from Panajachel have to take their turn on the plantations their women do the watering and weeding, even the harvesting and selling if need be. But when we have to go there's nobody to do our fishing and crabbing for us. Not fair!" He jammed his husking peg into an ear of corn so hard the wooden peg broke. "Chicken shit! Broke it," he confessed, knowing that his father would think it served him right for letting anger enter and then get such a hold on him. "I'll fill up from your bag and head on down to get another peg."

"Of course it's unfair," replied Vicente helplessly, ignoring the husking peg. "I told you years ago there's no justice in this first life. Each of us has to wait 'til our next one. I lost my temper completely when the mayor asked us again for plantation work next month. I told him about your marriage, but he just threw down the sixty-five centavos pay and walked off. I know well enough how hard it is to do the choosing, but it sure seems like we get asked more than most. At least they won't be sending crews from here again for several months after this coffee harvest."

"Really think the forced work on plantations will continue that long?" pondered Jose as he tied his bag closed. "With President Barrios dead, Father

Rodolfo Luis said that if enough of us refuse to work then the government will *have* to change the law."

Vicente helped him lift the bag into his carrying net and onto Jose's back. "Well, a few priests have been protesting, and you see what's happening to them. First just the Jesuits had to leave. But now with all the priests being kicked out, I fear the law's here to stay. Let's pray that it doesn't get worse!"

With a helpless wave of his hand Jose trotted off, head and eyes forced down by the weight of his load. He had given little thought to the priests leaving. As long as he was married before Father Sebastian left he hadn't felt that their going made much difference. But that was before learning that it had become a dying matter. And his uncle, of all people, working with that kind of priest! Hardly made sense. Must have been because of his cousin's fatal fall. Children dying had become so common that Jose hadn't given much thought to losing even his cousin. But it had made him more careful. He hadn't had a bad fall yet, despite carrying from farther up the mountain than did most. Of his reputation for carrying with a head strap, Jose was justly proud. He could tell that the girls admired his manly neck muscles. They helped compensate for the youthfulness of his baby-cheeked face, still completely hairless.

After an hour of contemplating life and death while carefully navigating the steep path, he stopped at the spring to rest, settling down on a well-polished log to let an uncomplaining boulder take the weight of his load off his neck before savoring the only spring water within easy walking distance from town. Such a relief to get back home to some decent drinking water after the questionable stream drainage they had to rely on at the Buenaventura. He was surprised to have the spring to himself — not a woman in sight — since fetching water was about the only way for girls to get away from home to talk with fellows. He surveyed the bay, looking for any fishermen. Just one still out, and that would be Esteban. Tired as he was from yesterday's walking from daybreak to dusk, he would have gotten a late start...too late for much luck this time of day. But nonetheless, Jose was envious...nothing quite like being out on the lake utterly alone with a little cloud cover from the sun and a mirror surface on the water. On just such a day as this, he once had paddled out far enough to view the whole panorama of the lake's length and breadth, some sixteen miles to the far west end.

The larger commercial dugout canoes coming across for Solola's Friday market had long since beached around the bend at Panajachel. For an hour or two — before returning canoes signaled early afternoon — nothing would be visible on the vast expanse of calm, sleeping water. But once those returning boats were safely on their way back from commerce with Panajachel and Solola, the inevitable crosswinds — the *chocomil* — would be kicking up in search of any hapless dugouts still at bay. But after ten years of doing little but fishing, crabbing, and hunting ducks, Jose knew well this treacherous end of the lake. It held no fear for him, despite his never having learned to swim. For the people of Santa Catarina, who depended on its resources more than any others living on its shores, the lake was a good friend despite the daily *chocomil* that occasionally would claim another Catarineco sacrifice to its Owner.

I interrupt the story for a moment to tell you that when I was growing up in Santa Catarina a half century ago I heard from my elders many stories about the *chocomil*. I listened to them during night-long wakes following deaths — especially deaths from drowning. The one that my fish spirit tells me is the true explanation for the *chocomil* is the one I want to share. The *chocomil* is guardian spirit of a Kaqchikel prince whose courtship many centuries ago of a daughter of the *cacique* (king) of Tzutujil speakers on the other side of the lake was so opposed by the *cacique* that he threatened to kill the prince if the couple continued to rendezvous. His daughter's response was to throw herself into the lake from a high cliff. And when her lover learned of this, he drowned himself to join her, his spirit becoming the dangerous wind that sweeps across the lake from south to north each afternoon at the time of day that he died. The *chocomil* seeks revenge through deaths of careless Tzutujil boatmen who return too late in the day from commerce with Panajachel and Solola to the north. But of course at times paddlers of the smaller dugout canoes used by Kaqchikel-speaking fishermen in Santa Catarina become victims of the prince's curse as well.

Returning to our story, Jose could see no other towns nestled in deltas around the lake from the spring. And from this distance the few fellow villagers he could make out far below were ant-like, methodically spreading freshly harvested reeds to dry along the shore. He had counted the houses in town from year to year, now more than the fingers and toes of five people. Apart from those scattered above town, those in town were crowded haphazardly around the church — three times taller than any other building in town. From here there was no hint of the paths winding among the homes, the latter walled off from passersby and neighbors by fences of stone, cane, or *chichicaste* burning nettles where soil permitted. It was a rocky and inhospitable hill once you got much above the church. Because of the citrus, plum, and avocado trees that his grandfather, and before

19

him his great-grandfather had planted, their compound was hidden with no need for a fence. Yes, those who lived near the moisture of the lake were the lucky ones.

"Sure glad that I'm not the one having to move!" he mused aloud, studying the treeless section of town where the Yaches lived and wondering how Rosa would feel to leave her home to come live with him. If, indeed, Rosa was to be the one. He was eager to have it settled. After his uncle Lorenzo, the marriage broker, was turned down by Marcelo, Jose didn't care much who it was he married. The important thing was to get into the new house with a woman to do his cooking. His patience was about gone — living with his lonely father and aunt Bacilia. He strained against the glare from the shimmering water, locating what looked like the flock of ducks that he'd spotted farther offshore yesterday while walking around from San Antonio. They would have arrived from the north while he was on the coast, and by the time he returned again from harvest they should be fat enough to hunt. Local grebes were fine, but after eight months of the tough little critters the larger foreign ducks were always a treat. "Can't wait!" he muttered, slipping under the head strap and struggling to his feet.

Out in the open again he watched the pair of thrushes he had startled at the spring flit back to reclaim their nest. The perfect wedding gift for Rosa's parents...he must remember to bring some birdlime on his return for trapping one or both of the pair. A sudden puff of smoke caught his eye to the west above the cliffs. He braced for the explosion and echoes off the cliff from the firecracker rocket. "That late already," he worried, concluding from a glance at San Bernardo that it was indeed midday. Anxious to get his three trips in before dark, he trotted up the rise to the outcrop, crossed himself at the cross overlooking Santa Catarina, and started down the final descent.

From high above, Vicente rested on his oak staff and strained with his one good eye to watch Jose scramble up the knoll and pause at the cross. Reassured that his son was showing such respect even when off alone, tears mingled with the sweat tracing the creases in Vicente's weathered face of fifty-some years. Exactly how many, he didn't know. He was the third of seven children, five of whom already had died. His parents had married soon after the independence fighting against Spain. His oldest sister knew that she was born after 1830, which meant that he had to be at least fifty. But the dull eye and bad ear from his fall when drunk, and hair now completely silver, made him look and feel considerably older. After serving as mayor three years ago his community services were done. He was the youngest of the dozen elders, the *principales* charged with Santa

20

Catarina's most important commercial and religious decisions. Being treated with that respect was pleasant enough, but getting old certainly was a mixed blessing. Those like his wife who had died before the *mandamientos* forced labor changed everything were the lucky ones.

He uncorked the bottle of cane liquor that he'd brought as a cave offering. Wetting his lips, he savored the few remaining bites of stale corn and black bean *totoposte* dough that had been his lunch during his single trip to the milpa every day this week. The morning's talk with Jose had been a good one...Jose's mother would have been pleased! Vicente had quarreled with his wife a lot in their early years, so much so that she'd lived with her parents much of the year before Jose's birth. Because Jose looked so different — cheekbones high even for an Indian and a much less prominent chin than his own — Vicente suspected that Jose wasn't his son. He always had suspected his brother, because of that chin. Both Jorge and Jose had unforgettable noses for their prominence between sharply slanting foreheads above and comparably retreating mouths and jaws below. Thick shocks of hair hid foreheads, but the thinness of facial hair failed to rescue their chins. With Jorge lost or dead, he felt guilty for how he'd treated his brother all those years...and for his resentment that overflowed onto Jose. Truth was that Jorge had been more of a father to Jose than had he. The second fire bomb's sharp retort reminded Vicente of his errand. Jose had agreed that burning candles in Judas Cave before their first marriage-proposal visit to Chepe and Maria Yach was a wise precaution.

———

The cave's four shamans nodded to Vicente — one of the more familiar faces at Friday divinations — as he labored up the last rough-hewn steps of the precipitous path and paused at the yawning, misshapen and blackened mouth of Judas to catch his breath. Within there were people numbering his fingers and half his toes: crowded, as it was increasingly becoming of Fridays with news spreading of the priests' exile. Judas Cave had become crowded even on the less strong but still auspicious Mondays and Wednesdays, with folks who heretofore had come to depend on the priests for intercession with the world of spirits now scrambling to renew allegiances to the shamans — curers and diviners — on whom they would perforce be dependent henceforth. From their garb Vicente knew their towns: those from Panajachel in brown, knee-length wool tunics, and from San Antonio in brown and white checked *rodillera* wool skirts. Jorge often had worn a *rodillera* over his drawers for warmth when fishing, but since wool

21

clothing had to be purchased in the market Vicente had decided that *rodilleras* were something that he and Jose could do without. Nor did he wear a straw hat. Most everybody did, but he preferred a head cloth. In his high milpa he'd lost too many hats to the *chocomil* winds.

He knew the four *zahorines* (shamans) and a few of their clients. No matter, he greeted them all, kneeling and kissing in turn the right hand of the several he judged to be older than himself. There was little visiting, the mood expectant. The youngest diviner, a Catarineco apprenticed to Marcelo, the oldest present, dutifully watched the shadow of an overhanging rock creep across the freshly swept floor. "San Bernardo is at his halfway point. We can begin." Three altars of blackened stones crimsoned simultaneously with the blood of three chickens as the third fire bomb swooshed skyward from its launcher. A family from San Andres crouching in the shadows tried to stifle the startled cry of a feverish child. Otherwise the audience was silent and mostly male, intently observing from respectful distances the *zahorines* they had hired as the petitioning and seed-reading got underway. In monotone the familiar unvarying appeals to Owners of Cave and Hill, to assorted saints, and to the ancestral spirits were offered up with blood (of fowl) and liquor, incense and candles, as smoke began to cloud the mouth of Judas.

At his favorite tallow-smooth ledge, in the deepest recess where years ago he had propped a small cross, Vicente crouched low to avoid the roof, blackened from countless candles. He preferred the beeswax yellow tapers he made himself from two hives he had tended faithfully for years. His prayers this day were brief, as his choking from all the incense and candles forced an early exit to the rock balcony overlooking a nearly vertical drop to the canopy of oak and pine below. Eager to start for home, Vicente was reaching for his staff when he overheard mention of a priest's death on the coast. Crowding in with the others he learned little more than Jose already had told him, holding his tongue rather than admit to his son having hired out on a harvest crew from San Antonio. Instead, he asked what the others had learned about their own priest's plans.

"Well, they say that the Solola bishop is quarreling with Father Sebastian again. Old 'Bald Pate' doesn't want any of his bishopric priests wandering around the countryside anymore. In fact he has forbidden Father Sebastian to say mass again here in Santa Catarina. He's even asking his priests to bring at least one of their sacristans with them to their remaining meetings in Solola. Imagine that — the bishop afraid that humble folks like us might do in Father Sebastian!"

22

Vicente joined in the laughter, but failed to mask his anxiety. "But what about the baptism and marriage blessings he promised to give after mass over here next week?"

Marcelo had suspected as much about Vicente: much more worried about the priest's leaving that he would admit. "Well," he drawled, rolling a cigarette on his knee while eyeing Vicente, "if you want his blessing, I assume that he'll give mass as usual in Panajachel. Or if it doesn't matter to you whose blessing it is, you can walk to Solola for the bishop's final mass on market day before even he puts his tail between his legs and runs."

The group was growing uneasy. Enough so that the Panajachel *zahorin* decided to be more charitable. "These are difficult times for all of us," he gently chastened Marcelo, his elder by a few years, "and it does no harm to receive the priest's blessing. To be sure, Father Sebastian hasn't stuck out his neck for us like the poor martyr across the lake," he deemed it prudent to add, "but let's not forget why even Father Sebastian has been told by Guatemala's Ladino rulers to go back to Spain: the nation's Ladino leaders think that they will have less interference in enslaving us if they are rid of our priests. Despite their poor opinion of us who worship in caves such as this, the priests have been the closest we *naturales* have to friends representing our interests beyond the borders of our Indian communities."

"Clearly we're in for some hard times," sighed Vicente, but now under his breath as he sadly began picking his way barefooted down the slippery path. Where to put one's trust henceforth? In the saints, abandoned now by their priests to a few Indian sacristans for who knows how many years...or in the likes of Marcelo and his fellow *zahorines*? Such a dilemma! Prudence dictated endeavoring for as long as possible to avoid the choosing, which meant keeping one's own counsel with diligence. But as a member of the Council of Elders, that would be a virtually impossible challenge.

The leaders of Solola's twelve *cofradias,* charged with care of the saints belonging to the capital city of the *departamento* of Solola, filed from the sanctuary of the Solola church and lined up in customary ranked order to make their homeward processional rounds. Apart from their silver staffs of office and tasseled red ceremonial head cloths, they were dressed in the usual Solola gray and black wool jackets and multicolored striped pants. It had taken an hour for their assembly and procession to the church; the *cofrade* of the lowest ranking *cofradia* —

once his fellow officers *(mayordomos)* had assembled at his house — beginning the silent, solemn trek from house to house of the other eleven *cofrades* in ascending order. Now, after an hour of discussion with their bishop, they would spend yet another hour dutifully reversing their trek back and forth across the city. There would be more complaining, were it not for Solola being adjacent to the county of Chichicastenango — to the north in the *departamento* of El Quiche — where such processioning took half again as long. Chichicastenango boasted sixteen *cofradias,* the most of any *municipio* in the highlands. And when custom called for not only the cofrades, but also for the four ranked *mayordomo* assistants of all sixteen *cofrades,* to procession to and from the church, the trek consumed over three hours commencing at 5:00 in the morning. But what a sight, those eighty men accompanied by drummer and flautist!

The *cofrade* heads of the Solola *cofradias* were pleased with their reception by the bishop. He had been more receptive than anticipated to their request to house the images of Solola's saints in their homes henceforth. With the priests' departure, people were especially worried about the care of their patron saint, La Virgin Maria de la Asuncion. To be sure, it would be bothersome to receive visitors at odd hours with emergency petitions, but building separate saints' rooms adjacent to the *cofrades'* residences would solve that problem for the town's most popular saints. The bishop's concern about the safety of the saints outside the church struck them as odd — did he really think that any Indian, or Ladino for that matter, would harm or steal a saint? After having been selected — the first of January — by the Council of Elders *(principales)* to serve as a *cofrade* for a year or two, the hospitality of the *cofrade's* own home surely would provide a saint more comfort and security than would the church.

—

The bishop had invited audiences this day with not only Solola's *cofrades,* but also with his four companion priests in the diocese of Solola. Rejoining his clerics in the rectory, he relayed the request of the *cofrades* and summarized his own position: "Let the *Inditos* take the saints' images to their homes for safekeeping in rooms or separate houses open to the public; leave the Indian sacristans in charge of the churches and any of the lesser saints left therein; and invest sacristans with the authority to baptize." It seemed a logical compromise: let the *cofradias* have their way, but insure that people still had to come to the churches for at least the baptism of infants — and pay alms to keep up the buildings.

"Separate saints' houses? Give Indians their own churches, in effect. You talk as though we'll never be returning! Surely we're only talking about a few years. The clamor for our return will begin soon enough when Indians start killing Ladinos for enslaving them!" Sebastian, the Basque poet and most passionate of the group, never hesitated to challenge his superiors.

"I can accept most of the images going to homes if we have the *cofradias'* agreement to leave at least each town's patron saint in the church," countered Rodrigo, always the voice of pragmatism from the lake's southeastern parish of San Lucas. "With their patron still there, they'll have to use the church. Otherwise I fear for its upkeep and the authority of our sacristans. The more traditional of these Indians already are saying that the sacraments can be foregone, and if the only reason they have to go to the church is for baptism I fear that it won't be long before the churches are completely abandoned."

"Rodrigo has a point," added Ignacio from San Pedro's parish at the lake's southwestern corner, "and if we won't be gone all that long, why not try to keep things as unchanged as possible? With so many Ladinos here in Solola it might not work, but in the outlying towns like the rest of us serve I can see the few Ladino residents agreeing to the lesser saints residing with Indians so long as they don't have to go to an Indian's home to be with the community's patron."

The bishop, already losing his tender scalp's eiderdown when arriving in Solola a decade earlier and now totally egg-headed from such tumultuous years ruling his roost, leaned back and again scratched his blotched and blood-stained pate in weary frustration. He would be less concerned if he could be as optimistic as his clerics about returning. But he was preparing for the worst and very much doubted that he, at least, ever would see Guatemala again. He had spared the others the details of his acrimonious meetings in the company of other bishops and their archbishop in the capital with the country's president and his generals. Only with the murder of Father Rodolfo Luis had they begun to understand the depth of Ladino landowners' anger. Hereabouts probably they didn't need fear for their lives, but the alms were certainly falling off and the mood was definitely souring. The sooner the rest of his priests were out, the better.

Capitulating, he shook his fists to quiet his colleagues and tried again to make the only point that really mattered. "Whatever else we do, can we at least agree to encourage the *Inditos* to continue placing their faith in the saints? If they revert to worshipping only their pagan spirits — make the caves their churches and the cave witches their priests — what will it mean, really, if they come to the churches only for baptism? Yes, protect the sacraments and maintain the churches we must, to the extent that we dare rely on the sacristans, but not at the expense of alienating the *cofradias*. They represent the hope of the Church in Guatemala. To be sure we struggle against the *Inditos'* idolatry of simply the wooden images, but pampering those images with food and liquor is a far cry from lining the pockets of cave witches. How ironical it is that the coffee growers find unwitting allies against us among the cave witches!"

"Not so strange, really," mused Rodrigo, "considering that they are the wealthy in both societies, and both at the expense of the poor souls who so desperately need our intervention."

"Exactly!" concurred Sebastian, "there are greater wealth differences among these secretive Indians than meet the eye. Indians hereabouts knew what they were doing when they named the cave above Santa Catarina 'Judas!' The cave witches are no better than common thieves."

Only Dominico, always the last to voice his opinion and more pensive and taciturn than usual, had not yet joined the heated discussion. From his southern parish of Santiago Atitlan he saw more evidence of the growing rift than did the others. Despite their representation of different dioceses, he and the slain Rodolfo Luis — in adjacent parishes — had worked together at times. Rodolfo Luis had convinced him that it was the wealth of the Church, more than the teachings of justice by a few radicals in his and other dioceses, that was the Church's undoing in Guatemala — just as had been the case earlier in Mexico. Dominico agreed with Rodolfo Luis: if and when they returned and found their authority eroded, they'd have only their own avarice to blame. He broke the silence following the bishop's impassioned plea. "We all suspect, I believe, that some doubting Thomases will refuse from the outset to accept baptism from a sacristan. If that will be the case, as I'm certain it will be in Santiago Atitlan, then it's only a matter of time before the refusal is widespread. Let them seek blessing from the saints wherever they choose to house them, and make that as easy for them as possible, but let's not burden Indians with indecision by suggesting that other than priests can administer the sacraments and thereby collect alms. They'll surely be accused of lining their own pockets."

The bishop could see that the issues would not find resolution that day. That was the principal reason for his suggesting that they bring their sacristans with them to Solola. "I believe that we need more of your sacristans' thinking about these issues. It is one thing to let them baptize if they are asked; quite

26

another to use them to pressure people into doing so simply to ensure the buildings' upkeep. Denying baptism to those faithful souls who desire it is the really painful issue. You need to discuss frankly with your sacristans whether they want the responsibility themselves and are willing to train successors. Then there is the issue raised by Dominico of the fee and how they avoid criticism of benefiting personally. I wonder how the Indians countenance the wealth of their cave witches? Do we know what fees they charge for curings and divinations?"

None of his companions knew the answer.

"Or the midwives and bonesetters?"

"I don't think they charge," chanced Dominico. "Rodolfo Luis often accepted tamales, eggs, and vegetables in lieu of the baptism fee, since his parishioners felt such gifts appropriate. And I'm constantly receiving gifts of food, my reason for asking only a nominal fee."

"Exactly why I have argued that we ought to keep to a uniform charge! If they want to add a gift of food, that's up to them. If Rodolfo Luis's bishop had done the same, and insisted on his priests keeping proper distance from these *Inditos,* we wouldn't be in this mess! And I dare say that Rodolfo Luis would still be alive!"

Their bishop's curiously heated retort surprised them all. The paradox was painfully obvious. In their zeal to protect the Church's authority and to turn these hopelessly idolatrous Indians away from their pagan ways, they hadn't come to know those beliefs and customs well enough.

"How sad," Dominico mused softly "— we are leaving because we have tried to protect these people, and yet we are arguing because we neither understand nor trust them ourselves. How many of us could count on even our sacristans to risk their lives in defense of either our churches or the saints' images we are so worried about protecting?" He didn't try to hold back the tears. Would that Rodolfo Luis were listening! How often he had despaired of his colleagues' insufferable insensitivity to their parishioners' traditional *costumbres*…and unwillingness to truly befriend even their Indian sacristans. Dominico had so envied Rodolfo Luis's friendship with the poor Indian assistant who loyally had died at his side.

The priests and their sacristans would meet again the next Friday's market day in Solola, before the farewell outdoor mass on Sunday, to decide finally on the bishop's response to the *cofrades* of Solola and the counsel to give the bishopric's sacristans.

27

Dutifully, the sacristans of Panajachel and Santa Catarina — Ciriaco Cuc and Chepe Yach — awaited Father Sebastian outside the rectory. "Forgive us, Father, we were worried... afraid that we'd stayed too long in the market and that you had started down the mountain without us."

"Bless you for your patience," replied Sebastian, looking with surprise at the position of the sun. "Had I realized we would be so late, I would have told you to go on down without me."

Chepe Yach looked worried. He had difficulty understanding his priest's Spanish, and from his somber countenance feared that they were being admonished. Ciriaco, from Panajachel and more conversant in Spanish, sensed his comrade's confusion and translated in full their Father's concern for them. Relieved, Chepe bowed respectfully, but Sebastian already had turned abruptly and started down the hill. He was tall, even for a Basque, standing and sitting ramrod straight to ease chronic pain from a fall from a horse in his youth. The curly hair, thick beneath his peaked hat, added to the distance between his own and the heads of his companions. His pace accelerated by the sun's decline, Chepe and Ciriaco began to trot to keep up. With their shoulder bags filled with market purchases it promised to be a grueling journey. Fortunately Chepe had purchased some cane liquor that the two men already had begun to share.

Sebastian seemed too preoccupied to visit with or to notice the plight of his hapless bodyguards. They had sensed from the trip up the mountain eight hours earlier that their priest would have preferred to travel alone, and he was even less communicative now. "Oh well, who knows what goes on in the mind of a priest!" murmured Ciriaco in their Kaqchikel tongue.

Chepe was less charitable, impatiently having watched the whole day slip away. He'd agreed readily enough to give up his morning, with errands requiring the trip to Solola's Friday market anyway, but here it was late afternoon and he was still a good three hours from Santa Catarina. "I, for one, won't miss the pompous ass!"

His frankness surprised them both. Before the recent fast-moving events, no sacristan would have voiced such sentiments even to friends, much less to a fellow sacristan. Ciriaco didn't know how to respond. Since his companion wasn't inclined to force the conversation, he fell silent. They caught up with and began passing the last of their countrymen returning to Panajachel, Santa Catarina, and San Antonio at the lake's east end....even some from the west end who were too drunk to take the shortcut down the precipitous Santa Cruz trail.

28

Solola lay perched on an escarpment overlooking Lake Atitlan 1000 meters below. As deep as its volcanoes on the opposite rim were tall and descending half the distance from the earth's surface to molten magma, the huge crater's restive waters were home to eight villages ringing the northern and western shores and four more at the feet of the three southern volcanoes. Soon after his assignment to the parish of Panajachel, Sebastian had walked around the whole body of water with Father Rodrigo to know the 'twelve apostles,' as the towns were affectionately known. In fact, most of the twelve bore the names of patron saints who had been Christ's disciples, making understandable the quaint fiction hereabouts that this was the world's center...where Jesus lived and the sun is directly overhead at noon. The trek with Rodrigo had required four days, and yet Indians living at either end of the north side managed to walk to Solola's Friday market by late morning, do their shopping, and return home by dusk. For the vast majority of the lake's people, Solola's capital was as far from home as they had need to venture throughout their lives.

Sebastian knew few of his parishioners by name, but he had no difficulty recognizing their towns. Conveniently they dressed quite differently in each of the villages he served: women's *huipil* pullover blouses with differently colored stripes and patterned figures; their carrying cloths shading heads and swaddling babies varying in color and design as well. Why men wore wool in this warm climate, while women sensibly used only cotton, no one had been able to explain to his satisfaction. And why Panajachel men wore knee-length sleeveless tunics and Sololatecos wore fitted jackets modeled on the garb of Spanish gentlemen, while in San Antonio they wore long wool skirts covering short drawers and in San Andres short aprons over longer drawers was still a mystery!

He acknowledged the respectful greetings of families as he swept past, his arms waving with such regularity that he appeared ready to lift off in flight. He and his two companions would come upon first the youngest children at the rear, most of whom he had baptized, then the older daughters and mother with infants on their backs and wide baskets of produce on their heads — all led by the father or perhaps an older son with shoulder bag or a load on his back suspended from the tumpline strap across his forehead. Sabastian's respect for Indians stemmed largely from the monstrous loads that they managed, barefoot, on these unforgiving trails!

With the priest by and out of hearing, friends called to the sacristans, and after stopping at first to try to explain their predicament the two gave up and pretended not to hear. But it wasn't a complicated puzzle: clearly the priest was afraid. Why else would he be in such a hurry to get down to Panajachel and have forced even his Santa Catarina sacristan to tag along?

But fear for his safety was hardly on Sebastian's mind. He loved the long walks that his dispersed parish required, especially these late afternoon descents to the lake from Solola. The clouds this time of year usually were cumulus, but they were unusually cirrus and uniform today — like furrows in a freshly plowed field. A number of his favorite poems had found inspiration on such treks, and he played with some ideas now to see if they held any potential for an addition to his collection. The deeper in thought he sank, the faster he walked.

Slaphappy from the pace, Chepe began to chuckle at the sight they presented. "We'd better grab ahold of his skirt-tails! If he goes any faster or flaps any harder, he'll soon be soaring like a turkey buzzard!"

"Or an angel," agreed Ciriaco, imagining the robed priest floating off the side of the mountain straight up to Heaven.

As luck would have it, the pace slackened suddenly when an oxcart loomed ahead, on their rounding one of the many turns of the serpentine road. Don Elisio, the storekeeper in Panajachel, had stocked up on provisions in Solola and was on his way down the mountain. Sebastian could not courteously pass his principal alms giver without visiting at length, so abruptly he decided that they should stop for a rest.

Ciriaco thanked him for his consideration of their loads and offered the sweating cleric a sip from his water gourd. To their surprise, Sebastian accepted! Then, smiling, he retrieved a small flask of whiskey from the folds of his robe. With that Chepe produced his bottle of rum, half emptied since departing Solola an hour ago. Settling down on the grass, Sebastian was pensive for a few minutes before asking if they would listen to his latest poem. Ciriaco had heard many poems on walks such as this, so wasn't surprised, but Chepe had to be told in Kaqchikel about the little song-like stories that priests apparently have to compose. In awe he listened to the first poem in Spanish that he ever had heard:

"Now leaves the sun his daily labor,
Plowing clouds in parallel
O'er soft-illumined terraces
Etched on a rural sky.

30

Now comes the daily breeze that rises,
Sowing fenceless sweeps of stars
That seek advancing shadows,
And in the darkness bloom.
Now thanks to ye who farm God's heaven,
Granting spring eternity,
We understand at last His need
For such infinity of room.

As usual, Ciriaco was complimentary, suggesting that this one be named, "Atitlan Sunset." He could at least grasp its general meaning. But just how his priest thought about San Bernardo and the *chocomil* wind of the lake, Ciriaco wasn't sure. He had made such a point of insisting that the sun wasn't God, and yet here he was, again, seeming to talk to the sun and the wind the same way others here did.

As for Chepe, the poem made no sense at all. Not knowing how to respond, he arose to signal his own readiness to resume the descent. Even on his feet he was little taller than the straight up and down body of the priest kneeling beside him. Lest his impatience be too evident, he squatted again until Sebastian extended his hand for assistance in getting his frame of almost two meters off the ground. As thanks, he handed Chepe with the other hand what was left of his whiskey before dusting off his frock. Such a difference...their hands. His own soft, long-fingered and manicured; the older man's gnarled, with nails broken and dirty beyond belief. Chepe's grasp was so strong that Sebastian had grimaced when pulled to his feet. And so large!...hands as well as their feet. With appendages so large, why then so short in stature? His fellow clerics attributed Indians' height to diet, but Sebastian suspected it had more to do with all their carrying on top of, or suspended from, their heads that commenced in early childhood.

Grateful that they were still a half hour from Panajachel, and eager to talk in particular with the taciturn ChepeYach whom he knew less well, Sebastian ventured, "Please tell me, Chepe, why so many of the parishioners insist on bringing me gifts of food at baptism or a marriage blessing, in addition to the payment the church asks for such service."

Warming to this unexpected invitation to instruct their priest in Mayan ways, Chepe did his best to respond in Spanish. "Us — us *naturales* that's to say — gives many gifts of food to each other. We always gives this way at fiestas, or

31

any special happening. And for favors, too — to Ladinos as well — we gives gifts. Would be sinful, not to give a gift, when you does us the baptism favor."

Sebastian had never heard Indians refer to themselves as *naturales*...the "natural people"...how quaint!

"But, Father," laughed Ciriaco, "people always ask me what you possibly can do with all their gifts of food. They know you can't eat all them tamales, chickens, and fruit. If you did, you'd be a whole lot fatter! I tell them the truth — that often you give me part of their gifts, and that sometimes the gifts I give my neighbors and compadres are those they have given you."

"People aren't offended when their gifts are given away?"

"No, of course not," replied Chepe. "Because one benefit of trading gifts is that sometimes you needs such help and sometimes not. Us children of Santa Catarina are very poor people, Father. When times is hard it helps to know the rich will share a few tamales or eggs."

"But surely people know that I don't need their food," acknowledged Sebastian.

"Of course, Father, but it's the custom. We gives to anyone who can help us."

"Then is this the way you pay for the assistance of midwives — and diviners?" Sebastian added quickly, careful not to call them cave witches.

"Yes, always. There was a Catrineco, they say, who was so powerful and famous that he tried charging money for doing divinations — like you charges for baptisms — but he soon had to stop because people complained so much. They complained that God gave him his powers to use for others, not so's he could get rich. Some curers lets it be known they prefers money, and that isn't bad so long as they still lets it be food if that's all we have. When you asks how much money to give, they always *says* that it isn't for them to charge. But you knows it's expected."

"But it seems to me that they become pretty rich either way," observed Sebastian.

"I suppose most do, agreed Ciriaco, "but not all. There is a very poor diviner in Panajachel, Celso Alinan —"

"Old Celso a cave witch?" exclaimed Sebastian, forgetting himself.

Both Indians smiled, forgiving him the unintended slight, and Ciriaco continued, "Yes, Celso's a very good curer, he is. But also very poor."

"I can see that," nodded Sebastian, "with so many *compadres* I don't see how he manages!" Celso was one Panajachel Indian whom even Sebastian knew by name, as often as he and his wife were asked by other Panajachel parishioners to be godparents to their children.

"Well, we seek out Celso because he's got the luck for keeping children alive. It's rare that a godchild of his dies."

Sebastian had been visited by Celso and some *compadres* of his with a sick child only last week, on the eve of the boy's death, but he thought better of contradicting his sacristan. Besides, clearly it was the faith that counted, whether justified or not. "Celso comes to me frequently, more often than other diviners. I sort of assumed that diviners wouldn't have anything to do with us priests."

They smiled sympathetically. Here, indeed, was a side to their priest neither sacristan had seen before. "Well, they're not exactly sorry to see you go, I suppose. They respect your power, though, and try to use the power of the church when they can," Ciriaco replied warily.

"But how do they use the power of the Church?"

"They use the power of the cross. And the wine you use in the communion service — that's like curers using liquor when doing *costumbres*."

At that, Sebastian chuckled. The reputation of priests for drinking almost rivaled the reputation of the cave witches.

"If I can speak frankly, Father, the diviners talk against you priests so much because they know how you try to turn us against *them*." Probably only Ciriaco could say so bluntly what everyone knew to be the case. "Some say that with the priests gone there'll be less quarrelling about *costumbres*," he concluded, confident that Father Sebastian wouldn't attribute this sentiment to him.

"But mostly I hears people worring — afraid how the saints gonna punish us after you priests goes," inserted Chepe quickly. "There's fear the pox comes back...maybe seeds doesn't grow or fruit trees doesn't give. There's worry, too, about the children. Father, what's gonna happen to them? What's gonna happen to us when we doesn't baptize children?"

"If you and the other sacristans baptize and give blessings," Sebastian explored cautiously, "would the people be willing for this?" He had mentioned the possibility in passing to Ciriaco, but didn't know, really, how Ciriaco had reacted. For his part now, Ciriaco was listening intently to Chepe.

"Well, Father," continued Chepe, "not to offend, but since you asks I can tell you with truth that we thinks only priests has the power. It's like the diviners. They has to have the destiny, the luck — not everybody succeeds at such dangerous work."

Ciriaco stepped in, with his better Spanish, to repeat Chepe's assessment of the thinking locally. "Yes, Father, I know that you've mentioned this, and I've thought about it. It — It'll be very hard for the people — and for me, Father — to continue the baptism ceremony after you're gone. I think I know how to do it, and of course I'll do so if you tell me I must. But I fear the people will accuse me of keeping the money. Your sacristan in San Andres feels the same way. And while I haven't talked with the San Antonio sacristan, people are saying that he's hoping that he *can* baptize! But, Father, you should know — since you're leaving — that the sacristan in San Antonio has close relatives who are powerful diviners. The sacristan envies their wealth. I fear that he'll keep the baptism fees, and that makes it all the more likely that people will accuse me of doing the same." He stopped, to see how the priest was reacting. Perhaps he had spoken too freely.

But Sebastian was grateful. He'd been listening so intently that he'd completely ignored the storekeeper, who had stopped to rest his oxen at the waterfall off the path when the trio had passed him earlier and now waved as his oxen lumbered past and on into Panajachel. Sebastian waved back, instead of responding to Ciriaco, peeved at himself for not suspecting such obvious explanation for the eagerness of his new San Antonio assistant to become sacristan when his predecessor had become ill.

Ciriaco had more on his mind to share: "The heads of the *cofradias* there, including some of the *zahorines*, don't like the Church mainly because it takes so much of their money. But the town is richer than most, and its people are very proud of that. So when the church fell in after the quake they built an even larger one to impress the rest of us poorer folk. They say that it will be better to leave the saints in the church and let the *cofradias* continue taking care of them there. They also say that they don't need a sacristan...say they can keep their saints satisfied in the new church and spend less money than they do now."

The church in San Antonio was, indeed, the pride of the parish. It was largely because of the cooperation that he had observed there that Sebastian had argued so vociferously for keeping the saints in the churches. What a revelation, to be told at this point that the town which had seemed most concerned for the welfare of the saints might in fact be less prepared to sacrifice on their behalf than their poorer neighbors!

They started down the last incline to Panajachel. Little was said the last few hundred meters before they went their separate ways. Each man was trying to comprehend what their frank sharing meant. In fact, the sojourn together — begun so inauspiciously — had decided for the bishopric of Solola the future of *cofradias* and their saints' care for the next quarter of a century.

Chapter Three — One Week Later

"**C**ongratulations!" Panajachel's storekeeper, Don Elisio, greeted Jose and Esteban in their tongue. "When your father ordered a full jug of rum, I said to myself, "Another marriage!" There have been so many weddings lately among you *naturales* that I had to go to Solola yesterday just to restock my liquor. I ought to thank Father Sebastian for leaving! Actually, though — don't know about you — but I'm going to miss the young thorn-in-our-feet. What will we do without him around to complain about?" The congenial storekeeper produced a large earthenware jug with the small mouth for easy pouring. "Need any empties?"

The jug would fill ten bottles, and Jose doubted that they had more than three or four at home. "We'll take six," he decided and put his money on the counter.

"Bless you! Since you're paying cash this time, I'll throw in the birdcage for nothing. I made the big mistake of selling on credit to my first customer this morning, and I've been punished by nobody having cash ever since. Now maybe my luck will change," he laughed, giving a generous view of more gold teeth than Jose had seen in one mouth.

—

"It sure would be different around here if all Ladinos were as friendly as is our 'Mr. Jolly'," Jose observed with a smile once outside the store and struggling to protect amongst the empty bottles in his net bag the birdcage that he had picked out for his parents-in-law. He had managed to snare one of the songbirds nesting near the spring above town and hoped yet to catch the mate. Esteban nodded agreement, wondering why the storekeeper and his wife took the time to learn their language, called them *naturales,* and even — folks said — ate what Indians eat. Positioning the jug of rum in his bag, he lifted it into place and headed off after Jose. Owning a store and tavern like this in Santa Catarina was Esteban's dream. But what Indian could save enough money to get started? There was a small store in San Antonio, but only because the owner found a pot of money buried beneath a flame he encountered in his milpa. He had found it after he'd lost half his corn to varmints when sickness had delayed his harvest. Varmints had told their Owner, and the lucky fellow had been rewarded for his kindness.

Such help from the Hill's Owner probably was the only way that a poor *natural* could do it.

At the river meandering through the Panajachel delta, whom should they see arriving from Santa Catarina but old Marcelo, staggering from the far side toward the bridge of a single shaved log. Judging from his unsteady gait, he was heading for Don Eliseo's store and tavern to cure a hangover. Jose flushed with embarrassment. The *zahorin* who had so rudely refused him his daughter in marriage the month before would see from their loads of rum and bottles that he was preparing to try again. "Quick, let's head downstream to the lower crossing before he recognizes us!" But before they had detoured more than a few running steps they heard a cry. Marcelo had lost his balance as soon as he stepped out on the log. Sober, he easily could have made it to shore, but his flailing limbs made clear that he was in trouble. Jose slipped out from under his load and bounded over the rocky riverbed to assist. Once safely on shore, Marcelo was a sorry sight, weeping and vomiting. He'd had a bad fright — enough to startle anyone's spirit — and would need to rest long enough to ensure its return.

But he tried to stand and embrace Jose instead. From what Jose could made out from his incoherent mumbling, the old man had been disappointed that Lorenzo and Vicente had given up so quickly in asking for his one remaining daughter. Marcelo had hoped for a second visit. "But you said we were too poor...told us to leave," Jose reminded him while helping Esteban lift the freshly purchased jug to his mouth for the liquor that could calm him down.

"Tha' I did...but only 'cause I wanted...only 'cause I hoped you'd conshent to live with me after marrying my daughter. Need her to do my cooking." Coughing and unable to continue, he slumped to the ground from exhaustion and vomited the rum. Jose felt that it was safe and probably wise to leave.

"Imagine that! Marcelo trying to shame me into living with them in exchange for his last daughter. And all because he lost his wife and with no sons. Better off poor with sons than rich with only daughters!"

—

The "five o'clocks" along the path had closed their petals for the day before Jose finally had gotten everything home — first dropping off his own load and then backtracking to Esteban's to get the jug of liquor. Vicente already had left to fetch Lorenzo. By dusk they were ready, after Vicente and Lorenzo had filled nine bottles and downed the rest to strengthen their courage for what lay ahead. Jose's resolve needed no rum after his reassuring encounter with Marcelo.

36

It was dark when they reached the Yaches, but they could hear voices within. Vicente and Jose waited on the path while Lorenzo called at the gate, "Pardon me, *Compadres*, it is I, Lorenzo. I seem to have lost my way home. I'll be obliged if I might borrow a cup of something to drink?"

"Oh, then you come with a hangover already?" replied Chepe, opening the door ever so slightly to study the situation.

"Yes, *Compadre*, with a hangover," replied Lorenzo, motioning to his companions "— and also with these two friends, Vicente Ajcojom and his son, Jose."

"Well, don't stand there in the dark. It's late, but since you're my *compadre* I can hardly say no." He turned up the lamp of castor oil and, feigning disgruntlement, offered their only two chairs to the eldest guests as Lorenzo confessed quickly the real purpose of their visit.

"So you have the nerve to ask me, the sacristan, for Rosa after going first to that cave witch, Marcelo?" responded Chepe dryly, crossing his arms warily as Jose opened and offered him the first of his bottles. "What d'you want with *two* wives?"

Concluding that he could argue his case more persuasively than could Lorenzo under the circumstances, Jose surprised even himself by reporting in detail his afternoon encounter. "We can go back to Marcelo to ask for his daughter, but as you can see that would be a mistake. It is unwise for us who are poor to mix with the rich." He hesitantly offered the bottle again, kneeling this time, and Chepe finally rewarded his directness and tact by accepting it.

"Yes," opined Chepe, "that's how those rich people always are. Because they have more land they think they can decide things." Then, turning to Maria, "Our *compadre* is asking for his goddaughter." Maria's wan smile conveyed her consent as she accepted her own proffered bottle.

Rosa, wide awake by now, didn't stir, afraid they would invite her out of bed for her opinion. Lorenzo was her godfather, and that was that. But she was not displeased...nor surprised. They had heard from a neighbor that Jose had been asking questions about her. Her thoughts raced to what lay ahead. The three would return the next evening with more liquor, plus food and money. Then Jose would start bringing firewood. It would probably be a couple weeks before the ceremony and having to move to his home. Would he have a hut of his own for her? Let her come home occasionally, and visit her friends? Strange how best friends, even sisters, usually drift apart as soon as one marries.

At fourteen years of age, Rosa had few questions or anxieties that her parents couldn't answer or alleviate. She trusted. If her parents couldn't help, there was her godfather. If he couldn't, then there were her aunts and grandmother. If they couldn't, then there were the saints in the church. Not that she had ever asked the saints for anything, nor her relatives — not even her godfather for that matter. But she knew that she could, and assumed that in time she would go to all these people for help with her children. In her experience it was only for one's children that parents needed help from outside the family, and children of her own had been until tonight the farthest from her thoughts. Children were gifts to married women. Now that she was to be married, the gifts would surely follow. What part she or Jose played in the receiving was still unclear. She knew only that today she could not become a mother, and that after the wedding she could and within a year or so almost certainly would.

She lay awake all night, more curious than apprehensive, straining for the conversation while it was audible but giving up when her father started on his second bottle of rum. When there was no longer any talking and she assumed they were all asleep, she got out of bed and crept to the hearth. Surveying the scene, she counted six bottles amidst the snoring bodies on chairs and floor. All were empty, or she would have tried the liquor. Before it was over she would have to drink with him. She settled down by the coals of the fire and sipped some maize gruel instead, studying her husband-to-be until her baby brother awakened and began to coo. To let her mother sleep, Rosa took him from the hammock cradle and climbed back in the bed of boards that she shared with a sister. She pretended that she was asleep when Jose awakened and helped his father and Lorenzo home.

———

The fourth day of the new year had dawned clear, like all others of late. But now, approaching mid-afternoon, clouds were gathering optimistically around the peaks of all three volcanoes across the lake. Sharpening his machete, Vicente paused to calculate that the fourth month would be April. With the halos forming around the heads of the volcanoes two-thirds of the way through the day, he predicted, "It looks like the rains will begin around the 20th of April, and that means planting by the first of April — only three months away. With all we have to do before then, Rosa's help is just what we need. Sure hope that she's as good a worker as Lorenzo says she is!" Vicente resumed his trimming of the eaves. Thatching the roof of Jose and Rosa's new house had been completed the week

38

before, except for trimming the eaves…a task that Vicente had been after his son to help him finish before the Yaches brought Rosa. Jose dutifully followed behind, sweeping and carrying off the trimmed straw to give the big pen a clean floor. They were interrupted by Lorenzo's call of greeting at the gate…the Yaches had arrived.

"How quickly you've come to bring my house servant," welcomed Vicente in jocular reply. "You must really be eager to be rid of Rosa!"

"It is just that we decided to bring her early in the day to avoid having to feed her yet another meal," laughed Chepe. "You know how poor we are. There will be no sense in Jose ever coming to us asking for a loan!" Then he turned to Lorenzo who had preceded them into the patio. *"Compadre,* now that you've done your part, it would be an embarrassment if we didn't bring your goddaughter to her new family right away. We don't want them or you displeased with us for any reason." With that Maria nudged Rosa who went to Vicente, kneeled and kissed first his hand and then Bacilia's. Lorenzo promptly led her inside to the hearth and bid her kneel on the new mat by the fire. "Here's your place now, Goddaughter, where you will make your tortillas for the rest of your life. For where a woman is born is never where she should die. Isn't that right, *Compadre,"* he said to Chepe who had now entered the room with the others. But Chepe was not the one to address, having dissolved in tears at the sight of his daughter's frightened face. Jose quickly handed his new relatives their bottles of rum for the day, to ease the sadness.

"You must respect the hearth, and it will in turn protect your family. Never move this stone," continued Lorenzo, pointing to the largest and eldest of the three sisters. "As long as this stone doesn't crack, you'll know that your house spirit is pleased." Lorenzo motioned to Bacilia for the new grinding stones. "Here are your new tools, my child: your stone arm and hand to prepare the maize you'll feed Jose and your children. Be respectful of these tools; if they don't break, your marriage will be a long and good one. Be sure to feed your tools maize of all three colors, to keep the maize spirits content. Rise early to revive the fire; it is a sin to let its coals die. Always have a pitcher of hot water when your father-in-law and husband awaken. If they ask for coffee, bring it right away. Whatever they and Bacilia teach you, learn quickly. But if you are mistreated, come at once to me and I'll complain to your father-in-law. This is why I'm here, to keep peace between you and your husband, to settle differences between your two families."

Then Lorenzo summoned Jose to kneel with his new wife on the mat. "You, also, should rise early, be about your chores promptly, and after breakfast leave Rosa detailed instructions on what you want her to do. If she won't obey you, you should come to me. Be careful with your money. Don't drink when away from home. Otherwise you'll not have money saved for your public service. To have to borrow for your services, even from us, will be a shame for us all."

Jose was as moved by the weeping of his parents-in-law as by Lorenzo's eloquence, and he hastened to reassure. Vicente did likewise, kneeling and kissing Lorenzo's hand before offering him his payment of rum. "Many thanks for this favor you have done us. Her parents and you need not worry. You know how much we have paid for the food and gifts. It would be a sin to treat her poorly and have her ask to return to her parents. Since I no longer have a wife, my sister-in-law will teach Rosa what she doesn't yet know. We don't want to lose her…we'll treat her well."

With that, Lorenzo accepted kisses on his hand from everyone present and took his leave. Bacilia ushered Rosa out to the cooking shed to show her where the utensils, dishes, and cups of family members were stored. Taking advantage of the lull, Jose presented the songbird in its freshly painted cage to Chepe and Maria. Then he invited them to look into the new two-room house. "If Rosa is embarrassed to stay here right away, she can sleep with Bacilia," he offered.

Too overcome to speak, they gave Jose an embrace before leaving. They couldn't bring themselves to say good-bye to their daughter. Maybe the strength would be there at the priest's blessing in the afternoon.

—

The feel of the sanctuary, toward day's end, was the same as the smaller church in Santa Catarina, just more pronounced — the drone of muffled supplications and scent of newly-cut pine boughs. The graying whitewashed walls were less bare than the church at home, and the saints in their cubicles were more visible due to twice as many candles. The Panajachel church was surprisingly full for so late in the day. But Rosa had never felt so much alone. Probably as alone as the thrush on her lap, she thought, stroking its quivering body with her finger through the cage. Poor thing! Maria said it hadn't uttered a note all day, suggesting to her the idea of offering it instead to their priest to take back to Spain.

As they had walked along behind the men to Panajachel, Rosa's conversation with her mother had been no different from that of any of their previous Sunday walks to Panajachel's weekly market. If Maria couldn't, or wouldn't, put into words what she was feeling, then Rosa was even more at a loss. They had been sitting together on the bench at the back of the church for an hour now, waiting for the priest's return from his evening meal. Maria knew the answers to most of her daughter's questions: Yes, there were more people than usual in the church because the priest was leaving and the people were worried about how the saints were adjusting. Yes, Vicente and Jose were burning only yellow beeswax candles in front of Saint Francis because Jesus had blessed the little bees. The Ajcojoms could afford this expense because Vicente kept his own hives. Then, suddenly, "Mama, are there things about being a wife and becoming a mother that you should tell me now? Without a mother-in-law, who will tell me such things?"

"Little by little, one learns." And the conversation that Rosa had been awaiting all week ended as abruptly as it had begun.

—

It was well past dark when the parents of Rosa Yach de Ajcojom — the name Father Sebastian had written in the book — arrived home. The young couple, now fully married (rather than simply *juntado*, joined as common-law partners without the benefit of a church ceremony), continued on with Vicente. Jose walked behind his father and Rosa brought up the rear. Bacilia, waiting at home because of her clubfoot, would want a full report. Rosa realized how useful she was going to be to her new aunt, handicapped with her clubfoot as was poor Bacilia. In return, surely she would be able to confide in Bacilia. About the ceremony, however, there wasn't much to report: very brief, but at least it was the private church blessing that her parents had hoped for. Father Sebastian said that it was the last blessing that he would give before he left. Rosa never had seen tears in the eyes of a priest, but tears they definitely were when her father, sacristan to Father Sebastian, gave him the wood thrush "as a daily reminder far across the ocean of the love the children of Saint Catherine have for you."

Jose's hand on its backward swing brushed hers. She didn't know what to do next. It could have been unintended, and she slowed a bit to take her proper place farther behind. But he slowed as well, and without looking reached back again. She giggled softly and took her husband's hand — the first time the newlyweds ever had touched.

Weary from the long day, Sebastian had stretched out on his bed but had not yet fallen asleep. The unexpected pealing of the bell in the church belfry startled and for a moment annoyed him. Ciriaco meant well — ringing the bell — and Sebastian sought what solace there was in that. The God-forsaken church bell he would not miss! — cracked since its fall in an earthquake over 50 years before. He had given up having it replaced once he understood his parishioners opposition. Legend had it that every bell contained a child, sacrificed when the bell was cast, and there was fear that someone would lose a child now if this one was replaced. How fearful these *naturales* were...how closed to the real meaning of Christ's sacrifice!

It would not have occurred to Sebastian to spend his final night on a poem, but as the discordant tolling ended he knew that it was not to be denied. He reached for pen and paper, and let the verses take shape — one for each toll of the bell. At least that was his intent, but the inspiration soon ran its course and he drifted off to sleep having penned just six:

> *Awaken, my children, and hark to the bell.*
> > *When bestirred, then be stilled by this shrouded knell*
> > > *Tolled in lament by a yet wakeful bell.*
> *A toll in the dark, your priest to depart —*
> > *In mourning not one on the quay — as tolled on their way*
> > > *All faith, hope, and love now embark.*
> *A priest's benediction, on this at least dwell...*
> > *Ring out, rural bell, in one resonant swell*
> > > *Tolled benedicities in far-flung farewell.*
> *Ah, world, so weary, too deep have ye drawn*
> > *Of draughts dissolving all dusk into dawn...*
> > > *Tolled blessings unheeded, a harsh requiem!*
> *Alas, ye ungodly, at least don the guise!*
> > *Clad this discordance! Dissembling lies*
> > > *Told the departing need fear no replies.*
> *Declare no dissentions, no willful mistakes,*
> > *Well learned this day's lessons — and yet, all too late,*
> > > *Told to a world no bell will awake...*

The usual babble of dogs and roosters greeted Sebastian's final dawn in Panajachel. Despite the short night, he awakened refreshed — unusually moved by the dream his late night ruminations had induced. His imaginings had included Father Rodolfo's last day...and how he had met his end. Rereading the poem's beginnings, he decided that the 'dirge' should stand, and titled it such. But he wouldn't let it rest at that. The last six verses would be redemptive — his final blessing. By the time Ciriaco and Chepe arrived to escort him for the last time up the road to Solola the 'psalm' half was done. He gave each of them a copy of the twelve verses as they parted, in envelopes bearing their names. They were the only *naturales* among his parishioners whom he could imagine might appreciate what the late night bells had inspired — even if they couldn't read the words.

Chapter Four — Three Years Later

Bacilia awakened with a start, the only sounds those of Rosa's breakfast clean-up across the yard. No voices, so Jose wasn't back from fishing. No tuberculosis coughing from Vicente's hut next door. He must already have left for the cave. She shouldn't have slept so long...not like Juanita to go the whole night without nursing. Rosa would be at her grinding in a few minutes, and for over-sleeping Bacilia would be the brunt of her teasing the rest of the morning. Better the woman's teasing than her complaining, however...if, after yesterday, she could possibly have any complaining left in that shell of a body. Rosa had railed against Jose from sunup until sundown and on into the night as well until he'd left in utter disgust to get some sleep in his dugout canoe before fishing.

The poor man was as discouraged and depressed as Bacilia ever had seen her step-son. Esteban finally had died two weeks before, from the bad water sickness that had first entered his body when he was at the Buenaventura. For four years now Esteban had pawned and re-pawned his wife's land near the border of San Antonio whenever they needed money, doing plantation labor to get it back. Because so much dirt was left over after burying him, his widow had hired Marcelo to do a seed-reading divination. The seed-reading left no doubt but that his dying was too early; his appointed time had not yet arrived. She was telling everyone that Esteban's patron in San Antonio had done black magic against him to weaken his body, to be able to keep the pawned land after he was dead. Jose had offered to go to the Buenaventura in Esteban's place, to help the hapless woman save her only milpa, and Rosa was distraught lest Jose also sicken there and die.

Bacilia gathered her blanket and got up to stir the embers of last night's fire, reviving enough heat to bring out flame in a splinter of pitch. A larger fire would be needed this morning. To make room for three sticks of oak she moved the two smaller hearthstones a bit farther from their eldest sister. Discarding her blanket, she shivered herself fully awake as she worked her head through the neck opening of the faded, too-small nursing *huipil* blouse that she never had expected to be using again. Exposing a swollen breast, she fetched her seven-month-old daughter and settled back on the bed. So began her every day: nursing, combing, and stuffing loose hairs into the soot-blackened thatch above her head. The lice and scabies were worse; the amount of hair she was losing from daily combings was worrisome. Nobody in the household was very healthy, the reason for Jose spending so much time fishing and crabbing for improving their diet and selling in the weekly Tecpan market.

While she combed she watched the hearth spirit weaken the darkness to take control of the room...and stared down at the misshapen foot that confined her more than most women to her one-room hut and patio. But today would be less boring. Vicente might learn whether Rosa was carrying a boy or a girl. Frankly, Rosa was more of a worry to the family than was Jose's offer to replace Esteban at the Buenaventura. After two miscarriages in rapid succession since having Julia, everybody in the neighborhood knew that she finally was pregnant again. It had become such an obsession that women were reluctant to let her be around their babies, afraid that Rosa's envy would give them the evil eye. "Now there's a woman who wants a heap of patience!" Bacilia mumbled as she shifted Juanita to the other breast. Sorry as Bacilia had been when her sister-in-law died, widowing Vicente, Bacilia had concluded within weeks of Jose's marriage that his mother was fortunate to go to an early grave. She would have had nothing but headaches with Rosa for her daughter-in-law. It was fortunate for Rosa that Bacilia's clubfoot had taught her such patience. Perhaps no one in Santa Catarina could have put up with Rosa's petulance and selfishness as patiently as had she.

It helped to know that, despite her thirty-five years and her crippled foot, Bacilia was considerably more attractive than poor Rosa. Four pregnancies already and more than her share of sickness had given Rosa a face and body much older than her eighteen years. Frankly, she looked ten years older. But this baby she was carrying would at least have the advantage of Rosa's long rest from nursing. Most women in town despaired of their being able to do much of anything to slow all the dying of babies in Santa Catarina — clearly poorer luck in this regard than the mothers in Panajachel and San Antonio were experiencing. There was a desperation that seemed new in Santa Catarina...that Bacilia didn't recall from her youth. Perhaps it was because the epidemic illnesses — like the pox — for some reason were punishing Santa Catarina more frequently, as Vicente believed. But Bacilia suspected that it was from couples trying to become pregnant so soon after losing a baby, not giving mothers sufficient time to strengthen their blood so as to have enough milk for the next baby.

45

The silence was broken by Rosa shouting at three-year old Julia, who — judging from her mother's invectives — had upset the maize left soaking over night. Bacilia smiled...maybe Rosa wouldn't get the early start on grinding after all! She returned Juanita to her hammock cradle, finished dressing, and hobbled out to relieve herself.

From the privy seat, Bacilia enjoyed a full view of the changing panorama above Santa Catarina. High cliffs had begun to catch San Bernardo's first rays, and within minutes his sunlight would reach the dark mouth of Judas. The cave was a couple hours climb above Santa Catarina — too far away to see those gathered at its mouth for daybreak divinations. Just one hour away, at the terraces near the spring, she could barely make out a Panajachel farmer at work — probably harvesting onions in readiness for Sunday's market. It had been six years since the Panajachel family had bought land below the spring. Everybody wondered why they would want a milpa field for maize and beans way over here. But when they terraced the land instead for planting onions, with the spring water permitting three harvests each year, it was clear enough. Jorge as usual had been right: Santa Catarina land could grow onions just as well as could the soil in Panajachel. He had been irritated with their neighbor for selling the land to outsiders, wishing that he had known they wanted to sell. The neighbor had felt badly...had told Jorge he would sell some adjoining land to the Ajcojoms for less money. But his brother Vicente was against it...said that Saint Francis had bestowed the luck of growing onions only on Panajachel. Buying the land would be a waste of money. That had been Jorge and Vicente's last, and worst quarrel. Bacilia had had a difficult time forgiving Vicente, suspecting that the quarrel was the reason for her husband leaving Santa Catarina.

Just how Bacilia felt about Jorge, missing now for almost six years, she wasn't sure. Not bitter really, and relieved to be spared his constant complaints about forced labor... about fishing getting worse and their always being poor. Vicente was probably right: it was a blessing that Jorge had been spared a long life in Santa Catarina. How could two brothers be so completely different?...Vicente so content despite being among the poorest men in Santa Catarina. And she apparently destined to be wife to them both! A year after Jorge's disappearance, she had received Vicente's first visit. "With your bad foot and my bad eye and ear, we deserve each other," he had told her as he climbed into bed. At first they had made love only rarely, mostly against her will, and with much shame on her part lest people learn or Jorge return. Vicente would come to her early in the morning,

46

catching her by surprise after Jose had left to fish. Even after she became pregnant with Juanita she still insisted on keeping her things and her bed in her own hut. For several months now, to avoid getting pregnant again and losing her milk, she had insisted on limiting her nights with Vicente to the safe times of the waning moon. They slept together only when she agreed to go to his bed. He didn't like it...complained that if people knew they would think she had bewitched him to make him so docile. In fact, she did lay an old skirt over his sleeping body the last night that he'd come to her bed, so demanding that they had fought. It seemed to have helped. He hadn't tried to force himself on her since then.

Vicente had gleaned only three-quarters of a bag of half-eaten ears, but enough to prove his point: Jose wasn't respectful enough of the maize. How could he and Bacilia entrust their milpas to such a son? Vicente spread a rope net over some stones which years earlier he had formed into a crude altar at the side of the field, and lifted his bag onto the net. Lifting from the ground had become too painful. Half-squatting in readiness for lifting his load he paused for one last sad look at Bacilia's field. He wouldn't be back until time to burn the cornstalks for planting next season. He would be just as careful next year to plant equal amounts of black, yellow, and white grain. And the spirit of the milpa could hardly complain; he had burned incense or candles every time he had visited the field. Satisfied that he had gleaned every ear, he struggled to his feet, resting the load again on the altar to bunch as much of his thinning hair under the capulin bark as possible. A leather head strap he couldn't afford. With head and eyes forced down by the load, and leaning on his oak staff, he started down the path. Just as well to have to look down, with only one good eye and all the roots the Hill's Owner uses to trip the unwary.

He had intended to save some candles for the milpa altar, but after Marcelo's seed-reading he had decided that the candles were better offered at the cave for Rosa's baby. Although it was a relief to have had his overdue talk with Marcelo, he wished that he hadn't asked for the divination. As usual, he had told the crotchety elder too much about the family! Marcelo had seemed respectful and cordial enough until the first two readings came out odd: three seeds left over the first time and only one the next. At that point Marcelo had threatened to end the divination. Said that something wasn't right, and then embarrassed him by asking if he'd had his way with Bacilia the night before. Of course he hadn't, so Marcelo then had asked if he and Jose were still harboring resentment over

Marcelo's not giving them his daughter. They talked for quite a while about Jose and Rosa, about Vicente's feelings toward Jose, until Marcelo said that he was satisfied that the anger in Vicente's blood was toward his son and not Marcelo. The last two readings came out even. And it was during the final reading that Marcelo's blood jumped strongly in his right leg. He had felt only weak movements on both sides until then. Probably Rosa would have a boy. But the four readings together suggested that Vicente's grandson would have a hard life. Vicente decided not to tell this to Jose...not even to Bacilia.

It was an unusually cool morning in March, and Vicente's tuberculosis cough had kept the whole family awake most of the night. Bacilia needed some mint for his tea, and with Jose still out fishing Rosa offered to make the climb to where Jose had told her he had found some above the Panajachel onions near the spring. The climb was arduous, but she welcomed the exercise. Despite Marcelo's prediction that this child would live, worry of miscarriage had kept her close to home. It felt good to be out. Exhausted, and needing a rest from the wind off the lake, she climbed carefully through onions to the thatched shelter built by the onions' owner. On reaching it, she kneeled and found herself face to face with her husband. A woman cowered half naked behind him.

Recoiling, Rosa choked on her scream and reeled down the mountain, sobbing and falling twice before she reached the path to town. Jose and his lover followed, for lack of any better idea, hoping that Jose would find Rosa at the house. But she was already on her way to the town hall when her husband reached home to await the consequences of what had become a regular rendezvous with Esteban's widow after his early-morning fishing when she was fetching water at the spring.

Rosa was hysterical when she rushed into the council room, interrupting the mayor and falling on her knees to kiss his hand. She continued around the table, kissing the hands of the councilmen, before collapsing at the feet of the mayor who had left his chair to try to calm her. When she could at last describe what she had seen, two errand boys were dispatched to find Jose and his lover. They would spend the night in jail, and their fines would be set on the morrow.

Vicente helped Rosa home where Bacilia had ready a hot drink with ashes and salt for the fright. "She told the mayor she fell down and is afraid for the baby," Vicente lamented. "What should we do now?"

"You should talk with Rosa's parents. As soon as they heard, they came to get Julia. They may be planning to take Rosa away from us as well!"

Vicente looked away, too angry at his son to weep but too ashamed to keep the tears at bay. His relationship with Rosa's father had become steadily more strained because of Jose's money problems. Bacilia didn't press the point, and decided to go for the midwife instead.

Rosa didn't return to her parents. At Bacilia's entreaty, she obeyed the midwife and stayed in bed for a week, insisting that Jose stay close by. At week's end there still was no bleeding. But diarrhea had set in and was joined by fever. For the fever Bacilia rubbed cold herbs on the soles of Rosa's feet, but not as frequently as the midwife ordered since Rosa's diarrhea was the cold kind that cold herbs seemed to aggravate. "We must bring a curer," Bacilia finally decided, and despite protests from Vicente, she sent him for Marcelo.

For all the talk that Bacilia had heard about Santa Catarina's most respected curer, she was not prepared for the diviner's deep-set eyes. No larger than frijoles amidst a maze of wrinkles, they weren't visible until you were up close face to face. And then they were piercing. She had seen him often enough, dutifully extending to him the greeting due all elders when meeting on paths about town. But Marcelo had never acknowledged her; their eyes had never met. Now, as Marcelo entered the patio he looked each of the household straight in the eye and addressed even Bacilia by name.

To her astonishment, Vicente was almost rude to Marcelo — sullen and subdued. But Marcelo was unruffled. He proceeded into the house without waiting for an invitation and asked to talk with Rosa, Jose, and Vicente together. For the first time Jose disclosed the details of his infidelity. Looking deeply into Rosa's eyes, Marcelo felt her pulse in each wrist, insisting that she return his gaze, until he announced, "She's had her spirit startled. It hasn't returned and must still be at the lean-to —"

"But we don't have the money for such a costly *costumbre*," interrupted Vicente, who already had anticipated the diagnosis.

"We can take care of that later," Marcelo assured him, motioning the others from the room and lowering his voice. "Jose can help me clear and burn my milpa next month. But we must do the cure soon. She and the baby could die from this soul loss. I can be ready by the next strong day. We'll need Rosa's father's assistance."

"I doubt that Chepe will come," objected Vicente.

49

Marcelo was firm. "Then I'll invite him myself. He's the sacristan and we'll need him *and* his church." With detailed instructions to Jose for the gathering of herbs and pine boughs, and to Bacilia for the meal to begin Friday's ceremony, he left.

The next two days reminded Jose of the preparations for his marriage. Vicente covered Rosa's floors with boughs and decorated the house altar with pictures of saints. The boughs that Jose collected for the church were accepted with a grateful nod; Chepe's anger toward his son-in-law was exceeded by embarrassment over the church's sorry condition. Jose volunteered to whitewash spots where adobe walls were completely bare of stucco. He had to agree with Chepe: it was a sad place to be asking for help from any of the saints.

Chepe and Jose were still readying the church when Marcelo arrived with Vicente carrying a bundle of beeswax candles and an incense pot. Marcelo was wearing his red ceremonial head cloth and an equally scarlet, newly woven sash. To Jose's surprise, Santa Catarina's most outspoken critic of the clergy and their expensive churches kneeled and crossed himself on entering the sanctuary.

Marcelo divided his candles among the few saints' images still in the church. The Virgin Mary and Saint Catherine had been moved to the homes of their *cofradia* leaders. As Chepe lit the candles, Marcelo prayed before each saint, swinging the incense burner in the sign of the cross while he explained Rosa's loss and the help needed to recover her spirit. The litany of petitions that followed required no concentration; he recited effortlessly from memory. Instead, his attention was on the sacristan sweating at his side. From the corner of his half-closed eyes, he watched Chepe's hands tremble as he struggled to light and plant the candles securely in their drippings on the freshly swept stone floor. Was the poor man really so afraid of him? Admittedly Marcelo had had no more to do with the sacristan and his church than absolutely necessary over the years. And he assumed that everyone, including Chepe, would know that his insistence on including Chepe in the rituals was calculated: if Rosa was going to recover and maintain any lasting peace of mind, her father's blessing was as important as any saint's. Marcelo had worried, needlessly it seemed, that Chepe would be cynical of Marcelo's visit to his sanctuary. Instead, Chepe obviously was not only pleased but worried that somehow he might offend and jeopardize the cure. Such a pious man, this sacristan!

Chepe's candles sputtered as if in protest; he hadn't yet noticed that the problem was the sweat pouring off his chin. "Why so nervous?" he chided himself silently, wiping his brow and glancing at Marcelo lest the curer be distracted by his clumsiness. But Marcelo's deep-set eyes appeared to be closed as he mumbled on in monotone. The saints' hearing must be better than his own, Chepe concluded, unable to understand a word. He had been amused at Marcelo's discomfort when the wizened curer appeared at his door to humbly ask Chepe's assistance with the ceremony. At first Chepe had refused — his reasons were many, and he assumed obvious to the curer — but when Marcelo politely reminded him that this was as difficult for the Ajcojoms as for him, Chepe acquiesced. It was more Vicente's than Marcelo's scrutiny that worried him now, as Chepe struggled to avoid offending the saints.

Marcelo abruptly ended his litany and reached into his shoulder bag. From a ball of beeswax he quickly formed two small figures, one male and the other female, and taking a pine needle he put it in the hand of the female.

"What's he doing with the pine needle?" whispered Jose to Vicente.

"We don't have an image of Saint Martin, the patron saint of curers, so the wax figures have to do instead. The saint's wife has a needle to prod him if he won't cooperate...if he won't agree to help Marcelo find the soul."

"But why wouldn't he be willing?"

"Perhaps because Marcelo is a sorcerer as well as a curer. Saint Martin might be jealous...knows that Marcelo will be asking help of Hill spirits to get the soul back." Jose was impressed. He trailed his elders home at a respectful distance.

After the meal, Marcelo helped Rosa out of bed and asked her to completely undress in front of the house altar. He took an egg in each hand from his bag and passed them over her forehead, neck, and arms. Then he stroked the inside of her forearms from elbow to wrist twelve times. With two more eggs he did the same: up the backs of her legs to her head, down again to her crotch, and finally over her abdomen and breasts to her mouth. Thoroughly engrossed, Jose moved to the side of the altar to see better. As the eggs were placed in a gourd dish amidst the candles, Marcelo paused to explain that the eggs now contained some of Rosa's sickness and could help him explain to the spirits the harm that had befallen her at the lean-to. "Now, will you take me to the place on the hillside, Jose?"

Jose hadn't anticipated this. Friday at midnight was the worst possible time to be out on the mountain. But when Vicente scowled he quietly accepted the pitch-pine torch from Marcelo and led the way. Surely Marcelo knew what he was doing. The men followed, carrying the eggs, digging sticks, two large candles, a

51

cigar, homemade cigarettes, a pitcher of gruel, some sweet bread, chocolate beans, and a bottle of rum.

From the position of the moon when they reached the lean-to, Jose concluded that it would, indeed, be midnight before they got home. While Vicente held the torch, Jose started digging a hole and Marcelo began to pray. Facing west and holding up the eggs as testimony of a missing soul, Marcelo addressed the Hills' Owner, "As a favor to me, oh *Compadre,* please help me restore this soul to its owner." After recounting Jose's story of what had happened, he asked Jose to help him lay the gifts and wax figures in the hole before burying them with dirt. Then, putting some pebbles from the mound in the gourd dish with the eggs, the old man got slowly to his feet and observed hopefully, "It should be midnight by now." As if in reply, a sharp breeze swept off the lake and sheet lightning brightened the sky above the volcanoes.

To Rosa's inquiry on their return Marcelo replied noncommittally. He lit new candles at the altar and explained to the saints in the pictures why it had been necessary to talk with the Hills' Owner. Then he asked Chepe to place a pot of coals under his daughter's bed. Expectantly, all watched Marcelo crawl through the smoke and place beside the pot the gourd of pebbles brought from the place of fright. The incense in the bowl of pebbles suddenly burst into flame, and Marcelo announced triumphantly, "Aha! The spirit is here!" In a large gourd half full of water he broke the six eggs with which he'd massaged Rosa. By the light from the few remaining candles on the altar he watched intently the slowly swirling shapes. He finally nodded with assurance and recounted the history of her fright, beginning with her first suspicions of Jose's unfaithfulness. As the egg whites sank slowly to the bottom of the bowl he pronounced that her series of fright had been cured…that the recent symptoms of illness soon would disappear. Only then did he finally sit down to rest and drink. It was almost daybreak when he and Chepe took their leave.

Marcelo didn't return; nor did he ask Vicente or Jose about Rosa. But within a few days she was up and about her work as usual, happier than Jose had seen his wife in years.

Chapter Five — 1890-94

As had become their custom, the rains again arrived earlier than usual in 1890. There was more rain that season than Vicente could recall, and the rains and wind also brought more than the usual sickness. They brought a new, much more deadly pox with smaller blisters that killed about everyone it entered. His own daughter Juanita was among the victims. "The good die young," Vicente consoled Bacilia as they buried the little coffin. The pain eased a little when Rosa bore them their first grandson six weeks later. Or so grandfather Vicente assured me on numerous occasions once I was old enough to learn the story of my birth and naming. At Jose's request and with Vicente's blessing, I was given the name of the martyred priest.

When I was two weeks old and could risk exposure to spirits out-of-doors, the martyred priest's crucifix was placed around my neck and I was taken to my maternal grandfather Chepe, the sacristan, for the closest thing available to a blessing by a priest. When Jose explained why they had chosen the name — showed Chepe the leaflet he had saved from the Buenaventura plantation — Chepe thought a while and in memory of both Father Rodolfo Luis and Father Sebastian offered a rhyming blessing: "Rodolfo Luis, remember grandson — the name of a priest whose work was not done. To the cross and the fish be faithful, grandson!"

—

The rains were heavy again the next year, and even heavier the year after that. I recall grandfather Vicente telling me that once in his childhood the lake had grown much smaller, even smaller than they were experiencing. Vicente told me that her Owner was lonely and wanted to move the lake. She lives in her castle at the bottom, as does her younger sister in the smaller Lake Amatitan near the capital city of Guatemala. When one sister is sad and goes to visit the other, her water wants to follow in the form of rain or perhaps a river underground.

"Perhaps," Vicente suggested in a meeting of the elders, "— the Owner's sister has come to live with her a while and has brought her water." So reasoned other elders, and to persuade the sister to go home they carried the patron Saint Catherine and the Virgin Mary to the lake shore to see for themselves the danger to the community. The stone weirs were so far from shore that they no longer trapped fish, and the hot springs were so far under water that the fish they attracted were out of reach of the basket traps. Unlike people, the elders explained to the saints, fish don't have permanent homes; they move to wherever the shore is shallow. The reeds also prefer shallow water and were becoming shorter and harder to find. The elders pleaded that without fish and reed mats to sell, the children of Saint Catherine were suffering more than the saints apparently realized.

But the saints either could not, or would not, intervene. The next season's rains were the heaviest yet, and Vicente's explanations no longer satisfied even himself. It was then that the elders began to listen to their sacristan. From the outset Chepe Yach had maintained that the problem was not with the lake's owner but with the saints themselves. They were unhappy to have been taken from the church, to be moved about from home to home of the changing *cofradia* leaders. How else could be explained that only Catarinecos had suffered from the lake's rising waters? Their neighbors in San Antonio had left Saint Anthony in the church, and their fortunes had worsened less than in Santa Catarina. Even the sicknesses that came with the rains had killed many fewer in San Antonio. Why not return the saints to the church for a year to see what would happen?

After whitewashing the church and repairing its door, they made the move in April. But to no avail: the rains and illness had been as bad again this year. The plight of many families had become desperate, and the elders could think of nothing else to try. As for Vicente's family, there were no resources left. Jose hired out whenever he could find work and made regular trips to markets in Solola and Tecpan to sell what fish, crabs, and ducks he could catch. Twice Vicente had talked the elders out of assigning them community services, pleading their dire straits, but because so many were refusing to serve he decided finally that the Ajcojoms should accept the next time they were asked, no matter what the sacrifice.

The request came sooner than expected. The *cofrade* of Saint Mary's *cofradia* drowned while crabbing, just two months before the Virgin's November fiesta of Concepcion. A family familiar with the fiesta's ceremonies was needed to avoid giving offense to the Virgin, and the elders asked Vicente and Jose.

"It comes at such a bad time!" Jose complained bitterly, "when everybody's out of maize and buying food in addition to going to the coast. I was only fourth mayordomo when I served before...and even then I had to pawn land. It'll cost twice as much if I am the *cofrade!*"

54

But Vicente had a plan. He met with the elders and proposed that the town's two *cofradias* combine their annual celebrations and give the community's saints a fiesta they would never forget. Perhaps, Vicente reasoned, the problem lay in less having been spent for the saints' care of recent years. If those in charge of Saint Catherine's *cofradia* agreed to the plan, he and Jose would take charge of Saint Mary and sponsor the Dance of the Conquest.

Within the week there was agreement, with pledges for the costs of marimbas, licenses for liquor sales, and for sponsorship of the Dance of the Deer as well. No one could recall a fiesta with two dances, even in San Antonio. The excitement was contagious, and to raise money three of Jose's dance group pawned land to families in San Antonio for a year. To raise his share Jose chose instead to hire out Rosa to the storekeeper, Don Eliseo, in Panajachel; she would grind maize in his store five mornings a week for three months.

Vicente had promised to accompany Jose and his *mayordomos* on the four-day round-trip journey to Totonicapan to rent costumes, but vomiting and diarrhea removed all desire to go. I was four years old by then and watched Grandfather carve small fish for me to sell during the fiesta — my first commercial venture.

Jose and Rosa's hut was the newest addition to the Ajcojom residential compound and had been converted to the home of the Virgin Mary for this special fiesta. That was where Vicente did his whittling by the light of candles kept burning at the Virgin's feet. Flickering flames illuminated Vicente's face, and the Virgin's, too...always awake, always praying, and more reassuring with each passing night. Vicente told the family that the red rooster's claw bromeliads and intoxicating smell of pine boughs and copal incense gathered by the *mayordomos* in the high country reminded him of the church in the days of Father Sebastian.

"Still carving?" whispered Rosa, returning from helping Bacilia with the *chicha*. "Would you like a drink?" For weeks Bacilia had been brewing the sweet liquor from Spanish plums donated by the first *mayordomo's* wife, and it was ready to sample. Rosa gave me my first sip of *chicha* before passing the gourd cup to Vicente and sitting down on the bench to inspect his latest carvings. The largest had been done with particular care, and she studied it approvingly. To my surprise Vicente said that he had made it for me to keep. "Your sacristan father says that the fish that Rodolfo encounters in his sleep could be the spirit of Father Rodolfo Luis. It might be that the priest's spirit keeps trying to take his namesake with him down deep into the lake. A fish charm seems a good idea, just in case."

Rosa listened without comment, distracted by the deep lines in Vicente's face and the vacant look creeping slowly into even his good eye. Shadows from the flickering candles accentuated deep creases beneath drooping eyes and sagging cheeks. He no longer plucked the few hairs on his face, and their grayness added to his sallow complexion. She was weary of the endless arguments over the meaning of Rodolfo's fish dreams. A fish charm was worth trying, although she inclined to agree with Jose: a priest's crucifix was protection enough for their son. And that he was unusually blessed there was no doubt. Despite his fish encounters at night he was healthier and happier than almost any child around. A nuisance — the dreams — to be sure; he always wet the bed when his fish visited. Out in his dugout the line would float over the hot springs near shore where schools of fish congregated of mornings. But none would take the bait. Then, when Rodolfo looked down to see why, the schools would suddenly be gone and in their place the strange fish would be circling right below him. It always was the same: the fish taking the bait and pulling him out beyond the reeds, beyond where a lad of four was allowed to fish, until suddenly the canoe was swamped. That's when he would awaken, always wet! Rosa assumed that when he stopped wetting the bed, or finally caught that fish, the dreams probably would go away.

To change the subject, Rosa asked Vicente why the dancers had to be married men.

"For the same reason that community service is asked only of those who are married. A wife's help is necessary to fulfill all the duties. My grandfather once told me about a neighbor who found himself short of money when the time came to go to Totonicapan to get his clothing for the Conquest dance. Since he'd already given his promise to the sponsor, he went for a walk along the shore to think. Distraught, he started crying like a child until a beautiful woman appeared from the lake and asked him the cause of such sorrow. When he told her, she consoled him by offering to provide everything that he would need for the dance. 'Turn around for a moment,' she told him, and when he obeyed and then looked again at the lake it had been parted by a lovely path adorned with more beautiful flowers than ever he had seen. Urged on by the woman, he followed her into the lake until they came to a great palace. She took him inside to a room full of costumes for every dance he'd ever heard of...the finest costumes available. 'Choose any costume you desire,' she urged, 'and then I'll also give you the money for liquor."

Transfixed, I had moved over to sit at Vicente's feet. "If I were him, I would have asked for every costume in the place!"

"Ah, but there was a condition!" Vicente replied with his good eye ominously narrowed. "Before the man could receive anything he had to promise to bring her two puppies. He decided that puppies were a small payment for such a favor and agreed to return with them immediately. As he left the palace he stopped to visit with some children tied to pillars of the building, but the woman was following and cautioned him to keep his distance lest they bite. Thinking no more about it, he returned home and chose the two largest and healthiest puppies among those in his patio. The woman was waiting for him at the palace, but when she saw what he had brought her she said angrily, 'That's not the kind of puppy I want! I meant a couple of your children who will serve to guard my house like these you see here before you.'

"Fearing what might happen to him if he didn't mind her, the frightened man went home again. On the way he bought some bread and sweets for his two youngest children, explaining to his wife that he was taking their children to work for a Ladina who promised to pay them well.

"This time when the lady in the lake saw what he had brought her she was satisfied; she picked up the children and led their father to the room full of dance costumes. After helping him pick out the best made costume available, she gave him the money she had promised and a bottle of brandy as well. She warned him not to drink — or give to his dance companions — more than a few swallows, however, lest they become drunk and die.

"As it turned out, this dancer was not only the best dressed, but the most able dancer present. His clothes gave him the ability, and since he had not gone with his companions to Totonicapan they tried in vain to guess where he had rented his expensive costume. But he told them nothing, offering them a few sips of his brandy instead. But even that small amount made them so drunk that they fell asleep immediately. And as soon as they awakened, their energy to dance all night had returned! So it continued for days — drinking and dancing — and to the man's surprise, no matter how much brandy he poured, the bottle always was full. When his friends asked him where he had purchased such remarkable liquor, he smiled but refused to tell.

"Meanwhile, in the palace his children were put to work sweeping out refuse in piles which they burned every evening. Those refuse piles become the crabs — tentacles hardened from burning — that come to the shore of the lake every night. The children must still be working at the palace, given all the crabs, and no one since has seen them, the path into the lake, or the palace's owner." Rosa smiled — patting me on the head — and teased, "Sounds like having a child or two to spare is all we'll need for performing our community services!" But Vicente reproached her — said that this was just as true a sign as were Rodolfo's dreams about the giant fish in the lake.

The rains were less heavy the next planting season. The level of the lake began dropping, and the fishing and crabbing improved. By year's end Jose was making trips to Tecpan every other market day during the months he didn't have to do forced labor. In his basket traps he could catch ten pounds of the *ulumina* fingerlings in an average night of fishing. If roasted properly they kept until there were enough for market. Having the coals right and roasting them just long enough was the secret to their drying. Since he could easily carry dried fish, he could carry twenty pesos worth of fish and crabs. Rosa did the roasting of fish after washing and stringing them on thin strips of cane. Crabs were a different matter. She refused to handle any except the dead ones that she cooked for the family. Jose had to tie the live ones on the sticks. By keeping them in water until noon on Wednesday, they could stand the nine hour trek to Tecpan for Thursday morning's market. Jose always sold out in time to make it home by nightfall...Always had, that is, until his first trip of the new year.

Tecpan's January fiesta was in progress, and Jose stayed to watch the Dance of the Negritos before starting home. An hour into the journey he overtook Luis Noj, the oldest Catarineco selling regularly in Tecpan. They seldom had been market traveling companions, because Luis preferred to stretch the trip over three days and two nights. But with his late start and the moon's face completely hidden this time of the month, Jose agreed to accompany the old man and to overnight in San Antonio. But, too late, they realized upon starting their descent to the lake that they should have over-nighted in Godinez instead. Stumbling along the narrow path, Jose was the first to hear it: a rustling in maize stalks above the path. They squatted to deny their silhouette to possible eyes out there in the dark, and waited. Jose fingered his machete. "Look out," he yelled, as suddenly a large form neighed and bolted toward them, veering at the last moment to gallop on down the path and out of hearing.

"What was that?" gasped Luis, more startled than was Jose who had convinced himself that they were listening simply to wind in the cornfield.

"Looked to me like a horse, and yet…I wonder…it acted so secretive. Why would a tame horse run off like that? Suppose that it could've been a *characotel* spirit? Seemed a lot larger than the normal horse."

"Could've been at that," agreed Luis. "Lots of souls in San Antonio have large *characotel* spirits. Powerful ones, too: bulls, oxen, even jaguars I've been told. There could be some people with spirits of horses, too, I suppose."

Jose convinced himself that it was, indeed, a horse *characotel*. Probably one belonging to a sorcerer, and most certainly from San Antonio on top of that. "What should we do?"

"Well, if it *is* a *characotel,* it's going to stay away from us. Look how it bolted. Probably knows that if it gets injured by us its owner will become sick or die. Let's just walk along like normal, talking so that it'll know where we are."

Jose had no better suggestion and to pass the time asked Luis about the Catarinecos with large or troublesome *characotel* spirits of whom people gossiped. To his surprise, Luis included mention of Bacilia…said that some nights she turned into a large black pig. The proof was all the nightshade bushes that thrived in the Ajcojom compound. Very few people knew the full secret of nightshade. Everybody knew its power to cause visions, but Luis had learned only from his grandmother that the bell flower bushes felt more at home around houses of people with *characotel* spirits. He went on about others with the ability until a cough ahead on the path alerted them to a lone figure approaching. With hands on their machetes they hurried past the man. He was from San Antonio and averted his eyes when returning their greeting.

"We're almost to the outlying houses of San Antonio; the cross by the big rock is just ahead," said Jose.

At the mention of 'cross,' Luis froze. "The cross — of course! He just made the change at the cross! That's where they always change…and change back again, too. That horse was the old man's *characotel!* After we surprised him, he hurried back to make the change before we arrived!"

Jose was incredulous. "But how do they change?"

"They turn four somersaults to the four directions. If anybody catches them before they're through making the change, they die. The animal's owner dies, too, if it is his last and strongest spirit-companion; otherwise the owner just gets sick."

Jose shuddered and picked up his pace. They began to pass darkened houses but saw no sign of life until they approached the church and town hall where animated voices had begun to draw a small crowd. Keeping to the shadows on the far side of the plaza, they listened. A lamp in the corridor of the council room cast eerie shadows among the men crowding around someone who was agitated and apparently hurt.

"I had a good hold on the bastard — could have wrestled him down — but he was shouting so loud he roused a neighbor. I tried to explain who I was when I let go of him, but the fellow macheted me anyway. Hit my belt, or I'd never have made it back."

"How much maize do you think he stole?"

"No idea," replied Anacleto. "No doubt he'll have stolen all that's left by the time I get back over there!"

"Going to take him to court in Solola?"

"Solola? Hardly! Them damn Ladinos would lock us both up! I'd end up losing more time than the maize is worth. No, I'll have to go confront him myself. The milpa's been legally mine now for over a month...including this harvest. I've got the papers to prove it, and that thieving Pablo Locon knows it! I'll need some help, though. Will some of you go with me tomorrow?"

A companion who had been wrapping the leg wound interrupted, "From the looks of this cut, you'll need to wait longer than that...no telling how much blood you've lost. Better get you home and filling up on beans to replace it before you die from weakness."

With that the group began to disperse, and Luis urged haste in getting out of town lest someone recognize them from their clothes. They didn't risk conversation and ran silently along a path now more familiar to them. Anxiety about *characoteles* had been replaced suddenly by fears unlike anything Jose had felt before. Poor Pablo, thought Jose, pondering what could have led him to such desperation. Pablo had been one of their *mayordomos* who had pawned land the year before to pay for fiesta expenses. He had told Vicente about missing the repayment deadline, worrying that the fellow to whom he had pawned it for this year's harvest would refuse to give him an extension.

Pablo's frightened wife was slow to answer their call from the gate. Only after she had heard their story did she acknowledge that Pablo in fact wasn't home...had gone into hiding, afraid that Anacleto's family might summon the authorities yet that night. "I don't think he's that badly hurt," Jose assured her, "but clearly he plans to come after Pablo and that maize as soon as he's able."

"There's maize in our shed for only a month," she offered, embarrassed that everybody now would have to know. "What with losing that milpa to Anacleto, it'll be like this every year. Pablo harvested only two sacks, the first one on his way back from San Antonio yesterday after Anacleto refused us an extension on the loan. He'd even offered to let him have all of this next season's crop as well, but Anacleto refused even that. So Pablo figured that we had the right to at least a couple of sacks. He went back for the second at dusk, afraid that Anacleto would finish harvesting by tomorrow. Didn't occur to us that Anacleto might also decide to pick through the night."

"All Jesus's apostles know that you deserve to have a little of your crop," comforted Jose. Vicente and I got you into this mess, so if you want to keep what you've got I'll round up men to be here at the house each night for a while."

No one from San Antonio to whom Catarinecos had pawned milpas dared continue harvesting that week. But because the moon was now waxing, Pablo surmised that this probably was as much due to the moisture content of the maize as to fear of more violence. The few who still had corn to harvest likely would wait until the moon was waning again to keep the spoilage at a minimum. But he accepted Jose's offer of reinforcements for a week on the chance that Anacleto would have the nerve to come looking for the one sack he knew they had taken.

With no sign of Anacleto that week, the volunteers had stopped coming except for Jose and Vicente. The Locons had spent the day at Solola's Friday market and were still drinking as Jose and his father approached their compound on the outskirts of town. The sound of laughter was audible even from the path continuing on to San Antonio as they started climbing toward the dimly lit Locon huts up the hill. "Stupid fools," Vicente mumbled under his breath as they neared the gate. He drew his machete to give them a much deserved fright for making it so easy for strangers to make their way to their door unannounced.

It was an unfortunate impulse. Anacleto and his five friends hiding in the fencerow thought they'd been seen. Anacleto's machete sliced through the darkness and caught Vicente's arm. His cry of terror and pain silenced the household as the attackers pinned both Ajcojoms to the ground. The house lamp went out. "Who's there?" Pablo challenged.

"We came in peace to talk about the maize you took, but this fellow drew his machete on us! We'll leave him and his companion with you and go if you return what you stole. Otherwise we'll finish them both, and their blood will be on your heart!"

Terrified at what he'd caused, Pablo blurted, "Take the maize and leave, damn you! But if you've killed a friend, you'll never step safely in my milpa again!" Already his wife was dragging the two bags to the door. Pablo heaved them over the darkened fencerow onto the path. His threat drew no response as the foreigners shouldered the bags and hurried off.

Jose helped Vicente into the house, his life ebbing from the nearly severed arm. He was barely conscious from the shock. They would have to carry him to the bonesetter...no one else could cure such a terrible wound. Pablo dispatched a child across town to alert the curer before following with Vicente as fast as his eldest son, Jose, he and his wife could stumble along the narrow path — two on each side of the blanket sling.

——

"There's no way I can save his arm," concluded the bonesetter quickly. "The only hope for his life is to cut if off and cauterize the stump as quick as possible." It was a valiant effort, stoking the fire to heat a machete while trying with pressure to staunch the remaining trickle of blood. But when the knife was finally hot enough Vicente already was dead.

Despite the hour, word traveled as quickly and inexorably to the ends of Santa Catarina as did chocomil waves each afternoon to the ends of the lake. By the time they had carried the frail body home, Rosa already was comforting Bacilia. She told Julia to get Rodolfo out of the house ...to take him with her to tell their other grandfather, the sacristan. Within minutes Chepe had his church bell tolling the alarm. Its urgent pealing stopped...replaced by echoes thrown back from cliffs high against an obsidian sky. An eerie, heavy silence carried on the January wind all its way to San Antonio, and by daybreak anxious waiting began as rumors of Catarineco sorcery thickened and people there searched for signs. An unfortunate burro, found wandering near Anacleto's home and feared to be a sorcerer's *characotel*, was beaten to death.

As Pablo had predicted, Anacleto did not resume harvesting his ill-gotten maize that month. It was rumored that his machete wound had begun to fester. Marcelo had thrown in the direction of San Antonio six oranges, one for each of the thieving attackers, after piercing them with six red pitch-pine splinters over which he'd done black magic. One of the oranges, bloodied, appeared in Marcelo's patio the morning that Anacleto died. His five companions fled to the coast, and no more oranges returned. Nor did any other farmers from San Antonio complete the postponed harvesting of pawned milpas that season. At dusk one evening a crippled woman with unkempt hair had been seen hobbling through those milpas screaming obscenities at the wind. And for several nights thereafter a large black pig rooted voraciously uprooting the stalks. Bacilia even boasted publicly of spoiling the maize, piling sin upon sin until not even Jose tried to defend her against the rumors. When it was learned that the *characotel* pig had been bludgeoned to death, no one was surprised that crazed Bacilia became ill. Marcelo said that he could try a cure to keep her alive a little longer, but that if that pig *characotel* was her last — or only — companion spirit, she would die as well. Jose and Rosa decided not to spend the money with death so probable. Within the week her agitated babbling ceased.

Dirt left over after filling her grave confirmed what everyone had assumed: it wasn't her time to die. Jose put the priest's crucifix above their door and lit candles every night for a month to keep her from returning to steal a grandchild to take with her to the underworld. It was a frightening time for everyone, but terrifying for me. Jose made a twine necklace so that I could wear Vicente's carved fish around my neck, and Rosa gathered rue in a pouch for Julia. Whether because of the fish charm and the rue, or because of the crucifix and Jose's fidelity in lighting candles, Bacilia's haunting ceased. Neither Julia nor I became sick from the fright.

State authorities from Solola eventually came to inquire into the rumors of sorcery and murder. Old Marcelo went into hiding in Judas Cave. Since those accused were dead or could not be found, the authorities departed, leaving a policeman in Santa Catarina and another in San Antonio. Anxiety grew on both sides of the border as time approached to clear and burn fields for planting. Folks ventured onto their fields in the border region only when a policemen could be persuaded to accompany them. The milpa pawned by Pablo Locon to Anacleto was sold by Anacleto's widow to Don Oscar Ramirez, the wealthiest Ladino in the region and owner of the small Primavera plantation west of Panajachel.

Chapter Six — 1914, Twenty-one Years Later

"Rodolfo!" called Elena from the back door "— come quick! Papa's patron is asking for you!" As curious as she was apprehensive, Elena rejoined her family in their front room peering out between its rough-hewn boards at the owner of the Monte Carlo plantation on the porch.

I swung down from the mango tree I was harvesting and brushed off my pants. "He doesn't seem to be angry," she whispered as I entered the house. "What do you suppose he could possibly want?"

"Can't imagine! Where's my shirt? I can't go out looking like this." She gave me a cloth to wipe off the worst of the sweat while my mother-in-law rummaged through the basket of freshly washed and dried clothing to find a shirt. Loosening my belt to tuck it in, I grabbed a straw hat and ventured out to join my father-in-law, Mateo, and his patron, the wealthiest Ladino in that southwestern region of Guatemala.

"Rodolfo Luis Ajcojom at your service, Sir," as I stopped several meters in front of the most intimidating Ladino I ever had seen: huge! I had heard that Don Ricardo was a big man, but there was no way I could have anticipated how muscular. His stern but not unfriendly gaze was nonetheless unnerving. I crossed my hands, hat in hand, and deferentially dropped my shoulders despite my studied efforts to shake the bad habit engrained in Indians to posture meekness around Ladinos. "You have some need of me, Don —?"

Mateo interrupted, I suppose to put me at ease. "My patron has come asking for you with news from his brother, Oscar Ramirez, in Panajachel. Is it true that you once lived under Don Oscar's roof and helped care for his children?"

"Y...Yes, Sir," I stammered "— I did live there, when I was a boy, for two years while I attended school in Panajachel." It had never occurred to me that Don Oscar and Don Ricardo could be brothers, and to think that Don Oscar even knew where I was working on the coast.

"Then you are indeed the Rodolfo Luis I am looking for!" Ricardo announced, his face widening into a broad and comforting grin. But just as suddenly he was serious again. "I'm sorry to bring you some sad news, Rodolfo. It seems that your father died in a fall from the church roof that the new priest is having repaired in your village of Santa Catarina. Because of the burial expense, your mother came to my brother to pawn a milpa of your family's. When my brother inquired about you, she told him that you were married to the daughter of Mateo Salanic here at the plantation. Oscar gladly loaned her the 300 pesos she needed, and since then he has decided to cancel that if you will come work for him at the Primavera."

But I was no longer listening. Dead...Papa? Poor Papa...the church of all things! And another priest, finally, on that side of the lake.

Mateo again came to my rescue, asking what kind of help Oscar Ramirez would be needing. Ricardo replied, "With all the chicken and smallpox, mumps, and measles sweeping this part of Guatemala of late, it seems that practically half the population of Santa Catarina has died the past few years. Survivors have sold or pawned at least 150 acres to my brother, much of it low enough for coffee. He desperately needs someone who knows Santa Catarina to manage his properties, preferably a native like Rodolfo here. With the schooling Rodolfo has had, Oscar thinks that he might be just the right person. Oscar will provide a new house on the Primavera delta near his own home and pay twenty centavos a day to begin with. And he can arrange for exemption from any form of labor required of you *naturales* now or in the future."

Exemption! The main reason I hadn't already taken Elena back to the lake was to avoid the *mandamientos*. "But, Sir, I haven't finished my obligation here to the railroad. I've got two months work left on this year's contract."

"I know the foreman," assured Ricardo "— he'll release you if I ask."

I looked at Mateo who in turn looked at Elena standing in the back doorway. Despite her mother's audible weeping within the house, Elena nodded her agreement to me saying, "My parents know that of course we should accept your patron's generous offer."

"Then, yes, Sir, I'll do it!" I virtually shouted. "How can we thank you for your kindness?" And again without thinking, I knelt to kiss the huge hand. But Ricardo graciously waved me to my feet, asking how soon we could make the journey.

"I can be ready by tomorrow morning," Elena offered.

"Good! I'll have two mules ready, and I'll send a muleteer with you to bring them back. I can see that you are with child, Elena. You shouldn't travel such a distance on foot, and the other mule can carry your belongings."

As their patron turned to leave, Mateo bowed his respect and walked him to the gate to thank him for the consideration of sending mules. What a different side of his patron he had just seen! And what a revelation to learn that his son-in-law was so well known to his patron's brother!" But to lose his daughter to the highlands, after having left there himself all these many years ago…that he hadn't anticipated. Such a sacrifice…

For her part, Elena was elated. Everything that Rodolfo had told her about the lake and the cool climate of the highlands was inviting, especially now that she was pregnant. And to have such a wealthy patron! She scurried about, gathering their few belongings and thinking about a new house all to themselves.

Needing some time alone, I returned to picking mangos. Memories crowded in. The six years on the coast had been good years. For most Indians the coast was prison, but for me it had meant freedom and becoming a man almost as soon as I had arrived. After my second year with the railroad I had met Elena at the Monte Carlo plantation store, and after another year of meeting there regularly I had begun to visit her at home. Then, one morning when I found her at home alone — her folks away at market — I asked if I could stay with her until they returned. It was the customary way of asking to marry her. They promptly consented and I helped Mateo build our sleeping room added on to theirs. There had been no happier years than the three living there with Elena. But I was ready to go home. The thought of the lake's cool breeze, of my mother and sisters, unleashed a flood of memories…

> "Wake up, Rodolfo…wake up! whispered Julia. "You've wet your blanket again! What a mess you can make!" I lurched into full consciousness and despairingly kicked free of the embarrassment. "Shit! Think I'd prefer the swamped canoe!"
>
> "What swamped canoe?" giggled Julia, tousling my hair. "It was pulling me through the reeds and I'd let too much water leak in —"
>
> "Feels to me like you let too much leak out!" she laughed, threatening to awaken their parents with her outburst.
>
> I pushed her off the bed, and from her lack of retort knew she wouldn't try to embarrass me. "Did I hurt you?"
>
> "Of course not, stupid, but you'd better watch it!" She straightened up with a glare and slipped her huipil over her head, tossing her hair defiantly.
>
> "Then you won't tell?" I asked, while turning away to pull on my only other pair of drawers.

Julia seldom held such an edge, and so said nothing while she slowly wound the fraying piece of skirt cloth around her waist. "Tell you what," I brightened in a whisper, catching her eye and with it regaining my brother's — even a younger brother's — usual advantage," let's both go down to the lake before the folks awaken. You can go out with me to fish for a while." Julia's eyes narrowed skeptically, and I wondered if it was a good idea after all. My embarrassment would quickly become hers if anyone saw her out fishing, and yet she constantly was pouting that only boys get to fish. This seemed a good time to risk it; it was still completely dark.

"Would you _really_" she whispered. "I can take the dirty clothes to wash in case someone's already there." I began to get cold feet, now that I knew she wouldn't tattle. But Julia wasn't to be dissuaded and smiled triumphantly. "I could even wash out your blanket and wet drawers!"

So artfully trapped, I could only smile sheepishly as I gathered my pants in place with the sash. Julia positioned the heavy basket of clothes and blanket on her head and followed me quietly across the patio, gliding barefooted down the path toward the lake. The morning star already was well above the volcano; Mama would be up within an hour or so. And a neighbor already was washing clothes down by the hot spring.

"That rules out fishing with you," Julia pouted "— she'd tell everybody! Washing clothes it will have to be." Tucking the bottom of her skirt into her sash, she waded out as far as modesty permitted and palmed the mirrored surface. I dog-paddled out as far as my toes could still touch. With the sky growing lighter, the only star spirits to be seen were in the western sky, reluctant to leave their moon grandmother unattended. The mist was lifting but still obscured the far shoreline and all but the peaks of volcanoes.

"Aren't those the ducks?" she whispered, elated with an excuse to postpone the washing.

She was right! There were a few grebes in reeds emerging from the haze. "Look for some smooth stones about the size of an egg." I had brought two avocado pits, and while she looked for suitable stones I waded out and chanced one of the seeds toward the center of the *covey. It fell so far short that the grebes didn't even notice. "Quick," I decided "— let's get the canoe!" We ran to the bushes where father's old avocado trunk dugout lay upside down. Together we struggled with it to the water, and when it was out as far as we could wade, I got in and crouched on the bottom. "Give me a push!" The secret would be to catch one just coming up for air, before it had time to notice, and with the slingshot partially drawn I steadied my arm on the boat. The dugout slowed and began to drift, still a good fifteen meters from the ducks. It had to be soon, or I would have to sit up and turn around. Even so, most of the grebes had entered the protective reeds. Only two were still feeding. When the closest dived it swam directly toward the canoe, surprising us both when it popped up barely five meters away. But I adjusted in time, and before the grebe could dive again my other avocado pit stunned it into unconsciousness.*

Julia was speechless, while I grabbed the hapless bird, twisted its neck, and flung it toward her. We pulled the canoe to shore, turned it over to drain, and sank down against it to catch our breath and examine the trophy. I couldn't have been more proud; less than one time in ten did I hit a grebe before frightening them away, and usually they were already well off shore by the time it was light enough to see them. The best time was before daylight on nights when grandmother moon was directly facing mother earth. But she was turning away this time of month. It was indeed my luck to hunt ducks!

"Tell us about your patron, Oscar Ramirez," urged Mateo, after the children had quieted from the day's excitement and crickets accounted for the only sounds beyond the patio.

I was stretched out on the porch, my head in Elena's lap, staring at the sky without seeing. I had given little thought since leaving the highlands to those first years away from Santa Catarina. Even Elena had not succeeded in unburdening me of unpleasant memories. I hadn't told her yet about my younger brother, Cirilo, or why I began coming to the coast at such an early age.

"Don Oscar owns the largest plantation on the lake's north shore. It's called the Primavera, on the delta west of Panajachel. It's small compared to these plantations here in the lowlands, but the coffee quality is better at that altitude. Even before I left Santa Catarina the Ramirez family had begun to buy up milpas in Santa Catarina and San Antonio. Even my father pawned a milpa to get money to hire others to do his forced labor."

"Why'd he do *that?*" asked Elena in surprise. "Why didn't he do his own work?"

"He did at first, both at the Buenaventura and then at the Esperanza after my grandfather was killed in the fighting with those thieves from San Antonio. The governor had Catarinecos go to the Esperanza after that. But we got the worst of that deal; conditions were even worse at the Esperanza. An immigrant from Germany, Don Herman, bought —"

"Bought it from the Barillas family," interrupted Mateo, "just before coffee prices started to fall and about ten years before I moved down here from up north. I stopped at the Esperanza to look into working there before I found this plantation. *Gracias a Dios,* I found out the truth about old Herman in time! What year was it when Catarinecos started working there?"

"Year of the bad earthquake. I remember, because Papa was on that first crew and was away when Mama had my sister, Victoria. Papa had hoped to be back home before the baby came, but instead of working four weeks at the Esperanza he ended up working twice that long. Don Herman made everybody stay after the quake and repair damage to the ditches and troughs that carried spring water to the plantation."

"Sounds like something that merciless thief would do!" said Mateo. "Don Herman started mistreating his workers as soon as coffee prices started dropping. The value of his Esperanza plantation began to plummet, and he decided to make everybody else suffer, too."

"Well, Catarinecos sure suffered," I agreed. "At first he made workers stay longer than they'd been paid for, but then when the governor made him stop that, he insisted that workers pay for anything they bought at his store with extra days of work. Either way, workers always ended up spending one or two weeks longer than they were paid for. That's what got Papa into trouble. Because he was the best in Santa Catarina at speaking and writing Spanish, the elders asked him to write their petition to the governor begging permission for the town to do its forced labor somewhere else again."

"And the governor let them?" asked Elena in amazement.

"Yup! Surprising, but he sure did. The president needed workers for the railroad, so the governor let Catarinecos do railroad work instead the next two years. Guess the governor figured that he would teach Don Herman a lesson by not letting him have enough help for a while. By the time Catarinecos had to work for him again, conditions were a little better. But because Papa had been the one who wrote the letter to the governor, the mayor advised him not to go back. At first Papa borrowed money to hire others to go in his place, but when people wouldn't loan him any more he had no choice but to pawn our family's only milpa to Don Oscar. Don Oscar let him work at the Primavera as a regular to pay off the loan. After several weeks of walking back and forth to the Primavera every day, Papa asked if he could spend nights there. Then he got the idea of having me stay there with him and go to school in Panajachel. There were three grades there then, but only one in Santa Catarina. I had finished my first grade so I got to continue in Panajachel where the teachers were Ladinos.

"We'd been sleeping in one of the workers' shacks, but when Papa finished working for Don Oscar, his wife Arcadia suggested that I move to the plantation house and help around the house after school to pay for my keep. I was the only servant the Ramirez family had staying in the house with them. I lived with them until I finished third grade, twelve years ago now. Don Oscar and Arcadia had two kids, Eduardo and Carolina, both younger than me. I spent most afternoons after school taking care of Eduardo. Spoiled kid...pure Ladino! I slept alone in a little room at the back of the main house. Ate alone, too, in their kitchen after they'd eaten. But I ate everything they did — lots of meat, I remember — because Don Oscar did some butchering."

"So that's where you got your appetite for sausage!" teased Elena as she pulled out a hair she'd missed the last time she had plucked my whiskers. "Never could understand where you learned to want Ladino food so much!"

"Don Oscar had a second woman for a while, more Indian than Ladina. She lived alone with several children by her first husband. When Don Oscar butchered an animal, he would always give me some of the best cuts to take home to my parents, telling me privately to be sure to leave most of it with his lover instead. I didn't tell my folks how it was that Don Oscar was so willing to share his meat with *naturales* like us! Perhaps because of this Don Oscar always was kind and helpful to me, even when I moved back to Santa Catarina. Since I wasn't baptized — didn't have godparents — Don Oscar and Arcadia were like godparents to me."

I paused, uncertain whether to continue, but knew there would never be an easier time. "It was the year after I moved back to live at home that my brother was born —"

Elena looked down at me in surprise. "But I thought you only had sisters?"

I rolled over and propped my head on one elbow to face her. "No, there was also little Cirilo. Don't remember much about him 'til he was taken into the sweat-bath for the first time. I recall asking, 'Who's that?' I'd known that Mama was sick a lot, but I didn't know the real reason. Papa had told me she had a bad stomach ache. I didn't know yet where babies come from; Julia didn't either. Now he told us he had *bought* the baby. 'Where?' I wanted to know. 'In Guatemala City. There they sell babies every day...'"

Mateo chuckled. "My folks told me the same thing when my sister arrived."

"Julia and I of course believed him, although I remember arguing that he hadn't been away from home long enough to go to the city. Then, when I asked why they were putting him in the sweat-bath, making him cry, Papa explained that Victoria had to introduce him to the sweat-bath, carrying him on her back in the carrying cloth even though she was only four years old herself. The midwife went in with them and talked with Victoria about how she would have to grow up now and be like a little mother to her baby brother. She gave Victoria a small loom that Mama had made for her. I thought it was so strange — Victoria not old enough to understand a thing they were telling her — but Papa said it was the custom.

"When Cirilo was about three years old, Mama sent him with me outside the village to gather some herbs for lunch. I had trouble with him on the way — didn't want to walk — but finally I got him there. After I'd collected the herbs, he didn't want to walk home either and began to cry. I hit him on the back of his head and dragged him when he cried harder and still refused to walk on his own. We didn't get home 'til real late, and Mama scolded me when Cirilo complained that I'd hit and dragged him. Next day he awoke with a fever. Didn't get any better by the end of that week, so they had to hire a curer. But a few weeks later he died anyway."

I sat up to wipe my eyes, glancing at Elena who now would understood why I never had had the courage to tell her. But our eyes didn't meet, and I stared out at the darkness to address the shadows. "I don't remember anything about the funeral. I just remember how sad everybody was...how Papa drank for a week

71

straight. He didn't scold me much, though....probably afraid that I would get sick, too. For a long time after that, whenever I passed the spot where I'd hit Cirilo, I would stop and feel really sad..."

Elena took my hand, as I struggled to continue. "After he died, Mama decided that whether I was strong enough or not I would have to go on *mandamientos*. She said that since I had killed my brother, I would have to help out more. So, when the mayor told Papa that it was his turn to go to the Esperanza I went in his place. He was too sick from sadness and drinking to go. I went with my older sister Julia's husband, Diego, that first trip."

Greatly relieved to have at last talked about it, I breathed a huge sigh and continued. "After Cirilo died, my folks moved in with Lorenzo. He was my father's father's brother-in-law and the oldest man in Santa Catarina by then. He also was my mother's parents *compadre* and the one who went with grandfather Vicente to ask my mother's parents consent to Papa marrying their daughter, Rosa. So Lorenzo was an important person in my early life. My folks owed him so much money that they had to do whatever he asked. And being so lonely and feeble, he needed for them to take care of him. I stayed there with them some in his house, but mostly I lived with Julia and Diego those years. Not for long, though, because when I was eighteen I decided to come down to work on the railroad. I don't know how much Cirilo's death had to do with it. I just remember how desperate I was to get away from Santa Catarina. You know the rest. It's been seven years now."

Chapter Seven

Victoria didn't recognize the stout, swarthy Indian in Ladino clothes standing with a pregnant girl at the gate until he removed the broad-brimmed sombrero and grinned mischievously. Her shout of recognition brought Rosa running. The first smile in weeks parted Rosa's thin lips, and tears that had refused to flow even at her husband's burial finally moistened her cheeks again.

"Oh, Rodolfo Luis! You heard about Jose..." That would be the reason her son had come home, she reasoned sadly, and he would soon leave them again. "But we buried him three days ago. Didn't know how to get word to you. The priest was upset when he found the church in such bad condition, and the men were rushing to repair the roof. Jose fell the second day... and now the work has stopped again —" Rodolfo's disbelieving stare made her pause.

His mother was not the woman Rodolfo remembered. Apart from her ragged *huipil* — the same blouse she was wearing when he left home, he surmised — there was little to remind him of the proud and spirited woman he had left. The *huipil* seemed much too large, so frail and shriveled she had become. Always petite, but now stooped, Rosa looked more the grandmother than the mother of the comely Victoria whose arm she held for support. But he had no way of knowing that his mother recently had buried not only a husband but twins born six years earlier, both victims of the smallpox. Embarrassed, Rodolfo stammered, "N — No, Mama, I didn't come to bury Papa, but I did learn about the fall. You did the right thing to go to Don Oscar. His brother is the patron of Elena's father down on the coast, and Don Oscar asked him to tell us. Mama, this is my wife. She'll have our baby soon."

Elena smiled shyly, deepening the dimples in her copper cheeks. Rosa reached out to take her hand, and Victoria couldn't resist patting her new sister-in-law's protruding belly. With that, Elena's infectious laugh bubbled to the surface. She and Victoria would be good friends!

As Rodolfo had hoped, Oscar hadn't yet told Rosa about the cancellation of her debt. He would save that good news lest she assume that he had felt obligated to come home to help out. He didn't want to spoil this homecoming.

The remarkable changes in Rodolfo would have a reckoning, but for the moment Rosa was in no mood to question anything he told her. Of course it had been necessary for him to stay on the coast all those years. Of course it was good that he got married. Of course he was the best person to manage Don Oscar's land. Even the new Ladino clothes that Oscar had suggested he buy brought no censure from a much-relieved mother.

No censure from Rosa, but the neighbors who observed the young couple on their arrival in Santa Catarina, and who quickly guessed Rodolfo's identity, were not so charitable. Anyone dressed so much like a Ladino landowner was up to no good. Word of his return preceded the couple's arrival at his older sister's, and because they had gone first to Rosa's house Julia was cool when she met them at the gate. "Neighbors tell me that my long-lost brother has returned home! Perhaps you've seen him hereabouts," she teased, her sarcasm barely disguised.

Rodolfo arched an eyebrow in surprise and pursed his lips. Elena was flabbergasted! What kind of sister would greet a brother like this after all these years? Rodolfo sensed that it was the clothes. Even Elena could pass for a Ladina if one looked only at her clothes. He had been away too long. He had forgotten how important such things were in Santa Catarina. Or rather, he had dared to hope that things would have changed.

Once inside the house, Julia was more her old self, and with no neighbors to hear she asked Rodolfo directly about the clothes. When he had related the surprising developments of the past three days, she relaxed, even laughed at her initial fears. But she didn't hesitate to tell her brother what, again, he should have anticipated: Don Oscar had tried unsuccessfully for months to hire a Catarineco to manage his land in Santa Catarina. Many were willing to hire out to work the milpas and plant the coffee and shade tree seedlings. But to be the person who decided which families would be loaned money and then perhaps have to take their land away — when there was so much sickness and so much poverty — that, no Catarineco had been willing to do. A Ladino from Panajachel had tried to manage the land for a while, but he had soon quit from the pressure of sorcery from angry Catarinecos. How possibly did Rodolfo imagine that *he* could do it after being away all these years, and only twenty-four years old?

"Perhaps you'll decide to go back to the coast," Julia advised finally. And that meant that Rodolfo had to tell her about the cancellation of their mother's debt. He was trapped, and suddenly wished that he never had lived in the home of Oscar and Arcadia Ramirez.

74

"At least take some Catarineco clothes," Julia suggested; "some of Papa's are big enough for you. My, but you've grown! You look just like Papa, especially in the face. Except you're so dark! Must be from all that sun down there. And you're bigger in the arms and chest than Papa...not so big in the neck, though. Must not do much head-strap carrying in the lowland."

"Nope, hardly none. But swinging a pick laying railroad tracks builds the body in a hurry."

The conversation was in Kaqchikel, but Elena understood Julia's allusion to Rodolfo's size. "He still eats like a Ladino!" she said in Spanish, warming finally to this fiery sister-in-law.

Julia had been studying Elena, wondering if she could possibly adjust to living in Santa Catarina. If Rodolfo was determined to try managing the Primavera properties, they definitely should live here rather than over on the delta. It was apparent that Elena didn't know their language, and Rodolfo explained that her Salanic family had come from the northwest where they spoke another Mayan tongue. But Elena caught enough to realize what Julia was asking, and added that years ago her parents had stopped speaking in their own dialect. She had spoken Spanish all her life. She also guessed at what Julia was thinking. "Perhaps we should tell your patron that we want to live for a while here in Santa Catarina," she offered. "Surely I could soon learn to speak Kaqchikel."

Julia decided that she liked Elena after all. They agreed to talk about everything again when Diego was at home. Rodolfo and Elena left for Panajachel, now more aware of staring faces behind cane and cornstalk gates and fences. Once out of town and on the familiar path climbing high above the lake Rodolfo lapsed into silent rumination. After these few hours in Santa Catarina it was clearer to him than ever before why he had had to leave. He could never again be a Catarineco. Either he would have to return to the coast, as Julia had suggested, or he would have to serve his patron well. He had no other choices. But to serve Oscar Ramirez well would mean gaining the respect, if not the good will, of Santa Catarina's Council of Elders. He couldn't make any more mistakes like he'd made with the clothing; he wouldn't wear Indian clothes, but neither would he dress in such expensive Ladino clothes. Sandals instead of shoes when in Santa Catarina would help. Living in Santa Catarina wasn't a solution; Elena couldn't learn the language soon enough. As for himself, however, he would always talk in Kaqchikel to Catarinecos. And it wouldn't hurt for folks to know he was doing all of this to help his mother keep her land. Julia had told him that their mother's loss of half the children she had been given by Saint Catherine was the norm now in Santa Catarina. But giving birth to just six was way below the average of probably a dozen children per couple in response to how rapidly the young were dying. Even another cemetery had been started, with long lines of tiny graves.

By the time they had reached the Primavera plantation that evening, Rodolfo had made up his mind: He would stick it out if Oscar Ramirez indeed intended to put him fully in charge. Oscar would have to let him be the judge of how to handle Catarinecos. If he could survive the first harvest, five months off, he was confident that he could do the job.

———————————

After three months of daily rain, the flowers and greenery surrounding the plantation house were lush. A pet scarlet macaw and a bevy of parrots — wings clipped — in shrubbery bordering the manicured lawn added jungle sounds to the rainbow of hues enveloping the white plastered, red tile-roofed house: lilies from white to pink; bougainvillea from pink to purple; fire flower blossoms from red to orange; and cannas from orange to yellow. The environs of the lake's small bay and the delta which composed the miniature Primavera were never more breathtaking than on sunny afternoons of *canicula,* those welcome days in August when God takes mercy on his children and briefly halts the rains. Elena was enthralled. "To think we get to *live* here! I don't care if our house *never* gets finished! With difficulty she rose from the warm grass, clapped her hands and ran barefooted around the lawn — despite six months of new life within her. Exhausted, she collapsed beside the hammock where Rodolfo lay bemused and smiling. Elena was such a cheerful woman...content with what she had and who she was... neither pretentious nor ambitious. She'd had two years of plantation school, yet wouldn't admit to any reading or writing. An obedient wife, eager to be a dutiful mother.

"It is a beautiful place," Rodolfo agreed. He had forgotten just how beautiful. "It was my job to trim the grass and bushes with my machete when I lived here. When you're born here, you don't think much about how pretty it is this time of year around the lake. It helps to travel and get a comparative perspective. Could be that folks who live only in one place all their lives, no matter how beautiful it is, never think of it as being anything out of the ordinary."

"And I love the red and purple colors of the Panajachel *huipil.* Prettiest one I've seen," continued Elena. "Wish that Arcadia would let me wear it, at least while I'm pregnant. Up here it's cool enough to be comfortable in a *huipil.* Down

76

on the coast Mama gave it up years ago. I like the houses here, too — aren't tile roofs nice? Even the thatched roofs are prettier than the palm leaves Papa said we had to be content with."

The thatched adobe house that Oscar Ramirez was having built for them was well under way, on a knoll above the path leading from the Ramirez house to the road connecting Solola with Panajachel. The outskirts of Panajachel lay only a kilometer's walk from their door. On the other side of the path, hidden by a banana grove, were a dozen smaller board shanties for the couple dozen workers that Don Oscar kept on the place year-round. Most were from San Jorge, the next lake town west. The others were from Panajachel, too poor to afford their own homes in town. Rodolfo had wondered if Don Oscar expected him to use these workers over in Santa Catarina, another of the questions he was eager to ask when his patron returned from Solola later in the afternoon. But until then he and Elena were free to enjoy the day, getting settled in the back room where he had slept years before. Being able to spend the first week or two in the plantation house felt more like coming home than did finding his mother and Victoria still living in the old compound of dirt-floored, cane and mud-walled huts with all their ghosts.

From a second-floor window, Beatriz — Don Oscar and Arcadia's teenaged daughter — watched Elena romp about the yard. Elena's charm lay more in her disposition than in her face, Beatriz had concluded. Elena almost had died from chicken pox in her youth and carried a number of large pockmarks. But true to her nature, she'd laughed when Beatriz had questioned her; said the blemishes were a daily reminder of how lucky she was simply to be alive. "Won't she hurt the baby, running around like that?" queried Beatriz of her mother.

Arcadia joined her daughter at the window and gazed wistfully at the winsome girl their little Rodolfo had married. "*Naturales* pay no mind to being pregnant. Maybe from working from sunup to sundown — with all that kneeling they do grinding and weaving — they don't have to worry. It's rare that you hear of a *natural* miscarrying."

"But she doesn't look very *Indito*," Beatriz observed, refusing to join her mother in referring to Indians as *naturales* given her father's Ramirez family's disapproval of her mother's deference to and inordinate interest in the Indians she had grown up with in her youth. "Funny how much more Ladina they can seem wearing dresses instead of their wrap-around skirts and *huipiles.*"

"Your father thinks it will help for the other workers to see them dressed like us. She looks so uncomfortable in that dress, though. I'm going to tell her that she can dress however she likes, at least until she's had that baby." She ignored the disapproving glance from Beatriz, who forever would side with Oscar — and especially their new priest — on denigrating everything Indian. From the front of the house Father Jacobo's deep voice had just called out in greeting.

Before Arcadia could respond, Rodolfo instinctively jumped from his hammock to receive the visitor as had been his duty as a boy. "Oh, to have children as dutiful and as genuinely eager to please as Rodolfo always was," she sighed as she went downstairs to meet their priest and regular visitor of late afternoons.

The Carmelite priest who finally had been reassigned from Spain to the Panajachel parish to replace Father Sebastian could not have been more different: short and stout, as red-faced as he was red-haired. His heavy eyelids and puffy jowls were outdone by the folds of chin that hid from view a cleric's collar he never could, but fortunately never had, to fasten. "And I'm as far from poetry as Panajachel is from the north of Spain," he had informed them when Oscar had told him about his Basque predecessor's love of poetry. After Sebastian's poetic, even irreverent, zest and wit, the Ramirez household found Jacobo to be a bit too priestly for their taste. But his predictability did have its advantages: he was a man of habit and utter predictability. Every Tuesday he stopped in at four o'clock for tea, and every Saturday he came for dinner and the evening, to relax before Sunday's hectic schedule. But whether his predictability extended to comparable loyalty, they had yet to decide. He was for the most part pretty inscrutable.

But he most certainly was a Ladinos' priest. As the stranger strode confidently toward him, Father Jacobo Rojas concluded that he was *Indito* despite his efforts to appear otherwise. "My horse will welcome a drink," he ordered before Rodolfo could speak, assuming the fellow to be one of the plantation's hired hands.

"Yes, Padre," Rodolfo responded cheerfully, "and I'll brush him down if you would like. Anything else that I can do for you?"

Astonished, Jacobo took another long, hard look at this agreeable, friendlier-than-usual Indian who seemed so much at home. "Who are you, if I may ask," he asked more politely, wondering if there had been a lapse in his self-proclaimed ability to smell out a man's origins.

"He's Rodolfo Luis Ajcojom!" Arcadia announced proudly from the doorway; "he has come home!"

Recalling Oscar's mention of the Catarineco they had invited to work for them, the priest's face brightened. "Yes, of course," he said, relaxing with this confirmation of his initial assessment, yet genuinely pleased to at last meet the son of the poor soul who had died in the fall from the roof of the church. "Your father was the first Catarineco I met...such a pity he fell. He has a place in Heaven," Jacobo added, not certain what more to say.

"Yes, Padre," Rodolfo responded politely, wondering if the priest assumed the same for any other *naturales* in Santa Catarina.

"He came to me right after I arrived...terribly worried about the sorry condition of the church. Said he wanted me to know before I saw it for myself. He told me about the old sacristan, Chepe Yach's, concern for their roofless church ever since the earthquake...said it made the sacristan so sick from worry that he drank himself to death. In January I'll have a new sacristan to watch over things there, but for now I'll be grateful if you will check the progress on the roof whenever you're over there." With that — to his mind — decided, Jacobo strode into the house with Arcadia.

"He's certainly a different sort of *Indito!*" Rodolfo heard the patronizing Spaniard exclaim before he was out of earshot. What to make of his request...or was it an offer? What benefit might there be in having *two* patrons when beginning work in Santa Catarina: the wealthiest Ladino around, and the new priest as well! There would be little chance of open opposition, at least, if even Catarinecos' access to the priest was through him. But would this only make them more envious and distrustful? Rodolfo determined to have a frank talk with Julia and Diego before having any more dealings with this red-complexioned and obviously besotted cleric.

Oscar Ramirez and Eduardo, the unruly youngster whom — at nine years of age — Rodolfo had tried to watch over when he himself was only twelve, rode in on their horses as Rodolfo was leading the priest's mount to the trough. Don Oscar hadn't changed: still lean, straight-backed in the saddle, riding as gracefully as his son. They brought their horses over themselves, and Oscar thanked Rodolfo for assisting Father Jacobo. "So you've met our new priest? But then, I'm forgetting that you never knew even his predecessor, Father Sebastian."

Rodolfo was respectfully quiet.

"Unfortunately for Rodolfo," chuckled Eduardo; "it might have been easier to take care of me if I'd had to worry about a priest showing up here twice each week!"

With that they all three burst out laughing, Rodolfo amused as much by Eduardo's high-pitched giggle. With his chubby, ruddy cheeks, Eduardo seemed scarcely older now than the mischievous youth Rodolfo recalled from their youth. Eduardo surprised him by offering to help brush down the horses to permit a swim before dinner. He wondered how much Eduardo might remember of their daily romps in the shallow water...such embarrassing times for Rodolfo when Eduardo had insisted on their undressing with young girls from the shanties, even showing themselves to older girls washing clothes at the shore. But Rodolfo could now be more charitable after observing such behavior among other Ladino youths on the coast. It wasn't just Eduardo.

"So you got one of my uncle's plantation girls pregnant and decided to be honorable and marry her!" Eduardo teased as they attended the horses. "At least you had the good sense to pick the best figured girl down there." Rodolfo blushed but was not to be outdone. "Oh, I'd gotten quite a number in that condition before I chose Elena. Actually, it's a great sacrifice leaving all my other women to come back up here."

Eduardo doubled over in his mirth, knowing secondhand from his cousin how rare Elena's comely body was among his uncle's impoverished, sickly families, and how unlikely it was that Rodolfo had fucked even Elena before they were married — much less anyone else. Rodolfo couldn't have changed *that* much! But Eduardo, too, was charitable, knowing better now what differences there were between Indians and Ladinos when it came to sexual talk and play. Rodolfo at least had learned how to joke. "I'm sure glad you're back!" he said, turning abruptly to give Rodolfo a slap on the back. "We really need you over in Santa Catarina, and it'll be fun having you living close by again!"

The signals were clear: good friends, to a point, but the "we need you" said the rest. Actually Rodolfo was relieved. To again be a close friend to Eduardo Ramirez would be more of a challenge than he had bargained for or wanted. "It's good to be back, Don —"

"Oh, Rudi, drop the 'Don,' — can I still call you Rudi? My father will expect to be addressed as 'Don' and around the other help you probably should use it to me as well, but between us it's just Eddy and Rudi...O.k? Race you down to the water and out to the old sunken stump!"

It was no contest. 'Rudi' hadn't been swimming for years, while Eddy's lithe body had been in the lake almost every afternoon of his twenty-two years.

———

Oscar was endeavoring, as usual, to match drinks with Father Jacobo on the back veranda, in good view of the young men swimming off shore. Rum was the one love the two men shared with equal passion. Otherwise they were as different in temperament as in appearance. Jacobo was as punctilious and proper as Oscar was lacking in ambition and convention, as scheming as Oscar was direct. Expansive and generous, Oscar was as undemanding of others as of himself. In reaction to such nonchalance, his son had the kind of single-mindedness that Jacobo admired in a young man. About Rodolfo, however, the priest had predictable reservations. The fellow wasn't deferential enough...looked you straight in the eye. But obviously, and luckily for this most fortunate youthful *Indito*, Rodolfo seemed to be everything that Oscar could have hoped for, except for his youth.

"But I think he can handle it," Oscar was saying. "He's big enough...looks years older than Eddy," he added, unable to hide from the priest his resignation over an only son's baby face. "The schoolteacher remembers him well. Tells me that Rodolfo was about the brightest Indian he ever taught. And he's been speaking only Spanish since he left for the coast. Looks to me like he's got just the right blend of Indian deference and our drive."

A smile traced Jacobo's thin lips at the suggestion that Rodolfo was deferent or that Oscar was among the driven. "Well, you know these brutish *Inditos* of this country better than I do, of course, but I'd be worried whether Catarinecos will ever accept one of their own in such a position, especially someone who left the village for so many years so early in his life."

The patriarch of the Primavera bit his lip pensively, concerned lest the cynical priest's doubts be justified. "He'll have enemies, to be sure," Oscar agreed, "but Catarinecos know they'll have to work with *someone* of my choosing. I wager that they'll decide they're better off with one of their own than with one of us." Hoping that Jacobo wouldn't press the matter, he refilled their glasses and added, "The best part of it is his good relationship with Eddy. It won't be long before Eddy's ready for major responsibility, and I'm thinking that the Santa Catarina holdings will be the place to begin. If the two of them get along well, it'll go a whole lot easier for Eddy."

But Jacobo wasn't satisfied. "Are you sure that you can trust Rodolfo with the hard decisions, when it comes to putting your interests ahead of those poor creatures he grew up with? After all, he still has family over there. He'll be forced to disappoint friends, maybe even relatives sooner or later...maybe even take away their land."

"Well, I'm not telling him this, but the truth is that I'm not expecting to increase our holdings over there for now. For the time being my problem is a dependable labor supply. Having more land does me no good if I can't keep what I already have in full production. Losing their land is bad enough, but it irritates the devil out of Indians to see it sitting there not being fully used."

"By Judas, Oscar Ramirez! I swear by all the black saints that you're too patient with these *Inditos!* Hiring one of their own as manager, even! Why under God's Heaven —"

"It's very simple, my friend. We're not a large enough coffee operation to be able to get labor dependably assigned to us by the government, so we *have* to keep on reasonably good terms with the people. With so many dying of late they're able to keep busy just with farming their own and dead relatives' land. The secret is getting them into debt with cash loans or the pawning of their land...then hoping that they have to work for us to cancel the debt. But if you loan them too much, they despair of repaying and give up on their land. Lots of land does me no good if I don't have the labor to work it. So part of Rodolfo's job is to learn what resources they have...how likely it is they'll be willing to work to pay off the loan. No, I won't be asking Rodolfo to squeeze them out of their land. Not now anyway. I'll be content if he can just get the coffee trees and milpas that I already have over there producing to capacity and fully harvested. If the population ever gets back to what it was a few years back — and the way *Inditos* breed I have no doubt but what it will — then we can think about more land," concluded Oscar, downing his third drink and rising from his chair in another effort to end the conversation. The swimmers were headed toward the house, and dinner was on the table.

But his persistent guest still wasn't convinced that all the dying in Santa Catarina didn't argue for buying up their land as rapidly as possible. "What about importing labor from other towns around to work your holdings in Santa Catarina?"

Oscar shook his head. "Santa Catarina may be the hardest hit, because of their abominable sanitation over there — drinking the same lake water their outhouses drain into — but every county in Solola has the same problem: not enough men to work the land they still have, after filling their *mandamiento* quotas each year."

———

As their voices drifted off into the house from the back veranda, Elena could again move freely about the spare room that Don Oscar obviously had forgotten was within earshot. Her report soon thereafter to Rodolfo of what she'd heard only further relieved his mind. He could at least reduce Catarinecos' anxiety in the short run over losing land from foreclosure. If he had a free hand in hiring, he could help those with pawned land get their loans repaid, and he could assure those needing to borrow that they wouldn't be risking their land. By never having quite enough men hired to fully harvest the crop he could forestall a change of Oscar's mind about adding to his holdings. He might even be able to control who got to glean the overlooked ears of maize in Oscar's milpas to protect himself against getting caught too short of harvest labor. Rodolfo kissed his namesake's crucifix that they already had placed on a make-do altar in the corner, concluding that what Elena had so fortunately overheard warranted sharing with Diego and Santa Catarina's mayor. His good fortune seemed to know no bounds. It might just be due to a companion-spirit after all, skeptical as he had been wont to be about his purported fish guardian until his luck had suddenly begun to change. Perhaps it had been all along his destiny to reside on the shores of this lake at the center of the world.

———

Santa Catarina's mayor had little recollection of Jose's son, and from the rumors swirling about he wasn't disposed to be charitable. But out of respect for Jose he received Rodolfo Luis cordially enough. As mayor, he had had many dealings with Oscar Ramirez, and after Diego explained the circumstances of Rodolfo's decision to accept the job the mayor had to smile at Don Oscar's good luck and ingenuity. But, at best, Rodolfo would not have an easy task. How helpful, as mayor, he should be to his prodigal countryman, he still was not prepared to wager.

"When faced with a bull, taking him by the horns is the only way," he was at least willing to advise, after pondering at length the intriguing news from the Primavera. "Your best bet is to meet with the Council of Elders and explain, just as frankly as you have to me, that people forced to have dealings with the Ramirez family will be better off with you than with anybody else Don Oscar might hire. But I wouldn't share what you've overheard about Don Oscar's intention not to foreclose. We never can be sure whose ears around here Ramirez money has bought. I'll help you make your case with the elders. But I'll leave it to you to offer some of the Primavera harvest earnings to finish our church roof, if you really think Don Oscar will agree to that."

Diego was impressed. Rodolfo wasn't about to give up. Six years on the coast had indeed taught him to think like a Ladino, and yet Diego could tell that his brother-in-law was still more Catarineco than he would care to admit.

When Rodolfo stopped in to tell his mother the circumstances of her loan's cancellation and asked permission to tell the elders, she was too astonished to say no. She had been devastated by the malicious gossip about her son and had assumed that he surely would go back to the coast. But clearly he planned to stay! Victoria was delighted. Elena would be the older sister that she'd never found in Julia.

Rodolfo got Don Oscar's agreement to more than a contribution for church repair; he also got his pledge to sponsor the Dance of the Conquest for November's fiesta. The elders of course saw through it all — Rodolfo expected that — but they were nonetheless impressed and pleased with his tact and eloquence. Rodolfo Luis Ajcojom knew how to use words!

So it was that, within two short weeks of his return to the lake, Rodolfo was firmly entrenched as the Ramirez foreman and in charge, as well, of seeing the church fully repaired in time for November's fiesta. "Oh, Jose...if only you could see your son now!" the mayor murmured, watching from the council room as Rodolfo directed work at the church. The clock that he had donated for the council room struck five o'clock. No longer could the Ladino secretary assigned to Santa Catarina from Panajachel leave early, claiming it was closing time.

Chapter Eight

Elena and Rodolfo had planned to name their baby Virgilio, if a boy. But to be born on the birthday of Panajachel's patron, Saint Francis, left them no choice. On October 4, 1914, Francisco Ajcojom Salanic joined the family. Beatriz Ramirez was thrilled. She chose to stay with Elena after the delivery instead of going into town for fireworks and dancing in the evening. With no need to be there to chaperon her daughter, Arcadia elected to join the happy Ajcojom household as well. Eduardo was elated; with no sister nor mother around, he stood a chance of bettering last year's record when he secreted a girl away from the dancing and had his way with her for half an hour behind the school.

Beatriz proudly announced to Elena that she finally had had her first period...not then understanding the midwife's apprehensive look. Elena explained about hot blood around a baby, when menstruating, but after discussion the midwife and Arcadia agreed that there was little danger of any *mal de ojo* (evil eye) affecting Francisco if Beatriz kept her distance.

The Ajcojoms were virtually adopted by the Ramirez household in the weeks that followed, and in early November Oscar and Arcadia became Francisco's baptismal godparents and thereby the compadres of Rodolfo and Elena.

Neither Oscar nor Rodolfo realized how jealous Eduardo steadily was growing of an Indian's place in his ailing father's heart. Oscar was too quick to support and defend any decision that Rodolfo made. And while Rodolfo was discreet, Eduardo had no illusion about the low respect Rodolfo had for especially his sexual exploits. The "Don Eduardo" relationship the two men held to in public gradually became their relationship in private as well. For his part, Rodolfo attributed Eduardo's greater reserve to increased responsibilities, not only in Santa Catarina but also for the smaller San Antonio holdings. Oscar was relinquishing control to his son more rapidly than Rodolfo had anticipated, probably because of his health, but perhaps also because things seemed to be going so well in Santa Catarina.

In Rodolfo's first January harvest, all the coffee got picked and maize yields were better than usual. But because Rodolfo had come too late for the critical pruning of young coffee seedlings, it would be another year before the effect of his rapport with Catarinecos became fully evident. All milpas were cleaned, burned, and planted by the first of April. In May the pruning was done and new coffee seedlings planted in time for the rains. Eduardo took note that all Catarinecos owing money had worked one or both months. He tacitly agreed with his father to Rodolfo's recommendation not to foreclose on families whose time was up on loan repayment. Oscar raised Rodolfo's wage to thirty cents a day and, unaware of the deteriorating relationship between Eduardo and Rodolfo, he turned Santa Catarina lands completely over to their joint management. Eduardo decided to hold his tongue, but to monitor closely the next year's harvest. Rodolfo went about establishing commitments for the next January's coffee picking among those most in need of the minimal income and, just as important, gleaning privileges in the extensive Ramirez milpas.

———

July 18, almost a year after Rodolfo and Elena had arrived in Panajachel, was the important fifteenth birthday of Beatriz. Panajachel would see the grandest party in its history. Arcadia asked Elena and Victoria to help with preparations. Rosa promised Victoria her first new *huipil* and sash in three years, and mother and daughter were weaving every spare moment.

"I haven't heard of anyone around here weaving a *huipil* in ages," said Victoria, watching her mother deftly throw the shuttle through the divided warp, draw the woof tight with the stick, then turn the stick in the warp to repeat the process. "I'm embarrassed to have a new one when everybody was feeling so sorry for us having to pawn your milpa...especially when folks learn what it's for!"

"People can think it's for the fiesta this fall. No one needs to know you're helping the Ramirez family with their party. I've told neighbors that you're going to Rodolfo's to help with Francisco for a week. Just be sure to wear your old clothes except for the party."

Victoria helped in the Ramirez kitchen, working late into the evening cleaning up after each day's bustle of food preparation. Over one hundred guests had been invited for the party meal. The excitement of such uncustomary activity was as exhilarating for Victoria as for Beatriz. She was fifteen — going on sixteen — herself and pretended that the party was for her as well. The family made her feel as much at home at the Primavera as they did Elena.

Especially Eduardo, whose attentiveness rapidly became a joking matter in Victoria's and Elena's absence. The girl's innocence captivated him. She was without pretense, ingenuous beyond belief to a youth whose philandering surpassed his father's and whose guile approached the cunning of the parish priest. Victoria not only failed to acknowledge his thinly veiled advances; she appeared not to recognize them as flirtations.

Not that Victoria wasn't aware of his hovering presence. She was very much aware of Eduardo Ramirez. She was as awed by this first youthful Ladino she had ever dared talk to as he was intrigued by his childhood friend's unreachable sister.

On the evening that Oscar and Eduardo slaughtered hogs, Victoria joined Beatriz and Arcadia to observe her first butchering. Stripped to his waist in the humid slaughterhouse, Eduardo was covered with blood and sweat. The earthiness of smells, the glistening light skin of Eduardo's broad back, and shadows cast on the walls by caster oil lamps transported Victoria. At a point where the men's four hands were not enough, and without their asking, she held the meat for Eduardo to cut until she was as wet as he. Arcadia and Beatriz left after the first pig, but Victoria remained for the second. She even offered to stay to clean up the worst of the mess when they had finished. Don Oscar was the first to leave, and after he had washed at the horse trough Eduardo left to do the same. Left alone, Victoria hummed with contentment as she cleaned the knives and table as best she could. Before blowing out the lamps she caressed the sleek loins on the rack and stuck her arms up to elbows in the barrel of warm blood and entrails. Her *huipil* was a mess. No matter…beginning tomorrow she could wear the new one!

Outside it was already dark. Eduardo kindly had filled the trough with fresh water. With no one around, she lifted her soiled *huipil* over her head. Kneeling over the trough she washed her arms and neck, lingering to enjoy the water and air on her skin, taut from the coolness. Her nipples tingled from their sudden erection, and she had started to rub them when she felt him standing over her. She knew it was Eduardo, even before his whispered reassurance, "I won't hurt you." His hands settled gently on her shoulders. Trembling, she stood slowly, hands still on her breasts, letting his own shirtless chest support her body. Her heart was pounding under her hands, then under his as they nudged beneath hers and began to massage. Her knees buckled, and she would have slumped to the ground had his one arm not dropped to her waist to support her firmly against his crotch.

The throbbing through his pants was frightening with its intensity. Regaining some presence of mind, and sensing what was about to happen, she uttered a faint, "N — No, please don't!" For the moment his tightening hold on her relaxed, to test her resolve. He knew so well what to expect...knew all the indications in an inexperienced girl's responses. Surprised, she, too, paused... mind racing with the realization that, if she struggled or called out and anyone came, there would be even worse consequences for her and probably for all relationships between the Ajcojom and Ramirez families. The important thing was not to be discovered. She let him resume caressing, relaxing again and not resisting as his hand moved slowly down her stomach. Muscles tensed and drew in, inviting his hand inside her skirt until probing fingers reached the moist hair. She was embarrassed with how easily his fingers slipped into the opening...never had she been so wet. She began to whimper, slumping as the loosened skirt fell to her ankles. She was too confused to resist as he lifted her free of the cloth and laid her on the grass, now wet with dew. Wide-eyed, shivering and sobbing from the cold and fright, she watched him lower his trousers before parting her legs and kneeling.

Assuming that it was her first time, he massaged the moist folds longer than usual, and only when her shuddering subsided a bit did he sink down on her stomach. His penetration brought a subdued cry. Only then did he unleash the excitement that had been growing since their sweaty arms had first touched three hours earlier in the meat shed.

Nothing was said as they dressed and walked quietly to the darkened house of Rodolfo. Eduardo squeezed her shoulders, to communicate she knew not what, before he disappeared back toward the plantation house, leaving her to decide the fate of her reputation and Rodolfo's future with the Ramirez family. Fortunately her brother was already asleep, and to Elena's faint inquiry, Victoria said simply, "I've just back from helping with the butchering."

Her shame was kind. It waited until Victoria had slept to descend on her the next morning. She awakened with a start, after Elena had given Rodolfo breakfast and begun to nurse Francisco. Joining Elena in the kitchen as soon as Rodolfo left the house, Victoria began to sob, giving up — with no more struggle than the night before — any attempt to keep it to herself. Elena guessed what had happened as soon as Victoria explained that she had stayed to clean up after the second hog.

"What stupidity! Didn't you know how Eddy's been eyeing you all week? Nobody will believe that you didn't outright invite him on top of you, staying late alone like that! If we tell, your reputation will be ruined and Rodolfo will be put in a terrible position! All of Santa Catarina will know, and no Catarineco will have you! What, oh what, were you thinking?" Obviously she hadn't been thinking, and Elena stopped fuming lest her milk upset Francisco. He already had begun to cry.

Victoria made no attempt to defend herself. There was nothing to do but to go about her work at the house the two remaining days as though nothing had happened. She shouldn't even have told Elena. But at least it was clear that Elena wouldn't tell Rodolfo. "Did anything like this ever happen to you on the coast?" Victoria finally mustered the courage to ask.

Elena stonily declined to answer, not prepared to share with poor, innocent Victoria the price that every attractive girl paid for being born on a coffee plantation. In fact, Eddy's older cousin, Pedro, son of Don Oscar's brother at the Monte Carlo, had forced her to submit even before her periods had begun. Her only reservation with living at the Primavera was worry over Pedro's occasional visits here with his parents. If Eddy didn't already know, it was only a matter of time before Pedro would be telling him in exaggerated detail of his conquest.

But Eduardo did, indeed, know, and because of this he also knew when he left Victoria that the next day would be just like any other. Victoria might tell Elena or even her mother, but no one would dare tell Rodolfo. As soon as his eyes met Elena's, Eduardo could tell that she knew. To her icy stare he even dared to return the trace of a smirk. He couldn't wait to tell Pedro that he now had had the buxom sister-in-law of Elena. As for Victoria, she didn't let their eyes meet, which disappointed but didn't surprise him. If he was to have her again, it would have to be by force. Struggling, she might be even more exciting. He began to consider the possibilities before she would return to Santa Catarina.

But Elena anticipated his thoughts; Eddy gave every indication of being just as reckless as his cousin. She resolved not to let Victoria out of the house alone until the party was over and she was safely headed home with Rodolfo. A second time could have even graver consequences. The mood of the household imperceptibly changed that day. Everyone sensed it, but only three gave it any thought.

That evening Don Ricardo's family arrived from the Monte Carlo. The next morning, the day of the evening party, Oscar asked Rodolfo and Eddy to take Ricardo to see Santa Catarina coffee groves for any advice Ricardo might have on treating seedlings showing the insect infestation. To Elena's relief, Pedro decided to tag along. In the afternoon the storekeeper, Don Eliseo, arrived with his family. Elena learned from Beatriz that Beatriz's mother and Eliseo had the same father but different mothers, but this of little consequence "since Eliseo nonetheless has been the bestest uncle a girl could possibly have!" The priest was next to arrive, and after five o'clock the house and yard rapidly filled with almost every Ladino family in Panajachel and the wealthier families in Solola. To Rodolfo's astonishment, even the governor rode in.

"I'm not surprised," boasted Elena. "When Don Ricardo's oldest daughter celebrated her fifteenth at the Monte Carlo, even Guatemala's president was invited!" They watched Solola's wealthiest and most powerful man dismount from a sweating stallion gleaming like polished obsidian. The governor's carriage was close behind with his wife and daughter. "What a beautiful girl," whispered Elena as Carmen stepped down in her white formal.

Eduardo, to be sure, took note of the governor's celebrated daughter, but it was still Victoria who had his full attention. Pedro was equally interested, after Eduardo's graphic report of the late night exploit. Victoria was radiant in her new *huipil*. Rosa had found time to add some embroidery, nicely complementing the blouse's vibrant red and purple stripes and the dark blue skirt. Elena had loaned her the best of her necklace and ear jewelry as well. Eduardo couldn't resist complimenting her even in Elena's and Rodolfo's presence when he came out to the kitchen.

"How can he have such nerve?" Elena thought angrily, as Victoria blushed so hotly that Rodolfo's initial smile drained from his lips. "Oh, dear Virgin Mary, don't let him suspect!" Elena distracted her husband's attention by daring to greet Pedro who happened in at that fortunate moment. The evening saw no more such incidents, but Elena breathed freely only when the three of them were at last walking home late that night, Francisco asleep on her back. The next morning Rodolfo needed to return to Santa Catarina; Victoria wouldn't have to walk home alone.

———

Eduardo had not given up, taking Pedro into his confidence. Assuming that Victoria would walk home with her brother, Eduardo had schemed to get Oscar to ask Rodolfo to run an errand a kilometer north of Panajachel before continuing on to Santa Catarina. Victoria wouldn't want to walk the extra distance, but Elena and Rodolfo wouldn't want her waiting around for him at daybreak in Panajachel. She likely would opt to catch up with him in Panajachel, relieved not to have to be up and about so early in the morning.

And the stratagem worked. After the night of partying and late night drinking, Eduardo and Pedro were still awake, watching from the banana grove across from the Ajcojoms' house before dawn when Rodolfo left by himself for

90

Panajachel. Impatiently they waited until Victoria started up the path as the sun appeared above the hills at the far end of the lake. She was wearing a folded carrying cloth on her head and carrying the new *huipil* under her arm. The cousins moved stealthily to the grove's far end, out of earshot even if she did make noise, and waited in the foliage a couple meters from the shaded path. Before she could more than gasp in surprise, Eduardo grabbed her from behind, wrapped her carrying cloth around her face, and with Pedro controlling her kicking legs they carried her into the groove. Holding her arms, Eduardo watched Pedro pull off her skirt and have his go at her first. She didn't have any fight in her by the time he was on her, so he took his time in coming, fancying that Victoria knew full well that it was him and was quietly enjoying the encore.

Victoria was still motionless when they left her, running through the grove out of view of the path and house. Convinced that they had gone, and free finally of the cloth that had kept her gasping for breath throughout the ordeal, she rose slowly to her knees and looked about. No one was to be seen or heard. Eddy for sure, and no doubt Pedro! She had dared entertain the prospect that Eddy actually was fond of her, but after this the truth was so painfully clear. How could even Ladino boys be so inhumanly cruel? But, again, at least no one knew. The old blouse was torn too badly to wear. So she cleaned the blood as best she could with it, pulled the new one over her head and rewrapped her skirt before limping on toward Panajachel. She had managed to straighten her hair and wash up a bit, collecting herself by the time Rodolfo showed up at Eliseo's store. While unusually quiet all the way home and fighting the tears, she was composed enough to convince him that he didn't need to see her all the way home and then to convince her mother that the old *huipil* had gotten torn too badly to continue wearing when she fell coming down the steep path to town. Never had home looked so inviting; the Primavera had lost all its fascination.

Eduardo's visits to Santa Catarina increased as Rodolfo forwarded to him the usual end-of-year fiesta and pre-harvest loan requests. "He thinks he's got to talk with folks himself! Doesn't trust me to tell him how much he can safely loan for repayment with work," Rodolfo complained to his brother-in-law Diego.

"Or maybe he's less interested in payment with labor than you are," Diego suggested guardedly. "I hear that Raimundo Sajbin asked to borrow only 100 pesos and yet had to pawn his two acres down by the new cemetery. You'd better be careful...Don Eduardo distrusts you for more than that! Rumor has it has he's been looking for someone to keep an eye on the maize harvest. He suspects that you'll purposely be harvesting light." From the way Rodolfo's left eyebrow arched, Diego knew the rumors were well-founded.

Curious as to whether any of the men who had agreed to harvest coffee in return for gleaning privileges in Ramirez milpas had been talking, Rodolfo asked, "Has anyone actually said that I'd be doing such a thing?"

"Nobody I know of, but when I hear who all's agreed to pick coffee for you, I figure that they see more in it for themselves than six centavos a day!"

Rodolfo returned Diego's grin and admitted that he did, indeed, plan to harvest light in at least the highest milpas where Eduardo would not likely bother to go checking. "It's the only way I can keep everybody who owes us money working off their debts. Besides, I figure that a good coffee harvest is more important to the Ramirez family than getting every last ear of maize."

"To old man Ramirez, maybe, but I'm afraid that Don Eduardo has his eye on another plantation in Santa Catarina as large as the Primavera. He wants more land, Rodolfo! Why else would he be making Raimundo pawn his land for just a 100 peso loan?"

Rodolfo had to admit that it didn't look good. "And here I've been promising folks that they don't have to worry about losing their pawned land if they just keep working off their debts!"

"And to your credit, dear Brother-in-law, they're beginning to believe you! Look how many are borrowing from Don Eduardo for the fiesta. You know as well as I do that some who say they need money for the fiesta are in fact building up savings for planting coffee trees themselves. I know at least four who will set out seedlings next year."

Rodolfo groaned. "If that happens I'll really have trouble with Eduardo. If folks aren't careful, he won't loan anything until he has gotten his hands on their deeds."

"But you can hardly blame them for trying to take advantage of the good price for coffee. I'd do it, too, if I had land at a low enough altitude to grow decent coffee."

Rodolfo pursed his lips, shook his head in submission and took his leave. On the way back to Panajachel he weighed his options, and then decided to talk with Eliseo. He was the one person Rodolfo could completely trust, who also was close enough to the Ramirez family to know their minds. Rodolfo found Eliseo's wife minding the store.

"He went to Solola to buy supplies," his wife said "— should be almost back by now. At least he'd better be! I've got better things to do with my time than tend store the whole day."

Thanking her, he hurried off. With luck he would find Eliseo not far above the lake.

Eliseo had stopped to water his oxen at the cataract off the road overlooking his half-sister Arcadia's and Oscar's Primavera plantation. In his opinion, the delta was too swampy for coffee. He had predicted that the Primavera would never amount to much, even before Arcadia surprised him by marrying Oscar. Arcadia's mother had opposed the marriage, but the father Arcadia shared with Eliseo thought there might be money for him in such a union. He'd been wrong. Eliseo had felt sorry for Arcadia ever since, especially after word got out about Oscar's other Indian mistress across the river. Arcadia hadn't had a very happy marriage...except for the day of Beatriz's coming-out birthday party. Eliseo had not seen Arcadia happier than she was that day. But Beatriz was off at school with nuns in the capital now, and it wouldn't be long before she found a city husband. And then what would his sister and Oscar Ramirez do?

He hitched up his oxen again and resumed the journey, encountering Rodolfo Luis a kilometer down the road. "Now here's a man who would have made my niece a worthy husband! Too bad you didn't come back to these parts before you found yourself an Indian wife!" Eliseo enjoyed teasing Rodolfo for being more Ladino than Catarineco.

Rodolfo blushed but was relieved that Eliseo's thoughts already were on the Ramirez family. He swung himself up to join Eliseo on the wagon and wasted no time explaining his dilemma. "If you will but do me the favor, Don Eliseo," he concluded, "I need to know whether you think Don Eduardo is planning to change Don Oscar's policy of not foreclosing."

"I haven't heard him talk about it," Eliseo confided, "but I can tell you that Father Jacobo thinks the family is crazy for not grabbing all the land they can while the numbers of *naturales* are down. He's told Eduardo what he thinks, and Eduardo listens to him even if Oscar doesn't! If you're asking me what I predict, then I say Eduardo will start foreclosing just as soon as he thinks you can find the pickers he'll need for expanded holdings in Santa Catarina."

Rodolfo nodded agreement and took his leave, begging Eliseo to treat the visit in confidence.

"No worry, my friend. Although he's my nephew, Eduardo has none of my sympathy! Rumor has it, I'm sure you know, that he even had your sister. I wouldn't trust him with his own." It was several moments after Eliseo rumbled off, Rodolfo trotting through the coffee trees on a shortcut home, before Eliseo's words sunk in. Victoria? Eduardo had *Victoria!* His pace quickened, taking him within a few meters of where she had been raped the second time. "Had to have been while she was here helping with the party," he muttered, rushing into the house to confront Elena. "Did you know about Victoria and that bastard, Eduardo?" he demanded.

Startled, Elena could think of no way to deny it. She nodded. For the first time in their marriage he hit her. He hit her again, throwing at his sobbing wife all the invectives intended for Eduardo that Eduardo would never hear. Nose bleeding, she didn't resist — relieved, in a way, that her husband finally knew. The least that she could do for him, for Victoria, for any future their poor family might have was to absorb the fury none of them could vent on Eduardo. At least she had managed all these years to keep from her husband the sorry history of Elena's abuse from Eddy's cousin, Pedro. Exhausted and crying himself, Rodolfo left her on the floor to walk off the rest of his anger. He almost hoped that he would run into Eduardo. Almost.

Elena even knew there had been a second time. She began to suspect the afternoon of the rape, when Rodolfo on his return from Santa Catarina asked her why Victoria had worn her new *huipil* home. But she had convinced herself otherwise, until she herself had asked Victoria about the *huipil* some weeks later. From the silent agony on her face, Elena knew, but she had the presence of mind not to press. For two months now she hadn't seen Victoria.

———

Victoria realized that something was wrong; she had gone three months without her monthly bleeding. But that it could have anything to do with Eduardo hadn't even occurred to her. She assumed that her bouts of fever were the cause. Like everyone else in Santa Catarina, Rosa and Victoria attributed the ever-present illnesses to the listlessness brought on by heavy rains after the *canicula* respite from daily precipitation. That lull this year unfortunately had been very short, and the rains were back with a vengeance. Rosa fed her a hummingbird heart to give her more energy, but to no avail.

When Elena next saw Victoria, at the November fiesta, Elena was herself six months into her second pregnancy. When she looked at Victoria and saw that she looked almost as heavy as herself, she knew what even Rosa had been slow to suspect. But Rosa assumed it would be Silvestre's baby. Neighbors had seen Victoria visiting with Silvestre at least twice at the spring above town, and so Rosa had prepared herself for the first visit from Silvestre and his parents. If Victoria didn't wish to tell her about Silvestre or the baby, she wasn't going to bring it up.

But Silvestre never came to ask for Victoria. He suspected that Victoria was pregnant, and if so, he knew the baby wasn't his. By the time that Victoria also suspected and got up her courage to talk with Elena, it was dangerously late to abort. Victoria tried the only herbal remedy that Elena had heard of: pomegranate skin. When nothing happened she waited until Rosa had gone to market one Sunday morning before trying a stick. Elena had told her that as a last resort some girls used sharp sticks on the coast. Victoria pushed it up inside…pushing harder, until the pain was too much. The bleeding had slowed by the time her mother returned, and she had covered the spot with new dirt. But the bleeding never completely stopped, and three days later her fever returned with a vengeance. Rosa brought the midwife and even hired a curer to burn candles at the cave. But by the end of the following week Victoria mercifully was dead.

As fate would have it, there was enough dirt left over on her grave to convince some that Victoria had not yet been summoned. If she had been bewitched, it would be because someone would benefit from her death. The only others who might inherit Rosa's land were Rodolfo and Julia. The reason for Rodolfo's coming back from the coast to protect against Rosa's land being lost to Don Oscar was finally clear. Even Rosa began to waver under the slander that Rodolfo had killed his own sister for no other reason than financial advantage.

Elena begged Rodolfo to let her tell his mother about Eduardo…to let her tell Julia about Eduardo…to let her tell *somebody* about Eduardo. But he couldn't bear for anyone to know. The shame was also his. No Catarineco knew Don Eduardo well enough to understand that he could be that callous or that cruel. Catarinecos would choose to believe that Victoria, or even Rodolfo himself, had let Eduardo have her.

So no one learned the truth. Eduardo heard the rumors about Rodolfo bewitching his own sister, but he had no understanding of the reasoning and shrugged them off. Victoria must have died from one or another of those sicknesses Catarinecos always seemed to have. Nor did Eduardo understand the intensity of Rodolfo's anger, nor the depth of Elena's fear that the anger would get the best of her husband. Eduardo knew only that they both assiduously avoided him. Elena even declined Arcadia's help when her second child, Margarita, was born. Oscar and Arcadia sensed that something was seriously wrong when the Ajcojoms didn't ask them to sponsor Margarita's baptism. They learned later that Rodolfo and Elena had asked this favor of Luisa and Eliseo, Arcadia's half-brother.

———

Whenever Eduardo found it necessary to travel with Rodolfo to or from Santa Catarina, he found Rodolfo civil enough but strangely uncommunicative. "Indians are impossible to understand," he said angrily to his uncle, Eliseo, as he downed a drink at the store after returning from such a trip alone. "I caught Rodolfo drinking over there today! Can you imagine? I say, that man is completely changed from the Rodolfo he was two years ago when we hired him! Even Catarinecos don't trust him anymore, and here I've been suspecting him of befriending them at our expense! The way Catarinecos are bad-mouthing him, I wasn't sure whether it was safe to leave him alone over there today!"

Eliseo could think of nothing charitable to say. Rodolfo had confided the likely cause of Victoria's death when he came to order her coffin, and Eliseo understood the beliefs of Indians well enough to know why Rodolfo was being accused of killing her. It was hardly surprising that he was buying a drink, if not a bottle, on his every trip to Santa Catarina. "If you plan to pressure Catarinecos into pawning land in order to foreclose on them whenever possible, then be merciful for God's sake and dismiss the poor fellow! He can't take the pressure of his own people thinking that he has betrayed them! He'll take his own life first!"

This was a firmness in his uncle's voice that Eduardo had never heard before. "Uncle, you're probably right," he replied deferentially, "but who could I possibly find to take his place?"

"That's your problem. There wasn't a better man for the job than Rodolfo, 'til you destroyed him!"

Eduardo reddened and stalked out, determined to have a stern talk with Rodolfo before deciding whether to follow his uncle's advice. He stopped at Elena's to tell her to send Rodolfo over as soon as he arrived home. But Rodolfo didn't come home that night. Elena didn't give it much thought; not uncommonly he stayed with Julia if there were problems that needed his attention the next day.

Chapter Nine

I recall, even now these many years later, that the "five o'clocks" lining the path to Julia's patio already had closed for the night when I began the long climb out of Santa Catarina that fateful evening. I reasoned in my stupor that if I could make the high point and get beyond the cliff by dark I would be all right despite the moonless night. But the climb was more exhausting than I had counted on...I think I was as drunk as ever I had been. Diego and Julia were right: I should have stayed to sleep off the rum and delay the return until morning. I stopped to rest every few steps, and had climbed only as far as the old cemetery turn-off when stars began to dot the eastern sky. My head was splitting, so I stumbled toward the rows of graves on the chance that someone might have left an offering. Desperate for a drink, I began to curse as cross after cross yielded nothing. By the time I reached graves familiar to me at the far end I was sobbing from frustration and shame. What would my father's spirit think, seeing me reduced to such a state? Exhausted, I remember sinking down between the graves of my father and grandfather, grasping with both hands Vicente's carved fish charm at my neck.

I had come to visit my family's graves numerous times since returning to the lake, but never had I been in the cemetery this late in the day. Anxious to leave but unable to move with head pounding, I just lay there and stared at the sky. A star raced across, and then another. My father had insisted that they were souls of the dead on errands for the saints. If he was right, and if the soul of my martyred Father Rodolfo Luis was tied to the strange fish I'd dreamed about so much in my childhood, would I become a soul star, too? Or did fish spirits stay in the lake to run errands for its Owner, as Vicente assumed? Despite the cold creeping through my clothes, I drifted off...jolting awake a few minutes later with the realization that I was wet all over. Lying in vomit, I had pissed in my pants as well. "That damn fish!" Shocked as much by the old dream as the incontinence, I managed to get to my feet wondering what it all meant.

When my head cleared and I remembered where I was, I staggered ahead...stumbling over first one cross and then another. I remember panicking with the realization of how late it must be. Childhood admonitions never to be caught in the cemetery when the time changed led to the fear that it already was midnight! Imaginings took control as bushes moved and voices rose above the gusts of wind. First my father's...then my grandfather's...and finally Bacilia's shrill babbling before she died. Terrified, my own sobbing became my baby brother's as I hit him...and graves began to open. On reaching finally the cemetery border I collapsed in exhaustion. The last thing I recall was hearing my namesake's shout of, *"Jorge, listen!"*

Jorge turned in time to see dim outlines of what Father Rodolfo Luis had heard: two horses rounding the turn only a few minutes behind them. "Quick! — into the trees," panicked Jorge, grabbing the priest's robe to pull him along.

It was too late. The lead stallion was reined in a few meters from their refuge in the ferns. "You stay with the horses while I find the bastards,"Don Carlos shouted to his foreman.

At the sound of the angry voice, Jorge's hand tightened on the priest's frock and began to shake from the cold of fear and heavy dew. The priest's hand found Jorge's as he whispered, "They'll find us for sure if we stay here, my friend. I fear it'll go badly for us. You at least can make a run for it into the underbrush while I —"

No, Father. We'll face them together."

"But I want no blood shed on my account," said the priest firmly, and he squeezed the fist clinging desperately to his robe.

"Here they are!" shouted Carlos, warily approaching the thicket. Rodolfo Luis got to his feet and stepped into the open. "You can put away your machete. We wish you no harm," he said quietly, his hand on Jorge's arm to insure that the machete stayed in his belt.

"Wish me no harm! You no good traitor!" scowled Carlos derisively. "You'd leave me with no one to work my plantation if you frocked foreigners had your way! Wish me no harm — like hell!"

The foreman had joined his patron and quickly disarmed Jorge before pushing the men toward Don Carlos. Rodolfo Luis took a step, then gasped and slumped down on Carlos's machete cutting into his bowels. Jorge's knees gave way in shock as Don Ramon savagely grabbed his scalp from behind and cut off first one ear and then the other with blows from his own machete. Jorge's scream rent the curtain of blackness dropping around him, and then again as the knife sliced deeply into the hand still clinging to the priest's robe.

"That's enough," decided Carlos. "Let the stupid Indio suffer a while! He can bleed to death out here with his papist friend. Buzzards will clean their bones tomorrow if the jungle hasn't devoured them by dawn!"

When the horses were out of hearing, Jorge crawled to Rodolfo. There was no life left. With his own fast ebbing, he lifted the priest's head into his lap and prayed for both their souls. First to Saint Catherine...then to the Hill's Owner and all its creatures. "May your buzzards be merciful."

Eliseo was the first in Panajachel to learn the news; the fisherman stopped at his store to beg a drink of water before running on toward the Primavera. Rodolfo had been found at water's edge below the cemetery. He was badly broken and bloody from the fall...unconscious, but still breathing. The Catarineco bone setter was bringing him to Panajachel by canoe.

Despite his fifty years, Eliseo was surprisingly fit. He ran the full kilometer downhill to the lake. Could Rodolfo really have tried to end his own life? Eliseo was as angry at himself for selling Rodolfo so much liquor the previous day as he was at his nephew, Eduardo. The canoe with Rodolfo had already arrived. A crowd was gathering to peer at the broken body in the dugout pulled up on the beach. If Eliseo hadn't been told that it was Rodolfo, he doubted that he would have recognized his bloody form. Rather than risk more harm to broken limbs, Eliseo suggested that they carry him in the dugout to the church for Father Jacobo's judgment on what to do. Five men on each side lifted the boat to their shoulders and started toward town. Eliseo shook his head sadly. "Looks like a funeral procession," he said under his breath as he instinctively removed his hat and followed along.

———

Father Jacobo waded through the crowd to the canoe that sat incongruously in front of his church door. He shuddered as he took a look at what they said was Rodolfo Luis Ajcojom. Quickly he dispatched his sacristan by horse to Solola to fetch the doctor. When horse and awkward rider met Elena and Eduardo running toward town, Eduardo insisted on making the journey himself. He took off at a merciless gallop to trade for his own horse at the Primavera stable. Elena reached the church just as Rosa and Julia arrived from Santa Catarina.

Eliseo had sent for the Panajachel bonesetter. After the local curer examined Rodolfo, he conferred with the Catarineo bonesetter at some length before they gave Eliseo their opinions in Kaqchikel. Eliseo interpreted for the priest: "They think that one hip is broken and at least one bone in the other leg. An arm is broken on that side, too. What's caused the unconsciousness they can't say. They think his heart beat is too weak to set the bones now. They want to bring a diviner." Knowing the priest's attitude toward curers and their divinations, he didn't add that the bonesetters feared that Rodofo's soul would have departed his body during such a fall. The diviner had the power to learn if it had found its way back during the night.

Further delay in setting such badly swelling limbs made no sense to Jacobo, but he held his tongue. This wasn't the time to show his impatience with cave witches. The last thing that Oscar Ramirez wanted was Catarinecos stirred up over church or Ladino opposition to Indian superstitions. Relationships with *Indios* were uneasy enough as it was. Jacobo saw a major dilemma in the making: Catarinecos would be convinced that Rodolfo was doomed by sorcery. As priest, he might make some headway against such nonsense by personally taking charge of his care and recovery. On the other hand, he also had much to lose if the poor fellow died. From the looks of him, he might well not make it through the day regardless of what they did for him. Jacobo needed a doctor's prognosis, but in the meantime he wasn't about to defer to Indian bonesetters — far less to a cave witch. The bones must be set. But it would be best if Rodolfo's family made the decision. "Personally, I think the bones that we can take care of ourselves should be set immediately, before his limbs swell even more. But such an important decision should be left to his family." He watched Rosa and Julia — Rodolfo's mother and sister — argue argue heatedly in Kaqchikel. Clearly they weren't of one mind. Hoping for the best he turned to Elena.

Elena had been brushing flies from the clotted blood on her husband's head. Now she was weeping quietly and fingering the crucifix and chain that Rosa had added to the fish around his neck. Elena agreed quickly that to do nothing until the doctor arrived would be unbearable.

Jacobo suppressed a smile and eyed the crowd inscrutably. Panajachel's bonesetter chose to side with his strong-willed priest, but the Catarineco just as predictably refused to assist and stalked off. Jacobo supervised Rodolfo's transfer to a table in his rectory, and the bones in the right arm and leg were set by the time that Eduardo and the Solola doctor reached the rectory. The doctor was

100

relieved to find that he had only a hip to attend to, and it, he concluded, was only dislocated. Fortunately for Jacobo, Rodolfo was still breathing when the doctor had finished. "He should be conscious by tomorrow. Then he can tell us himself if there are problems that we can't see more serious than these bones. He shouldn't be moved for several weeks in any case." Before leaving, the physician suggested that Father Jacobo continue to look after him in the rectory. Jacobo couldn't have been more pleased.

Eliseo promptly invited Elena and the children to move in behind the store temporarily.

—

After two days of anxious waiting by family and friends in the rectory, my consciousness did return — at first only briefly and at long intervals. Frightening dreams began to come and go. If it wasn't horsemen chasing me, it was a fish, and always with the same outcome: milpas ending and then the long fall — tumbling down, down, down, into the cold water.

"I can't talk to Father Jacobo about my dreams," I admitted to Eliseo, who had stopped in after everyone else had gone to bed. He had come to the rectory every few hours on the chance of finding me conscious and able to talk. Eliseo had sensed from the outset, when Jacobo first told him about my frightened mumbling and tossing in my sleep, that he was the one who might be most able to help me.

I learned that Eliseo's father had been raised an Indian, something his father had told no one after he moved to Panajachel with his family. He'd changed his name from Aju to Lopez when he moved, and when thereafter he had the affair that produced his daughter, Eliseo's older half-sister Arcadia, her mother assumed that she was Ladina. His father later in life, after fathering Eliseo in time told Eliseo the truth of his ancestry, but they both agreed that probably it was wise never to tell Arcadia. His father had lived in fear that somehow someone, especially Don Oscar after his marriage to Arcadia, would learn. But Eliseo wasn't as worried and wasn't a bit bothered by being half Indian. He even had persuaded his father to teach him Kaqchikel so that he could converse with Indian store customers. When Eliseo married Luisa, whose mother was herself an Indian mistress of Luisa's Ladino father, Eliseo felt no embarrassment in telling her of his similar mixed ancestry. For twenty years they had lived peacefully in Panajachel, accepted as well by the *naturales* as the Ladinos.

101

The fears and imaginings that I described while convalescing from the fall reminded Eliseo of the talks he had had with his father over the years. Having divulged to me his ancestry, he was quick to assure me that he well understood the significance of my dreams. "Few Ladinos know what we *naturales* learn in our sleep, and even though we know that folks would laugh at us, Luisa and I nonetheless talk each morning about the nightly wanderings of our spirits. Sometimes there are important signs in what Ladinos call dreams."

"But Rosa is convinced that my dreams can't end until we hire a curer. She thinks my spirit's still there where I fell. I tell her that the priest won't let a curer come near me, far less do the long ceremony needed to bring back my soul. And maybe it isn't lost. Father Jacobo says its not unusual to have these long sleeps after such a fall...he says there is nothing to be done but to rest. What do you think, Don Eliseo?"

Eliseo was slow to respond, pondering how much to confide. "Well, I know how strongly Catarinecos feel. Some say there's no way you can recover without the ceremony, and others say there's no way you can get well even with it because of the sorcery they believe someone is doing against your soul. But I also know what the priest and the doctor say. They think your signs are good. You seem completely yourself when you're awake, and your memory's good. As for the dreams, I don't worry about them. The problems you've been dealing with in Santa Catarina were enough to make you have bad sleeps, even without a fall. And I'm convinced that you fell simply because you were so drunk. I don't think for a moment that anyone was chasing you. Diego, too, says that you were probably just imagining that. Says you were talking nonsense even before you left their house. He was afraid about your walking home alone, but you wouldn't listen. Even so, the business about your soul being startled worries me...it could be that you should, in fact, have the curing *costumbre* done. I've thought a lot about it...even talked with Elena and your mother. We have a plan, if you are willing. The doctor says that we can move you to our house in a few days to be with Elena. We can have the ceremony done there without Father Jacobo or the Ramirez family knowing. If you feel up to it, I'll make the arrangements."

But Rodolfo had slipped out of consciousness again, crucifix and fish still nestled against his chest. Eliseo dabbed at his own tears and, before leaving, kissed the ugly scar tracing Rodolfo's cheekbone. Eliseo didn't know what to believe anymore about one's soul leaving during sleep or being dislodged by a bad fright. But it surely wasn't going to hurt to have that ceremony. Clearly Rodolfo would wel-

102

come it. Just to be on the safe side, he would hire a diviner from across the lake in Santiago Atitlan. No one in Panajachel or Santa Catarina would need to know. Rodolfo and Elena could keep their peace with all concerned.

Father Jacobo kept the Ramirez family fully informed of his patient's progress. Since he judged that Rodolfo wouldn't be able to walk to Santa Catarina for several months, Eduardo realized that he would for the first time be overseeing the harvest himself. He would be able to ensure a full maize harvest, but he wouldn't be able to learn whether Rodolfo had expected to cheat him of some of the yield. In the interest of ensuring enough coffee pickers he would have to follow Rodolfo's advice: he would exempt pickers from any threat of foreclosure, at least for this season.

Through his brother-in-law Diego's periodic reports of goings on in Santa Catarina, Rodolfo learned to his satisfaction that his accident was working to everyone's advantage over there except Don Eduardo's. Those who had agreed to pick coffee only if they could glean in the milpas got out of working. Fortunately Rodolfo hadn't felt it necessary to obtain their signed agreement. They denied to Eduardo having every agreed to work, and there was nothing he could do. To Eduardo's chagrin, Rodolfo's list of pickers dwindled to half the needed number of men as January's harvest approached. He had no choice but to offer higher wages. The mayor advised Catarinecos not to hire on until the offered wage had increased from six to at least ten cents a day. The pickers were finally lined up in December, but at almost twice the usual cost.

"We must *never* let this happen again!" fumed Oscar to his son as Father Jacobo sat listening to their frustration over the limited options left to them. "It's clear to me that Rodolfo was keeping secret the agreements he had with pickers who backed out on us. But I'm beginning to suspect that he was doing exactly what he had to do to ensure the coffee harvest he knows we must have. Could be that he has been working in our best interests even when he didn't level with us completely. In any case, Rodolfo is one smart *Indio!*"

"One frightened one, as well, you are forgetting," added Father Jacobo. "Rodolfo still isn't convinced that he wasn't being chased by angry Catarinecos when he fell. I gather from what the sacristan over there tells me that half of Santa Catarina still expects him to die. They think he can't endure the sorcery, especially since they know that we've kept his mother from bringing in a curer. Eliseo swears that no curer from either Panajachel or Santa Catarina has been to see him. And if he pulls through, I trust that I will have made some headway against those who are so afraid of all this sorcery talk. I do believe that sorcery's the only thing that Catarinecos think about! They're convinced that everybody's out to cheat them. They don't trust even their own relatives or neighbors. Imagine! — thinking that Rodolfo caused his own sister's death just to get more of her mother's land, when Eliseo tells me that she died trying to abort!"

Eduardo's face froze. Abort!...*Victoria!* Could he or Pedro have gotten that girl pregnant? Must have! Elena had told Beatriz that Victoria didn't have a serious boy friend. Eduardo struggled to regain composure before his father could sense his consternation, but from the priest's half-closed eyes he couldn't tell what he might have noticed. Eduardo had to say something: "I've heard nothing of the sort, and I'm over there several times each week!"

Jacobo's eyes widened in surprise at Eduardo's uncustomary retort to his father. "Well, Eliseo says that he heard it from Rodolfo himself, and I reckon that the girl's brother ought to know! But why Rodolfo didn't tell folks over there, I can't understand. Could have saved himself a heap of trouble by letting Catarinecos know the truth about how she died."

Eduardo meekly nodded agreement with the priest and lapsed into silence to let the matter drop. He understood immediately why Rodolfo hadn't wanted to tell, especially if he'd found out that Eduardo might be the father. Rodolfo *must* have learned! When the priest left, Eduardo was still deep in troubled thought.

Oscar was less concerned about Victoria's mysterious death than with finding enough workers in the months ahead. "Maybe we're worrying too much about getting Catarinecos to help us. Jacobo may be right: perhaps there's a way to get cheap labor from other towns around."

Eduardo was again attentive. He had agreed with the priest about that for a long time, and added, "Jacobo told me on the way back from Santa Catarina the other day that there's a move afoot to force German plantation owners out of the coffee business, now that Germany is at war with the United States. Don Herman didn't get all the *mandamiento* pickers he asked for on the Esperanza this year, and if the governor intends to bankrupt him by cutting off his help, we might be able to benefit."

His father's sudden smile caught Eduardo by surprise, as did the suggestion that followed: "Of course, Eddy, that's it! The governor can give us some of the laborers who usually go to the Esperanza if he wants to! And the way to insure that he wants to is *you!* Have you given any thought to marrying his daughter?"

At twenty-three, Eduardo hadn't given much thought to marrying anyone. As the most eligible Ladino in Panajachel, he had his way with most any younger girl in town. No Ladina in Panajachel could reasonably expect to become his wife, given the lesser wealth and position of local Ladino families. But to become Eduardo's mistress was within the reach of many. While not adverse to marriage, he was in no hurry. He hadn't given the governor's daughter, Carmen, much thought. In fact, since Beatriz's fifteenth birthday party, he realized that he hadn't even seen her. She'd had her own coming-out birthday at least a year before Beatriz, and might be as old as eighteen by now.

From his lack of response, Oscar judged that his son hadn't given Carmen any serious consideration. "Someone else you've been thinking about?"

"No, it's not that...it's just that I haven't expected to marry for several years yet."

"But with the responsibility you've been taking for our land, anyone can see that you're ready. You may not be thinking about it, but I dare say a number of girls around are thinking of little else! Any objection to the governor's daughter?"

"No, not really...especially with what we've learned about the Esperanza. No question but that the governor could be a big help to us. Maybe Carmen and I will be invited to the same parties over the holidays; first step is to learn if she is involved with anyone else."

On learning of the men's discussion, Arcadia suggested that they have their own end-of-year party at the Primavera. "Beatriz has been asking for one out here before January and her new school year in the city. But without Elena's help I haven't been very eager to oblige. This is just the excuse we need to get Eliseo to let the Ajcojoms move back here to their own house! Frankly, I think that he and Luisa are keeping Rodolfo there just to have Elena's free help with their store!"

———

But Oscar was too intrigued with his son's marriage to the governor's daughter to leave such a potentially valuable union to chance. He confided in Father Jacobo, who agreed to do some discreet inquirying of his own in Solola. What Jacobo learned was hardly surprising. The governor had designs on the Esperanza himself and would be doing all he could to force the German owner to sell. He had told the new Solola bishop only the week before that he expected the Esperanza to be up for sale within the year. He would indeed welcome appeals for workers on smaller plantations in the diocese. "I think you could even have help for pruning this season, or for planting seedlings at the very least," Jacobo added with a twinkle, hoping that Oscar finally would give Eduardo a free hand to increase their holdings.

Oscar caught the twinkle, and bit his lower lip pensively. "I know, I know. Everything that's happening of late seems to argue for buying up land as rapidly as we can. I still have my reservations, but it'll be hard to argue with Eduardo that we shouldn't. I'll see how Rodolfo comes along. If he won't be able to work for us any more over in Santa Catarina, and I turn our holdings there completely over to Eddy, that will pretty much decide it."

"Maybe the governor will need such experienced help even with the Esperanza within a year or so," said Jacobo with a sly smile.

"Well, that assumes that Eduardo becomes his son-in-law," laughed Oscar.

"Of course he will!" chided the priest. "It's a perfect match!" The bishop's on good terms with the family and has offered to get the governor's reactions to several eligible men in the diocese. I'm prepared to wager that Eduardo will be married to Carmen within the year!"

———

The bishop learned that the governor was indeed interested in the Ramirez family. As for Eduardo, a New Year's Eve party was all the time that he needed to make up his mind. Carmen was tantalizing. The only way to have the woman would be to marry her. They were married the next May.

———

"Some affair!" exclaimed Eliseo, who had stopped in with Luisa on their way home to report to Elena on the biggest wedding anyone in Solola could remember. "If I didn't know about the scheming that went on to get this marriage arranged, I'd even say they love each other. Handsome couple, I must say…almost allowed myself to be proud he's a nephew!"

Luisa was even more complimentary. Given her humble origins, to be a guest of honor at the governor's home was no mean accomplishment. She had thoroughly enjoyed the day, climaxed when Carmen called her Aunt Luisa in the reception line. "Imagine! The governor's daughter *my* niece-in-law!"

Elena drank in every detail, envious of Carmen to a point but feeling sorry for her — so naively ignorant about Eduardo. *I might be poor,* she thought to herself, *but at least I can trust my husband.* "Did you learn where they'll be building their home?" She had overheard Arcadia say that Carmen's father had asked the couple to delay that decision for a while. Rodolfo hoped that this meant the governor was trying to persuade Eduardo to live in Solola.

"No, not a word," replied Eliseo. "All I know is that Oscar and Arcadia are really upset with having to hold off the decision. They want to get started so they can get the house finished by the end of *canicula,* just four months away. Personally, I enjoy watching them stew! It isn't often that Oscar has to! Eduardo did ask me to tell Rodolfo that he'll be away for at least a week. They've gone to Antigua to honeymoon. Rodolfo's over in Santa Catarina, I suppose?"

"Yes, he thought it might be best to be over there the day of the wedding. Didn't want Catarinecos to think we might have been invited."

"I wish your husband would listen to me!" scolded Eliseo. "I keep telling Rodolfo that there's nothing he can do anymore to make Catarinecos believe he isn't good friends with his patron. He might as well accept the inevitable: he's considered more Ladino now than he is *natural.* Especially after all the attention he got from us and especially from Father Jacobo while he was recovering from the fall. Catarinecos were so sure he would die. They're saying now that the sorcery didn't work because he's too Ladino, or because his blood's too strong. They're now calling him '*El Coyote.*'"

"Yes, we've heard, and Rodolfo doesn't know what to make of that. But I think he's becoming more resigned to the ambivalence Catarinecos feel about us," said Elena. "With the trouble Eduardo had finding pickers this past harvest, he and Oscar have decided to go outside the county for workers. Rodolfo knows that this means that they'll be pressuring him to increase their holdings there. Catarinecos will have even more reason to hate him..."

"Un huh," Eliseo pensively agreed. "I think it's pretty clear what the future holds for anyone around here who's poor and has land that will grow coffee. But Rodolfo shouldn't feel responsible. He's been as sensitive to the problems of Catarinecos as anybody could be. Tell him that I think he should take the bull by the horns and assure Oscar that he can support the stricter policy on foreclosures. It would be a shame for Oscar to assume otherwise and perhaps replace him after all you two have gone through these past two years!"

—

On my way back to Panajachel, I climbed to Rosa's milpa. I hadn't been up to the field since my fall, and with the limp it was a tiring climb. The hip they thought was dislocated had turned out to have a fracture after all. It hadn't healed quite right and short steps were all I could manage with that leg. The prominent scar on one cheek, a front tooth missing and another chipped were more visible reminders of the fall. Elena told me I look positively fierce when I grin. I don't mind having the scar and reputation for toughness, when 'El Coyote' is more rabbit at heart!

The maize and beans I had planted in April were up and in need of weeding. This would be the last milpa crop that I would have to worry about. Rosa reluctantly agreed to sell or trade her land after this harvest, to let me start a small coffee grove closer to the lake. I had waited a whole year since Victoria's death to raise the matter. I would have waited even longer if it weren't for the Ramirez decision to start grabbing land. Between Eduardo and the several Catarinecos starting their own groves, all land low enough for coffee would be gone within a year or two. Diego had no land left to sell, or he would be doing the same.

Diego and Julia had been much on my mind of late, and after my visit earlier in the day I was even more worried. Diego seemed distant and nervous. When he left to prepare for the night's crabbing, Julia confided her fear that he was involved with another woman. He was always leaving like this to get ready for crabbing or fishing, and she knew that there wasn't that much to do. But, then, she supposed that it was partly her own fault, unwilling as she was now to risk losing her milk with another pregnancy. After having lost three children, and then finally having succeeded in successfully birthing a son to join their six-year-old daughter, Julia was doing everything she could think of to keep him healthy. I had to agree. She was acting in her son's interest, but she hardly could blame Diego for looking at other women if she hadn't let him have her for six months. I felt sorry for them both but had no counsel to offer.

When Eduardo returned from his honeymoon, Oscar learned the unexpected price he was to pay for the marriage of his son to the governor's daughter. Carmen stayed at home while Eduardo rode down to share his father-in-law's proposition. "Herman will have a fit when he learns who has purchased the Esperanza," exclaimed Eddy gleefully. "The price is less than half what Herman paid for it, despite the acres and improvements he has added. But the real news concerns us. It seems that Carmen's parents have had in mind all along to buy the Esperanza for her and her husband, whomever he turned out to be. Now that the purchase is final, they told us this morning. They hope I'll be willing to manage it for a while to decide whether we want to settle there permanently. Carmen's as surprised as I am. Her father never had said a word about it...probably afraid that

108

you might object if you knew before the marriage."

"Well, I reckon!" sputtered Oscar. "What's he expect me to do with my holdings here, I wonder? I suppose he thinks that our 600 acres aren't good enough for his daughter!"

Eduardo gazed across the lake toward Santiago, too excited with the prospect of the Esperanza to be very worried about the Primavera. "But you must admit...it's quite a wedding gift."

"That it is," his father murmured, tears welling. "You'll have as large a plantation as my brother's! No more talk about trying it for a few years. Once you leave here, you'll never be moving back..."

Eduardo didn't comment. "What will you do with the Primavera?" he finally asked instead. "Any chance that Beatriz's fiancé, Pancho, might be interested in living out here?"

"They may spend weekends here from time to time, but that will be all. Pancho won't leave his family's business in the capital for no larger a plantation than I have to offer. With Indian parcels of land so small we'll never have a very large plantation, no matter how ruthless we're willing to be. And the more hard-hearted we are the more trouble we have keeping good managers!"

Eduardo had reached this conclusion months ago. Frankly, he found the offer of the Esperanza a perfect way out of his troublesome dilemma: how to extricate himself from managing the Primavera without completely rupturing the uneasy relationship with his father. What the Primavera needed was an owner with large lowland holdings who could afford to live at the lake while making weekly trips to the coast. Maybe someday...

———

But there was another alternative, and Oscar was quick to seize upon it once his anger and disappointment had subsided. At least Eduardo hadn't asked, and wasn't likely to ask, for Rodolfo's help at the Esperanza. A few days later Oscar went to the city to talk with Beatriz and his prospective son-in-law, and upon his return he sent immediately for Rodolfo.

Elena quickly concluded that the summons for an important meeting with Don Oscar meant that Rodolfo was to be replaced. And this after Eliseo finally had convinced Rodolfo to try to stay on. She watched as he limped home from the meeting, wiping his eyes. She prepared herself for the worst. Somehow we'll manage, she thought, and she decided to be humming when he came in. She didn't look up from her work. When finally she glanced at him furtively, he was all smiles.

"Elena, the saints have been merciful! Eduardo and Carmen will move to the Esperanza, and Pancho will come out with Beatriz a couple weekends each month to help Don Oscar oversee things here. But guess who's going to manage the Primavera here as well as the Ramirez holdings in Santa Catarina!"

Chapter Ten — Twenty Years Later

S pray off the bow misted across the Primavera's launch, adding to the late October chill. Rodolfo, his son-in-law Lazaro, and ten-year old grandson Virgilio were perched atop sacks of maize, relaxing in the early morning sun. Below them and less protected, Margarita was snuggling up to Elena against the cool breeze. Rodolfo looked down and smiled. Margarita was a constant pleasure, albeit fully as stubborn as her mother. She had Elena's large liquid lake-green eyes but otherwise looked more Ajcojom. Less comely than Elena had been at that age, due largely to the unfortunate birthmark high on Margarita's neck that was the first thing to catch one's eye. But she was also taller...taller even than her father and almost as tall as her brother, Francisco. Their mother's cooking — a largely Ladino diet with plenty of meat all their lives — had seen to that.

As usual, because of her birthmark, Margarita had insisted on wearing a dress instead of the collarless *huipil*. Had he — her father — asked her, perhaps she would have complied. But saying "no" to her mother was so habitual that Margarita had made up her mind before Elena had been able to explain the importance of blending in with other Indian vendors. This was not the time to risk giving the impression that Ajcojom children thought that they could pass as Ladinos. But Rodolfo hadn't intervened; it really didn't matter that much what Margarita wore since her husband, Lazaro, looked so Ladino with shoes and even socks. As long as Elena, at least, in their entourage was in her Indian clothing from head to feet, Rodolfo was satisfied. He was too pleased with Lazaro's and Margarita's unexpected request to join him and Elena for the day's outing in San Antonio to be critical about much of anything. Don Pancho at the Primavera plantation and his brother-in-law Eduardo Ramirez at the Esperanza plantation south of the lake had obviously selfish motives. But they might be perceived as less blatantly self-serving with Rodolfo's entire Ajcojom family joining in the celebration.

"I think Pancho and Beatriz should have done this selling themselves here today to really make the impression they're after," he mused aloud.

111

"That would be something to see!" Lazaro chuckled in agreement. "If people had that to look forward to in San Antonio, it would be a memorable first market day for sure."

Rocket firebomb explosions diverted their attention skyward, announcing the market's inauguration. A few moments later they rounded the bend in full view of San Antonio Palopo, sister village to Santa Catarina Palopo since their founding in antiquity, spread out on the hillside of Lake Atitlan's eastern shore. Just how long ago, no one had been able to tell Rodolfo. They were founded by descendants of Kaqchikel-speakers to the east of Lake Atitlan who assisted Pedro Alvarado in subduing the Tzutujil-speaking kingdom across the lake after the Kaqchikel kingdom of Iximche was conquered about 1525. But that was centuries later than the region's oldest Mayan ceremonial center discovered to date outside the town of San Andres Semetebaj, perched several hours above the Palopo sister villages on the dirt road snaking its way from Panajachel toward eastern Guatemala and the capital. Why neither of the Palopo villages prior to today had established a market day tradition for this end of the lake between Panajachel and San Lucas Toliman, all the way around to the southeast corner several miles south of San Antonio, Rodolfo could not say. Thus ended his brief recounting to the children of the extent of this region's history that Rodolfo knew as the launch slowed in preparation for its beaching on the sandy shore.

The high walls of the church, still roofless from the earthquake at the turn of the century, dominated the village center. Strains of a marimba reached them from the market area in the churchyard. It would be an exciting day, an unexpected fiesta added to this year's round of *municipio* celebrations bordering Lake Atitlan.

The first day of San Antonio's experiment with a weekly market was off to an auspicious beginning. The mayor at last count reported twenty-two vendors from other towns and half again that many from San Antonio selling local produce. Sections had been marked off on the ground, with a booth available only for meat — some chickens and two hogs that the mayor had donated and roasted for the occasion. Vendors from across the lake to the south were the most popular, selling their papayas, platanos, melons, pineapples, and mangos from the coast. Vegetables in profusion had arrived from Panajachel and San Andres; fish and crabs from Santa Catarina. Venders from Tecpan had brought salt, chile peppers, and lime. There was even a pottery maker from Totonicapan. Cloth was the only thing missing; weavers farther north apparently hadn't yet gotten word.

There was one straw hat vendor, and the sandal-maker with his tire carcasses from Godinez, the largely Ladino village at the intersection of the roads heading east and south of the lake high above San Antonio. Not surprisingly, there were hardly any Ladino buyers or sellers from Godinez or Aguas Calientes, the closer Ladino settlement on the hillside to the east. Ladino shopkeepers would be understandably uneasy about the potential competition of an Indian market in the area.

There had to be at least 300 people milling about in the churchyard, and the morning was still young. "I happily admit that I was dead wrong," said the wizened First Elder with a rueful grin to his five companions, the *principales,* in San Antonio's Council of Elders. "It looks like Monday has the saints' blessing after all." He was leaning on his staff, surveying the crowd from the church stairs above the improvised market. "Truth is, I had doubts about trying a market on *any* day of the week...and I still predict that it won't last more than a few weeks. But at least people don't seem to be afraid of Mondays."

With their closest market on Sunday in Panajachel, and markets within same day walking or boating distance all other weekdays except for Mondays, Monday had been the logical choice. This despite the poor reputation for Monday; it was a risky choice for initiating any undertaking of importance. "If no other towns have a Monday market, it's for a good reason!" the eldest among them had argued, "— even the hens don't lay on Mondays." But after hearing him out the elders had chosen Monday anyway. They worried less about a strong day's bad luck than trying to have a market without wholesale buyers and sellers from other towns around. With many such wholesalers in Panajachel on Sundays, and with no other Monday markets to compete with, it made sense that many of those wholesalers eventually would opt to stick around this end of the lake through Monday to include San Antonio in their weekly circuit. And it seemed to be working. There were more canoes lined up on the shore than they could recall for any Saint Anthony religious fiesta.

But it was the Primavera launch, the only motorized boat of the lot, that had made the most impression. It had brought much needed maize that Don Eduardo had sent across from the Esperanza below Santiago Atitlan, being sold for only a centavo per pound. That was a half centavo less than anyone locally could afford to sell it for.

"That must be the eighth bag they've unloaded," mused the Third Elder. "Wonder why they're doing it? Can't be making money at that price. With maize so scarce they must know they could sell it for half again as much."

Aware that the question was to him, the mayor chose his words carefully. "I don't really know, but it couldn't come at a better time for us. Don Rodolfo said that they wanted to do their part to promote our market, but since a neighbor tells me that they sold it for the same price yesterday in Panajachel it obviously isn't just a favor to us."

The First Elder's eyes narrowed skeptically as he listened. Surely their young mayor couldn't be this naïve. "Come now, you all know good and well what's happening! Our dear Ramirez friends at the Esperanza and the Primavera plantations know that time's running out for getting us to settle our work debts before next May's deadline. If they can't get us to their plantations for the December harvest coming up, then they stand to lose all that we owe them besides having to pay a decent wage to those they *can* find to harvest for them!"

"Now who's being simple-minded?" laughed a companion. "You can't believe that anyone around here is going to volunteer to cancel his work debts out of gratitude for this cheap maize...when all we have to do is keep from being caught a few more weeks!"

"Of course not!" retorted the old man. "It's us elders they want to befriend...especially our mayor here...and they know we want a good first market day. If we help, or at least don't oppose them, they might stand a chance of finding some who still owe them work. But without our compliance, they'll get nowhere!"

Their taciturn mayor smiled faintly but declined to comment. The First Elder was right, of course, as anyone should be able to discern. For his part the mayor would be as noncommittal with his friends as he had been when Rodolfo sought him out immediately upon disembarking to present the flowery letter from Don Eduardo hinting at how the leadership of San Antonio might show appreciation for the "gift" of inexpensive maize sent to celebrate their new market. The hint was painfully clear when he discovered the fifty peso bill in the envelope, too late to refuse it without a scene. He couldn't be sure that Rodolfo even knew the money was there. But whether he knew or not, Rodolfo would have been reluctant to take it back. So the money was in the mayor's pocket as he pondered just how much help the Ramirez family had had the good luck to purchase with their 'gift.' "Let's celebrate with a drink....I'll buy," he said after it appeared that the others might be ready to drop the subject.

As he started down the steps who but Rodolfo came toward them from the crowd. The polite thing would be to include him in the invitation, but with only

114

the fifty peso bill to use the mayor was embarrassed. Nonplussed, he retreated to the top of the stairs. Hoping no one would sense his nervousness, he dutifully repeated for his companions' benefit the speech of welcome and appreciation that he already had delivered to Rodolfo in private.

As Rodolfo listened, sensing the mayor's discomfort, he concluded that Don Eduardo's money had been found and accepted. He smiled graciously and accepted for a second time the community's thanks. His day's assignment was as distasteful to him as it had to be to the mayor, but at least the poor fellow was cooperating.

"Who has come with you from the Primavera?" inquired one of the elders, probably wondering whether Lazaro and Margarita were *naturales* or Ladinos. Margarita *was* an incongruous sight! She never had stopped carrying Indian-style on her head — to adopt the Ladina preference for baskets with handles for hand-carrying — and in deference to Elena, Margarita at the last moment had left her shoes in the boat to walk barefoot. "Yes, I guess we're a strange-looking group of merchants!" Rodolfo chuckled politely. "The older woman is my wife, and the younger one's our daughter. It's her husband, the hefty one in the white shirt, who's been helping the launch operator carry the maize from the boat. My hip won't let me carry much anymore, and since Lazaro has never been over here before, he and Margarita offered to come along. I think that's the last sack he's bringing up now, so we'll soon be heading back." In the awkward silence that followed, Rodolfo braced for the question he had hoped to avoid: the reason for the Ramirezes selling so cheaply.

"Is your son-in-law from Panajachel?" the same elder asked.

Relieved and pleased with the informality of the banter, Rodolfo brightened. "No, he's from Patzicia...son of Capo Tonon who has the new store in Panajachel. They moved here four years ago. Margarita had about given up finding herself a husband in Panajachel. Within a year Lazaro came asking for her, and she lives with him and his folks behind — "A chorus of sharply raised voices near Lazaro, Margarita, and Elena suddenly quieted the churchyard, as Elena emerged from the throng and waved frantically for help. The mayor followed Rodolfo's limping gait, more apprehensive even than Rodolfo on reaching his flushed and frightened wife.

"That last bag, the weak one you hoped we wouldn't need...it split just before Lazaro could get it to us from the boat!"

"Is that all," sighed Rodolfo with relief, lifting his sombrero to wipe his brow. "I was afraid maybe some of the maize was spoiled."

"But some of the women are crying —" urged Elena, "saying it's a bad sign...that the spirit of maize will be angry."

By the time the two men had forced their way through the onlookers to the mound of maize on the ground, the magnitude of the disaster had begun to sink in. The mayor visibly was shaken, as prospects for the successful market day suddenly dimmed. Far from scrambling to salvage some free grain, no one was touching it. The spill was the bad sign that some were expecting. There were mumblings about returning the grain already purchased lest the maize's spirit punish her buyers as well.

"Should we offer to buy it back?" Rodolfo asked meekly, suddenly numbed by the crowd's hostile reaction. The mayor didn't answer but moved quickly to back the crowd farther away from the maize before any more dirt mixed with the grain. Fortunately, the group of elders that had followed them into the crowd included Domingo, the *zahorin* diviner who had done the seed reading that finally had convinced them it would be all right to experiment with a Monday market. "What do you think, Domingo —," whispered the mayor, "has our luck changed?"

"No...don't think so," Domingo answered in his broken Spanish, to keep the conversation private. "The signs were good, and everything has gone smoothly until now. I think the thing to do is to make sure all the maize is picked up...every last grain. Tell them that you will supervise the clean-up yourself, and let them know when you're satisfied that none has been wasted. As for offering to let them return what they've already bought, I think that would be unwise. That could offend her spirit even more. Tell them that I'm going to the church to pray to Saint Isidro and our Saint Anthony. With their help, surely the maize will have mercy."

Rodolfo marveled at the crowd's acquiescence after the mayor made his announcement. Within minutes most people had moved back to resume their buying and selling. Several even offered to help with the clean-up. But Elena's agitation was slow to subside, and leaving her and Margarita to assist the mayor in recovering the grain Rodolfo left for the tavern across from the church to buy a cup of cane liquor to calm Elena's nerves.

From beneath the tavern's shaded overhang Diego watched his brother-in-law approach. They had not talked for some time, their friendship strained when Diego finally left Julia to take up with a widow living across town. Things had worsened after Rodolfo agreed to approach Don Eduardo on Diego's behalf to see if his labor debt to the Esperanza might be cancelled because of his arthritis. His indebtedness had grown rather than decreased over several years, due to the debilitating condition that had kept him on the plantation barely able to work sometimes for days at a time. The law called for a son to assume debt obligations when a father could not comply. But with Marcos angry with his father for deserting Julia, Diego had had nowhere to turn. Rodolfo had convinced Don Eduardo to forgive half the days owed, but only after either Diego or Marcos had worked off the balance.

And that had been almost two years ago, just before General Jorge Ubico, the country's new president, had announced that the law would change. Ubico had granted plantation owners two years to claim any labor debts still outstanding, and the deadline was rapidly approaching. Marcos and Diego had so far managed to elude the Esperanza contractor who showed up unannounced in Santa Catarina every few weeks. Most Catarinecos with debts had left home to work outside the area for the two years. Diego worked for employers in San Antonio more than in Santa Catarina, but today he had come over solely to observe the market — and to drink. He wasn't too drunk to figure out that it was the mayor's help in locating foreigners like himself hiding in San Antonio that Don Pancho and Don Eduardo were after in providing low-priced maize. But Diego was in no mood to leave the tavern simply to avoid Rodolfo. His brother-in-law obviously had too much on his mind at the moment to be concerned about debts to the Esperanza.

"For a moment I thought I was gonna have to rescue a brother-in-law from a hanging!" Diego drawled consolingly, catching Rodolfo totally by surprise. "That had the makings of an ugly situation. Must say I'm impressed...you and the mayor handled it well."

Pleased with a friendly greeting, even if it did come from a relative, Rodolfo accepted the bottle Diego offered. "I'm disgusted with myself! I could so easily have avoided the whole mess. We knew that last sack was weak, but I didn't think about the consequences of possibly spilling maize over here...especially today!"

"Yup, lots of people will be disappointed if today doesn't go well, and not just folks here. Did you know that the elders brought old Father Jacobo over by canoe last week to bless the marketplace? Then later they decided to invite the Panajachel Protestant pastors to come and offer their prayers as well. Elders wanted everybody satisfied, Evangelicals as well as Catholics. Looks like they will be, what with you selling maize for a centavo a pound. Was that the elders' idea, too?" taunted Diego.

Rodolfo smiled sheepishly. "I reckon you can guess why Pancho sent me here with maize of his brother-in-law's from the Esperanza. Tell me, loyal Brother-in-law, was it a good or a bad idea to sell it at our cost?"

Rodolfo's candor pleased Diego. He savored another swallow before answering. "Oh, definitely a good idea! Several here in the tavern who owe days on the Esperanza say they're so grateful that they're ready to volunteer in January for working off their debts. And I can't wait to get home to tell Marcos that he should be signing up as well."

The two men looked at each other straight-faced for several moments before bursting into laughter. With that behind them they settled down on the ground to share family news. By the time Rodolfo remembered why he'd come to the tavern they had finished Diego's bottle.

"Gotta get back to help the wife and the kids," said Rodolfo. "Elena was mighty upset... worried that some maize will be left in the dirt. She's as respect-ful of maize as is anybody...gets after me for dipping tortillas in coffee or feeding leftovers to the dog. And it doesn't help for Margarita to keep telling her it's all silliness! After today it'll be interesting to see how Lazaro and Margarita feel. You should've seen the look on Lazaro's face when the *naturales* began scolding him! He doesn't understand much Kaqchikel and couldn't imagine why some women started crying. I'm not sure he understands even yet what they're so 'fraid of! Maybe now he'll be more careful with what he says...especially 'round Elena. He's slowly turning Margarita against us over this religion business. She's more *Evangelico* now than she is *Catolico*...a *big* worry to Elena."

But neither of them was sober enough to be of help to Elena, who was sell-ing the last of the salvaged maize when they staggered up. Diego was in no condition to walk home, and Lazaro helped Rodolfo get him down the hill and into the boat.

Elena collapsed in the boat as well, too exhausted to argue religion. To Margarita's surprise her mother agreed with Lazaro after he had harangued them most of the way to Santa Catarina about the need for Catholics, and especially Indians, to stop being so afraid of everything.

"I think that you Believers are right about the fear," Elena conceded. "It's a pity not to have enough faith in God — the good things in life — and stop worrying about the power of the bad all the time. Respect, though, that's another thing. There can't be harm in showing respect to maize. It might be a sin to be so afraid, but it's just as sinful not to show respect. There's bound to be some maize still buried in the dirt back there...I know that. It makes me sad. Sad partly because I know how much those poor women are afraid, but mostly because Saint Isidro — the patron saint of crops — tries so hard to have enough food for us to eat. The least we can do is to take good care of what we are given. That's what I mean by respect. Whether it's you Believers or us Catholics that are right about spirits doesn't matter. It doesn't matter much to me if each kernel of maize has its spirit — like these *naturales* were claiming — or just the three sisters of black, yellow, and white maize have spirits. Doesn't matter to me if all maize has just one spirit, like I've heard Father Jacobo say. It really doesn't matter —"

At the mention of the three sisters, Diego began to sob and mumble in Kaqchikel. Rodolfo bent over to listen. "He's remembering a dream he had. The spirit of black maize came looking for him...angry and complaining...because he had planted only white and yellow this year. She told him that that's why his maize stalks are putting on so few ears."

"Poor, superstitious fool!" muttered Lazaro. "I've heard *naturales* in Papa's store talk the same way. They blame last season's harvest and the poorer prospects this year on the laying down of Saint Isidro's *cofradia* in Panajachel some years back. Do they think that God punishes everyone because one person doesn't plant black corn...or one town lays down a *cofradia?*"

By now the liquor had loosened Rodolfo's tongue, even around a son-in-law. "Who's to say what God has in mind? If it's so clear to you Believers what God's thinkin', then why all the arguin' amongst yourselves 'bout the truth? Folks living near the chapel say there's more arguin' there on Sunday evenings than there is the whole week in the town's council room!"

Lazaro blushed beet-red. The Tonons and a few others recently had left the congregation of Centroamericanos to set up a new group called Pentecostals. To the delight of Catholics, the separation had not been amicable. Margarita gave Lazaro her "Let it drop!" look and quickly interrupted. "Papa has a point. No one knows when God or some saint will lose patience with us sinners and decide to punish us. Papa has seen so many injustices to the poor in his life — what with

119

mandamientos and now the debt labor and road work — that it does seem some-times like we all get punished for the sins of others."

Neither Lazaro nor Rodolfo responded, so Margarita turned conversation to the grebes in the reeds they were passing. "Look how unafraid *they* are."

"Because it's against the law to hunt them this time of year when the young need their mothers," Rodolfo observed. "People all around the lake started to hunt ducks when there was so much hunger in the depression years. Grebes about disappeared, so the governor made a law...a wise one for a change! It's like the *cofradia* of San Isidro. Because we're hungry we do things for which we get punished later. I was asked to serve in the *cofradia* before they decided to lay it down. And like everyone else, I refused. Now we all suffer with poor crops...Catholics and evangelical Believers alike —"

"But Saint Isidro is well cared for in the church!" Elena interrupted, hesi-tant to let her husband get started again on laying down the *cofradia*.

"And probably feels like you would if we decided not to take care of you and had you move in with someone else!" Rodolfo countered.

But Elena continued undaunted. "If you ask me, Father Jacobo's right. All the *cofradias* should take their saints back to the church. Then saints couldn't complain about some being treated better than the rest."

Lazaro smiled but held his tongue. What a surprise to learn that Rodolfo felt somehow responsible for poor milpa yields of late! Clearly it would be some time before Margarita gave up her faith in saints when her parents were still so very Catholic... .

The small and rapidly deteriorating dock that Rodolfo had had built for servicing Ramirez coffee holdings in Santa Catarina was fast approaching. Diego still was sleeping soundly. Rodolfo announced that he would see him home and stop to visit Julia before walking back to Panajachel. Despite her weariness and coughing, Elena decided to go along. There was too much risk of her husband drinking some more with Diego and trying to walk home. His limp and face were constant reminders of his last trek home alone at night from Santa Catarina.

"If I ever become a Believer, liquor will be the reason!" she said under her breath as she gathered her things to leave the boat.

Margarita overheard. "It is sad that the poorer and more fearful people become, the more they seem to drink. Look at Uncle Diego there! Not a care in the world 'til morning."

"All Catarinecos are like him, if you ask me!" Elena continued. "You can't judge your father too harshly when you realize that he grew up in this ghost town." With that, Elena let the Primavera launch operator help her off onto the dock.

"I hope, too, that we found all the maize back there," called Margarita, as the motor caught and drowned our the rest of her good-bye. Elena waved a kiss and started after the men. It was the first time she had returned to Santa Catarina with Rodolfo since his mother's funeral six years earlier. Elena could hardly bring herself to glance in the direction of the abandoned Ajcojom compound, generations old, as she hurried through the silent grove, deserted except for its ghosts.

———

It wasn't altogether deserted. Julia and Diego's son was watching Elena from within his grandparents' dilapidated shack. The launch motor had awakened him, and he watched until all three were out of sight before settling back on the rotting bedstead. Marcos surmised that the man helping his father was his uncle; the woman, therefore, must be his aunt. Would his father have told them where he was hiding? Should he leave…go home, maybe? No, they might go to visit Julia. It wasn't likely that Diego would have said anything. Probably they had found him drunk in San Antonio and were just bringing him back to his new lover's house. The wisest thing would be to stay put and try to get back to sleep.

"Rodolfo, I don't like this town one bit!" complained Elena, coughing from the exertion of running to catch up. "Can't we start home as soon as we've helped Diego to his place?"

Rodolfo was too winded from struggling with Diego's unsteady body to respond, so she continued: "Please!..Julia won't know we were here if we leave now, at midday. Everybody 's indoors! We haven't seen a soul since we left the boat. Catarinecos are so afraid of being out when the time changes…they're even making *me* nervous." Rodolfo still wouldn't answer, so she trudged along counting the few Catarinecos in sight — only two women and four children by the time they reached the hut of Diego's mistress. It was empty, so they laid Diego on the bed and took their leave.

"It's not just the fear of midday," Rodolfo replied finally after catching his breath. "The kids in school went to Panajachel today to practice there for the graduation program Wednesday. And most men are out of town. I doubt if there are any men younger than me around today, what with market in San Antonio and so many working elsewhere. It's always like this over here this time of year when everybody's running out of maize. But, you're right...Catarinecos do stay indoors at midday. They seem to fear the bad luck of strong days and time changes more than folks do in Panajachel. I can remember as a kid being scolded by my mom just because I gave some coals from our hearth to a neighbor who came to ask for some at noon. Mama always was careful not to take trash out at midday...or even comb her hair. She was afraid...of everything and everybody." Rodolfo paused, contemplating how it might have been had he never left Santa Catarina.

"As for visiting Julia, you don't have to go with me if you don't want to, my love. You can rest in the church. It's cooler there. But I've got to talk with Julia. Before Diego got so drunk he told me how worried he is about the family. They're still afraid that Marcos will have to work off all of Diego's debt to the Ramirezes. Eduardo does expect me to get one or the other of them to harvest for at least a month, so I need to find out just how desperate they are. If they can't do it, then I'll have to hire someone else to go instead. I tell you, Elena, I'll be so relieved when the May deadline is here! Trying to get people in debt so that you can force them to work has been just as inhuman as the old *mandamientos*...just one kind of slavery replacing another! Why we had to wait until a depression and change of presidents to get a better law I'll never understand."

"Well, if you have to go I'm coming with you. I'm not spending a minute alone in this cemetery of a town!"

A dog, too weak to stand, was vomiting in Julia's patio as they approached her dilapidated gate. A pair of buzzards reluctantly flapped out of the avocado tree to circle patiently above the high pitched roof of soot-blackened thatch. The stillness and humidity were stultifying these days at the end of the rainy season. The stink of vomit was almost too much for Elena. She jumped when the door suddenly opened and Maruca threw out a bowl of water. Julia's only daughter, married briefly but already widowed, gasped at the sight of the well dressed man and woman standing at the gate.

"Uncle Rodolfo!" she exclaimed almost inaudibly.

Julia quickly appeared, clearly nervous as she met them at the gate. Elena rarely came with Rodolfo, and Julia's Spanish was no better than the first time Rodolfo and Elena had surprised her at her gate over twenty years earlier. Even in Kaqchikel it took Rodolfo several minutes to reassure her that he wasn't searching for Marcos. Julia finally invited them indoors, apologizing for the dog in her halting Spanish: "Sick several weeks now...hard to put her out of such misery."

122

Rodolfo quickly explained the purpose of their visit. From Julia's reaction he realized his mistake in communicating only with Diego about the understanding he had reached with Eduardo. Julia had indeed become convinced that Diego was lying when he told her the debt had been reduced. She assumed that once Eduardo Ramirez had Marcos at the Esperanza he would keep him the full ten weeks. Convinced now that Rodolfo spoke the truth, she eagerly sent Maruca to fetch Marcos. "He's in the old house. Thinks no one will look for him there. Sleeps days and works nights. He's gotten more and more afraid with the deadline approaching. I doubt that even Maruca can calm his fears."

Bur Maruca soon returned with a slight, timid youth whom even Rodolfo would scarcely have recognized. Elena hadn't seen their nephew for several years, and while she knew he was at least twenty, he looked more like fifteen. How much smaller than Rodolfo at that age, she thought to herself, smiling to try to put him at ease.

Rodolfo wasted no time. "How is it, Nephew, that you suspect your uncle and even your own father of deceiving you? Your father came to me over two years ago, asking me to do him the favor of talking with my patron. I did this for a sister and her son. I tried my best to get all the debt cancelled. But you probably have heard how it is between Don Eduardo and me. He always has to remind me that I'm a *natural* and can expect only so much in favors. So he said, 'Only half will I cancel, and that only because Marcos is your own blood.' He also made me promise that the remaining debt would be paid...even if I had to hire someone else. Later Diego told me that you had agreed to do it. But now, after these many months of never seeing you around, I realize that you did not so agree. I understand from your mother that you didn't believe your father in the first place and thought both of us were lying to you. Can this be true?"

Marcos was trembling violently, weary from being up all night to have crabs enough for the Tecpan market, and confused by feelings of both relief and lingering uncertainty. Tears began to flow from bloodshot eyes. As Rodolfo's gaze softened, he lowered his head and kneeled to ask his uncle's forgiveness. "We don't know no more when Father tells the truth," he whispered. In Kaqchikel Julia broke in, in her own as well as her son's defense: "It's as much my fault... We're so poor now that if we lost Marcos, even for ten weeks, I fear we'd starve. It shames me to tell you, Brother — forgive me, if I offend — but Marcos sometimes begs..."

123

"Stand up, Nephew," Rodolfo insisted, almost overcome himself and interrupting his sister so she couldn't continue. "Why haven't you come directly to me? Why beg?" he asked gruffly, angry as much at himself for letting so many months pass without coming to visit. "What must the Catarinecos I hire here to work in the Primavera coffee groves think of a fellow Catarineco like me who lets his sister's family starve!"

He was really asking this of Julia, but she didn't try to explain; just bowed her head and began to weep — silently at first and then unrestrained as her brother put both arms around her and commenced to sob himself. Elena didn't know what to do or say. She wished she'd gone home, or at least had waited in the church. The memory of her first encounter with Julia, in this same house, came back to her. Such a fiery, proud and independent woman! So different from her cowering daughter busying herself with who knows what in the corner. Julia would die before she would come to Rodolfo for help. But even after that thought, Elena was unprepared for Julia's next words. Although they were in Kaqchikel, Elena understood snatches.

Julia straightened suddenly, kissed Rodolfo on the cheek and said, "If it wasn't for the children…I'd stop eating and die. I know that would be a sin…but it's just as sinful to try to change one's destiny. There's nothing to be done, Brother, if God wills us to be poor. It's the luck of the spirit. Some are rich and some are poor…some of us are Ladinos and some are *naturales*. Some live long lives and some die young. Like I told Maruca when her little Joselino died last year, he'll be born again sometime, and live a long life then — maybe as a Ladino. There's justice in the end, but for now what can one do, Brother? Really…what *can* one do? No, it's better to leave things in the Virgin's hands. We're children of Saint Catherine, and if we're born poor, that's how we should die. At least I'm not going to complain, Brother…not to the saints, not even to you. If you spit at the sky, it just falls back in your face!"

Overcome, Rodolfo nodded meekly and decided not to argue. Instead he turned to change the subject with Marcos. Julia remembered she hadn't yet offered them coffee. "Coffee at least we have, thanks to your husband," she said to Elena cheerfully, sensing her discomfort. Rodolfo had told them years ago to pick what coffee they needed from his small grove. Maruca dutifully set about heating coffee while Julia took the baby and kneeled on the frayed floor mat beside Elena. The baby's swollen belly suggested worms, and flies hovered about his runny eyes and nose. Julia smiled proudly nonetheless, remarking on his

124

beautiful long eyelashes and reddish hair. Elena hadn't the heart to tell her that those were the tell-tale signs of poor nutrition, signs that Marcos and Maruca — even Julia — clearly exhibited. Elena counted five front teeth gone, and Julia was barely forty-five.

Marcos was embarrassed to admit in Elena's presence how desperate their situation had become, so he answered his uncle's questions in Kaqchikel. From the deepening furrows in her husband's forehead as he listened, Elena could tell he was alarmed at what he was hearing.

It was late afternoon by the time they started home. "The reason I didn't see anything of Marcos for such a long time this year was because he was in jail in Solola!"

"W — Why? How could we not have known?"

"Don't know, unless Julia asked local officials here to keep it quiet. Seems that Marcos was so in need of money that he stole a couple sacks of coffee."

"From Ramirez groves?" exclaimed Elena in astonishment.

"No, of course not. I'd have learned that for sure. He took it from Don Mencio who has a small grove next to ours. Since he is a Ladino, the mayor unfortunately decided that the case should go to Solola. They kept Marcos in jail until Holy Week. I asked him to tell me what he has been doing since then, and I must say it tore me apart to hear what he's been through, poor lad! I couldn't bring myself to tell him that he has to work on the Esperanza. I will hire someone else."

"Yes, I could tell that," Elena replied softly.

"During Holy Week he cleaned the milpa that they rent and rethatched the old house where he's been sleeping. The first week of April he did one of his two weeks of obligatory road service. The rest of April he repaired their onion terraces and planted milpa for themselves and a neighbor widow. In May he went to the coast to plant maize. Had to cancel a debt that Diego has had down there for several years. It took him four weeks to cancel two and a half weeks that Diego owed, because he didn't have money for food and ended up with a fever. He got back just in time to plant onions before the hard rains. He'd hoped to do his second week of road work then, too. They couldn't take him 'til late June, though, so he had to work when it was the coldest and wettest. Got sick again and wasn't able to cultivate his milpa before the Day of Santiago. He's afraid he'll be punished by Santiago with a poor crop. Can you imagine? He didn't earn a centavo for three months after he got out of jail. Then he fished nights during July to pay back what he borrowed for half a pound of onion seed. Said he sold fish in Tecpan every week that month. Got home early on Fridays but was too weary from all that walking to do any work on his onions 'til Sundays. In August he worked two weeks for a neighbor at eight centavos a day plus food, and two weeks for Don Mencio — part of his punishment for the theft. By September he was worrying about the Esperanza debt, so he spent most of that month hiding across the lake in Cerro del Oro cultivating maize owned by the San Antonio patron they rent milpa from. The patron gives him a choice between sharing the crop or working off the rent. Trouble is, when he works it off the patron scoundrel pays only six centavos a day for work that should pay eight! Now, this month he's been crabbing and hunting grebes to sell in Tecpan, hoping the authorities there won't learn it's illegal this time of month to kill them here."

They walked most of the rest of the way in silence, awed by the brilliance of the setting sun beyond the volcano of San Pedro. Elena struggled to reconcile such beauty with the squalor of Santa Catarina. She hadn't been inside a house as run-down as Julia's, nor seen clothes so patched and worn. Maruca didn't have to open her *huipil* to nurse the baby, so large were the holes in the blouse. And Marcos's frailty was evident through his threadbare shirt, too. "It's no wonder he is so frail!" she murmured. "I don't see how he can keep going."

"I know. I asked him what they've been eating. He said tortillas and salt with prickly pears most days this month. They eat meat only when they can afford to keep one of his grebes. He's grateful not to have to work off the Esperanza debt mostly because he won't have to hide and can now work during the days. And he'll be able to go to the cemetery for All Souls Day. The rumor's out that plantation owners will have spies in cemeteries to catch debtors on All Souls. At least we've spared him the worry of having his grandparents' spirits haunting him because he didn't show up to pay his respects! Poor kid...he's so afraid of everything, To think...afraid even of me."

The aroma of oak from countless hearth fires greeted them as they approached Panajachel's outlying, haze-enveloped compounds. Reluctant to call attention they walked quietly, catching snatches of patio conversation behind cane and nettle fences lining the deserted path. Panajachel's river was only a stream this time of year and permitted easy fording without taking the longer path up to the log bridge. They removed their sandals and let cold water soothe weary feet. Eliseo's store was still open. His kerosene lamp cast bright images of door and window across the intersection of the path to Santa Catarina and Panajachel's main street. A Ladino couple was out strolling, the descending dark-

126

ness not the worry it was to Indians. To the right a cluster of rowdy youths kicked around a soccer ball in front of the lamp-lit pharmacy. On beyond, the church loomed ghostly, dwarfing the few shuttered homes and shops between the pharmacy and deserted town hall.

Pancho and Beatriz's Model A Ford rumbled by, then stopped and backed up as their son, Chico, recognized Rodolfo. "Guess what! Your son's home. I told him where you'd gone. He decided to go across the lake to see Max and Carolina. He'll be back tomorrow evening. Want a ride the rest of the way?"

"Francisco came home for all Saints and All Souls, bless his heart!" exclaimed Elena. She was more excited by the news than was Rodolfo as they climbed into the rumble seat.

"Don't you mean for the drinking and to see Eduardo's daughter!"

"Oh, don't be so hard on him," she coaxed. "And you're forgetting the school program. It could be Mario's graduation that brings him home. Or have you forgotten that our youngest is about to finish school?"

"Too much on my mind," he acknowledged "— hope he got along all right with the rehearsal today."

It was dark when they crossed the threshold, the same house they had occupied since moving up from the coast. Mario already was asleep in the back room, added when he was born and they had all three children at home. After Francisco had enlisted in the army and Margarita had married and moved out, they finally had the main bedroom to themselves. Elena had surprised her husband by buying a mattress bed. She collapsed in it now, pondering aloud how they could have become so blind to what was happening to even their closest relatives...a nephew jailed in Solola no less!

But Rodolfo's thoughts were of Francisco and Lazaro: two such totally different men. Even with Lazaro's strong-mindedness and troubling religious ideas, the son-in-law was easier to be with than was Francisco. How would he have managed the past two years had Francisco not gone off to the army barracks in Quetzaltenango? Rodolfo had encouraged him to re-enlist. Perhaps an army career made as much sense for Francisco as it did for Max...except for Max's advantage of being Ladino and enrolling in the military academy in the capital. If only Francisco weren't so admiring of Eduardo's son...and so in love with his daughter. Rodolfo did not look forward to the week ahead, and with so much on his mind Elena's coughing kept him awake most of the night.

Chapter Eleven

Mario was more interested in finishing his kite than in parading for graduation from fourth grade. Last year he'd won the prize for the largest, and this year he was counting on Francisco's help in flying his the highest. Francisco, however, was skeptical as to how the judges would know which kite was the highest. "Simple," beamed Mario "— Don Eliseo is donating balls of string that are all the same size, handed out to everybody just before the competition begins. First one to reach the end of his ball wins. So if I hold the kite and you run with the string until it catches the wind, nobody can beat us! Boy, am I glad you came home!"

They were gluing the paper to the string border with pine resin. "Here, let me finish while you get dressed for the parade," Francisco suggested. "After all, it's your graduation that I came home for, not to run my ass off on that rock-strewn river bed!" Mario reluctantly obeyed, and Francisco winked at their mother. Elena had been cajoling Mario to leave the kite until after the ceremony, but to no avail.

"How many kids are graduating?" Francisco asked her.

"Six Ladinos and four Indians from fourth grade."

He couldn't resist teasing. "Is Mario one of the former or the latter?"

"As long as he's in Panajachel, he's a *natural*," she retorted, "and the same goes for his older brother!"

Francisco chuckled and let the matter drop.

"They honor the kids finishing second grade, too, Elena continued, "since so many drop out then. *Naturales* especially."

"That's new, recognizing second graders," mused Francisco. "How long have they been doing that?"

"Ever since the Santa Catarina school joined with ours for graduation. They still have just one grade there, and most from there who want more schooling here stop after second grade when they can read and write a little Spanish. Did we ever tell you that your father was the first Catarineco to come to Panajachel after first grade there? He had his second and third grades here before they added fourth."

"It's about time that Panajachel added fifth and sixth! Then you get to learn about places besides Guatemala. You know, Mom, until my lessons in the barracks I didn't realize that Mexicans speak Spanish, too. Somehow I thought they talk like Gringos. I've learned that Indians are mostly gone in the Central American countries south of us; they've all become Ladinos. Won't be long 'til Indian languages are gone here, too, I bet. To think...Guatemala will be the last country to get civilized!"

"So that's what they teach you...that we're not civilized?" Elena said quietly.

Francisco blushed. "Didn't really mean — not us, anyway — but you should listen to most of the Indians when they first arrive at the barracks! Hardly able to talk understandable Spanish, let alone read or write. One or two years of school is all they get in the small towns, and after being out of school for ten years they've forgotten everything they learned! If you ask me, army training is just another name for school. Unless you reenlist. Everything changes then. Finally we're beginning to learn important things: more about fighting than just cleaning and shooting a gun. The best part of it, though, is getting to share quarters and training with Ladinos. We're all treated alike, and if it wasn't for this Ajcojom name nobody would know I'm Indian." He waited for her reaction, before venturing the question he finally had decided to ask. "Do you think Papa would object if I changed it to Rosales...or Lopez? With a name like that I can be Indian or Ladino when I want to...either way."

The question surprised Elena. She had never thought about his wanting to change. "What you do at the barracks is your business, I suppose, but it's no kindness to make an issue of it here with your father."

Rodolfo caught the end of the conversation as he entered the house. "Make what an issue with me?"

"Nothing important," said Francisco with a shrug, busying himself with tying the cross pieces to the paper. "It's just that if we had a surname used by Ladinos as well as Indians, I wouldn't be thought of right away as an Indian at the barracks..."

Unlike Elena, Rodolfo was not surprised by the question. He had been expecting it to come up at some point. Even so he had to struggle not to overreact. "I can't believe that you suddenly become a Ladino just because you change your name. A bird can't change its feathers...a parrot's always green!"

His father's reaction was milder than Francisco had feared. "But that's just the point, Papa...when you're in uniform everybody does look alike. If I gave my name as Rosales, I bet people who didn't know me would assume I'm probably Ladino."

129

Rodolfo realized that his son's mind was made up. "Well, change it if you must. It doesn't matter to me," he lied. "But please don't embarrass your mother and me by using any name other than Ajcojom around here!"

"Of course I won't," said Francisco, pleased to have the conversation end on no more unpleasant a note and anxious to change the subject. "Papa, I didn't know that you were the first from Santa Catarina to finish school over here. How'd that happen?"

Rodolfo remained silent long enough to let Francisco know he was displeased. "My parents decided...but I think the school teacher probably suggested it. Papa had learned to read and write about as soon as anybody did there, and he was determined that I would, too. Best thing he ever did for me. My life would have been totally different if I hadn't come to Panajachel when I did. I think about it every time I see Julia's family. You don't know how lucky you are! And here you are complaining that you can't be somebody else. I do believe you are mostly Ladino already...never satisfied with what you have."

Rodolfo's voice was taunting, and with his broken, missing teeth even the faint smile wasn't very reassuring to his conflicted son. Only when his father signaled an end to the unpleasant conversation by reaching out awkwardly to embrace, did Francisco begin to relax. But he returned the hug eagerly and for the moment felt sorry to be doing this to his father.

Mario was dressed and ready — new white shirt and new black shoes to go with the blue pants and cap. "Very patriotic, I must say," complimented his brother. "Does everybody dress in blue and white for the parade nowadays?"

"Yup. President Ubico says we have to dress this way on Independence Day and for graduation."

"Sounds like something Ubico would do," Francisco said approvingly, as the Ajcojom brothers proudly set off for school. Ajcojom more or less. Francisco weighed Francisco Rosales and Francisco Lopez as they walked, before deciding that he might as well use both henceforth when not in Panajachel: Francisco Rosales Lopez. Rosales for his father's side; Lopez for his mother's.

———

The parade struck Francisco as a sad affair compared to barracks parades. Even the flag was torn. But most discouraging was the number of children ending their schooling after only two years: several dozen, including the Catarinecos. Only ten were graduating from fourth grade. One of the four Indian fourth graders had him completely puzzled: a young woman who had to be in her late teens. In her blue skirt and white blouse she looked oddly out of place. Pretty though! He would have to ask Mario about her.

Rodolfo wore a white shirt, but not blue pants; nor did the other councilmen, despite Don Eliseo's suggestion that the town's officials dress in patriotic blue and white for the occasion. Rodolfo felt sorry for Eliseo, now mayor of Panajachel, whose uniform was the topic of good-natured jests all day. Especially in the afternoon procession of the town's saints where he was the only person dressed in blue and white...and the only Ladino. Rodolfo volunteered to help carry the image of Saint Isidro in the procession from church to cemetery, commencing the celebration of all Saints and All Souls Days. At each intersection of paths, the procession halted to rest while the sixteen *mayordomos* of Panajachel's four *cofradias* served drinks to onlookers and those bearing the saints. There was beer for Catholics and fruit juice for Believers.

The gossip centered on Calixtro Queche, an aged widower who had been attending church services with Pentecostals but couldn't resist the carousing of a fiesta. He had embarrassed Protestants with his drinking at the fiesta for Saint Francis the month before, and youths were tempting him again today as the procession got underway. He was unsteady by the time the procession reached the river, and he had to be helped across the bridge. Only as the procession approached the cemetery a half hour later, did a group of Believers finally arrive to rescue him. Words were exchanged between one of the Believers and a Catholic cousin of Calixtro who was not unhappy to see Calixtro drinking again. In the ensuing scuffle Calixtro was knocked to the ground. He bloodied his nose, and after the cousin thought he had the bleeding stopped he helped Calixtro to the shade of a tree by the path. Calixtro promptly passed out and was left to sleep off his stupor. When the procession passed the tree on the way back to town, he was gone. Folks assumed that Believers had come to get him, and he promptly was forgotten.

The next morning, November second, was ideal for kite flying. The rocky but treeless river delta swarmed with children and assisting adults until noon when the cemetery began to fill for afternoon visiting, eating, and communion with the dead.

Margarita and Lazaro were already at the small cross marking the grave of their first born, a stillbirth, when Elena, Mario, and Francisco arrived to lay flowers on an adjacent grave — the child that Rodolfo and Elena had lost between Margarita and Mario. "Where's Papa?" Margarita inquired.

131

"Left early for Santa Catarina to decorate family graves. I feel sorry for him every year on this day, but he always wants to go alone...to be with his sister Victoria's spirit in particular, I think." Elena's eyes filled and she looked away toward the coast...toward another cemetery too far away to visit. "I wonder who'll be with my Mama and Papa —." She couldn't continue for another of her coughing attacks. Her tuberculosis was taking its toll. Margarita crawled over to pat the frail back of the strongest woman she knew.

Lazaro, always ill at ease around Francisco and unable to deal with the emotions inexorably settling over the cemetery, broke the silence: "How'd you two do in the kite contest?"

"Lost," said Mario dejectedly, equally glad to have something to talk about now that he had finished wrapping the two infants' graves with crepe paper.

"All my fault...fell down running," Francisco admitted. "Sprained my ankle on the rocks and couldn't continue. By the time we traded places for me to hold the kite, somebody already had reached the end of his ball of string. Next year we'll win it, though, won't we?" he comforted Mario. With that he was off, limping toward the lake's shore below the cemetery. He had caught the sound of an approaching launch. It would be Eduardo's family from the Esperanza, arriving to help Arcadia's family decorate her husband Oscar's sepulcher, the largest in the cemetery.

Not until he almost stumbled over the body did Francisco see the man at the edge of the tall grass, blood caked on his face. After determining that he was still alive, Francisco hurried to help dock the launch and assist Carolina and her mother-in-law to shore. "Max, come help me, quick! Some drunken Indian is out cold over there. People in the cemetery will know who he is."

As they approached carrying the body, people at once recognized Calixtro. Lazaro told Fransicso about the scuffle and how his father and another Pentecostal had gone to Calixtro's home last evening to check on him. He wasn't at home, so they came back without searching further — assumed that relatives had him. But obviously he had become disoriented and lost, passing out from loss of blood or too much liquor.

"Ugh!" whispered Mario "— look at all them flies in his nose...are you sure he's alive?"

Max saw his chance to drive his uncle's Model A Ford and quickly suggested that he and Francisco take Calixtro to the Primavera by boat and drive him from there to the Solola doctor's house. Carolina jumped at this unexpected chance to be away from the crowd with Francisco and offered to go along to help. Under the circumstances her parents couldn't very well object, and Calixtro was hurried off to the launch. The crowd dispersed among the several hundred graves.

Not long thereafter Rodolfo arrived with Father Jacobo. The elderly priest had gone on horseback to Santa Catarina to bless graves before returning to Panajachel's cemetery for the balance of the afternoon. His bald head was badly burned. The wind he had prayed for earlier to please kite enthusiasts unkindly had carried his felt hat far out over the lake. Eduardo reported on Calixtro, and Jacobo decided to continue on into town to telephone the doctor. With rumors fixing blame for Calixtro's fate already circulating among Protestants and Catholics, each sect blaming the other, the sooner everyone could be reassured that the old man was conscious and would recover, the better.

By mid-afternoon the cemetery contained all the town's living as well as all its dead. The one time of year when all children of Saint Francis found themselves in the same place. For color, the occasion was unsurpassed, with poinsettia hedges still vibrant from recent rains and multicolored streamers linking family crosses. Smells equaled those in the church during fiestas: assorted incense aromas, carpets of pine boughs, bouquets of white lilies, and wreaths of other, assorted freshly cut flowers. It was the fiesta that Margarita most enjoyed. So tranquil and solemn in contrast to the others. With no flutes nor drums, not even a marimba, it was a welcomed change. Margarita had little use for the monotonous traditional Indian music.

Not that she felt much attachment to Panajachel either. Her parents and grandparents, her parents-in-law and even her husband had been born elsewhere. And it certainly wasn't Panajachel's dead who made the day so meaningful...even her stillborn son rarely brought her to the cemetery. No, it was the unity of the living — Ladinos and Indians, rich and poor, Believers and Catholics — all brought together by their common mortality. True, Ladinos tended to be to one side of the cemetery and Indians to the other, in life as in death. But not altogether so; some crosses marking Indian graves were interspersed with the blue, white, green and pink vaults of Ladinos.

When she was a girl her godfather Eliseo had shown her where he would be buried when he died...among Indians, in the ground, with only a cross as marker. That was the childhood memory of her godfather that she cherished above all others: Don Eliseo confiding to his favorite godchild that he, too, was at birth an Indian, and would so proclaim with his death. Margarita was the only person in Panajachel, apart from his wife and children — and Rodolfo — who would know until then. If ever she had shared her brother's misgivings about being Indian, they had vanished when Eliseo had told her his secret. She had come to wonder if that wasn't the reason he had told her. He didn't want her soul to be troubled like her brother's. Poor Francisco...so discontent with whom he was. Why couldn't Francisco be more like her husband: able to pass as Ladino away from home when it was useful, but perfectly content to be Indian in his own mind? Francisco wouldn't be content until he changed his name, left Panajachel, and married a Ladina!

If it were just Francisco, she wouldn't worry so much, but his influence over their younger brother already was evident. Mario had no more to do with Indian schoolmates than he had to, and he outdid Ladinos in ridiculing them. It made her sad...and her father angry. So angry that he had finally told Francisco to reenlist, go back to the army, because of what he was doing to his brother. Francisco was almost insolent. Said he wouldn't care if he never saw his family again, so confident he was that he could gain acceptance anywhere as a Ladino. But could he, really? Margarita dreaded the day that he decided to try becoming more than just a family friend to Carolina. Margarita doubted that either Max or Carolina — far less their parents — realized how much in love with Carolina her brother had become.

She jumped with the sudden realization that Lazaro had rejoined her and was watching, puzzled by her pensiveness. Though flushed and eager to interrupt, he was uncharacteristically restrained. "Margarita, dear...Father just learned that the priest has gone to Solola to be with Calixtro. The poor soul hasn't regained consciousness, and they're afraid that maybe he won't. Father wants to get Protestants together for a service while the priest's away. Both Father and the pastor will speak, to show Catholics that we Protestants are not quarreling anymore amongst ourselves. Will you come with me to sit with the Believers?"

Margarita hadn't anticipated having to make this kind of decision today. She resented having her reverie ruined so abruptly. But her husband's tone was urgent. Using today to force all of Panajachel to listen to Believers did make sense. No one apart from the priest or maybe Eliseo — as mayor — would be bold enough to interfere, and Eliseo had left with his wife to visit her parents' graves in Solola. Margarita concluded that she had no choice and went with Lazaro to join the small group of Believers assembling almost unnoticed at the cemetery's east end.

People had finished their ceremonial meals, and some already were leaving when the crowd began to quiet at the sound of singing. Margarita was uneasy under stares of the couple hundred people who were standing to see what was going on. And yet she couldn't help but smile at the opportunity the day presented. The Catholics were awestruck. Enough Believers, Ladinos as well as Indians, had gathered in this public testimony that virtually everyone straining to see the hymn singers could recognize at least one friend or relative. Caught unprepared, even the most ardent Catholic opponents were unwilling to risk the spectacle of trying to interfere with the Protestant service suddenly underway in their midst. So everyone listened to the hymn.

With the closing "Amen," a silence settled over the cemetery as deep as the silence of any midnight time change. There wasn't a sound...until the pastor stepped forward and invited anyone who wished to, to gather closer and hear what he and brother Capo Tonon felt led by the Lord to share. They would hold their service quietly, so as not to disturb others who wished to continue communing with the dead. They hoped not to offend and would be brief. With that introduction he commenced preaching, albeit in less strident tones than members of his congregation were accustomed to. Clearly he was speaking to Catholics, and while most Catholics resumed their visiting — deliberately turning their backs and raising their voices — enough edged toward the group of Believers to encourage him to continue. He stayed away from theology. Instead he talked about the excesses of Catholicism that had led him to convert: the drinking, the money spent on wooden images instead of on medicines for relatives who were sick, and the distance between saints and the people — between even priests and the people.

Then he mentioned Calixtro. Margarita's heart stopped. Why in Heaven was he bringing in Calixtro? But instead of accusing Calixtro's family he blamed the Believers themselves for letting Calixtro down. They should have been more understanding and less quick to judge, just as Jesus was forgiving. Surely God in his mercy was understanding of the temptations of fiestas — yes, even of the drinking. And as pastor he blamed himself for being hesitant to go with those who had crossed the river the night before to check on Calixtro. Protestants had gathered now to pray for Calixtro's recovery...for his soul if he should die. "Won't you who love our brother — your brother — join us in prayer?"

The cemetery quieted again. Lazaro's father led the assembly in a prayer so simple, yet so eloquent in his halting Kaqchikel, that Margarita couldn't hold

135

back her tears. And when her eyes welled up, even Rodolfo softened. He had never heard Capo speak in Kaqchikel. Until this point Rodolfo had become steadily more agitated, lest Jacobo or Eliseo blame him and other councilmen for not putting a stop to these goings on. But the spell cast by the prayer relieved his mind. Silence continued through the closing hymn, and then the pastor thanked his audience for their patience and forbearance. Catholics as well as Protestants let the end of the service signal an end to the afternoon. Within a half hour the cemetery was deserted...except for the usual group of Ladino youths making their rounds of Indian graves drinking liquor left for the souls of loved ones. The priest usually stayed behind to at least delay such sacrilege, but in his absence the youths knew that no one would give them any heed. Even Rodolfo gave them only passing thought; Francisco, at least, was away in Solola! For years he had spoiled the day for the rest of the family by ending up drunk, if not in jail.

Chapter Twelve

A Solola errand boy from the communications office brought the doctor the news: Panajachel's priest was on his way.

"Then we don't need to stay," Max decided. "Let's head back. There's nothing more we can do for this sorry fellow."

Carolina ran skipping ahead, hair bouncing, and climbed in the back.

"Looks like I'll have to put up with your sister in the rumble seat," said Francisco, trying not to sound too pleased.

"Oh, we can leave her back there alone. You can sit up front with me if you don't want to be bothered by her," Max said, loudly enough to tease his sister. Then, in an undertone to Francisco: "Now I see why she wanted to come along, you old goat!"

"My reward for holding the old man all the way here," Francisco retorted. "Hope your sister shows more life than he did!"

Max snickered, then laughed aloud as Francisco piled in beside Carolina. "Just remember she's a virgin! And our mother's going to check to make sure she still is when we reach home."

"Oh, shut up! How awful! Can't you show your sister a little respect?" pouted Carolina. "You know that isn't true!"

"Which?" grinned Francisco "— you're not a virgin, or your mother won't check?"

"That's *terrible!* You're as bad as he is," she giggled, trying to slap him but ending up in his lap instead by an unexpected blast from the horn. Max was shaking so hard with laugher that he had squeezed it by mistake as he tried to start the engine.

"Scared the shit out of me!" he choked. "How am I supposed to drive this thing with you two carrying on like that?" As the engine caught, he peered down at the gauge. "Damn! Wouldn't you know? In all the excitement I forgot to fill up with gas at home before we left. With All Souls' Day, I bet we won't find any here in Solola. Looks to me like we scarcely have enough to get down the mountain. What d'ya want to do?" he asked, turning to Carolina "— try it, or go to Gramma's to spend the night?"

"But what about Francisco? She'll wonder why we show up with him. She gives me a hard enough time about men without our bringing home such a handsome one to spend the night!"

Max smiled, and with eyes a twinkle decided to tease them both. "But she also wants to see you married. We could pretend that Francisco's a *serious* suitor!" He couldn't tell which of them was blushing more, until Francisco turned crimson as Max added, "Of course his Indian name would give her a start. Can't you just see her?"

To Francisco's chagrin, even Carolina laughed. His own embarrassment was beyond disguise. "But if that's a problem, you could call me R — Rosales" he stammered, "or Lopez". It was out before he realized, and Max and Carolina were suddenly quiet.

Finally Carolina concluded, "No, that wouldn't work. She would know...says she can smell Indians' strong blood. And if she isn't sure, she looks for the dark spot in the corner of the eye. She's convinced every Indian has it."

Francisco was bewildered. He couldn't tell whether they were teasing or not. Beads of sweat began to form. He had thought that Max was serious about going to their grandmother's house, but now he wasn't so sure. Max's teasing could be pretty subtle at times...and pretty biting at others. But Carolina...she had to be serious. Damn it! he scolded himself. Why so quick to suggest that I pretend to be Ladino?

"We'd better try for the Primavera," decided Max. "We can coast in neutral much of the way... as long as the brakes hold!" he added mischievously. "We'll at least get close enough to walk the rest of the way before dark." With that he put the car in gear and they rumbled off. Francisco wanted desperately to say something, but he was afraid his nervousness would show no matter how much nonchalance he mustered. He was trembling and tried breathing deeply to calm down.

Carolina didn't know exactly why Francisco was nervous, but feared that something they had said had hurt him deeply. Early on she and Francisco had talked about his being Indian, and about that no longer mattering to her. So maybe it was how Max felt about it that was the problem; she had no idea how much Max and Francisco had discussed the race issue. Surely Francisco would not find it surprising to learn that their grandmother — the governor's widow after all — was pretty old-fashioned in that regard. Not that Francisco looked that different from the darker Ladino men around, especially with his army fatigues and cropped hair. He certainly was tall enough, had a full moustache and enough hair on his face to have to shave. Even spoke good Spanish, with none of the Indian accent. But, admittedly, there was still something... maybe her grandmother was right about it being in the blood...certain tell-tale signs that never go away.

To make amends for whatever it was that she or Max had said, she snuggled closer to the suddenly taciturn Francisco. "Put your arm around me," she coaxed aloud. "I'm chilly." Then, raising her chin to his ear she whispered, "You know I don't care. Gramma, though, she's too old to change."

It wasn't their grandmother that Francisco was concerned about, but he said nothing and obligingly did Carolina's bidding with the regained nonchalance that he had learned to feign so well in those occasional moments when they found themselves alone. Neither of them had ever let true feelings show physically; it was safer just to joke. And Francisco wanted Max to assume that in private they carried on just as they did when he was around. True, they all three realized that Eduardo and Carmen were concerned; they joked about that frequently enough. So far he had done his best to act like any such concerns were as groundless as Max assumed them to be. But had things now suddenly changed? Had he betrayed his truer feelings by suggesting that he thought of himself as Ladino — even able to pass as Carolina's Ladino suitor? The resentment that he sometimes felt toward Carolina was creeping in, denying him this unexpected opportunity to hint to her his deeper feelings. He resented her freedom to admit so openly to him, to Max, even to her parents that she liked him. Somehow in her flirting it was acceptable to show her tender feelings. He could flirt, too — just as Max could tease him about Carolina — but only so long as it was coarse. If and when he ever did speak his true feelings to the woman that Carolina had become since their childhood friendship commenced so many years ago, he sensed that things would change very rapidly. And that was just the problem. He didn't know how Max and his parents, or even his own parents for that matter, would react if they knew how he really felt about Carolina Ramirez.

The familiar restraint that Carolina now felt in his arm, resting lightly around her shoulder, was reassuring. Maybe nothing had changed after all, she concluded with a sigh, and nestled closer. Max mentioned the free cane liquor they were missing at the cemetery, and as the men reminisced about Days of the Dead of years gone by, Carolina drifted off to sleep.

Only then did Francisco relax his arm, his hand caressing her forehead, neck and cheek ever so lightly as he chatted with Max. If Max had been momentarily alarmed, he seemed his usual, casual self now. Maybe nothing had changed after all.

As if in confirmation, Carolina let him know his caressing had awakened her. She kissed the fingers on her cheek. They froze momentarily, until she kissed again to encourage. And with that he gave her the hug that had been building. His tender squeeze had a different feel, and her emotions began to swirl within a breast she realized had begun to pound.

Francisco felt her tremble and was pleased.

"We're not going to make it," Max announced, as the engine missed once, and then again. They had passed the cataract above the plantation and had a kilometer — two at most — before the shortcut path down through the coffee trees. "Want to walk, or should I leave Francisco with you while I go for gas?" he asked. This time neither of his passengers knew if he was teasing.

Francisco was feeling reassured, and to allay any lingering suspicions Max might have about his motives, he quickly offered to go instead. "You stay here with your sister; she's sound asleep," he lied. "I'll run down and be back in an hour at most."

"No, I'm not," Carolina yawned, as if just awakening. "We might as well all walk." She gave his hand one more kiss as she straightened up and looked to see how far she had volunteered to hike. "Oh, it's not far at all! Beat you both there!" Before Francisco could respond she was out of the rumble seat, again skipping off with that beautiful black hair bouncing so provocatively.

"Sound asleep, eh?" Max grunted knowingly.

Francisco could not come up with an appropriate response as the fear momentarily returned. He gambled and slapped Max appreciatively on the shoulder as he hopped out to start after Carolina. "Come on! I may not be able to outrun that rabbit you have for a sister, but I can at least beat the tortoise she has for a brother!" But after only a few steps he was wincing. "Damn! Forgot all about this ankle!"

With that, Max chuckled at the result of Francisco being the one that would stay with the car, all alone while he and Carolina went for fuel.

It was so reassuring to hear Max laughing again that Francisco joined in laughing at his predicament. He finally had reached out a bit and Carolina hadn't drawn back. Even Max probably realized that this time they would have preferred to be alone. Did he approve? That was probably too much to expect, but at least he didn't seem to be upset.

140

Max was pondering the same question as he loped along, catching up finally with his sister.

"Where's Francisco?" she asked with concern when she realized that only one pair of feet was gaining on her.

"Forgot his sprained ankle! You should have seen him….a picture of dejection sitting there beside the road!"

"Oh — that's right — poor thing! I'd better go back and wait with him."

"Think you should, Sis?" Max asked, and from his tone of voice and the "Sis" she knew that he was asking several questions in one. They stood uneasily side by side in the dusky evening, preferring to look out over the lake rather than at each other. The sun had slipped from view, and the brighter stars were sprouting in the eastern sky. "You know what I mean," he continued with an apologetic shrug, not having intended to ask so much. "It's just our folks that I'm concerned about. If I tell them you two stayed in the car, you know what a scene there will be when you get home."

"I know exactly what you mean," she replied darkly…frightened more than angered by this unexpected seriousness in her brother. She clasped her hands behind her newly trimmed hair, left longer than usual for Francisco's benefit, and pensively walked a few steps before turning abruptly to face her brother. "I really love Francisco…I guess you know."

"Well…you've been telling me long enough that he's your boyfriend," he smiled, hoping to reassure her. "I guess I should know by now. But I…we —"

"The folks, you mean!"

"Well, yes — folks, too — all of us," he stuttered, "w — we haven't taken you seriously, what with Francisco so many years older, and —"

"And an Indian?"

Max didn't have to reply. After a pause, he continued: "While it has been clear that you've liked Francisco for a long time, we've assumed he was just letting you be the flirt you are…so as not to hurt you. I mean, he didn't seem to —"

"You mean, he didn't let you know how he might really feel?"

"Well, no, not to me anyway…he never has. Has he to you?"

"Not really, not until today, anyway…and I — I still don't know for sure," she stammered. "He seemed nervous, frightened, by your comment about us pretending, just for Gramma's sake, to be really in love."

"Yes, I could tell that he was upset. I thought maybe it was because of all that talk about his being Indian."

141

"But what if we...what if he really *is* in love with me, Max? Does that change anything?"

It was Max's turn to pace. "You *know* that it does, Sis...and so does he. That's why he's frightened...and why you and I are, too, for that matter," he added quietly. "I really don't care that he's Indian. Francisco is as much a brother to me as I'll ever have...just as his dad and ours were practically brothers for many years growing up together until they drifted apart. There isn't much about our thoughts that we don't share. But I've never asked, and he's never offered to tell me, how he really feels about you. We've gone out with girls together, and he tells me when he's been with someone he finds attractive. But whenever I ask him if she's someone he could think about marrying, he gets embarrassed and says, 'How could I? She's a Ladina and would never have me.' So I've assumed that he was just kidding around with you because you so obviously were flirting with him all the time. We all have assumed that he was just playing along to avoid hurting your feelings."

"But what if he was testing you...wanting you to argue with him that marrying a Ladina would be okay. Maybe he wants to know how you really feel about his loving me...maybe *I* want to know how you really feel!"

"Carolina, I —"

"No, Max, I really want to know!"

"All right, damn it, I really want to tell you! And what I want to tell you is that it really doesn't matter what your brother thinks. But that it *does* really matter what our parents think, and you know what they think just as well as I do!"

"No, Max, you're so wrong! Of course I know how Mama and Papa feel!...not that different from how Gramma feels. What matters to me — to Francisco, too — is how you feel! Or perhaps what you're telling me is that it ought to be as obvious to me how you feel as how the folks feel!"

Max raised his arms and shook his fists in frustration. "No, Carolina, that's not what I am saying...at least I don't think so..."

His pause was reassuring. She knew he was now ready to be as honest about his feelings as he could be. Perhaps he didn't know how he felt, when it came right down to it.

He read her thoughts, and ended the conversation. "Carolina, my dear, dear sister, are you any surer than I am how you will feel if he asks to marry you?"

Tearfully she nodded her head, but only after she almost shook it instead — her hair not sure which way to bounce. At last they both knew that she understood clearly how she *should* feel and, despite this, had firmly made up her mind.

———————

Carolina had two reasons for choosing not to go back with gasoline to the car with Max: to put her parents' minds at ease, and to have some say about where she slept. Back at the house an hour later — when Eduardo told his uncle, Pancho, that he would prefer to discuss their business yet that evening rather than leave it until morning — she saw her chance. "If you two are going to be up talking half the night, I want to be at the other end of the house. I'm exhausted!"

"Take my old room, then," said her aunt Beatriz. "You can't hear anything from there."

It had worked! Carolina said her "good nights" and went to the end of the hall. Max would be up front with the others until late as well. She would be able to get out without anyone hearing. She opened the window to have a look. It was about eight feet from the ledge to the ground, easy enough to let herself down. She collapsed on the bed to calm down and think things through. What could go wrong? There was the cook's son; she didn't know him very well, and conceivably he could tell someone. But at least he couldn't read her Spanish, even if he opened the note to see what was inside. The fact that he was reluctant initially to undertake delivery of the envelope to Francisco upon his return home — afraid that he would get caught and get his mother in trouble — augured well. He wouldn't be telling anyone, anyway. So the worry was Francisco himself. He might not come. He might still be upset, or might have talked with Max. And who knows what Max might have told him. But that's what she had to find out: what difference it would make to Francisco if her folks or even Max disapproved. If he didn't come she would be worried sick, with no way to find out how he was feeling until he came home for Christmas. And even she might not get back to the Primavera for Christmas, if her folks decided to stay at the Esperanza for the end of year holidays this year. "Francisco, you just *have* to come!"

She listened to what sounded like an engine and jumped up to extinguish the lamp and peer out the window. Only Max got out of the car, meaning he had already left Francisco off at the Ajcojoms. So far so good. After Max had come indoors she saw the cook's son start up the lane. She threw herself on the bed again and prayed. For an eternity she lay there. From the moon she guessed that an hour, at least, had passed since her mother and aunt had gone to bed.

She couldn't tell what Max was doing. But Eduardo and Pancho were still up and drinking; they would keep everybody awake if this continued. Even so, nobody would have reason to come check on her. She would go as soon as the church bells rang again. "By midnight I'll be at the launch," she'd written, and it had to be almost eleven by now.

She slipped on a sweater she knew that he liked. He never said much about her clothes, but when she wore this low-cut one his eyes were always there! The talking in the parlor had not abated, but outside there wasn't a sound. The moon seemed uncommonly bright...anybody looking out would be able to see her once she was away from shadows of the house. Maybe meeting down at the shore wasn't such a good idea...Oh, stop your worrying! she scolded herself — nobody's going to be looking. And he *is* going to show up! Faint pealing of the church bells in Panajachel put an end to her impatient waiting. She dropped her shoes and let herself down from the ledge before she took a deep breath and let go. Before picking herself up she listened again. Then she was off, hair now streaming behind, running breathlessly for the launch.

She had counted 436 laps of gentle waves against the boat when she saw him coming down the beach. He had gone the long way around to avoid her house, as she supposed he would. She stood up and waved.

"Aren't you chilly?" he said calmly.

"Positively cold! I was too nervous to think of a blanket."

"Figured as much," he chuckled as he reached the boat and paused to look at her standing there hugging herself in the moonlight. That sweater again...a good omen, indeed! "I can't believe we're doing this," he said. She held out her arms, and he threw her the blanket.

"It's not the blanket I want, silly! I want *you!* The blanket I needed an hour ago."

He stepped into the boat and after an awkward silence he reached out to grasp her hands. At arm's length they gazed deeply...he looking down, eyes shaded from the moon. Her face was luminous in its frame of loosened hair, and he thought he saw the sparkle of tears. He bit his lip.

"Let go and cry a while with me," her anxious eyes frankly pleaded. Moved by such beauty, his eyes also filled. He had spent the two hours worrying about what he should and shouldn't, would and wouldn't say. Now, after years of only joking, there seemed no need to talk. They gazed joyously, still at arms length, until his arms began to ache and he assumed hers must be about to break. He started to pull her toward him, but she smiled and resisted.

"No, please, not quite yet. I haven't had enough of just looking. I can't see your eyes as well as you can see mine...you have our grandmother moon's help. Not fair!" She chose her words purposely...it was only *naturales* who addressed the moon as 'grandmother.'

He smiled appreciatively, adding, "But you're embarrassing me! It's hard not to talk!"

"But we *are* talking, Francisco...just listen to my eyes! They're telling you 'I love you' for all the times I couldn't find a way. I'm so weary of the kind of talking we've always had to do...never serious, always joking. I could stand here looking into your face all night and my eyes still not have told you all they have to say."

So they gazed a while longer, until she thanked him with a smile and yielded finally to the pull from his arms. To kiss would be enough for him; even for that he'd waited all these years. They kissed, caught their breath, and kissed again until Carolina couldn't continue and started to gasp. "Please, Francisco, I can't breathe!"

"I'm sorry, "he said tenderly. "I feel so desperate. I've waited too long just to kiss you, Carolina. Now I hurt all over..."

But Carolina didn't understand. She was ready to talk and pulled him down to sit beside her on the board seat. "Maybe women talk with our eyes more than you men do. We certainly cry more. Or maybe it's just me...my family. Mama cries easily, and Gramma does, too. Our family's always been that way. Does your mother...and Margarita...do they cry easily?"

Francisco realized that he never had given it thought, but he wanted to reassure. "They're sentimental, I guess...more than me and Papa, anyway."

"But do they *cry* easily?"

"Well, no...not a lot, really. Like at the cemetery today, before you arrived...Mama was talking about Papa going to the Santa Catarina cemetery alone, and then she started to think about her own folks — both dead, down on the coast. She was real sad, but she didn't actually —"

"That's what I mean," Carolina interrupted "— I think your family is stronger that way than mine. Or maybe it's that Indians are stronger that way than Ladinos."

145

Francisco was silent, troubled to have this coming up again. Why was she doing it?

"Oh, Francisco, you're getting quiet again...just like this afternoon. Don't be so self-conscious! You don't have to be embarrassed about yourself, about being Indian. I felt that I had to talk with you about that before we separated again for such a long stretch. I have to know how you and I are different...if we really are. In important ways, I mean. Not in the little things like how we talk, or dress, or what we eat...but how we *feel* — how we love. And if we are different like some say, I want to know why that's bad."

"Well, you really are in a serious mood," he smiled in an effort to be forgiving. "What's gotten you all worked up about Indians and Ladinos all of a sudden?"

"Max. He got real serious before we came down to the house together. Asked me if I knew what I was doing...if I was prepared for you to get serious about your feelings. But I can see he didn't talk to you."

"No, he was oddly quiet after he returned with the gasoline. Hardly spoke a word."

"Well, I guess I'm glad that he didn't —" she gave his cheek a kiss, "or you might not have come! Max doesn't seem to be against us being in love...we *are* in love, aren't we? I mean *both* of us?"

Despite her twinkle, he knew it was a serious question. After all, he had never told her. "Yes, Carolina, I love you very much — too much, I fear."

"Good! Just needed to make sure," she giggled, and curled up on the seat with her head in his lap. "Max can deal with it," she continued, "but I guess he wanted to be sure I knew how opposed the rest of the family would be."

"Just because I have Indian parents? Or also because I'm me? Do your folks not like *me?*"

"How can I know which it is? They're so busy letting me know I shouldn't love an Indian that I can't tell how they really feel about you...personally, I mean. I think they like you...Max certainly does. After all, dearie, you're a very likeable person — so witty, smart, and — so good-looking!" She pulled his head down and gave his chin a kiss. "D'you know how your folks feel about me?"

Francisco had to stop and think. Like her, he really didn't know, so he laughed and admitted, "I see what you mean. They're too worried about what might happen to us to say what they think of you. But I know who they *don't* like in your family, so I think if they didn't like you, I'd know it."

"You mean my father!" she retorted, hurt a bit at his frankness.

"No, no, Carolina, I was thinking about your cousin, Chico. He's pretty obnoxious. Your uncle Pancho isn't easy to be around either. As for your dad, he and my dad have a strange relationship. Not really friends any more, but very careful not be let themselves become enemies, if you know what I mean."

"Uh huh, I think I do. Okay, you're forgiven. And I agree: Chico is obnoxious! Anyway — back to my folks — I expect that they object to our getting serious simply because you're Indian. And I want to know why. Whether it's just because most Indians are poorer and have less school than Ladinos — obvious things like that, that don't apply to you —"

"No, Carolina, the point is that Ladinos think we're poor because we're just basically inferior — dumb! And when someone like me learns how to work with Ladinos and maybe even pass as Ladino, then they say it's because they helped us out. Like we're not capable of bettering ourselves on our own. Or, take what you were talking about earlier: the business of not crying so much. I think that you are absolutely right. Indians probably *don't* let themselves cry a whole lot. If they did, they'd be crying all the time — what with all the hungry kids, and dying they've got to put up with! But I bet your folks say Indians are less sentimental because we can't feel things as deeply as Ladinos...like we don't have the same emotions you do. Do your parents, or at least your grandmother, think that? Might Max, or even you, my dear, think that at some level?"

"Of course not," she murmured, feeling terrible to have unleashed such a torrent of feelings. Clearly her Francisco was deeply conflicted, referring to Indians as "they" and then "we" practically in the same sentence. And here she was so eager to blur whatever differences there were between them by wanting to learn how to think more like Indians did!

But Francisco wasn't through. "And how can I know how different, or alike, you and I are? I'm me, and you're you. I don't think I'm any different from Max in the important ways you talk about; it's just that he doesn't have to worry about how others think about him, while I worry a lot about what people, like your family, think of me. Every Indian who wants to get ahead in this life *has* to learn how to avoid offending or angering Ladinos, and since we never know when that may happen we learn very early in life to seem simple-minded. We purposely act around Ladinos like we're dumb, so that they will be more forgiving and not feel that we are any threat. It's so dishonest, and *that* is what makes me the angriest at Ladinos." He didn't add that this lie was what made him so angry at himself as well.

But he didn't need to...Carolina understood that much about Francisco's anger. He was trembling, and they sat quietly until he had calmed down. She decided to let him know that she'd had enough talk by caressing his fingers as they lay cold and sweating on her waist. It was silly of her, she supposed, but she needed to know he felt this way...could say these things. Even she had begun to wonder just how deeply this man she had come to love really could feel.

Francisco, too, was feeling oddly pleased with such outpouring of thinking about himself. While Carolina, of all people, should know that he felt things as deeply as anyone, he had to admit that he didn't show his feelings easily...least of all to her. Maybe it was harder for Indians to do, after all they'd been through...and maybe he wasn't as free from that kind of Indianness as he liked to think. In any case, he suddenly felt very tender toward this unusual woman who insisted on unburdening him as well as herself, even though she knew it was hard for him. It was becoming clearer how much she did, in fact, care. He wanted to shift his legs to spare her the embarrassment of the erection that would soon be unmistakable, but she lifted his hand to her lips to say, "Don't worry...it's all right." So he didn't worry and let it lift, pressing against her head. "It hurts," he pleaded.

"Good," she whispered, "I want it to...for a little while longer. I don't want anything about tonight to be over...yet. It's too delicious!"

With that he lifted her head closer to his and said firmly, "And if I say a donkey's bald, it's because it's bald."

"What on earth does *that* mean?"

"If I say it hurts, it really hurts. You want to know how we're different? Well, that apparently is one way. You obviously don't hurt down there like I do, or you wouldn't stay so relaxed!" And he kissed her with such force that she started to struggle to her feet. "I'm sorry, Carolina...I didn't mean — but we've been out here a long time, my love, and the night isn't going to last forever just because you don't want it to end."

"I know...it's just that I'm a little nervous. I know what you want...I do, too, but with all that we've been through emotionally already today — I'm too nervous." She walked to the front of the boat and gazed at the powdery swath of stars across the sky. Santiago's Road is so bright tonight."

Francisco, frankly, was relieved. "It'll get colder by morning, then. Indians call it 'The Cold Road' because the brighter it is, the colder the dawn will be."

"Really? I didn't know you have other names for stars! What do Indians call 'The Seven Marys'?"

Francisco didn't know which constellation she meant, and joined her in the front of the boat to look where she was pointing. "Oh, those," he chuckled "— they're 'The Seven Ladinos,' because they always stick so close together."

"I don't believe you! You're teasing. "She turned to give his face a playful slap, but caught sight of the moon. "Look! There's going to be an eclipse."

"You're right. I'd completely forgotten with all the excitement of today. They told us at the barracks that there'd be one tonight. Total, too. Pretty soon we'll hear the noise from town."

Suddenly she panicked. "I've got to get back! What if they awaken with the noise and come out to watch?"

He thought about it a moment, and then relaxed. "They probably *will* awaken and come out, if they're not still awake anyway. But what's wrong with that? It'll be pitch black about then, and when you reach the house you can say that you woke up before anyone else and came out to watch. They won't suspect a thing with your already being outdoors."

"How'd an Indian get to be so smart?" she mocked, reassured for the moment at least. She let his body support hers as they both watched the slowly dwindling sphere. Left hands clasped at her side, she trembled a bit from the touch of his other caressing her neck, then her breast through the thin sweater. "I get mixed up," she continued, nervous lest the talking cease and he convince her to throw caution to the wind. "What's the difference between this and the sun's eclipse?"

"I think that with the moon the earth comes between it and the sun, while in the daytime the moon passes between us and the sun. That's what they told us in the barracks, anyway. And it's the earth that moves in the sky, causing day and night; not the sun. My grandfather used to say it was San Bernardo riding from the east end of the lake to the west each day. When the sun stopped shining for a while during the day, or the moon darkened suddenly at night, Rodolfo told us that our grandmother, Ixchel, was fighting with San Bernardo. Like now, the sun is angry with the moon, and to protect her everybody makes noise until he stops. It works; he always does!" laughed Francisco, caressing lightly still but with increasing confidence.

"It isn't dangerous to watch, is it...like we're not supposed to watch the sun's eclipse?"

"Depends on if you're pregnant. You're not yet, are you!" he teased, sliding his wandering fingers to her stomach to feel.

She laughed nervously and decided to hold both of his hands. "But why pregnant?"

"Because it can make you lose the baby..."

"But how can it do that?" she pressed.

"Dunno...just does." He didn't tell her the rest: that he'd been told it was because the moon wanted to take babies with her if she was going to die from the beating. "I know it's true, though," he added, "because that's what happened to Margarita. Their first was stillborn simply because she had looked at an eclipse a few months before. Just for a moment, until Mama warned her to come indoors, but that was enough to do it."

Carolina didn't know what to think. Hurting your eyes by looking at the sun made sense, but how possibly could looking at the moon cause a miscarriage? She would have to ask their Indian cook about it. Must be something to it, though, if Margarita — "Listen! It's begun!" Pots and pans, church bells, and crackling of firecrackers were discernible in the cacophony that was mounting in Panajachel. "We'd better be going. The plantation help will join in the noise soon, and our families are sure to awaken."

Reluctantly Francisco had to agree. He turned her around to give her one more kiss. They agreed to meet again during Holy Week, if not at Christmas, and parted. "I love you!" he called, but she already was out of earshot, running through the rapidly descending darkness of their grandmother's beating at the hands of San Bernardo.

A light went on in the house as she approached, and then there were voices from the back yard. "Carolina isn't here," came Max's surprised call from her open window.

"Here I am, silly...you don't have to yell," she said calmly from the edge of the lawn. "I saw it begin and have been watching it down on the dock for the last half hour." She wouldn't even have to use the window to get back in.

Eduardo was the first to go back to the house. He checked rooms to confirm that his wife was still sleeping. Leaving quickly by the front door, he hurried toward the Ajcojoms. Their house was dark, but they, too, could be outdoors awaiting the moon's reappearnce. Half way to the house he crouched and darted from shrub to shrub across the clearing toward the oldest coffee grove. He might yet cut off Francisco if his suspicion was correct. Carolina wouldn't have gone all the way to the boat dock just to watch an eclipse!

He chose some bushes beside the path that Francisco probably would stick to in the darkness. Within minutes he heard soft whistling, but not until the fellow had passed did he follow. The blanket was proof enough, and from behind he grabbed Francisco with a crushing arm lock. Eduardo had the advantage of surprise and downed his startled victim easily, pinning him with arms and knees. Savagely he pounded his head into the dirt — "You miserable *Indio*...you filthy pig" — a different epithet with each blow until he was out of words and out of breath.

Francisco had ceased struggling and lay motionless. Eduardo began to fear what he might have done until a groan, barely audible, gave assurance that he was still alive. Eduardo stood up and paced a few meters up and down the path, mind racing. What to do now? He hadn't intended to hurt him badly....It wouldn't do for people to know that he'd beaten Rodolfo's son. Rodolfo mustn't find out...even his own family couldn't know. He'd have to make sure of that. As soon as he knew Francisco was going to be able to walk — he had rolled over and gotten to his hands and knees — Eduardo took him by the shoulders and helped him unsteadily to his feet. "Now you listen to me, you uncivilized savage! Don't you as much as *look* at my daughter again before she's married! You stay at your barracks, and you stay away from this lake, or I'll see to it that Rodolfo's fired and the whole lot of you goes back to the coast! If I have to, Francisco, I'll kill you to keep you away from Carolina! Now, if you've got any sense left in that sorry head, you'll not say a word and you'll be off to the barracks before your household stirs in the morning!" Satisfied, he kicked Francisco to his knees again and stalked off.

CHAPTER THIRTEEN

Eliseo brought his oxcart to an abrupt halt on the bridge, in spectacular view of one cataract cascading above and another plunging below. To his consternation and his companion Father Jacobo's chagrin, a baptism was underway in the pool beside the road. Spray off the jumble of rocks lining the watering hole would be his oxen's only relief from midday heat. For Father Jacobo was not about to approach any closer to the Believers crowded around Calixtro and yet another of his Pentecostal converts.

Calixtro Queche had recovered from his hideous throat infection, to the relief of Protestants. After Capo's cemetery prayer for his recovery, his dying would have been difficult to explain. Less difficult to account for had been the maggots that started hatching in his nose and throat. He had lain in the deep grass too long with the flies before Francisco's discovery undoubtedly saved his life. When he finally returned home from Solola, a large scar marked the removal of his badly infested voice box. A reddish scar in the shape of a cross. Able only to whisper in punishment for his sins, and with the cross plainly visible, Calixtro had become a legend. He had insisted on being baptized anew in the lake — totally immersed, like John the Baptist — and since then immersion had become the way the *Centroamericano* Protestants distinguished themselves from the newer Pentecostal sect.

Jacobo grimaced as he studied the motley assortment of Indians. "I rue the day I so worried myself over that man!" From their dress Jacobo recognized families from at least three of the counties in his parish. The majority were Sololatecos, meaning that the convert probably was from several kilometers up the road as well. Otherwise Calixtro would have used the lake.

Eliseo couldn't suppress a smile over the cleric's frustration. "Life around here would have been a good deal simpler if we'd just let the old codger die," he suggested, pulling at the few wisps of hair he fondly called a beard. "Have you wondered at the irony of your being in Solola on his account the fateful afternoon of that cemetery prayer meeting?"

"Work of the Devil to be sure! I hear the old coot's getting to be known as far away as the capital. Have to admit, that red cross on his throat is a powerful sign. Maybe I need to have my larynx cut out and talk in a whisper!"

"Come on, Father! They'll make a Believer of you as well if you let down your guard," laughed Eliseo, but more at the impossibility of such a cross scar ever being visible beneath all those chins. He snapped his whip, and the oxcart loaded with market purchases creaked across the bridge and down the road. "As for me, I worry mostly about the *cofradias*. Calixtro's cousin has asked the elders to have Sacramento's *cofradia* taken over by someone else. He hasn't turned Protestant himself, but his wife has. She refused to do her part in the *cofradia* ceremonies, and the duties of the *cofrade's* wife are pretty important. I wasn't going to mention it until we had someone else to take over, but we haven't been able to find anybody. The elders are ready to return Sacramento's images to the church, at least 'til next year." He paused to await Jacobo's reaction.

Jacobo tried to hide his satisfaction with this unexpected consequence of Protestant success. "And the others?" he asked casually "Do you think the elders will want to return all of the *cofradias'* saints images to the church before long?"

Eliseo caught Jacobo's sideward glance, belying his nonchalance. "Well, I don't really know, Father, but I doubt it. Most don't want to give up the closeness they feel to the saints when they're housed in the homes of friends and relatives. It's clear to me that much of the appeal for Believers also is getting together in homes — for prayer meetings a couple evenings each week. Indians seldom visited one another in their homes previously, but even Protestant Ladinos go to Indian Protestant homes now. Indians also go to evening meetings in Ladino homes, all calling each other brother and sister. Catholics don't have anything to match that, but at least they have the saints close to them in their homes where worshippers drop in now and then."

Jacobo listened intently. Eliseo was as faithful a parishioner as he had. For years Eliseo had given him sound advice on how to treat Indians. If only he had listened to the man before pressuring elders to lay down the *cofradia* of Saint Isidro. Then, too, elders had asked to return the saint's image only temporarily. In his eagerness to get Saint Isidro back in the church once and for all, he had insisted that they lay down the *cofradia* instead. Even Rodolfo had remonstrated with him, before the elders finally acquiesced — only to find themselves blamed ever since whenever crops were poor. Jacobo suspected that the elders were using Eliseo this time to feel him out before they risked more public outcry. If so, he would be obliging. "Tell your elders that the church is available for as short or as long a time as they wish."

153

Eliseo nodded appreciatively; his irascible companion was in an expansive mood! Before raising a more delicate concern, he again shared the half empty bottle of rum with which he had been plying Jacobo since leaving Solola. "Father, we have a problem with Believers more serious than Catholics' reluctance to house the saints. Because town council service sometimes involves ceremonial drinking of liquor, Believers are arguing that their religion won't permit them to do that public service anymore either. Indians have the idea that they show respect and work together better when they drink. It's so strong an idea that I've seen them pretend to drink by pouring liquor into a funnel and bottle around their neck rather than risk giving offense to the saints."

"Really!" said Jacobo in surprise. "Had no idea...I thought they just like to get drunk."

"Well, some do, I reckon. That vice isn't restricted to Indians. But for most it's just a sign of respect. As I see it, we have two choices unless we decide to exempt Believers from all community service —"

"God forbid that we do that!" exploded Jacobo. "We'd soon have nobody willing to admit to being Catholic." It's bad enough that Indians can get out of the *cofradia* expenses just by saying they're Believers."

"I know, I know," added Eliseo quickly, afraid that he'd gotten off on the wrong foot.

"Either we have to take the drinking out of council service, or we have to get Believers to contribute part of their tithes to running this town."

"Can't believe we would ever get any of their tithes!" Jacobo snorted. "The precedent would worry me, too. Pretty soon even Catholics — those who could afford to, anyway — would want to pay instead of taking time to serve." Jacobo wet his lips and chuckled knowingly. "No wonder you keep getting elected mayor, Eliseo. You could talk honey from a bee tree. Here I am downing your liquor while you tell me that I've got to join Believers in preaching against their drinking!" He handed Eliseo the bottle and shook with laughter. "And the irony is, you're quite right. There's much too much drinking by *Inditos* around here. What surprises me is that where it's the biggest problem, over in Santa Catarina, there's so little interest in Protestantism."

"That is strange," agreed Eliseo. "The Catarineco couple back there at the cataract, Rodolfo's brother-in-law Diego and his new woman, are the only Believers over there so far. Rodolfo says that ever since Diego decided to get out of *cofradia* service and try to stop drinking, the town's done nothing but hound

154

him and his woman with threats of sorcery. Lazaro Tonon, Capo's son and Rodolfo's son-in-law, told me the town of Patzicia was like that when his father first converted. Capo used to drink a lot 'til once, about five years ago, he was drunk and dropped their last baby —"

"Dropped his child! *Capo?*" exclaimed Jacobo in disbelief.

"So I'm told. Baby died. Capo was so shaken by what he'd done that he decided then and there never to drink again. But people began giving him such a hard time for not drinking in the fiestas that he decided the only solution was to leave Patzicia. When his family moved here, it soon got around that he didn't drink. And if you don't drink here, people automatically think that you're a Believer. So you might as well join! In my opinion that's the main reason why Indians convert: to avoid drinking and save the money that the rest of us spend taking care of saints. They certainly don't convert because they agree with every-thing the pastor says. In fact, most Believers here don't care much for their pastor. That's why Pentecostals broke away in the first place. And a lot of these Believers aren't very faithful. I'm told that Hilario Churunel still does divinations for his old clients hereabouts, and yet he calls himself a Believer! You would be surprised how many Believers secretly buy a bottle from me now and then, asking me not to tell anybody. Some of them don't mind drinking; they just don't want to have to buy it for their friends and the saints! That goes for some Catholics, too, though. At Ana Chuc's funeral wake last week, her family invited some Protestant neighbors just so they wouldn't have to buy liquor. Served gruel instead, and the Chucs are no more Protestant than you are."

Jacobo winced. "But, like you say, the drinking's so much a part of fiestas. Do you really think that you and I, even with the help of elders, can change all that?"

"We've got to try. Got to talk with the pastor and Capo to get assurance that Believers will cooperate if the elders do agree."

Jacobo reached for the rum again and shook his head at the unlikely com-plicity that Panajachel's wily mayor had just talked him into. He knew better than to trust any Ladino as popular with Indians as Eliseo, but he couldn't help admir-ing the man!

At the insistence of hungry oxen, the cart stopped at a knoll, lush with grass, where one of several roadside crosses between Panajachel and Solola marked a death from falling over the precipice. Here the cause had been a landslide during the rainy season several years back that took several lives at the spot, but for others the more common cause was liquor on market and fiesta days.

"I wonder why Indians put branches by these crosses," Jacobo pondered aloud.

"Those are branches of snake nettle. It's a *secreto* for weariness."

"A *secreto?*" Jacobo had heard Indians use the word for assorted remedies, but didn't understand why they were called secrets.

"Indians say that the leg aches you get when walking long distances are caused by snake-of-the-road." To humor the priest, Eliseo added, "They believe that the Hill's Owner sends it, so they make brooms of snake nettle to send it back! They brush their legs and leave the brooms at the cross." He stopped short of adding that he'd done it himself, with good results, on many a trip.

"But why at the cross?"

Eliseo didn't know how much more he could safely divulge. "With a cross, Indians talk to all powerful spirits...to the Hill's Owner as well as the saints."

The rum was getting to them both, and Eliseo's effrontery annoyed Jacobo. "But the holy cross is a symbol of our Lord Jesus's death for our souls! It doesn't belong to the Devil, too!"

"Pardon me, Father — I know that's what those of us who are very Catholic say. But what most Indians say is that crosses are simply 'strong'...not good or bad...just strong." Then, to move the discussion away from crosses, he added, "But the *secreto* isn't only this. You can brush legs to cure 'snake-of-the-road' whether there's a cross around or not. The secret is to leave your broom where somebody else will find it, like at this cross here. If you're lucky, somebody who doesn't know better will use it after you have and take your tiredness into their body instead!" He laughed nervously. "Indians say that if you're smart you'll never use another person's broom."

Jacobo was staring at him so incredulously that Eliseo couldn't resist telling him the rest of what his father had taught him. "Then, for really heavy tiredness, the *secreto* is to make a broom from thorn vines to prick you skin and let the tired-ness drain. Some say that's why a crown of thorns was placed on our Lord Jesus's head when he got tired carrying his cross."

Dumbfounded as much by the logic as a Ladino's familiarity with Mayan superstition, Jacobo's eyes narrowed as he studied his companion — the first time, really, that he had taken the time to look closely at Eliseo's features. The high cheekbones of his almost hairless face belied the Ladino ancestry that Jacobo, like

156

everyone else, had never questioned in view of his relationship to the Ramirezes. Eliseo's half-sister, Arcadia, looked Ladina enough, so if there had been an Indian in her and Eliseo's past, it must have been several generations back. Few Ladinos, after all, were protected from that likelihood. Perhaps the rum would further loosen Eliseo's tongue.

But Eliseo's amusement changed suddenly to wariness under the priest's stare, and he ended the conversation with an angry crack of his whip. He had talked too freely! Its retort startled Jacobo as much as the oxen, and as the cart lurched forward the priest settled back to enjoy the rum's effect and to ponder. Sensing his companion's uneasiness, he handed Eliseo the bottle and proffered a genuine compliment. "Panajachel owes you a lot, my friend. There aren't many towns hereabouts where Indians and Ladinos — Protestants and Catholics for that matter — live together as peaceably as they do here. You should hear the tales told by priests farther north where Germans have dominated Indians so. Even worse than down on the coast. I tell you, Eliseo, this country is a volcano in more ways than one! Anyway, there's been many a time that I've asked myself, 'What makes a brother-in-law of Oscar Ramirez so concerned about *Indios?*'"

Pleased by the praise, but skeptical of any solicitousness from Father Jacobo, Eliseo thought better of the temptation to reveal his ancestry. "It's a complicated story, Father. Perhaps you'll hear it in the confessional before I go to my grave," he offered with a grin. "Running the store and learning their language is a large part of it. I've made lots of friends here and in Santa Catarina. Rodolfo for one...he's a large part of the reason. He's taught me a whole lot, that man has. Impressed me the first time I met him, and my respect just continues to grow."

Jacobo had to nod in reluctant, albeit genuine, agreement. "I remember when I first saw that lad at the Primavera. Wasn't sure if he was *Indito* or Ladino then, and I'm just as undecided now."

"Oh, he's Indian enough! But Rodolfo's a survivor. How a native of Santa Catarina could survive all these years as foreman of the Primavera is a genuine wonder of this world."

"Why do Catarinecos call him *'El Coyote'* behind his back?" Jacobo ventured, in hopes of a story.

Eliseo happily obliged. "They began calling him that after he survived his bad fall, because it's so hard to kill coyotes. Clever animals, coyotes. People say you can't kill 'em with a gun, unless you put salt on the bullet and make a cross on the barrel. Otherwise they change your aim. Strong animal, too. Never know what they're going to do. Have you heard it said that the coyote is the only animal without a saint to look after it? Doesn't need one."

"Humph!" snorted Jacobo. "That describes Rodolfo all right. Never have known him to use the confessional. Respectful enough, though. It's just that he never seems to need my counsel."

"Exactly. Wise and totally self-sufficient is what he is. Elena, too. Did I ever tell you that Rodolfo was named for a priest?"

"No! *Really?* — who?"

"Rodolfo Luis...never learned his last name. A Spaniard, murdered at the Buenaventura plantation about the time I took over the store. He was stirring up Indians against the forced labor, the *mandamientos,* after our President Rufino Barrios was killed in El Salvador. Rodolfo's father was mightily impressed...heard the priest talk to the workers the evening he was macheted."

"Well, I do declare!" mused Jacobo. "How'd you find out?"

"Back at the time of his fall. When he learned about people calling him *El Coyote,* he told me that perhaps he had a coyote *characotel.* But it was his mother who convinced him that he survived because of his namesake priest looking after him. Seemed to think that because of the fish that the priest had drawn under his signature on the leaflets he was handing out, this meant that his receiving the priest's name resulted in his receiving a fish spirit in his soul as well. That's why he always wears that fish charm around his neck. Something else," Eliseo recalled "— remember the crucifix that Rosa put around his neck when we all thought that he surely was going to die? His father apparently rescued it from around the priest's neck when buzzards were finishing him off."

"Well, I declare....That's quite a story. I had no idea he was so devout a Catholic."

"That's why it's such a pity that Margarita married a Believer. It's a constant worry to Elena, and I think that it bothers Rodolfo more than he lets on. But Margarita isn't nearly the worry that their son is. Now *there's* a troubled soul who needs your prayers, Father. If Francisco didn't have some of his father's luck — not to mention the luck of being born on Panajachel's patron saint's day — I believe he would have gone to his maker long ago."

"How so?" queried Jacobo, sensing that the rum was about to answer a question on many minds in Panajachel: why Francisco never came home to visit his family.

"Something happened between him and Eduardo the night of All Souls Day a year ago. There was an eclipse…remember? It was total, and you know how much noise Indians make when it's total. Noise woke up the Ramirez household, and they all went out to watch. Max realized that Carolina wasn't there, and when he went to check on her she wasn't in her bed…with the window open. About then she came walking up from the lake. Since she'd been with Francisco earlier, Eduardo figured they'd snuck off together. But with her being so head-strong and the boys such friends, he decided not to let on like he suspected anything. Instead, he snuck over toward the Ajcojoms. Sure enough, he caught Francisco coming up from the lake. I reckon he would have killed the fellow if it wasn't for him being Rodolfo's son."

"Eduardo actually *beat* Francisco? Strange that I never heard about it."

"Oh, not so strange, Father. I only learned because of my sister. Eduardo apparently felt badly enough to have to tell at least his mother, but he made Arcadia promise not to tell anybody else, not even Carmen or the children. But my sister Arcadia was so distressed for especially Carolina that she had to tell somebody…and finally told me. Guess it's because I feel that *somebody* should be confessing this to you, that I'm telling you now. But Rodolfo and Elena must never know! Rodolfo told me later that something happened to Francisco that night, because he was gone by the time they awakened in the morning. Francisco left them a note so that they would at least know where he was, but as far as I know they've heard nothing since. Eduardo must have put the fear of the Devil in the poor —"

"But why didn't Eduardo simply go right to Rodolfo if he was worrying about their respective children getting involved with each other?" interrupted Jacobo.

Eliseo hesitated, not sure how much to divulge, then smiled faintly: "That's another long story, that it will be for Eduardo to confess on *his* death bed. Everybody respects *El Coyote,* but Eduardo has the most cause to fear the man."

———————

Capo Tonon surprised Eliseo when Eliseo stopped by the store to chat. Not only had Capo and the pastor already discussed the community service problem; they had agreed to ask their congregations to accept the town council services and bring fruit juice when ceremonies called for drinking. "To expect Catholics to give up liquor for us is unreasonable. People should give up liquor only when their hearts tell them to," said Capo. "If we can drink juice at wakes and funeral processions," he added, "then we can honor the deceased together as well."

Eliseo in turn surprised Capo with the warmth of his grateful embrace.

The elders had a much easier decision to reach when Eliseo took them Capo's proposal, and at the end of December when several Believers were asked by the elders to serve as councilmen, night watchmen, and errand boys the following year, only one refused to accept. To Capo's chagrin, it was his own son, Lazaro.

"It makes absolutely no sense to agree to be Fourth Councilman this time, and then Third, Second and maybe even the First later, only to have to refuse when eventually I'm asked perhaps to become mayor," stormed Lazaro to his father. "It's the principle of the thing. In God's name, Papa, the mayor is responsible for the image of Saint Buenaventura. Eliseo keeps it in his home! It all goes to prove that town hall and *cofradia* services are so intertwined that there's always going to be resentment toward us Believers for not helping with the saints. I say the whole system needs to be reformed! If enough of us Protestants refuse to serve, we can force the changes for the good of everyone. Even the government is on our side, by saying that those who enlist in the army are exempt from council service. Look at Francisco...he'll never have to serve. And if Rodolfo Ajcojom's son won't have to serve, then why should his son-in-law?"

"So I suppose you're going to enlist and leave Margarita for us to care for!" Capo was irate. He had promised Eliseo that the elders could count on his support for a compromise, and here his own son was the first to turn them down.

"Maybe I <u>will</u> join the army, if that's what it takes to get out of this service," Lazaro retorted. "All I know is that I'm not going to be a councilman and lose money from not being able to work half the weeks next year! Already we're tithing for our church. Catholics never think about that! I'd have to borrow money from you or my in-laws before the year was even half over. I won't do it, Papa, even if I have to move back to Patzicia. Maybe at your age you have to compromise and do what the elders tell you...but I sure don't. Nor do I have to stay in Panajachel!"

He was out the door before Capo could reply, leaving the household stunned. Capo knew it was not an idle threat. Grandparents and Capo's brother would welcome him home, and Patzicia was large enough than an outspoken Protestant like Lazaro probably wouldn't have to do community service even if he didn't enter the army. Lazaro was a faithful Believer, but not a devoted citizen of Panajachel. And if Capo had to choose one or the other for his son, that's how he would have it. He resolved to go himself to the elders to apologize for Lazaro and try to explain.

But the damage had been done. Word circulated rapidly, and within days the Tonons' store was boycotted by most Catholics and even some of the Protestants. Eliseo's store — the only other in town — of course benefited, and Capo began to wonder if Eliseo himself hadn't put people up to it. Not that he didn't have good reason.

In fact, however, Eliseo did his best to discourage the boycott, disturbed though he was with this unexpected resistance to a sensible compromise that Believers in general had agreed to. But by the time that cooler heads had prevailed to end the boycott, Lazaro had left for Patzicia. Margarita waited two weeks for her husband to reconsider before she finally packed up with their son Virgilio and took the bus to join him.

Even the stillborn loss of a child had not been so hard for Elena and Rodolfo to bear. "This is absurd!" he said to Elena for at least the tenth time since Margarita had left that afternoon. But for the moment he could think of nothing to do.

It was December of 1936, seven months since the Debt Law extension had ended and the Vagrancy Law had been substituted. The new law called for every Indian without a trade or business to prove that he had enough land to keep busy. If one couldn't show title to more than two acres of farm land, 100 days of plantation work were required each year. If one couldn't show title to more than one acre, the requirement was 150, half the work days in a year. In Panajachel, irrigation farming in the delta and on hillside terraces kept owners busy most of the year farming fewer than two acres. Concern was mounting as the May deadline approached because so few Panajachel landowners could show in their record books that they had been working on plantations. It fell to their hapless mayor to decide who had complied, proof being signatures of Ladino employers who entered numbers of days worked for them by Indians.

Eliseo went to the governor, his half-sister Arcadia's in-law, to ask for clarification of the law. Many in Panajachel worked for each other or Ladinos in farming and construction, building Ladino homes. Eliseo didn't know whether to count those days. A month later the governor responded: only work for Ladinos on plantations would count. He couldn't afford to make an exception just for Panajachel's distinctive advantage of having river water for convenient year-round irrigation of onions and garlic; he would never hear the end of it from other towns in the Department of Solola. No punishment would be given for the months already gone by, but henceforth every Panajachel adult male Indian would have to abide by the law.

It was a heavy blow, and promptly the other Protestants and one of the Catholics who had tentatively agreed to accept community service the coming year went to the elders to complain that they couldn't comply and work on plantations as well. When Rodolfo learned the news, he was more troubled than Elena had seen him since Margarita left. "Somebody needs to go to the head of Agriculture, or to President Ubico himself, and explain the dire situation here!" he shouted in desperation, pounding his fist in his hand as he paced about the room.

"Well, *you* sure can't!" Elena replied angrily. "We've already lost our daughter, and you'll lose your job — probably your *life* — if plantation owners around here get the idea that you oppose the law they depend on for their labor! You, a plantation foreman of all things! Already Ladinos complain that you're too soft on your workers. If the Primavera ever gets big enough to have labor problems, you know good and well that you'll be the first one blamed!"

"Nobody knows that better than I do!" he shouted. Their frustration was more than either could handle in the wake of Margarita's departure, and he left to walk off his anger. As his head cleared he was even more convinced that he was right. Ubico was the kind of president who would listen, especially if the elders themselves went to him. Everybody had heard what happened when leaders of Chichicastenango's sixteen *cofradias* walked all the way to the capital and complained personally to Ubico about their overbearing priest. The priest was ordered to leave! Ubico was no fool. Actions like that benefiting a few Indians made him popular even while he imposed a Vagrancy Law to help the plantation owners more efficiently exploit all the rest! But Elena was right, of course, With all that they had at stake, he had no business becoming involved. He was tempted to share the idea with Eliseo, but Eliseo couldn't afford to be credited with such a radical idea, either. In fact, no Ladino could afford to be implicated.

Finally, it was Elena who came up with the solution. Even though she sensed that it could be dangerous for Lazaro, anything that might bring Margarita home was worth the try. But she didn't tell her husband even, surprising him that evening by announcing that she wanted to pay Margarita a visit. She would take the bus next morning and be back in two days. She hadn't felt like making love since their daughter's departure. With emotion born of thinking that she had lost Margarita, but now renewing hope, Elena threw caution to the wind. Defying her mother's counsel early in their marriage — that she should never let any of her clothing or any part of her body be on top of his clothing or, worse, Rodolfo's body — she mounted her startled husband and unleashed a passion that surprised them both. Hearts pounding, they clung to each other and pondered what it all meant.

Chapter Fourteen

Hissing and a flurry of sparks in the hearth's early morning fire announced a visitor. When Pedro Noj saw that it was Lazaro Tonon standing at his gate, the First Elder sensed that this would not be an ordinary day. The swarthy, petulant Believer stood deferentially, hat in hand, not the way Pedro remembered Lazaro when he had come to the elders several weeks earlier and flatly refused their request to serve as Fourth Councilman.

"Good morning, Don Pedro," said Lazaro respectfully in Kaqchikel. "I arrived last evening from Patzicia to seek your counsel, if you will but do me the favor. Can I please join you for a few moments inside your house?"

It had to be important for Lazaro to ask to talk privately, so despite the minor annoyance, Pedro ushered him in and offered him their only chair. Seeing that Lazaro was uncomfortable with this, he pulled up their storage box and sat down formally himself. His wife, squatting at the hearth, served coffee, and they sipped as Lazaro outlined his proposal. The plan was simple: determine as exactly as possible how much work it took to work an acre of garden plots planted with the vegetables most commonly grown in Panajachel. Then take this information to their country's president with a request that he make an exception for their kind of intensive year-round irrigation farming.

Pedro was incredulous: go to the city and ask to see *President Ubico!* What was wrong with Lazaro, to come all the way from Patzicia to suggest such a thing? But Lazaro reminded him politely of Indian elders' experience in Chichicastenango, and Pedro began to understand the strategy he had in mind. "You mean that even the mayor and secretary wouldn't be involved?"

"They can't even know about it. Ubico has to hear the idea first and only from you elders. Maybe he'll figure it would be useful to him to help us *naturales*...just like in Chichicastenango where elders became so fed up with their priest's efforts to destroy traditional divination by *zahorines* that they successfully petitioned Ubico to remove him. Since our governor has turned us a deaf ear, just maybe our president will listen instead."

As Lazaro walked slowly back to the other side of the river, he had no idea what to expect in the way of Pedro's support. Pedro had heard him out attentively enough, but he had had very little to say. He agreed only to discuss it with any of his companions who came to that Sunday's monthly meeting of elders before mass. Until then there was nothing to be done...but to pray. If he went back to Patzicia, it was clear from talking with the mayor there that he would be classified as a vagrant and would have to work the full 150 days down on the coast.

Five elders joined Pedro in front of the church. As he'd anticipated, they laughed in disbelief when he first broached the idea, even before he added to their mirth by admitting it had come from Capo's son. He explained the rationale, reminding them of Chichicastenango elders' experience with Ubico in ridding themselves of an overbearing priest. But he did not press further. After the meeting had ended and he had rejoined his wife selling in the weekly market, the Second Elder stopped by to chat. Pedro had hoped for as much.

"Tell me frankly, Pedro, what do you think of Lazaro's idea?"

Pedro had rehearsed his response. "My reaction when the fellow came unannounced to see me was the same as yours. I had trouble taking him seriously after all we've been through with him. But the more I've pondered it, the more sense it makes. If I just forget that it's his idea — young, willful Believer that he is — and ask myself how I would have reacted had it been the idea of one of you wise elders, I must say I would think it worth the try!"

His friend looked at him intently, then smiled. "Well, wisest of the wise, I agree! No matter how we look at things, our biggest problem is these damn Believers. Like them or not, we've got to keep them from using liquor, the army, this law...or whatever else the Devil comes up with...as excuses for not doing their part to keep this town going. If we lose their support, we're in for trouble with Catholics as well."

"I know...I know," said Pedro sadly. "I've never felt so trapped between a machete and its stick. What makes the plan so intriguing is Lazaro, of all people, coming back here to help! If the president thinks our request is reasonable — and they say that he's a reasonable man — it won't hurt at all that Capo's son was the one who suggested the idea. Ladinos will be angry, but that pushes *naturales* who are Protestants and us Catholics closer together. Once you've got one finger in the honey pot, the rest of you is stuck there, too!"

His companion smiled again. Pedro had a way with words. "Then what's the next step?"

"We call a special meeting of heads of households, I reckon, but not here at the church. We can't afford for anyone to learn who might think it his duty to tell Ladinos hereabouts."

"You mean even Don Eliseo, or the priest?"

"Especially the priest, and Don Eliseo as well if we can manage that."

"What about Rodolfo? Won't he learn, with Lazaro being his son-in-law, and feel that he needs to protect his skin by letting at least our mayor and perhaps even the Ramirez family know what's up?"

Pedro smiled shrewdly. "Lazaro told me that this idea was actually his wife's. But he also mentioned that his mother-in-law had come to visit them recently. I have a hunch that Margarita's idea is really Elena's, and that Elena's idea is in fact Rodolfo's. But that's strictly between you and me," he warned. "And if I'm right, Rodolfo wouldn't be exercising such caution unless he realized how much risk he, of all people, is running on behalf of the likes of his son-in-law. But if I'm wrong and Rodolfo doesn't know, Lazaro is trusting that when he does get wind of it he'll not stand in our way. And if Lazaro trusts Rodolfo, then I'm ready to trust the old coyote."

Pedro came to Lazaro's house behind the Tonons' store three days later to report to Lazaro that the elders had met. A few remained skeptical, worrying about retaliation from Solola's governor if their petition was denied or from Ladino landowners if it was granted. Enough were in favor, however, that the final decision was to proceed. "A group of four of us will meet tomorrow morning before sunup to talk about the amount of time our work takes. We'll be obliged if you'll join us to write down what we decide."

The meeting at Pedro's house stretched into the afternoon. Most of the other elders stopped in at least once to see how work was progressing. The constant interruptions were annoying at first, but by afternoon Lazaro welcomed all the inputs he could get to settle disagreements about time requirements for the different vegetables folks in Panajachel had begun experimenting with. By day's end, he was convinced that they had reasonable figures, and from his quick calculations it was clear that an acre of irrigated vegetable beds needed, on average, easily three times the work required for an acre of milpa. Even at twice the time, their petition made sense. With just an acre and a half of irrigated land, an average family could keep busy the whole year.

They disbanded, to meet again next evening. The news had spread, however, and when Lazaro approached Pedro's house after an exhausting day of typing and retyping on his father's old typewriter, it looked like most of the men from that wholly Indian side of the river were awaiting his reading of the document. By flashlight he slowly read the long list of tasks required to farm an acre of crops grown in Panajachel. The crowd listened patiently until he finished. Their murmurs made it clear that they were satisfied, and the elders quickly gave it their approval. Pedro signed first, and the others from oldest to youngest followed. Three signed with an "X", after which Lazaro printed their names. To himself he proudly admitted that with all those signatures, it was a most impressive document! His parents knew of the plan, but he had decided that the less they knew of the particulars, the better. As for Rodolfo, Lazaro avoided him assiduously.

Ten companions left with Pedro in the direction of San Antonio the next Monday morning. All except Pedro carried small loads of onions to sell. Pedro carried a sack of assorted vegetables for their president. They were dressed in their best tunics and carried their elders' ceremonial silver staffs. Otherwise they blended in with the usual stream of Indians heading toward San Antonio's weekly market. Before entering the market area, however, they took the path toward Godinez and began to climb. They spent the first night in Patzun, the second in El Tejar, and entered Guatemala City the evening of the third day. Bus had been ruled out, even though that had meant two had to stay behind; the trip would be too much for the eldest of their number. Bus was expensive, but Lazaro was right: Ubico had been impressed by the delegation from Chichicastenango walking all that way. As younger men, all had made the trip many times to sell in the central market. One even had seen the national palace when visiting the adjacent cathedral, but none of their group ever had been inside.

They decided to spend the night in the small park in front of the palace, where they would be clearly visible the next morning. The gray building was impressive, even frightening — a silent fortress in the waning light. Windows were shuttered with steel. Cannons stared at them as they tried to sleep.

Before palace doors opened to start the day, eleven bare-footed and weary-looking Panajachel elders were waiting patiently outside. As cathedral bells tolled eight o'clock, the huge doors opened and army guards took up positions with no more than a glance at the motley group of their countrymen on the steps. Having come this far, Pedro was not to be intimidated. He climbed the steps and handed their carefully folded petition to the most official looking of the guards. "If you will do us the favor, sir, we wish to have this delivered to our *Presidente."*

Palace staff were accustomed to groups large and small with a grievance arriving without appointment and expecting to see *"their* President" forthwith. And Ubico obliged whenever possible. The guard nodded condescendingly and

167

promptly went inside. No words were spoken by guards or elders as the group stood waiting, waiting, waiting for something to happen. Others came and went through the big doors, and one by one the elders sat down again on the steps. The cathedral bells struck nine, then ten o'clock before the messenger reappeared and whispered to the guard in charge. He motioned to Pedro and announced that their audience had been granted for two o'clock. With that much time, they decided to take their onions to the central market. They left Pedro sitting alone in the park with their gift sack of vegetables.

———

Ubico was delighted when he read the petition. He hadn't yet replied to the Solola governor's telegram of several weeks previously, informing him of Panajachel's request for exemption from the law. Ubico had waited to see what the governor would do. Obviously, according to the letter, the governor had decided on his own to deny the request, for lack of a presidential decision. The perfect opportunity had presented itself to teach Solola's obdurate governor a lesson!

Promptly at two o'clock the president's receptionist himself appeared at the palace entrance and announced that the General was ready. Inside at the front of the building there were officials milling about and other people waiting, but within moments the elders were filing noiselessly down marbled corridors where guards standing at full attention were the only other people to be seen. Deeper and deeper into the labyrinth of stairs and hallways they followed the receptionist, past manicured gardens in courtyards open to the sky. Not a word was spoken. The interior of the fortress was as silent as an empty cemetery. When the second elder slipped on the smooth stone steps, his staff of office sounded like gunfire as it rolled down the stairs. Only then did their guide turn and frown a bit, as he stopped to wait for everyone to catch up. The elders, wearing now their ceremonial home-woven head cloths tied behind their heads, paused in anticipation outside a huge carved door behind which their president must be waiting.

The receptionist was immaculately dressed but not in uniform, so Pedro wasn't prepared for the eye-level chest of medals and ribbons of the tall, slightly balding and bespectacled man who opened the door.

Ubico, by contrast, was fully accustomed to the mixture of reactions he read on the awestruck faces that filed past him into the large room. Eleven pairs of eyes turned furtively upward in greeting as their passing heads bowed briefly, before adjusting to the bright lights of hundreds of bulbs in the chandelier. The room — his favorite in the palace — was breathtaking, and before the usual formalities of introduction Ubico started talking about the tapestries covering the walls.

"This one may interest you," he suggested, pointing to a tapestry depicting the fateful meeting of their respective ancestors, Pedro Alvarado and the leader of Guatemala's Indians whom he was in the act of spearing in battle. "Here is your valiant ancestor Tecun Uman."

Pedro wasn't sure what about the Indian leader was supposed to impress them; certainly not his clothes, half naked as he was. Clearly Ubico looked more like his ancestor than they looked like theirs.

"And the chandelier is from France," Ubico concluded "— in Europe...across the Atlantic Ocean," he thought it helpful to add.

Since he was pointing up, Pedro assumed that he was talking about all those lights.

The incongruity of the one Indian standing in the center of his reception room trying to look at the chandelier with a sack of vegetables still suspended by rope from the poor man's forehead, produced a chuckle that Ubico could not suppress. "Here, Sir, please allow me to help unburden you. If those vegetables are for me, I thank you, and — gentlemen, all of you — please be seated."

Dutifully they sat, but on the edges of the deeply recessed, ornately carved chairs. All eleven leaned forward — otherwise they couldn't reach the floor — supported as much by their staffs as the chairs, bare feet planted for the moment that Ubico might tell them to rise. Pedro was remembering, by sharp contrast, the miniature wobbly chair he had offered the young visitor who had gotten them into this!

He didn't know who should mention the petition first. After they had introduced themselves and Ubico had asked them when they left Panajachel, Pedro began. He felt surprisingly relaxed, perhaps because their president clearly was enjoying their wonderment and didn't seem at all upset with them for coming with their unusual request. "Honored President, Sir," he began in measured words he had been rehearsing the past three days "— we are but poor peasants who ask your forgiveness for taking your valuable time to meet with us. We were hesitant to ask for a meeting with you, Sir, but we heard from others that you sometimes listen to even the poorest of your countrymen."

"You were right to come," broke in the General, "and I am the one who is honored. You have taken much time from your important work to come all this way to see me. I have read your petition — all of it, in fact — including the detailed description of labor required to farm your beautiful delta. I must say, I am impressed! I had no idea that so much work is needed to grow your famous onions. You have given me a valuable lesson in vegetable gardening, and you have made it abundantly clear that you cannot raise vegetables as you do and still help on the plantations of your region.

"Therefore, I already have talked with the Director of Agriculture. We have decided to issue an order to your mayor and governor to reduce by half the amount of delta acreage that will exempt landowners in Panajachel from the Vagrancy Law. And we'll permit your vegetable farm work hired out to other Indians to be entered in your record books as well. As for carpenters and tradesmen improving Panajachel for visitors to the lake, if they are employed full time in their trade, they, too, shall be exempt. When the work is for a Ladino, he is to enter the days in your books. When the work is for an Indian, then your mayor should sign for those days.

"Do you understand and find this acceptable?"

Pedro already was off his chair and kissing the hand of their president, as the Second Elder translated in Kaqchikel to be certain everyone had understood. Smiles erupted, even tears. A bit overcome himself, Ubico rose from his chair to signal an end to the audience and suggested that they wait outside in the corridor for the signed order. They filed out, each in turn kneeling on one knee to kiss their president's hand. Alone in the corridor, Pedro asked for a repetition in Kaqchikel of what the others could agree they had heard, still afraid to trust his understanding of the president's rapid Spanish.

"Won't the governor be astonished when he learns *this?*" still speaking Kaqchikel lest anyone be able to hear. "As Ladinos say," he added with satisfaction, "you've got to talk with the owner of the circus, and not with the clowns!"

Their laughter was interrupted by the receptionist approaching with the order. In turn the eleven gratefully kneeled and kissed his hand as well, before Pedro secreted the valuable document in his shoulder bag and they quickly retraced their steps to the palace entrance and out to the park. "To think!" exclaimed Pedro "— even our work for other *naturales* will count, at least as long as we have Don Eliseo signing our work books! Between working our own land and hiring out to neighbors, most of us never will have to work on a plantation again!"

Instinctively they turned toward the cathedral to seek out the image of St. Francis. Even the one non-Catholic who had become an elder before converting

170

to Protestantism ventured inside, to add his prayer of thanks to Panajachel's patron on behalf of Protestants.

––––––––––––

The streets were deserted by the time Pedro reached Eliseo's store late Saturday night. Except for reporting to their mayor and perhaps Father Jacobo, the elders had agreed to keep the news to themselves until market the next morning. Eliseo would then decide whether to tell any other Ladinos before taking the President's order directly to the governor. Now that the Indians had gotten what they wanted, it would be prudent to do all they could to keep their relationships with local Ladinos as respectful and calm as possible.

No one responded to his knocking, so Pedro went around back and called over the fence: "Begging your pardon, Don Eliseo, but are you still awake? I am Pedro Noj —" The dog was up and barking at the fence drowning him out. A flashlight appeared at the door. "Get in here, hound! Pay her no heed, Pedro. Any hound that barks as much as she does lacks the energy to bite. Come around to the store and I'll let you in."

Eliseo lit the kerosene lamp and the two men sat down at the table, Eliseo in his night shirt and Pedro in his best tunic with silver staff across his knees. Even his ceremonial head cloth was in place, for the warmth it provided. Taken back by Pedro's incongruous late-night appearance, Eliseo only half-heard what the elder breathlessly blurted out.

"Say that again! You've just come from the city...and you saw *UBICO!*" Pedro nodded, and Eliseo headed for the liquor cabinet. "I need a drink before you go any further!" He poured each of them a full glass of rum, then downed his own before starting to pour another.

"Begging you pardon, but should you drink any more?" warned Pedro. "This town will need a very sober mayor tomorrow."

But Eliseo insisted, before sitting back down and staring in continuing disbelief at Pedro while the full, incredible story unfolded. By the time Pedro had finished, Eliseo had gone from bewilderment to anger, then to admiration for this man who earlier had lacked the gumption to go with him even to see their governor. Eliseo was too disoriented from the news and rum to grasp the full implications of what he was learning, so Pedro tactfully reviewed why Eliseo hadn't been informed, why no Ladino yet knew, why Lazaro was likely in danger, why even Rodolfo might be accused.

171

"But *did* Rodolfo know?" interrupted Eliseo, as what Pedro was relating began to sink in. The realization that his best friend might have known and kept from him something as important as this was numbing.

"I think not," assured Pedro. "But whether he knew or not doesn't matter. Plantation owners who know that Lazaro is his son-in-law will assume that Rodolfo knew and chose to keep quiet ."

"Not to be misunderstood, Pedro," said Eliseo, his irritation growing, "but they'll be saying the same about *me!* They will certainly assume that Panajachel's *mayor* had to know about anything *this* important!"

"I know, but we had to go. We've done our best to protect you. Here's the president's order to you and the governor and the document that Lazaro helped us to prepare. Now, if you'll excuse me, I'm very weary. Haven't slept much all week, and hardly at all since we left the city Thursday. May Saint Francis give me the strength to see this through to its end."

"May he have mercy on *all* our souls," agreed Eliseo as he closed the door behind the old man and poured another drink. He slowly read and reread the document Lazaro had written, pondering his predicament as mayor. That the elders so mistrusted him...that an entire Indian community could keep this from him this long was hard to accept. Landowners like Eduardo Ramirez wouldn't believe it for a moment. Whom to tell first, at this time of night? Father Jacobo, at least. Warmed from the liquor, he trudged to the rectory in nothing but his nightshirt, sandals, and straw hat. He knocked at the door and windows, but couldn't arouse the priest. Rather than wake up the neighborhood he gave up until daybreak and returned home to down another glass of rum and try to sleep.

Pedro was hungry and exhausted to the point of collapse. He had drunk only half the glass of rum, but on his empty stomach that was enough. He vomited a block from the store and had to lie down. When he saw Eliseo's flashlight coming back from the church he called, but too feebly to arouse even the dog. He feared falling asleep on cold ground more than the agony of continuing to his house across the river, so he staggered on toward the bridge. Lest he lose his balance, he crawled across the log. But despite the precaution his left leg slipped off, dragging with it much of his heavy woolen tunic. Too weak to pull it back, his other leg slipped into the current as well. He knew then that the weight of body and soaked tunic was too much. He clung to the log long enough to remind himself that Eliseo at least had the papers. Before reaching Panajachel that evening he had concluded that even Saint Francis could not protect him from the probable

172

fate that was unfolding. His patron was kind to intercede, at least, and let it end this way.

Eliseo was with Jacobo soon after daybreak, detailing his unlikely story of Pedro's late-night visit, when news of Pedro reached the rectory. People washing onions at the mouth of the river had found his body.

"I wouldn't wonder that the bastard took his own life," scowled Jacobo, after they sat speechless for several minutes.

"If so, he had the charity to do it before anyone could be accused of killing him," mused Eliseo, wondering if that wasn't the real reason that Pedro had gotten him out of bed to deliver the papers. "His dying may be sobering enough to prevent violence to others over this. He was worried about Lazaro, and even concerned for Rodolfo —"

"As well he might!" stormed the priest. "Rodolfo knew this was going on and let it happen without —"

"Pedro said he didn't know. It was Lazaro's —"

"May have been Lazaro's idea," Father Jacobo interrupted, his usually half-closed eyes flashing, "but you can't tell me it could go this far — Lazaro meeting with all the elders, typing papers, and all — without his family knowing! Everybody's been wondering why Lazaro came back, and you know his own relatives would have found out why!"

Eliseo started to repeat what Pedro had told him, until Jacobo smiled sardonically. "My mayor doth protest too much, me thinks!" Eliseo didn't know about Hamlet, nor even Shakespeare for that matter, and continued to protest. But neither did Eliseo know that Jacobo had learned some months after Rodolfo's fall that it was none other than Eliseo who had hired a curer from across the lake, after assuring Jacobo that no curers from Panajachel nor Santa Catarina had been allowed to see him. If Eliseo was willing to deceive his priest to help Rodolfo then, he was lying now! Of course Rodolfo knew, the old coyote! About Eliseo, Jacobo was less certain. That the storekeeper had tried to awaken him, he was prepared to believe; noise outside had aroused him momentarily during the night. In any case, to alienate the man before the facts were fully known served no useful purpose. Jacobo pretended to be convinced of Rodolfo's as well as Eliseo's innocence until Eliseo at last departed with the president's order. "If only that venomous decree had been swept down the river, too!" said Jacobo aloud as he prepared to go to the Primavera and on to Solola. He would leave word for his sacristan that he was ill and had gone to see the doctor. If ever there was a day not to be in

Panajachel, this was it! He crossed himself as he asked forgiveness for missing mass and for the thought that had just occurred to him: what if something happened to Eliseo before anyone knew he had that order?

Lazaro hadn't given the consequences of Ubico's granting the petition as much thought as had Pedro. Like Rodolfo, Lazaro assumed Ubico to be capable of granting such a petition simply because it was just. Pedro had been more cynical, especially after pondering Ubico's obvious delight in granting every one of their requests. Pedro could think of only one reason why: Ubico wanted to embarrass the governor. If correct, then the governor and his supporters would be outraged. Pedro had prayed that he was wrong. But if he was right, then the implications for himself and the others responsible were grave indeed. He had reached these conclusions on the way home while talking with the Second Elder.

The day after Pedro's death, the former Second — now First — Elder asked Lazaro and Rodolfo to meet him at dusk where the river entered the lake. He could think of no place so safely away from any other ears to share with them Pedro's fears. "I think that Pedro would have wanted me to tell you these thoughts," he concluded. "Do they make sense to you?"

"I'm afraid that Pedro was right," Rodolfo responded, going over the sequence of events in his mind. "Why else would Ubico have decided then and there to give you a decision without talking it over first with the governor? He could so easily have let the governor save face."

"Excuse me, Father-in-law, but there might be another explanation. Ubico may be less concerned with this governor and his supporters hereabouts than with how the country in general reacts to his making these decisions. With the decision to throw out the Chichicastenango priest, Ubico has told the Church that he's the boss. Now with this he says the same thing to every governor in Guatemala. We know that he wants to bring more central control to the government. In Patzicia my uncle overheard two landowners talking about a plan of Ubico's to appoint new mayors to replace the ones elected locally."

"You mean that mayors would be appointed by *Ubico?*" Rodolfo asked.

"Or at least by governors loyal to him, I guess. It's no secret that Ubico wants to get control over those governors and plantation owners who try to run the country themselves."

"I think there's probably some truth in what you both say," said the new First Elder, "but either way, it seems to me the result is the same: plantation owners will be mighty angry when they hear about this. I'm advising elders not to

174

leave town or to work in fields alone. If we're going to get killed, we want it to be obvious — not some accident like drowning. Perhaps the two of you will be wise to be vigilant, too. That is what poor Pedro would want me to tell you." With that he took his leave and hurriedly disappeared into the trees.

"Could be we're off the griddle but into the coals! My concern about not being associated with the plan in any traceable way seems foolish now...even selfish. I was implicated as surely as were you, Lazaro; if the elders so assumed, everyone else will, too. If I am honest with myself, I've known this from the beginning. I am so, so sorry!"

"I'm not afraid," Lazaro responded, with an assurance Rodolfo had to admire. "It was the right thing to do, don't you think? Even if it *has* cost poor Pedro his life —"

"You mean even if costs some other lives as well, like yours or mine," Rodolfo added, putting his arm around his son-in-law's shoulder.

"Yes, if God lets it come to that."

"I wish I had your faith," Rodolfo mused, somehow not having much confidence that even his fish charm and crucifix could stop Eduardo Ramirez if he had finally found the excuse he needed to have Victoria's brother killed.

Chapter Fifteen

Panajachel was remarkably calm in the weeks following 'Bittersweet Sunday,' that fateful day when the town learned simultaneously of Ubico's decision and the First Elder's drowning. In part because of the persisting rumor that Pedro's death had not been an accident — that powerful Ladinos some how had learned what was afoot even before the delegation had returned home — all of us who might similarly be targeted for vengeance remained wary...watchful. I made Lazaro promise to stay close to home unless accompanied. Since he found construction work near their Tonon family store, that wasn't a problem for the moment. Besides, Lazaro had become such a hero with Catholics and Believers alike that it would be a long time before anyone risked trying to get at him. I didn't worry much about myself for the time being either, since it was apparent that at least Don Pancho and Beatriz weren't upset. Arcadia had confided to Eliseo that Pancho and Beatriz didn't mind if workers *did* assume my involvement. It would incline those who couldn't get out of Vagrancy Law forced labor to work for us at the Primavera — from gratitude for the effort made on their behalf — rather than to meet their labor requirement farther afield. The euphoria enveloping virtually everyone in Panajachel was a wonder to behold. And Lazaro and I became much closer in the course of his disclosing in full detail how things had proceeded in the aftermath of Elena's visit to Patzicia to communicate the strategy which Lazaro all along had assumed was my idea.

It was Elena who concerned me, nerves worn worrisomely thin. She was babbling almost constantly over fears about one family member or another, mostly about whether Francisco would finally come home to visit during Holy Week. If he didn't show up this weekend, I was ready to go seek him out at the barracks. I had confided this decision to Eliseo, but not to Elena.

But unlike Rodolfo and Elena, Eliseo was hoping desperately that Francisco still had the good sense *not* to come home. Rodolfo's readiness to hunt Francisco down in Quezaltenango was worrisome. Arcadia finally had shared with her brother why Eduardo was so anxious for no one else in the family to learn of Carolina's tryst with Francisco: it was Eduardo's wife, Carmen, who would be utterly appalled if any of the family got involved romantically with an Indian. With that, Eliseo better understood why Eduardo was so afraid of Rodolfo. If

Carmen would be upset over her daughter lying with Rodolfo's son, there was no telling what she might do if ever she learned about her husband's rape of Rodolfo's sister! Francisco *must* not fan the flames by coming home, even if it would take his learning about Eduardo and Victoria to keep him away.

The next morning Eliseo told his councilmen that he needed to go to Chichicastenango to do some buying for Holy Week. He took the bus north, but before reaching Chichicastenango he got off at Los Encuentros and changed to a bus from the capital heading west to Quetzaltenango.

"Carolina," her aunt Beatriz called from the front door, "there's a messenger here from Eliseo at the store asking if you'll be willing to help them work tomorrow on the flower carpet for Good Friday's procession.

"For how long?" yelled Carolina from the back bedroom, pleased that her great-uncle wanted her help but anxious to finish her dress. "I've still got some work to do on this dress before the procession as well."

"No more than a couple of hours," he says, "and preferably first thing in the morning before it gets so hot."

"Sure! Tell him I'll be there by eight o'clock. Do they want me to gather flower petals from here, too? Beatriz turned to the errand boy and then yelled, "He says they probably have enough, but it won't hurt to bring a small basket full."

It was Ash Wednesday. By Friday morning the main streets of Panajachel would be covered with flower carpets that Jesus Christ — dragging his cross — would pass over on his way to Calvary. They would be further disturbed when the procession bearing his coffin to the cemetery followed the same route. For years Eliseo had volunteered to supervise preparations for both the processions and the crucifixion. It was his happiest time of year. Because he put so much money and time into Holy Week, the judges always awarded his family's carpet a prize in one category or another, usually the largest. Carolina had helped every Holy Week since she was a child, her excuse of recent years to come over from the Esperanza even ahead of her family. So she was up early Thursday morning, picking petals just in case. On her way into town she passed Mario Ajcojom, playing *taba* with friends in the street. "Any news from Francisco?" she asked with as much casualness as she could muster.

Mario didn't recognize her at first. It had been a year since he'd seen Carolina, and she'd put on some weight. Her hair was different somehow, too, but she was just as pretty, he decided. He refused to answer immediately and took his turn throwing the heads-and-tails bone to let her know he didn't appreciate how sad she'd made Francisco. Mario had no idea what she'd done, but whatever it was, it had meant his brother never came home anymore. The bone came up heads and Mario won another centavo. He tossed the *taba* again.

Carolina stood awkwardly, not knowing what to make of his rudeness. Elena, too — at Christmas — had seemed strangely aloof. Whatever the reason for Francisco staying away, it was making them angry with her. She had asked Eliseo about it, wondering if Rodolfo and Elena had put their foot down about Francisco seeing her, but he had been reassuring on that score.

"Haven't heard much," Mario said abruptly, as she started to walk away.

"Is he still at the barracks?"

"Sure, he's still there. Must like it real well, 'cause he never comes home!"

"But how is he?"

Mario didn't know what more to say...it wasn't any of her business! "Dunno. He doesn't write much. We got a letter finally a few days ago, though. He can't get away even for Holy Week, it seems."

"So that's that!" she sighed under her breath and marched off. She grew even angrier as she approached the store and saw that the carpet was virtually finished! She let her feelings show to Eliseo, working behind the counter. "Why didn't you send someone to tell me you don't need me after all?"

"Because that wasn't the real reason I wanted you to come," he said mysteriously. "Come inside quickly; I need to talk to you." Nobody else was available to mind the store, and after locking up he sat down with her in the kitchen. "It's about Francisco...I went to see him."

She trembled with excitement, or fear, and braced herself for she knew not what.

"Not a soul except Luisa knows I went, and I wanted to get you away from the Primavera so I could have the kind of talk I should have had with you months ago."

The tone of his voice had Carolina on the edge of her chair; clearly he'd found out and was going to tell her what had happened!

"I gather that you still haven't been told by your grandmother what happened the night when you and Francisco met on your launch, the night of the eclipse?" He knew the answer from the color draining from her face. "Eduardo suspected that you two had been together at the boat, so he went looking for

178

Francisco. He found him before —" Carolina wasn't listening. She had slumped down, and he lifted her from the chair to lay her out on the floor, propping her feet up on the chair. With his handkerchief he brought some water from the sink and wiped her forehead until the color began to return and she opened her eyes.

"Eliseo?" she finally whispered, "tell me, honestly, is Francisco all right? Did Papa hurt him? How...*how* could my father do anything to him...or to *me*, his own *daughter?*"

"Don't know, Carolina...I *really* don't know. Never could understand your father. But there isn't time to talk about why he did what he did. The fact is, he did hurt Francisco terribly, more in his mind than his body, and it's because of this that Francisco doesn't come home."

Carolina had stopped listening again, daring to imagine what must have happened to produce such fear in as stubborn a man as Francisco. But at least she understood now why there had been no word...or *did* she understand? No, it still didn't make sense. He might have had sufficient reason to stay away, but he certainly could have found some way to at least get a message to her, to explain. It had been eighteen months after all! "But why has it taken this long for him to communicate with even you? He couldn't have been *that* afraid of Papa!"

"No, not really afraid of him. But Eduardo threatened him...said that if you two ever got together again or if Francisco even came home before you had found a suitable husband, he would see to it that Rodolfo lost his job."

"Oh, Papa, how *could* you? Eliseo, how *could* he threaten something as cruel as that just because we —"

"Carolina, you simply don't understand how nervous you've made your folks all these years by making over Francisco so much! Eduardo feels uncomfortable about the whole Ajcojom family. It's not primarily about their being Indian. I'm convinced that it isn't even primarily about Francisco. It's about Rodolfo. Your father, and your mother even more so, never would be able to accept your being in love with *Rodolfo's* son."

"But *why?*"

Eliseo didn't know how much he ought to tell the poor woman, but decided it best to stop at this. "I don't fully understand myself; I just know I'm right. Now, Carolina, I didn't sneak you in here just to tell you why Francisco has stayed away. The painful thing I have to tell you is that Francisco's changed. He isn't like he used to be...so good-natured, so witty. He's grown old since you last saw him. I'm not sure you would recognize him. I didn't at first. He's also very discouraged with the army...knows that he'll never be an officer like Max soon will be. Francisco's had all the spunk taken out of him, Carolina, pretty discouraged with who he is. He's resigned to never being happy again, and that's about the worst thing that can happen to a fellow his age. And the *reason* for this is his thinking all these months that you probably learned what your father did and said...and that your folks convinced you it was best for things to be this way. Since he never heard from you...not even a letter...he's become this way. He couldn't even tell his folks. After all, he knows his folks weren't too excited about the two of you, either! It would have been hard for him to admit even to them about the eclipse night."

"I hadn't thought about that...even his *parents* don't know why he has stayed away?"

"No, no idea, and that's why they've suffered so, thinking that you decided you didn't love him and probably told him so that night. So, Carolina, what I need to know now is whether, after learning all of this, you wish for Francisco to know that it was only because of the misunderstanding your father wanted to create that the two of you have been so disappointed with each other? You see, I haven't known how you really feel down deep about Francisco. I haven't known whether at some point you learned what happened and decided that it *was* for the best that it worked out this way."

Carolina now was sitting on the floor, hands clasped around her knees. Eliseo was at the table, shifting uneasily lest he hadn't explained things well. What would the poor girl be thinking? How *did* she feel about Francisco after all these months? He had heard rumors of her being courted by the school teacher's son in Santiago Atitlan.

"I want to write to him," she said finally in a steady, determined voice. "Maybe he has changed, like you say, but somehow I think not really, not permanently anyway. If he knows that I have suffered in my heart just as much as he has...that surely will help. You don't *know* how much better I feel already, just knowing that he didn't choose for it to be this way. I had decided that he didn't really love me, hard as it was to believe after...after being with him that night...." Her voice trailed off, and she bowed her head sobbing.

Eliseo had to wait even to regain his composure, before announcing, "Then, my dear, I have a very big surprise for you! You won't need to write that letter to your love! Francisco is in the yard out back. He walked down from Los Encuentros last night. We arranged it when we talked. But *no one, absolutely* no one, can know he's here! I'll leave the two of you alone while you talk all this over. He's going back on the noon bus."

She didn't listen beyond the "yard out back," and got slowly to her feet in utter disbelief. She was trembling violently, and Eliseo feared that she was in danger of fainting again. "Come now, Carolina, get a hold of yourself! You look like you've seen a ghost."

She stared at Eliseo while fighting back the tears, then threw her arms around his neck and kissed him on the lips. "Oh, thank you, *thank you,* and she was out the back door. Eliseo wiped away his own tears, glanced through the window at the couple standing with hands clasped at arms length, and left the kitchen.

"Hope this isn't a big mistake," Eliseo sighed, as he locked up the store again and left to join the group of Ladino youths who had volunteered to be the 'Jews' in that evening's betrayal and capture of Jesus. He would need to be back in an hour and a half to make sure that Francisco was on that bus. Since it appeared that Carolina indeed was *not* over her infatuation with the fellow, she might be capable of confronting even her father. At least *Francisco* now knew about Victoria and Eduardo, understanding the full implications of why he and Carolina simply must not be seen together for the foreseeable future. Perhaps Francisco would decide to tell Carolina about Victoria. But despite all the risks, Eliseo was pleased with himself for thinking of this way to get the couple together. At least they would now stop blaming each other.

Eliseo was so deep in thought that he had walked on two flower carpets before the pharmacist's wife yelled at him from her doorway. He apologized and stopped to repair the damage. "I've had to repair it twice already," she said, joining him to help. "Believers carrying benches acted like it wasn't even here."

"Carrying benches? Where to?

"Other side of the river. Seems they're going to have a prayer meeting at Calixtro's house tonight and again tomorrow while we Catholics are processioning here."

"Glad you told me," said Eliseo. "I was going to hide Christ's statue over there for the capture this evening. To avoid trouble I'll hide it at the Primavera instead." He hurried on to the town hall, arriving in time to settle an argument about whose turn it was to play the part of Judas. Solomon would do it, and the next fifteen minutes were spent rehearsing lines.

181

"Where do I lead the Jews to find the statue?" Solomon asked "— other side of the river again, like last year?"

"Nope," smiled Eliseo mysteriously. "All I'll tell you is that he'll be somewhere in the Primavera coffee groves. Look for the candles. After you fellows find him, put a rope around both the statue and Solomon — our Judas for this year — and bring them back to the church. The secretary will be here in the office to unlock the jail. Then, after the procession tomorrow morning, come to the church to help with the crucifixion."

"What's this we hear about Indians quarreling over the cross for the crucifixion?" asked Solomon.

"Well, for years old Santos Locon has been head of the group that puts up the cross and takes it down. He keeps the cross and tools at his house along with the Virgin Dolores, saint for the cross. He's been making it hard for anyone else to take over that duty, I expect because of the money and liquor he gets for doing it. So finally the elders marched over and took everything away the other night. Santos took after them with a machete, and now he's in jail."

"You mean I have to be locked up with *him!*"

"Just for a few minutes," laughed Eliseo "— long enough for the crowd to tell you what they think of Christ's betrayer!"

"Seems like we ought to make Santos be Judas!"

Eliseo had to admit that wouldn't be a bad idea.

"What do I do after I'm let out of jail?"

"You get killed on Saturday!" snorted a companion.

"Come to the churchyard around ten o'clock Saturday," said Eliseo, "where the Judas straw dummy always sits. Let kids pretend to beat you before we set fire to the dummy. Act like they're really hurting you, and I'll treat you to a drink at the store afterwards."

The bus driver honked to announce his departure from the town center. Leaving the boys to talk about costumes, Eliseo hurried back to the store, straw hat in hand. He reached the corner in time to see Francisco wave down the bus. Carolina wasn't in sight. She must have left the store ahead of him. Eliseo breathed a sign of relief.

———

At the edge of town Francisco smiled at Carolina who barely looked up as his bus passed. She must still be pouting. "You could get off the bus above the Primavera and wait in the coffee until dark," she had begged as she left him at the store "— and I *am* going to be at the launch tonight, in case you change your mind!" To make sure she didn't say something foolish to her father when she got back to the plantation house of Pancho and Beatriz, he'd promised to think about it. Such a dilemma! He hadn't told her about Victoria, lest she not be able to control her anger at her father. And yet, to spend the evening with her was almost too tempting. Especially since she was so convinced that it would be perfectly safe. Her folks would be going up to Solola with Beatriz, Pancho, and Arcadia for dinner and the evening with Carmen's mother.

But how Carolina really felt about him now, he still wasn't sure. It could be that she was just feeling sorry for him after all her father had put him through. And while they might be able to rendezvous safely this time, there was no way it could go on without Eduardo eventually finding out. Eliseo was right. He had to stay on the bus and get back to the barracks.

The driver shifted down to begin the climb from the delta. As they approached the Primavera turnoff, Francisco leaned out the window to get a good look at the plantation house, his family's cottage almost hidden by banana trees, and the launch moored at the dock. The bus rounded the curve, and suddenly there was his sister Margarita right below him walking toward town. Their eyes met for a second, before he quickly leaned back. Could she possibly have recognized him through the dark sunglasses? If only he hadn't looked so startled himself. And in a few minutes she would meet Carolina returning from the store. Damn it! He couldn't leave without knowing if he had been recognized; if he had been, Margarita certainly would be quizzing Carolina about what she knew. A half kilometer above the turnoff he went to the front of the bus to explain that he had left something behind. As the bus disappeared around the next bend he hurried down the embankment into coffee trees.

Later that afternoon, Eliseo went to the church to get the statue of 'Christ on the donkey' to hide at the Primavera. The *mayordomos* of Panajachel's three remaining *cofradias* were washing the feet of the Apostles, twelve young Indian boys chosen by the elders. Their mothers stood behind them while the *mayordomos* took turns washing each boy's feet with water and sour-orange blossoms. "Not like the old days," thought Eliseo as he watched the perfunctory washing and kissing of feet. The sacristan dutifully distributed to the apostles the tools used in Christ's punishment and crucifixion: hammer, small cross, a branch, crown of thorns, small ladder, the wooden sword and spear, a whip with six points, and then a nail for each hand and foot to the last four Apostles. While

Father Jacobo explained their responsibilities during the procession, his sacristan gave their mothers small loaves of white bread.

"Depressing!" said Eliseo to Jacobo when the others had left the church. "Remember back before the depression years when the *mayordomos* for San Isidro *cofradia* used to kill a bull and send *pulique* stew to the homes of all the Apostles and Jews?" Jacobo nodded, for the moment wishing that the *cofradia* for San Isidro were still active. The *mayordomos'* wives also had made crowns of flowers and hand-woven clothes for the Apostles to wear. Now it fell to him to buy the bread and pay a Ladina to make their costumes on her sewing machine.

———

Francisco was resting in the coffee grove when he glimpsed someone wandering through the trees. He crept closer until he saw to his consternation that it was Eliseo, looking for someone. That someone surely was himself, but why Eliseo would be spending his time looking for him made no sense unless for some crazy reason Carolina had told him...maybe through Margarita...that she anticipated he would be hiding out here. He considered simply announcing his whereabouts and facing Eliseo's anger for so unwisely ignoring his advice. But he retreated instead deeper into the grove, weighing whether he shouldn't just get back to the barracks as soon as possible. That would mean the early morning bus, and spending a long cold night right where he was. Damn!

After Eliseo had chosen his spot and made an altar of stones supporting the statue, he decided to pay Arcadia a visit at the plantation house. He found her sitting alone on the veranda. "Came out here to get away from the brothers-in-law," she said by way of greeting. "Just listen to them! Like two cocks after the same hen. Been at it ever since Eduardo's family arrived yesterday, and there are still two days left of the weekend! At least this evening will provide a lull in their squabbling...we all are invited up to Solola to the governor's mansion."

Eliseo warily mounted the stairs to survey the situation. He had no stomach for encountering an angry Eduardo. "Max here, too?"

"No, he wisely stayed in the city to avoid the tension. It's been this way ever since January's harvest when Eduardo couldn't find enough pickers. Ubico's cursed order on behalf of local workers is tearing this family apart! Pancho offered to send some of our Primavera regulars over to help with pruning at the Esperanza, but that just made things worse. Truth is, Eduardo has gotten spoiled, letting Pancho and Rodolfo do his recruiting for him this side of the lake. Serves him right for relying on Panajachel workers so much in the first place!"

"Well," added Eliseo, sitting down beside his half-sister, "Eduardo doesn't help matters by making Indians work longer than they've agreed to before he'll sign their work books."

"It's worse than that," whispered Arcadia. "Pancho told me that a fellow from San Jorge who sometimes works here was telling our workers that when he got sick and asked to leave the Esperanza early, Eduardo's foreman agreed to sign his book but then refused to pay him a single centavo!"

Eliseo was too nervous to sit and suggested that they take a walk. After helping his frail sister down the stairs, they walked to the statue to light the altar's candles. En route he shared with her his decision to bring Carolina and Francisco together.

"But you're sure he left?" she said anxiously when it sank in that Carolina had been with Francisco all morning. No wonder that the girl had seemed so distracted since returning from town.

"Positive. Saw him off on the bus myself."

Arcadia carefully looked around before continuing. "The way Eduardo is behaving, no Ajcojom is safe around here if you ask me. He's so convinced that Rodolfo and Lazaro are the cause of all his woes. Pancho has seen to it that Rodolfo is needed over in Santa Catarina every day 'til Sunday when Eduardo's family goes home."

Eliseo stopped fanning and returned his hat to its customary perch at the back of his head. The din of a crowd was rising in town. "The Jews are coming, so I'd best be joining them. Do you really worry about Eduardo doing something to Rodolfo?"

She waited to respond until he had helped her up the steps. "Maybe not Rodolfo, frightened of him as he is, but it worries me the way he talks about Lazaro. And I hope you are right about Francisco heading back...this would *not* be the weekend for Eduardo to meet up with him here!"

———

Francisco was still hiding when the Jews and accompanying crowd descended on the grove. He retreated still deeper toward the Solola road, totally panicked, as a group of young men fanned out through the trees. "He's not over here," yelled one to a companion as he ran by, barely five meters from Francisco. Francisco began to shake from fright. But just as suddenly the crowd erupted into laughter. He made his way cautiously back toward the banana grove, spotting a youth bound with rope being pushed along the path. And then he remembered what day it was: "Jews with Judas!" Chuckling with relief, he watched them pass before picking a banana and lying down to collect himself.

It was dark an hour later when Pancho's car started up at the plantation house. "The family invited to Solola," Carolina had told him, and while she had promised to stay at home and be at the boat, she might have changed her mind if needing to reassure Margarita that everyone at the Primavera had gone to Solola for the evening. He moved within view of the lane to watch the car pass, but to his surprise it stopped before reaching the grove. There was no one in the rumble seat, where Carolina would have opted to ride. Eduardo got out and walked quickly toward the shacks of Pancho's regular workers. Staying within cover of the grove, Francisco moved to where he could see Eduardo talking to one of the men. They were walking slowly toward him to seek the privacy of the grove, and Francisco caught a few words. Eduardo mentioned Ubico, and then it was talk about road work. Eduardo pointed toward the back of the Primavera, then took out his billfold. They shook hands after some money appeared to change hands and before Eduardo hurried back to the car. Francisco noted the shack to which the fellow returned and stood pondering the little he had heard until the car lights disappeared up the road.

Before he was really ready for her, Francisco heard Carolina running toward the beach. Partly to tease but mostly to hide his uncertainty over being with her again like this, he moved to the rear of the launch — behind the pilot's chair — and knelt out of view.

"Oh, Francisco, *why* aren't you here," she fumed in exasperation as she stepped from the wharf to the bow, then sat down on the bow to study the growing darkness for some sign of movement. For five minutes she sat, her back to Francisco, who — not knowing what to say — on an unkind impulse pushed the starter to turn over the motor.

The poor woman almost tumbled out of the boat, catching herself just in time and straightening up angrily to let Francisco know she was not impressed with his gallantry. For his part, embarrassed, he untied the mooring rope, put the boat into reverse, and eased it out to head toward the center of the lake. Neither of them had yet said a word, and didn't until they were well offshore and he had cut the motor.

"I didn't expect you to be here..." she ventured finally, unfolding one of the two blankets she had brought and putting it around her shoulders.

186

"I shouldn't be, but I was afraid that Margarita recognized me when the bus passed right by her going slowly up the hill. The window was open and I was looking out at the delta. Our eyes met — just a few feet apart — but with my sunglasses I couldn't see her expression to be able to tell. I figured that within minutes she would be meeting up with you as you were walking to the Primavera. I had to know, lest I was leaving a real mess for you and Eliseo here."

"We passed each other all right, but she ignored me — like she has ever since you left all of us the last time. She would have acted differently if she suspected that you were on that bus. There's another blanket here, if you're cold and feel like joining me."

"I'm more nervous than cold. It isn't the same, is it? And I didn't help matters with that scare...can you forgive me?"

She answered only his first question. "No, but then there's probably no way it could be like that again, after all we've both been through," she said flatly.

"That was both the happiest and saddest night of my life. I don't know how to feel about it anymore," he said simply.

"That's such a shame," she murmured, softening. "It was pure joy for me. Do you know, Francisco, I waited out here all night a year ago tonight? But then at the procession on Good Friday I learned from Margarita that you weren't coming home. I was devastated...decided you must have fallen in love with some girl in Quetzaltenango."

"Would've been a hell of a lot easier if I had..."

"I've tried to fall in love," Carolina admitted slowly "— a fellow across the lake has been persistent. We met a year ago. Mama finally convinced me I was getting too old to wait any longer for the perfect man to come along. And I couldn't tell her that I had already found you! So I gave in and started dating Daniel Mazariegos, a teacher in the school there. He proposed last month...and I finally told him I would —"

"Too *old!* You're only twenty," interrupted Francisco, as though he hadn't heard the rest. "To think, I've been in love with you at least six years, and here he's known you only one..." His voice trailed off, as he stood up to revive the circulation in his legs.

"Does it help to know that I don't love him as much as —"

"You're just saying that! Of course you love him...you'll soon forget all about Francisco Rosales —"

"Rosales?"

"Yes, Rosales Lopez. That's who I am now, which is the same as saying I really don't know *who* I am anymore."

"Oh, you're just feeling sorry for yourself, stupid!" she pouted, pulling him down beside her. "Don't you care that I love you, have always loved you, and *still* will, even when I'm married with a family? Francisco, tell me truly, doesn't that matter to you anymore?"

Francisco was silent, thinking, until she wondered if he was falling asleep. She lay down herself, her head in his lap. "Of course, Carolina...that's all that really matters to me anymore," he sighed finally "— but I've got to get on with things and find a wife myself. I'll go out of my mind if I don't."

"Well of course you do, silly, but for tonight can't we just forget about my Daniel and your whoever-she-turns-out-to-be? Let's forget about these past terrible eighteen months and pretend the eclipse didn't happen that night." The stirring beneath her head was all the answer she needed, and smiling at the memory she sat up so they could kiss.

They took turns kissing, exploring with their lips until abruptly he stood up and began to undress. As startled again as she had been by the motor, she rose to protest. But he quickly, gently laid a finger across her lips to silence her and continued disrobing down to his shorts. Then, as she was asking herself if he could possibly be expecting her to do the same, he abruptly turned and dived over the side of the boat.

Once recovered from this third shock in rapid succession, Carolina giggled in relief and — on her own impulse — followed his example. And not to be outdone, she left even her bra on the seat before climbing to the bow to give him a good, full look before arching her back and artfully launching her lithe body in his direction in a perfect swan dive. She was a long time in surfacing, and he was worrisomely treading water when she suddenly popped up right in front of him, doubly startling him with her hand at his crotch. She got a good hold through his shorts, said that now they were even, and refused to let go until he enveloped her in his arms. She in turn put hers about his neck for a very wet kiss.

Then they turned over on their backs — the water perfectly smooth — her left hand in his right, to float and enjoy the celestial panorama of Santiago's Road (the Milky Way) stretching from the southern horizon of cliffs damming the lake and continuing directly overhead on north as far as their heads could strain to see. Carolina got a nose full of water in the process and let go of hands to regain her equilibrium. Grabbing onto his shorts to help her stretch out prone again, she teased, "Not fair! You have an extra leg down there to help you keep afloat!"

"Thanks to that look at you on the bow. God, Carolina, but you're beautiful!" and he returned to treading water to admire her breasts in the moonlight on her floating body. He couldn't resist, and she didn't object, as he slipped his arm under her back to kiss the closest nipple, erect from the cool water.

"If you find me so, my love, I am grateful! But in this setting, on such a perfect night, I dare say that you would find just about anybody attractive! Just look at this sky, these volcanoes..."

"And I, my love, dare say that we're the only souls out here...certainly the only ones floating around stark naked to entertain the firmament. For tonight, Carolina, Lake Atitlan is its Owner's gift to just you and me...our own private lake at the center of the world. Could there be anything more perfect? The water isn't even cold, after that initial shock of the dive. I do believe that I could swim to shore from here. And perhaps I should, Carolina, for we both know what is bound to happen if we return to the launch together."

"Um hmm!" she said, squeezing his hand.

"So, Mrs. Carolina Mazariegos-to-be, wouldn't it be best if I started swimming?"

"Well, Mr. Ajcojom...I'm not at all sure that I know you well enough yet. But since I have never driven this boat, I guess my *slight* preference is for you to climb back in with me." And with another squeeze, she let go and started swimming toward the launch. But upon taking a good look at how far it had drifted, she suddenly panicked. "Help, Francisco, I can't make it that far!"

"Not to worry, Carolina...You'll be just fine. Just dog paddle for a moment while you relax and calm down." He caught up with her, and from behind adroitly slipped his right arm under her right shoulder and laid her out prone — his left arm across her chest. Before she could panic any further, her head — nose and mouth above water — was supported firmly against his chest as he commenced side-stroking toward the launch.

"My, but that was close! How did you learn to do this?"

"They taught us life-saving techniques in our first-aid class at the barracks. At the time I couldn't imagine ever needing to save someone's life in the water, but I'm glad I paid attention!"

"Sure is cozy," she murmured, now fully relaxed and helping with her own legs. "The lengths to which a girl won't go to find herself in *this* position. You can tow me all around the lake if you wish, soldier."

"Afraid not, Ma'am. We're taught not to take advantage of people whose lives we save. Your only options are my swimming to shore alone after depositing you safely on board, or we *both* use the boat!"

"Hmm...but in the boat can we still maintain this position?"

"Well, if you insist, Ma'am. But I'll be tuckered out by the time I get you to the boat, so from then on you'll have to do all the work. Okay?"

Once in the launch, they used one blanket to dry themselves — she him, and then he her.

They laid the other blanket out on the floor for their bed. Then they resumed where they had left off before his sudden dive into the lake: kissing and caressing until Carolina sensed that he was in need of a more vigorous full body massage to relax adequately from her rescue. That was the beginning of the most pleasurable hour of Francisco's life. Her patience with him taught him a valued lesson. He reciprocated with her, providing Carolina a glimpse of how it would be for her when it could be in a comfortable bed without any worries. But even on the floor of a gently rocking boat she was hopelessly adrift in emotions utterly new to her when his final thrusting bore down deeply. So deeply that each sensed the bittersweet sobbing in the other's soul.

Francisco fell asleep, so soundly that Carolina hadn't the heart to awaken him. She savored their closeness, he still comfortingly within her, until the church bell tolled ten o'clock.

"Francisco, you must wake up, sweetheart...I'm getting cold and need to get back to the house before long." He didn't respond, so she eased out from beneath him and gently caressed him awake.

"Oh, Carolina, that feels *so* good. Don't stop. You're ready again so soon?"

"Well, *you* sure seem to be, soldier." she replied tenderly. But we can't take the chance. Mama said to expect them home around 11:00. Luckily we'll have at least a half hour's warning. We'll begin seeing car lights soon after they leave Solola. We have been so lucky. It would have been impossible to take the launch out like this — to be this relaxed — if it hadn't worked out for me to be home alone. Max could so easily have decided to join us for the weekend, and if he had I now would be sharing the evening with a brother rather than with you — feeling mighty sorry for myself!"

190

"Not to mention this morning's luck of my running into a sister. Otherwise, I would be in Quetzaltenango by now feeling a whole lot sorrier for myself than I am."

"Don't tell me that after these three hours with me you're *still* feeling sorry for yourself?"

"Afraid so...does Daniel know yet how blissful his nights are going to be the rest of his —"

She kissed him quickly to stifle the question she preferred he not ask. As with Francisco now, she had made love with Daniel only once — on the ground — after agreeing to marry him. She had hoped that making love with him would give her more of the passion she felt for Francisco, but he had been too eager...too impatient. Tonight's experience with Francisco wasn't going to help with *that* dilemma.

Francisco sensed that she didn't want to talk about Daniel and changed the subject. "Carolina, remember what I told you about eclipses causing miscarriages?"

"I certainly do...why?"

"I've decided that they don't. I think it's just a superstition."

"I decided that, too," she said, "after asking the cook here about it. She said that her mother told her the moon wants to take the babies with her. But if Indians believe that the moon is a spirit, like you say, then thinking that way about eclipses is reasonable enough." She was delighted to have an opening to tell him what she had been doing. "I've asked the cook here and our Indian help at home to tell me everything like this that they can remember. And when Grandma Arcadia realized what I was up to, she confided that she also is fascinated with Indian beliefs and customs. Her brother, Eliseo, has been even more so all of his life. But with not only Oscar, but Max and especially Beatriz joining her husband in denigrating Indian ways, she early on in her marriage decided to keep that interest to herself. Now, sharing my secret, she has taught me much of what she learned growing up in Argueta among mostly Indians. So, *mi amor,* you would be surprised with how smart a *natural* wife I could be!"

With that he pulled her over for a final deep kiss, before getting up, pulling her to her feet, and getting dressed. "Well, I guess that I won't feel sorry for myself after all...me wanting a Ladina wife and you wanting to become a *natural.*"

"Francisco," she said quietly after they had moored the launch and were walking to the house, "I hope that you marry an Indian. Seriously, I truly fear that

191

you'll be disappointed with any Ladina other than me. May I tell you that I believe you still are very Indian in your soul? There can't be many Ladina women who would understand and appreciate that quality about you as much as I do."

He knew she was serious, and didn't respond. When he took his leave, he said, "I have a favor to ask. Find out who lives in the third shack from the east end, behind the banana grove. Then ask Eliseo if he knows any reason why whoever lives there might be an enemy of my family. If he does, tell him to warn Rodolfo and Lazaro to be on their guard around that man. Write to tell me what you learn."

"But why?"

"I can't say more, just a hunch."

"All right, I'll do it right away. *Vayas con Dios,* my love, and remember, marry a *natural!*"

It was the kindest thing she could have told him, and he thought about it all the long, lonely walk up the mountain to Solola to catch the early morning bus back to Quetzaltenango.

A week later her letter awaited him following afternoon field exercises at the barracks.

> Dearest Francisco,
>
> I did my own checking and learned that Juan de Dios Quenum lives in that third shack. He is a Catarineco who used to work for Papa on the Esperanza. Papa arranged for him to trade with one of Uncle Pancho's workers when Juan married a Catarineca and wanted to move back to the north side of the lake. Since Eliseo knows the financial status of almost everybody in Panajachel and Santa Catarina, I asked him what he knew about Juan's situation. Eliseo says that his family lost their land when they pawned it to my grandfather years ago. Juan complains a lot about that when he gets drunk at the store. Juan stays in debt at the store almost constantly, but he paid off his debt right after Semana Santa. Whether Juan had a run in with Rodolfo over Primavera work, or blames Rodolfo for his having lost his land over there, Eliseo can't say. But everybody knows that my father bribed a few Catarinecos to spy on Rodolfo over the years, and since Papa seems to con-

sider Juan an especially dependable worker, Eliseo wonders if perhaps Juan wasn't one of those informers. Eliseo doesn't want to say anything to Rodolfo, however, until I can tell him why I'm so suspicious!

After our talk I decided to tell Daniel and the folks that I wanted the wedding as soon as possible. That way you can start coming home again soon to see your family. The wedding will be June 1, and we'll be moving to the capital. Daniel will work in my uncle's store there. Maybe I can see you again on All Souls' Day? I'll wait for you in the cemetery! I love you, Francisco...always will. And can either of us ever forget the precious gift of that night alone on our lake at the center of the world? It was pure bliss!

Your Carolina

Chapter Sixteen

Francisco did not have to wait the half year until All Souls to next encounter Carolina in the Panajachel cemetery. They met, standing on opposite sides of his mother's grave, just two months later. He hadn't realized that Elena was failing so rapidly. No one had. For several years they'd known she had tuberculosis, but coughing had become so much her habit that not even Rodolfo thought much about the blood that she'd mentioned from time to time.

"Papa, I'd have come home in a moment if I'd known Mama was this sick!" "he repeated, back at the house after her burial. He bore his father's outbursts with patient resignation. It wasn't the time to explain his absence of almost two years. Not with Eduardo, the cause of it all, only one uncontrollable impulse away.

As for himself, Francisco had felt surprisingly relaxed around Eduardo at the cemetery. Casually greeting the Ramirez family had not been difficult, made easier by the diversion of the pet monkey that Carolina had brought along. Surely Eduardo would be satisfied that he had nothing to worry about from Francisco. And if Eduardo and Carmen had come to pay their respects to the Ajcojoms with any suspicions about Carolina's feelings toward Francisco and his family, they would have left reassured. Carolina had been so coolly formal that Eliseo had taken Francisco aside to ask if their meeting at his store had ended on a different note from its beginning. But when Carolina's eyes had first met his across the grave, the trace of a proffered kiss thrown his direction as her eyes dropped to her hands on her belly suggested that nothing had changed. Was she telling him that she was pregnant...so soon! But as Francisco crawled into bed that night and relived their love-making, his resignation embraced never knowing Carolina that way again. She might be pregnant, but it more than likely was Daniel's child.

But it was those same memories of love-making that had enabled Carolina to hide so convincingly her contrary assumption. If she could have one baby with Francisco, she would find a way to lie with him again. Carolina had come to the cemetery determined that absolutely no one, on thinking back months later, could suspect the baby to be Francisco's. She had missed one month's period, and while it would as likely be Daniel's as Francisco's, she had not again lain with Daniel. She supposed she felt guilty, but in any case had told him she wanted to await their wedding night. Regardless of the father, the baby would resemble

194

Francisco given her feelings. Pregnancy hadn't even occurred to her after lying with Daniel, but she'd thought about little else the day after truly making love with Francisco. Skin color would likely be darker than hers in either case. Daniel was dark for a Ladino. But if exceptionally dark because of Francisco, then everyone would assume that her unwise attachment to a monkey was to blame.

Carolina was a happy bride the first of June. Francisco thought better of attending, but Rodolfo and Margarita accepted the family's invitation. Eduardo couldn't resist telling them that Carolina already was expecting.

———

Francisco's second two-year stint in the army ended in September. He decided that he'd had enough of barracks life and came home a few days before his 25th birthday the day of Saint Francis, October 4. Despite its persistent honking, people ignored the bus as it inched toward the only parking area police could keep clear in front of Panajachel's newly refurbished town hall. Francisco got off and climbed the stairs to survey the scene. He was noticed immediately, and Indians cautiously edged toward him. "They think that you're one of Ubico's soldiers," laughed a policeman standing on the porch. "Are you?" he quickly added, worried that he might have misjudged this stranger in soldier's uniform.

"Me? Hardly!" scoffed Francisco. "I just got out of the barracks in Quetzaltenango. Didn't have clothes of my own clean enough to wear home, so I walked off with my uniform! I'm Francisco Ros — Francisco Ajcojom...catching himself — son of Rodolfo Ajcojom who manages the Primavera west of town." He shook hands with the stranger, pleased that he'd been taken for a Ladino. "And who are you?"

"I came down from Solola to keep this crowd under control. Guess you haven't heard: Ubico's supposed to come through here on his way back to the capital."

By the time Francisco went to look for familiar faces in the market, he had learned more about Ubico's Solola visit than anyone else in Panajachel would know by day's end. For their president never came. Ubico had become famous for his sudden visits to remote communities. Accordingly, every town within twenty kilometers of the state capital had half expected him to come driving in. He had, in fact, planned to go down to the lake to accept the thanks he was assured from a grateful citizenry in Panajachel. He had so written Solola's governor several weeks before. But after his cool reception by the governor and leading families of Solola, no one — not even his own soldiers — knew what he planned to do. He had thought better of further antagonizing Solola officialdom by rubbing their noses in his Panajachel decree, and instead had gone up to Chichicastenango to meet with *cofradia* leaders and the elders who had walked to the capital to see him the year before. Since he had told Solola's chief of police that he might return in time to visit the lake by late afternoon, the market and adjoining streets were still crowded in eager anticipation. Eliseo had invited the elders to greet their President Ubico in full ceremonial regalia, but they were not about to announce their identity so flagrantly to a vengeful Solola governor's spies who undoubtedly would accompany Ubico on any appearance in Panajachel.

The market square lay adjacent to the side of the church, and on a low wall jutting at right angle from the front of the church Francisco found a spot to squeeze in for a look around. He had hoped to be inconspicuous, but to no avail. "Francisco!" shouted his brother from among the couple dozen boys also sitting atop the wall. "We didn't know when to expect you. The *President* is coming!"

Francisco shared with Mario and his friends what he had learned from the policeman before asking Mario about the rest of the family.

"Papa seems lots older...from his drinking. He drank for a whole month after Mama died. Seems to be less depressed now, though, largely because he knows that you're finally coming home to stay! Margarita was here buying meat a few minutes ago," Mario added, pointing toward a booth almost empty of pork and beef strips hanging in the window.

"I see her," said Francisco, jumping down to make his way through the throng toward his sister standing as tall as most men, even without a basket atop her head. She had stopped to talk with two women selling tortillas.

"If you're so sure that money is out there in the hill, then let's empty our baskets and go get it." Margarita said with a nervous laugh.

"Yes, let's do!" exclaimed one of the women, as she got to her feet and started to empty her basket.

"No, Juana. She means that if *you* know where there's money, then she'll go with you to get some!" laughed her companion.

Juana scowled when it became clear that she'd become the brunt of Margarita's teasing. She was about to retort when Francisco stepped forward to rescue his sister. After they were beyond earshot of the women, he asked, "What on earth was *that* all about?"

"These *naturales* are so ignorant and gullible! Somehow they've got the idea that Protestants get money from the Owner of the Hill. All we can figure is that somebody saw our tithe money being collected and assumed it was being passed out instead. Newcomers aren't allowed to attend business sessions, which makes them think that's when we divide up the money. Last Sunday Juana and her husband came for the first time, and now she wants me to take her to find all that money out there on the mountain! Why Catholics think we Protestants have all these dealings with the Hill's Owner is beyond my understanding."

"Oh, not so hard to understand, Sis. Our ancestors have been talking for a long, long time about buried money that the Hill's Owner lets lucky poor folks find. If it looks like someone's getting wealthy, what else are they supposed to think? You Believers *do* tend to be richer than the rest of us poor souls!" he teased.

"Well, only because we don't spend money on liquor, fireworks, and candles burning for the saints all the time!" she rejoined.

"It's not just that, and you know it," he countered with a smile. "It's as much because of all the Ladino jobs that you Believers have. Take your parents-in-law's store...and the barber over there by the wall. He's a Believer. The butcher is, too. I bet most of the carpenters out in the street buying lumber from cutters up in the valley are as well. Lazaro's boss is, isn't he?"

"Uh huh, Mariano is Pentecostal like us. How about soldiers at the barracks? Are many of them Believers?"

"A few, I reckon, but not many. Our officers make fun of Protestants, so even those who are don't talk about it."

"What a shame," she added, "when all we want is for people to be better able to help themselves."

"That's just the point. The president and his generals don't want Indians feeling independent and acting like Ladinos! Harder to keep us doing *their* work if we have hopes of keeping busy with our own."

The "us" and "we" weren't lost on Margarita, and she smiled. Her brother really *had* come home! "Speaking of work, dear Brother, what are your plans?"

"Haven't any."

"If you're interested in construction, Mariano can use some help. They're building a chapel for Pentecostals. Pay won't be much, but you can probably start right away if you want to. Lazaro's starting his two weeks of road work for the county next week, and Mariano needs someone to fill in for him."

Suddenly Francisco straightened. Ubico and road work, the only two references of which he was certain in Eduardo's late night exchange with Juan Quenum at the Primavera! "Road work? Where will he be assigned?"

197

"You passed it coming down from Solola, just beyond the cataract where the hillside slid down during this year's heavy rains. Buses have made a new road right over it. Earlier we were told it wouldn't be cleared 'til after Christmas, but I guess the governor changed his mind when he received Ubico's order exempting most everyone in Panajachel from plantation labor."

"Strange that they would ask Indians from here to work that far from home when San Jorge is so much closer. Must be an hour's walk each way. Why didn't Lazaro just pay the fine and be done with it?"

"We wanted him to, but he's stubborn...said people would think he's afraid to leave town. Half of the crew *is* from San Jorge...only five from here."

Francisco promised to give some thought to working for Mariano and left for home on the run. It made no sense to ask Indians to walk all that way from Panajachel, and it hardly could be a coincidence that Lazaro was assigned to the first road crew of the new dry season. Eduardo had pointed toward the back of the plantation in the direction of that landslide. If Eduardo had hired Juan Quenum to harm Lazaro, and a road crew accident was the plan, then either Eduardo had bribed someone in Solola or the governor himself was involved. Eduardo was, after all, the governor's daughter's father-in-law! By the time Francisco reached home he had decided what to do.

His homecoming visit with his father was the most relaxed and pleasant he could remember. After Mario's forewarning, Francisco wasn't surprised to find Rodolfo looking haggard. With no one to pluck his whiskers, there were more gray patches than Francisco recalled.

———

Francisco asked me if I felt as sad as I looked. I explained that I had just lost another tooth and maybe was avoiding smiling more than before. "I'm feeling pretty positive, actually — haven't had a drink for over a month now. I'm managing the Primavera again. We've gotten behind in the pruning, but are gradually catching up." Then, to my pleasant surprise, Francisco offered to help for a few days.

"Anyone from Santa Catarina working for you? I would enjoy getting to know another Catarineco."

Francisco certainly had changed! I couldn't recall his ever acknowledging that he was, at birth, a Catarineco. "Only Juan Quenum. He's not much more of a Catarineco than you are anymore, though! Hardly ever goes back to Santa Catarina. Doesn't get along that well with his wife's family. Still wears Catarineco clothes, though...the old style, red and white stripes without embroidery. He's

198

pruning back by the road to be close to where he's cutting firewood of evenings after work."

———

The next morning Francisco already was at work pruning when Juan arrived. They worked together until Francisco finished a day's assignment and pretended to start for home. Instead he followed the stream flowing from the cataract toward the deepest recesses of the Primavera. From there he would be able to observe Juan when he climbed to where he was cutting wood above the road. The fellow couldn't have been friendlier. Nor calmer, Francisco thought, recalling their conversation about the Vagrancy Law and Ubico's decision to exempt most of the men hereabouts. He showed no irritation that Catarinecos weren't included. Even when telling how his family had lost all their land to Oscar Ramirez, he showed no rancor. But then, if he was complicit in any plan to harm Francisco's brother-in-law, how else would he behave?

Within a few minutes after finding a comfortable spot to sit and wait, not far from where he had hidden when avoiding Eliseo and the Jews, Francisco spotted Juan walking up the road. Where the cut in the hillside above the road sloped gradually enough to be able to climb, he made his way up the exposed dirt and rock face of the incline. He disappeared into underbrush fifteen meters or so above the road, and within moments his machete could be heard. He was indeed cutting firewood. A half hour later he emerged carrying a load of wood. He carried it a considerable distance along the tree line to where Francisco could make out a large pile of neatly stacked wood. It was obvious that Juan had been cutting for a number of days. Francisco waited until he had cut a second load and watched him start down the incline for home with that load on his back. He would carry stacked wood down only as he had room to store it under his eaves. This was how *naturales* always did, and it seemed normal enough. Francisco was relieved.

The next afternoon it rained, and although Francisco decided to seek shelter, Juan kept on working. Said he wanted to finish his firewood cutting by week's end. When the rain abated, Francisco walked back toward the road to watch again. The woodcutting was a repeat of yesterday. Only as he was returning home after Juan had started down the hill with his final load, did Francisco ask himself why the fellow was stacking the wood so far away from where he was cutting. Why stack it where the embankment above the road was so steep that he would have to detour unnecessarily when ready to transfer that pile to his shack?

199

On Wednesday Francisco again started and finished work ahead of Juan by an hour. He waited in the grove until Juan had not only done his woodcutting but would have returned home far enough to be out of sight of anyone climbing to the stacked pile. It was dusk when Francisco reached and climbed the path up the embankment. He hoped he was mistaken, but on reaching the neatly stacked wood above the road his worst fear was confirmed. The wood looked innocent enough from below, but all that kept the pile from toppling and cascading down the steep embankment was a large log on the embankment side that could easily be kicked away. A cursory look at what lay below made clear why he'd selected this spot: boulders supporting tons of dirt were exposed below the wood, while below the boulders the bank had eroded away to make an avalanche both inevitable and deadly if the largest boulders could be dislodged. Even without a landslide, his wood was directly enough above the road to badly injure or kill anyone passing below.

It was an ingenious trap, the more so because he had made no effort to hide the fact that he was stacking it there. He could disappear in the underbrush after releasing the wood and be back across the road before anyone arrived on the scene. The only risk he ran was a landslide before he was ready, so precarious was the overhang. Francisco stepped back quickly lest his own weight spring the trap. Clearly the resumption of daily rains after this *canicula* interlude would increase the likelihood of the hoped for avalanche, but just one heavy rain also increased the likelihood of the land giving way even without a woodpile's assistance. While he was digesting the planning that had to have gone into such careful timing, the road crew came into view a couple minutes away. He watched Lazaro and his companions pass, dumbfounded at the sudden realization that Juan was prepared to sacrifice them as well to collect whatever money Eduardo had offered.

Francisco had trouble falling asleep that night, realizing the trap might be sprung any day now, conceivably even tomorrow morning or evening! Juan had said that he would be cutting wood through the week's end, but the rain's return might change that. It would happen when traffic along the road was the lowest, probably at dusk. But with people returning from Friday's Solola market even into the late afternoon, Juan wouldn't choose Friday. The work week ending at noon on Saturday ruled out the weekend. But the morrow — Thursday — even in the morning as the crew reported for work, couldn't be ruled out.

He was awake long before daybreak. Lest he awaken Mario and Rodolfo he didn't bother with breakfast and left the house to watch Juan's hut from the banana grove. Only after he saw the crew pass on the road...after he knew they were well past the woodpile...did he go back to bed. Then, to his relief, at noon Rodolfo announced to his workers that Pancho wanted the pruning done by week's end. With everybody diverted to pruning until dusk, Juan hardly would attempt anything even if this evening was his plan. Still weary, Francisco gratefully settled into the hammock for the rest of the afternoon. Nothing would happen before Monday.... Yes, in all likelihood it would be Monday at dusk.

It rained off and on throughout the weekend, and Monday promised more of the same. Francisco had promised Mariano, Lazaro's employer, at least half days of construction work the remaining week of Lazaro's road work; they had settled on nine o'clock until two o'clock each day before the rain commenced of late afternoons. Accordingly, by four o'clock on Monday Francisco had made his way to his accustomed hiding place in the coffee grove, just as a gentle rain commenced. Judging from the sound of machetes, only a few were still at work completing the pruning that hadn't gotten done on the weekend. As the rain grew heavier, first one and then another left for home, until one machete could still be heard. To make certain it was Juan's, Francisco crept toward the noise. Within moments Juan stopped working, hid his machete under a pile of newly cut limbs, and ran toward the road. Without his machete, clearly today was the plan!

Francisco followed and watched Juan look up and down the road before scrambling up the embankment. Part way up he tripped and slid in the mud several meters. Only when he had made it to the top did Francisco run through the grove to a point in the road where he could cross out of Juan's view.

Church bells were tolling five o-clock by the time Francisco finally was within sight of the woodpile. On hands and knees he approached until he could see Juan huddled beside the stack trying to keep out of the rain. He was rubbing his leg, bruised probably in the fall. Even with Juan thus distracted, to get close enough to avoid a fight was going to be risky. At least Juan had left his machete behind. He was about as tall and certainly stronger than Francisco. Had to be, to work at such a pace all day and then spend a couple more hours cutting oak each evening. He was facing pretty much toward Francisco, so with eyes glued on him Francisco snaked slowly through the underbrush until he judged he was twenty meters away. Still too far to avoid a fight, and only a half hour or so before the work crew would be heading their way. A stone beneath his stomach gave Francisco the idea. He felt around for others. He threw the largest well beyond

Juan, and fortunately it hit a tree. Juan froze. The noise of the second in a nearby thicket brought him to his feet, and he limped over to investigate. It was as much time as Francisco needed to reach the near end of the woodpile. Juan returned and sat down again, satisfied that it was only an animal. When Francisco leaped at him with his stick of wood, Juan had time only to look in disbelief.

Francisco couldn't be sure that the poor fellow was dead, but nor could he bring himself to hit him again. During four years in the army he had pondered how it would feel to kill with a rifle, and here — little more than a week out of the barracks — he had done it more cruelly with his own hands. He felt sadness more than remorse, sad to think that need for money or fear of a Ladino could bring a poor soul to this. How many others could Eduardo control this way? Would there be other Indians whom Lazaro and all Ajcojoms would now have to fear?

He went quickly through Juan's clothes, pocketing his workbook with its identification paper for any use it might be. Then he went to the edge of the cliff. There was no one in sight, no excuse to delay any longer. He rolled the body over the side of the embankment, sprang the trap, and leaped back as a deafening roar rose from below. The boulders must have gone, with so much ground around the woodpile continuing to slip away. But he couldn't risk looking and began the arduous walk, now without a path, around the hillside through underbrush protecting him from the multitude of eyes that must already be studying the avalanche. He was surprisingly relaxed, satisfied that the next road crew would find the remains of an unfortunate woodcutter who unwisely had picked a dangerous spot to stack his wood. When he finally reached the road and joined people rushing toward the cloud of dust, even he was dumbstruck. They might never find Juan's body!

—

Others who surveyed the debris thought it odd that Juan had chosen to stack his wood in such a precarious place. There was talk of little else that evening at the store, and Eliseo closed up early to go to the Ajcojoms. Never had he seen Rodolfo so disconsolate. No one had seen anything of Juan Quenum since morning; his poor wife was distraught lest he'd been buried in the slide. And Pancho was enraged that Rodolfo had let Juan cut firewood in the first place, since they were behind with pruning. Francisco held his tongue. His only suggestion was that his father take Pancho to see how much pruning Juan had done; Pancho didn't need to know that Francisco had helped him.

202

Eliseo decided not to worry Rodolfo with his fear that the slide might have been intended for Lazaro. Eliseo hadn't forgotten Carolina's inquiry about Juan Quenum. Obviously she had heard something that made her suspect he might be up to no good. Eliseo did mention it to Francisco, however, after Francisco offered to walk him to the end of the lane.

Francisco in turn was sorely tempted to share what he had overheard months earlier in the banana grove, but then Eliseo would know of Francisco's second night with Carolina. With Carolina pregnant, no one could know about that night. Instead, he suggested that Eliseo inquire in Solola how it was that the composition of that roadwork crew came to include men from Panajachel — Lazaro in particular. And since mayors usually did the actual choosing, why was it that Eliseo was bypassed this time?

———

Eliseo already had been chaffing under the latter slight, and welcomed the encouragement to inquire discreetly of the road administrator's Indian secretary — with whom he routinely conversed in Kaqchikel. To his satisfaction, since her boss was out of the office, she retrieved from his desk files the folder for the current crew. Eliseo was startled to find that Lazaro's name hadn't been on the initial list. In fact, there was nobody from Panajachel on the initial list, confirming what Margarita said had been rumored. "But how, then, did it get decided to make it a joint San Jorge and Panajachel crew? And why was I — as mayor — not asked to suggest names from Panajachel?" he asked.

The secretary shrugged, saying that her initial list of men — all from San Jorge — had been returned with a note to replace half with workers from Panajachel. Since time was short, the administrator had suggested that she choose men who had not been needed from Panajachel's last work crew roster. She had done that and returned it to her boss. That was the last she had had anything to do with this current work crew. She went to her own desk to retrieve her copy of that final revised roster.

Eliseo accordingly asked no more questions when, on perusing the final list, he noted to his dismay that one of the Panajachel names she had entered had been crossed off and replaced with 'Lazaro Tonon'! And there were copies of the subsequent letter, signed by the governor, that had been mailed to the ten men selected...the reason why the mayors of San Jorge and Panajachel had on this occasion been bypassed. Shaken, he gave the secretary ten pesos for her assistance, and left for home. But was it the governor who substituted Lazaro's name?

It probably was the administrator, but at whose request: the governor's or Eduardo's? Either one would have had the motive of revenge for Ubico's order. Eduardo would have had the additional, more personal motive for fingering Lazaro. Without knowing for certain who had been responsible for including Lazaro, both Lazaro and Francisco would have to be warned to be constantly vigilant. But telling Rodolfo, in his state of mind, would be too unkind.

———

At Lazaro's home that evening Francisco listened to what Eliseo had learned, but said little. Francisco's guess was that the governor might well have been miffed enough at Ubico to help Eduardo settle a score with the Ajcojoms, but that it wasn't likely that he had been involved in such detailed plotting against Lazaro. It was Eduardo they had to fear, but for now there was no harm in Lazaro and Eliseo believing it was the governor. About Eduardo Ramirez, something would have to be done. Lazaro's family could go back to Patzicia. But Rodolfo had nowhere to go. Sooner or later Eduardo would avenge himself on Rodolfo, if he couldn't get at Lazaro. At just how much risk he, himself, might be, Francisco spent little time pondering as he walked along the lake shore back to the Primavera to join Rodolfo for the night. Probably Eduardo would be content to let Francisco's fear and paranoia persist indefinitely, always uncertain as to what Eduardo might in time have in store for him. But the only eventuality that Francisco really needed to fear for the time being would be the Ramirez family's suspicion that Carolina's baby was, in fact, not Daniel's.

In this regard, upon Rodolfo's receiving from Eduardo confirmation of Carolina's pregnancy, Francisco had concluded that in all likelihood the baby was his. He might never know for sure, but Carolina certainly had enjoyed being so coy with her belly! Not long thereafter the significance of the pet monkey suddenly had dawned on him as well. If Carolina suspected that the baby was Francisco's, she would be worrying about how dark-skinned it would be. And she was counting on the Ramirezes and Daniel's family to blame darker skin than Daniel's on the monkey. It was commonplace among Ladinos to caution their pregnant women against emotional attachment to any dark pets, monkeys in particular, lest they be cursed with an *Indio*-appearing baby. In welcoming a baby that she suspected would be Francisco's, she was doing everything she could to protect both herself and Francisco from her family's suspicion and consequent wrath. In pondering whether he could bring himself to kill again, Francisco was really asking whether he could kill the man who might well turn out to be grandfather to his own child. It was almost too much to contemplate.

––––––––––––––––––

Francisco's prediction proved correct: after the next road crew had pushed enough of the debris down the hill to make the road passable, there was still no sign of Juan Quenum's body. Father Jacobo decided to pronounce him dead anyway. His widow planted a cross atop the remaining debris. It might be years before enough dirt eroded away to reveal his bones for removal to the cemetery in Santa Catarina.

Francisco grew steadily more despondent in the weeks that followed. Rodolfo was drinking again because of Margarita and Lazaro's talk of again moving back to Patzicia. Even Mario wanted to go. Unable to confide to anyone the depth of his anxiety, Francisco began to join his father in daily drinking. In his stupor, he concocted scheme after scheme for rendezvousing with Carolina, desperate to reconnect in any way possible. But it was the depth of their mutual love and anticipated parentage that prevented him, as well as her, from actually initiating any contact.

Ironically, it was the governor himself, who came to Francisco's rescue as he spiraled downward in self pity. Every town the size of Panajachel was supposed to have a militia corps of volunteers, but after the last drill instructor moved to the capital, the local volunteers stopped coming to their weekly practices. With the new mayor appointee due to take office the first of the year, it wouldn't do to have a poorly trained corps. The governor ordered Eliseo to appoint a new drill instructor, and Eliseo promptly appointed Francisco.

Within days of his first Sunday afternoon drill in the churchyard, the number of volunteers doubled. Eliseo was relieved and saw to it that in their free time the town's errand boys appointed by the elders whittled the likenesses of two dozen rifles for the corps. Although Francisco wasn't allowed a gun under the law — no Indian was, except while in the army — Eliseo sought permission for an exception in Francisco's case. "Without ammunition, what can be the harm?" he reasoned with the Solola district commander. A few days later an old rifle was assigned to the new Panajachel drill corps. With a rifle and dressed in his barracks uniform, everyone began calling Francisco *El Comandante*.

After the second week of exercises, one of the volunteers got up his courage to ask *El Comandante* to help him learn more reading and writing in Spanish than he had been able to get from four years in the Panajachel school. Andres began coming to the house three evenings a week, and it wasn't long before a cousin had asked to join the class. Then a somewhat older woman showed up one evening with the two cousins. *"Comandante,* this is my sister, Simona," said Andres. If you will do her the favor, she wishes to study with us, too."

"Have you finished school?" he asked, a bit skeptical about complying with the request.

"Yes, Sir," she answered politely. "I finished fourth grade three years ago."

"You remember Simona," called Mario from the other room. "She was in my class. Remember, in the parade?...you asked about her."

Simona, as well as Francisco, blushed, she wondering what Mario might have said, and what Francisco might have thought back then. That parade had been difficult for her, and so embarrassing for her mother that she had refused to watch. After arguing with her mother to let her go to school, and after persevering through all four years, Simona had been determined to walk in the parade no matter how much people gossiped.

"Simona Cosme?" laughed Eliseo, in response to Francisco's query the next day, "of course I know her. So stubbornly independent that her husband couldn't handle her! Twice she came to town council meetings to complain about his beatings. Finally left him. Has a baby and lives with her folks down by the lake. Her father's decent enough, but her mother's a real viper!"

Simona was as attracted to Francisco as he to her, but they had no chance to be alone until her brother's illness gave Francisco a chance to walk her home after class. Strolling along the beach, they talked about his life in the barracks and her difficulty with parents, living at home with a baby, until an hour had passed. When they reached her house he realized too late the trouble she was in. He listened outside to the berating her mother gave her. When the words turned to blows and he heard Simona crying, he sadly returned home and concluded it best to put her out of his mind. He wasn't surprised that she didn't come back to class until her brother was well enough to attend again. It was a week later, on a Wednesday. When she mentioned that her family was going to the Friday market and she wouldn't have time to come to Friday evening's class, his resolve weakened and he lied that he needed to go to Solola as well. Perhaps he would encounter her there.

He took the early morning bus and passed the Cosmes half way to Solola. He waited outside town at the tavern until they walked by. He waved to catch Simona's eye. She smiled her surprise, and he followed at a respectful distance while the family started their buying. When they were as close to the church as they likely would get, he walked by in a way to insure that she saw him, and entered the church.

"I didn't think you were serious," she said with a twinkle when she soon sat down on a back bench beside him. "Told Mother I would nurse Laurita here."

"I wanted to apologize for getting you into trouble last week. I had no idea it had gotten so late."

"No need to worry about that," she tried to reassure. "It was just that Laurita was colicky and Mother was at her wits end with her by the time I got home. She only made it worse, though. I was so upset by the time I fed her that my milk made her even fussier. Served both me and my mother right; Laurita kept us up half the night."

"Served us *all* right," Francisco laughed "— I didn't get much sleep that night either!" He could see why her husband had had such a time with Simona. She *was* spunky! Talked like a Ladina! But she was *natural* enough, and certainly beautiful. She shifted Laurita to her front and parted her *huipil* to expose as full and well proportioned a bosom as Francisco had imagined. The baby was plump and seemed healthy enough. Went after her nipple with an eagerness Francisco could understand.

"Does her father live in the area?" Francisco asked, feeling more awkward than she — even asking questions to which he already knew the answers.

"He lives on the other side of the river with a new wife. Works for a Ladino family up toward San Andres. We rarely see him. He doesn't show much interest in Laurita here... does he?" she said lovingly to the large brown eyes returning her gaze while sucking away. "But his mother does, so I'm glad we gave Laurita her name...I really have come to love that woman."

"Do you still love h*im?*" Francisco pressed, surprising himself with such bluntness.

Simona looked him full in the face a while before replying. "He didn't understand me very well. If he had? Yes, I think I could have loved him. We weren't together long enough for much love yet. Loving someone takes time. Have you been married...or in love?" She knew the answer to the first question, but not to the second.

Francisco answered only the first: "No, not yet."

207

"Well, you're old enough, I would judge, to begin contemplating such things!" she teased as she got up to leave. "I've got to get back. Mother will come looking if I stay any longer!"

"Would that matter?" he asked, puzzled by her apprehension.

"You don't know my mother!"

Francisco didn't know what to say, so simply touched her arm in appreciation for her coming in to talk. He followed after several minutes, assuming it safe. But unfortunately the Cosmes had not moved on. When her vigilant mother followed Simona's furtive glance and smile as a very Ladino-appearing Indian exited the church, she turned on her. Francisco felt he had to apologize, or at least explain, and started toward them to introduce himself as Simona's Spanish teacher. But the irate woman turned on him just as vehemently: "You lazy, good-for-nothing would-be Ladino! Get away from my daughter! She's never going to marry anyone who thinks he's too good to be a *natural!*"

Francisco said not a word. With one long, desperate look at Simona's agonized face he walked out of her life as abruptly as she had stepped into his. As buoyant as he had become in those three short weeks of knowing her, no attraction could bring him to become involved with another women whose parents wouldn't have him. Hurt more deeply than he was willing to admit, Francisco marched with fierce determination down the mountain.

His family all knew about his interest in Simona. Leaving now, after what had happened, would be as understandable an excuse as ever he would find. Fortunately, Rodolfo wasn't at home. Francisco left a note, relating what had happened in Solola and explaining that he had decided to leave Panajachel for at least a year or two of work down on the coast. He gathered his few clothes, his father's net bag and tump line for carrying Indian-style, the rifle, and wrapped them all in a blanket. He would stop by Eliseo's and sneak some bullets off the shelf.

Chapter Seventeen

Julia was as surprised to see her nephew standing at the gate as she had been some twenty-five years before when Rodolfo returned to Santa Catarina with Elena from the coast. And it took as long now to realize that it was Francisco as it had then to recognize his father. Francisco never had visited her, and he was embarrassed to admit that he'd had to ask directions.

"I have several favors to ask, Aunt Julia...hoping you'll find it in your heart to help your brother and our family." He brought her up to date on what Eliseo had learned in Solola, Margarita and Lazaro's decision to leave Panajachel — taking Mario with them for his protection as well, and Rodolfo's depression. Then he told her about the fiasco with Simona's mother. "I need to find myself a wife," he said with strange resignation "— and no families around here will have me. I'm too Indian for Ladinas, and too Ladino for Indians. Maybe I'll find someone in the low country."

Julia of course knew all about the Juan Quenum tragedy, and Rodolfo's drinking, but nothing about Lazaro and Margarita moving back to Patzicia with Mario.

"Rodolfo agrees to that?" she asked in surprise. "And now you're leaving him, too? You can't keep filling a jug without it overflowing sooner or later!"

Francisco was having doubts about his decision himself. He didn't know how to explain why he had to leave, or why he had sought her out in Santa Catarina. "It — it's not just because of Simona," he stammered. "I've been wanting for some time to get back to the coast for a while. Just have to hope that sometime everybody, especially Papa, will understand and forgive me. But for now he desperately needs you to stay with him."

She already was prepared for that request, but not for his second.

"Aunt Julia, I need to find a woman who is *natural* through and through. I think it will help if I wear Indian clothes in the low country, but I don't have any. And looking for them in Panajachel would be a bit awkward, never having worn such there. Frankly, with my Santa Catarina origins, I really would prefer to dress as a Catarineco."

Julia smiled, then chuckled, then laughed heartily. "Bless you! I tried so hard to get your father to go back to our clothes, when he first returned from the coast, and here you come begging to! As a matter of fact, I still have the same clothes that I gladly would have given to Rodolfo twenty-five years ago. They belonged to our grandfather, and I couldn't bear to throw them away. As well-woven as clothes were back in those days, using the natural cotton they used to grow hereabouts, they still should do." She went to the dilapidated storage box and felt toward the bottom for the shirt and pair of pants. "These were your great-grandfather Vicente's. He had this shirt on when they macheted his arm. See…where the sleeve's been mended? You can still see his blood stains. This is all I have that might fit you. My son, Marcos, is much too small. Do you mind the old red and white stripes without the embroidery everyone adds nowadays?"

"They're fine, Aunt Julia," he assured her, having hoped for as much. "And I have a third favor to ask, if Marcos will be so kind. If he can take me across to Cerro del Oro in his canoe, I'll be grateful. I plan to walk to plantations from there."

"Why not have him take you to Santiago? That will put you closer by a couple of hours."

He had hoped she wouldn't think of that. He didn't want to be seen in Santiago; too many people knew him there. Cerro del Oro would mean a long climb over or around the volcano of San Lucas, but approaching the Esperanza from the saddle between volcanoes San Lucas and Santiago would be much the safest. "I have a debt to pay off in Cerro del Oro ," he lied. "I'll gladly pay Marcos for his time."

"No need for that; he'll welcome the excuse to see what grebe hunting's like over there. He's been going out every evening. That's where he is now. There's just one more week before the law says he's supposed to stop for a couple of months during their breeding." Julia was pleased that Marcos would have that time with his cousin. She hurried about preparing to grind enough maize for the two men. "The two of you can do your planning over breakfast. If you're going to be up early and walking all day tomorrow, best to get some sleep!"

Francisco stretched out on the platform bed and noticed that it faced east. Probably everybody in Santa Catarina still slept with their heads toward the rising sun.

They got off by 4:00 the next morning, after Julia had finished making enough tortillas to last him for a couple of days. "I'll tell Rodolfo that it was your request that I move in with him temporarily; proud as he is, I doubt that he would agree on just my say so."

210

Marcos had slept only a few hours, and curled up on the narrow floor of the dugout while Francisco paddled the first half of the three hour crossing. For so early in the morning the breeze in his face was uncommonly strong; only by glancing back could he be sure he was making headway. Marcos needed a wider paddle! By the time he no longer could make out any landmark, he already was weary from such unaccustomed exercise. The realization deepened that there would be no hope for him if they capsized. He wouldn't even know in which direction to swim for shore! Life certainly was fragile. And now it seemed so much more so, having taken one life and preparing to take another. "How ironic," he thought, "— here I am even wearing the clothes of a murdered man."

Rodolfo had told him years ago about his paternal great-grandparents' violent deaths. Rodolfo himself had been too young to remember the details, but Julia had told him. Especially about their grandmother Bacilia going mad and haunting the family after her burial. Until now Francisco hadn't thought about even his own mother's ghost. No one had suggested their moving out of their house or burning candles. Maybe ghosts were more of a problem when people died violently or went mad. Nor had he given Juan Quenum's spirit any thought until Julia mentioned that Juan's widow had moved back to her folks' house in Santa Catarina for fear of his ghost haunting their shack at the Primavera. Did spirits *really* haunt the living and take loved ones with them? Ever since concluding that the moon didn't take babies during eclipses, he had questioned that the dead or dying could summon the living. Whether ghosts could even be seen, he'd doubted ever since the time he and Max had spent most of one All Souls' Night in the cemetery drinking cane liquor and watching the graves. Max was convinced that spirits couldn't eat and drink. That was why stealing from graves on All Souls Day had never seemed a sin.

One think was certain: if the dead *could* haunt the living, Eduardo's spirit surely was going to...his body lying out in the open for weeks, maybe even months, while buzzards cleaned his bones. He became so engrossed in his morbidity that he forgot to alternate sides paddling, and suddenly realized he probably was going in a circle. Frightened lest they be badly off course, he shook Marcos awake.

"Just keep facing the wind," his cousin reminded him. "I'm sure glad that you awakened me before I started to dream. I'm afraid of having the same dream I had early Friday morning. Being the strong day that Fridays are, I worried all day that it might come true. I dreamed that Diego died and I was at his wake. But only

Believers like him were there. Suppose it could be true that Believers are the only ones who know how to get the Owner of the Hill to let them come back to life? At the wake folks talked a lot about 'eternal life'…said they had the secret for living forever."

"Well, I know only that my father is convinced that some people — maybe all people — live two lives," agreed Francisco. "That's probably true for Catholics and Believers alike. You can tell whether you are in your first or second life by the way your hair grows. That cowlick some have? Papa says that it's the sign of being in your second. But about what Believers say, I haven't heard. Except, come to think of it, a soldier at the barracks told us about a Believer in Nahuala who died and was about to enter the Hill when he was met by an angel. The angel told him he could live another life if he *gave up* his new religion. He agreed, and now he's back at home living as a Catholic again. So where the truth lies, I can't say."

"My sister, Maruca, has gone to some of the Protestant meetings in both Panajachel and San Antonio," Marcos added. "You ever gone?"

"Went once while at the barracks, with a friend. Couldn't agree with what they said about forgiving everything…or their lies about the meek eventually inheriting the earth. The Catarineco who died in the landslide, Juan de Dios Quenum? I spent a week working with him at the Primavera pruning coffee. He told me that he went to the Centroamerciano chapel for a while, and they told him that the land his grandfather used to own here in Santa Catarina would sometime be his again. Juan said he tries not to blame the Ramirez family for his being so poor, knowing they'll receive God's judgment. But that's not the way things are, if you ask me! I agree it's bad to be greedy like the hoe — always pulling things in and never giving back — but I don't see many Ladinos getting punished for being rich…if *that's* a sin! If you act like you don't care how you're treated, then you'll be treated like shit! Look what happened to Juan Quenum for trying to be a friend to Eduardo Ramirez. There's no way his soul can get out of all that dirt and rock to have another —"

"But nobody knows for sure that Juan's buried there," objected Marcos. "His relatives say that they think he caused the landslide to make it *look* like he died so he could get away from the woman he's with. They think he's on the coast and will never show up."

Francisco was pleased to hear this from Marcos, confirming what Eliseo had told him that Catarinecos were saying. In fact, this was what had given him the idea of arranging for Eduardo's remains to be found in some out-of-the-way spot south of the lake. Eduardo's bones with a Catarineco's clothing. How fitting! And with Juan's workbook hopefully still intact enough in those clothes, who would suspect otherwise? But Marcos and Julia needed to think that Francisco, at least, was convinced that Juan had died in the avalanche. "Perhaps you're right. But as I said, I was working with him every day the week before the accident, and he sure sounded like he was expecting to be around throughout this rainy season...almost desperate to get enough firewood cut to get them through. And he already was carrying some down each evening to stack at their shack. Don't know why he would have gone to all that bother if he expected to be leaving for the coast."

"I've been thinking about going to the coast for a while myself," mused Marcos. "Mama's against it, but if she's going to move to Panajachel to take care of Uncle Rodolfo, then maybe she'll not object so much. If I stay here I have to put in 150 days of vagrancy work and two weeks of road work besides. At least as a plantation regular, I can stay put and think about getting married myself."

"Well," mused Francisco "— the way I look at it, by the time I've spent a year or two on the coast this Vagrancy Law will have changed. With all the talk against Ubico, I can't imagine that he'll be our president much longer. Until that happens, though, I'm going to get as much pay as I can for working down there. Do you have any desire to move away from Santa Catarina for good?"

"No, not really. Wouldn't know how to do the work of any other town around here, and wouldn't want to raise a family down on the coast. They say the girls all get raped down there, and more children sicken and die even than in Santa Catarina. Besides, I like to fish, and folks in Santa Catarina say we only have that luck when we are faithful children of Saint Catherine and stay at home." With that his conversation turned to fishing and duck hunting, neither of which Francisco had ever done. "But, cousin Francisco, now that you've decided to be a Catarineco again, wearing our clothes and all, you'll have that luck of fishing, too! Having Saint Catherine on your side can be a big help in lots of things. Who knows?...in those clothes, Saint Catherine may have a say about when even *you* die."

It hadn't occurred to Francisco that Saint Catherine ever had figured in anything he had done thus far in this life, or in anything he might yet do. What if Eduardo killed him instead? It certainly hadn't occurred to him that Saint Catherine might have some part in deciding whose corpse would end up wearing his grandfather's clothes! And how was she already feeling about his having just killed a Catarineco? And would she assume that a Ladino at heart, who then reverted to wearing the clothing of her town, was still worthy of her care? Would it help that his clothes had been his great-grandfather's, who certainly had been a faithful Catarineco? How foolish not to have taken time before leaving to light candles for Saint Catherine in the church!

—

By dusk that evening, the 'Catarineco,' after asking directions from every *natural* he met in fields beyond and above Cerro del Oro, knew that he was totally lost. Francisco had not seen another person for a couple of hours since starting to cut his way through branches and vines thicker than any growth he'd seen on the coast. He had begun to fear that it would, indeed, be his own body that his great-grandfather's clothes would claim. But at least he wasn't climbing any more, so he must be on the saddle. But in which direction he was headed he had no idea. With the foliage so dense, he wouldn't be able to tell much about direction even in the morning. The few thorn trees he failed to avoid tore at the old cloth so badly that finally he changed back to his army uniform.

The worst problem was his feet, blistered from his tire carcass sandals he hadn't worn in years. Once in the cool, wet humus of the cloud forest, he took them off, sinking to his ankles with every step until he didn't know which hurt worse, his feet or aching legs. The barracks should have a place like this for training exercises! With that thought he wished he'd never left Quetzaltenango. To sleep on the ground in such dampness would be impossible, so he kept on until he spotted one of the few moss-covered outcroppings of lava not yet wholly reclaimed by the jungle. Atop the rock he frightened away a beautiful blue-green lizard with a golden head, assuming that it would be back during the night to investigate! There was enough moss to cushion the sharp edges, yet not enough to make the moisture unbearable. He settled into position for the night and munched several of Julia's tortillas before falling asleep.

The next morning, as light began to filter through top and middle layers of the canopy, he lay motionless studying the occasional movements within the foliage. He'd been surprised with how few birds he'd seen or heard the day before, but now a song completely new to him was close enough, hopefully, to be able to spot its owner. Eventually giving up, he jumped down from his stone bed, startling the bird whose bright green plumes swept away from the tree closest to him. "Quetzal!" he gasped "— and so close!" He had seen only pictures of the national bird with its scarlet breast. Tail must have been half a meter long, he reflected, and then realized the person he would most enjoy telling would be Carolina.

Carolina! How could such a buzzard of a father have such a quetzal of a daughter? At the comparison, the first chuckle since leaving Simona escaped his lips. In relief he lay back down and laughed until he sobbed. He would have only buzzards to thank if it would be his fate to escape apprehension for the murder of Don Eduardo. And if caught, like the quetzal's legendary inability to survive in captivity, his days would be numbered. Such a creature of innocence, of passion for freedom, the quetzal! So like Carolina....But to liken Eduardo to the buzzard missed one important difference: Ladinos lived on the labor of Indians, day by day snuffing out lives cut short by want and sickness. Buzzards at least didn't exploit...had the decency at least not to feed until all signs of life were gone. The image Francisco savored of Ladinos was of the rat he had watched feed relentlessly on a hobbled pig, clawing at its nose until it squealed and then quickly sticking its head in the mouth to tear out one more mouthful of tender flesh and tongue. Would that Eduardo's buzzards would do his killing for him — draw it out, let him bleed to death slowly as Rodolfo's dreams told him his namesake priest had died. But Carolina...she was her father's daughter. Francisco didn't yet know if he would be able to bear watching Carolina's father suffer.

It was difficult to be certain, but it seemed that he was going up more than down after an hour of trudging through the changeless vegetation. As the canopy's top layer began to thin, yielding glimpses of sky from time to time, he was sure of it: he was near the vegetation line. Where he was, when finally he left the last of the underbrush and climbed high enough to see over the stunted trees, was about half way around the western side of volcano Santiago Atitlan. The saddle was well behind and beneath him. Farther yet behind rose the peak of San Lucas Toliman. "I've come one hell of a long way, farther than I need to!" Almost all of the lake was blocked from view by Toliman behind him to the north and by the volcano San Pedro rising on the other side of the bay of Santiago to the west. Far below, looking west, the sprawling city of Santiago, largest of the lake's towns, nestled against the bay. To the south, only clouds obscuring the boundary between sea and sky. Probably the ocean's shoreline would be visible on a cloudless day. "No wonder folks say this volcano holds up the sky!" he said in awe, calculating the considerable distance to its summit. From the sun's position it already was midday — too late for any side trip. Could Rodolfo be right?...that the sun is directly overhead at midday only above these volcanoes and our lake Atitlan? Is, indeed, our lake at the center of the world?

He stumbled through the deep ash several more meters before concluding that the most direct route to the Esperanza, farther on around the peak and then straight down, would not be the fastest. Even after he had made it through the ash, he would have hours more of cloud forest to cut through below. The milpa clearings there didn't reach nearly as high up the slope. Straight down from here he would have only an hour or two of cloud forest, and then maybe two or three hours along the top row of fields before starting down to Esperanza coffee groves visible in the far distance. He sat down on a boulder to eat more of Julia's cold tortillas.

It was late afternoon by the time he finally found a sheltered place to spend the night, in case the clouds that had gathered steadily throughout the afternoon finally spilled over. It was a small grotto, not a cave actually, but from the evidence of can and bottle litter it offered shelter enough for several farmers. The last cultivating for the season had been done weeks before. Probably the grotto wouldn't be visited again until harvest. As he thought about it, the place would be ideal for disposing of Eduardo's body. A fugitive like Juan Quenum would have looked for just such a hiding place, and buzzards cleaning the bones would not be obvious. But could he get Eduardo all the way up here? He would have to force him to walk almost the entire distance; carrying him very far would be impossible. If they were going to walk without being seen, their meeting would have to take place in the late afternoon and at considerable distance from the plantation house. There was a spring on the plantation's eastern border, about an hour's walk above the house. He and Carolina had walked there once with Max to look at the aqueduct that Rodolfo said his father had helped rebuild for Don Herman after the earthquake.

That night proved to be the longest and loneliest of Francisco's life, sitting without a fire, thirsty, in the place where Eduardo's body would soon be lying. How would he face his family or Eliseo if ever the truth came out in Panajachel about Eduardo's death? Could he ever look Carolina in the eye again?

But what else could he do? He couldn't stand helplessly by until fear or Eduardo killed Rodolfo. At no point had Francisco seriously doubted his decision, and he didn't doubt it now. It was just the emptiness he felt and the fear creeping in, knowing what sadness and anger he was going to cause Carolina and Max. The hardest part was not being able to talk to someone about it. If it had worked out with Simona, maybe he could have confided in her. Surely she would have understood....Yes, Simona would understand!

———

Eduardo Ramirez was awakened from his afternoon siesta by a hesitant knock at the door. One of his new men stood nervously on the veranda. "Begging your pardon, Don Eduardo, but I have a message from a Catarineco. He surprised me while I was burning trimmings out east. Name's Juan de Dios Quenum, and —"

"Quenum! Are you *sure?*"

"Yes, Patron, he showed me his work book. Said people think he's dead. Told me to mention the name Lazaro Tonon if you find this hard to believe."

"Where is the fellow now?"

"He said he felt uneasy coming to the house, but needs to see you right away. He'll be waiting up by the old spring around 5:00. Want someone to go with you?"

"No, he's harmless enough. I'll be all right."

Eduardo didn't know what to think. When news of the landslide and Juan's disappearance had reached the Esperanza, Eduardo had no doubt but that the careless fellow had died in the slide. Over a month had passed, and Eduardo had put Juan Quenum completely out of his mind. There was plenty of time yet to deal with Lazaro and the Ajcojoms. What possibly could have happened to make Juan run away and stay in hiding all this time? Well, no alternative but to meet with him and find out. It would be a walk of two kilometers at least, and a fair climb besides. If Juan wanted privacy, he knew where to find it! The spring was seldom visited any more, now that water was piped down the hill.

He was exhausted when he reached the spring. After receiving no response to calling Juan's name, he enjoyed a drink and settled down to rest.

Francisco could see that the man was too weary to do any more walking for a while, so he stayed out of sight while Eduardo rested and shadows lengthened. When Eduardo's patience had run out, replaced by shouting Juan's name and swearing his frustration, Francisco left his hiding place and started toward him. "Good afternoon, Don Eduardo," he greeted him calmly, enjoying the astonishment grow as a soldier approached.

Can't be Juan, thought Eduardo, the figure still too far away for recognition. He had to be Ladino; no Indian would be carrying a rifle. Not until the soldier was a few meters away did Eduardo finally recognize Francisco. Before he could turn to flee, even shout, the rifle was leveled at his chest.

"We'll talk while we walk," said Francisco tersely. "As long as you feel like walking, you'll stay alive...I've got all the time in the world." He nudged Eduardo with the rifle and motioned him up the hill.

"W — Where'd *you* get a rifle?" fumed Eduardo, appalled at how easily he had been tricked into venturing so far from home alone.

"Solola's militia commander."

"Damn fool!" Eduardo retorted "— both of you! How do you think you can harm me and get away with it?"

"Not you I'll be harming, sir," Francisco said calmly. "Eduardo Ramirez will simply disappear, and it will be Juan Quenum's bones they put to rest in an Indian's grave in Santiago Atitlan or Santa Catarina, if in fact your bones ever *are* found! Here, change your clothes! Think my great-grandpa's clothes here will fit you?" He had to smile at the consternation in Eduardo's frightened eyes as he turned to look aghast at the torn garments Francisco had pulled from his bundle.

Eduardo was incensed and started to protest, until Francisco cocked his rifle. While he undressed and fumbled with the strange pants and sash, Francisco continued his monologue: "Maybe you didn't know that my great-grandfather was murdered trying to hold on to land that had been pawned to Indians of San Antonio...same land that your father grabbed to start your family's plantation over there. That's the first reason why you're going to die and be found in his clothes. Look, there on the sleeve, where they cut off his arm! You're lucky I'm not ending your life that same, painful way!

"My aunt Victoria, who you raped and killed, is the second reason —"

Stunned, Eduardo looked at him in disbelief.

"And the third reason is my brother-in-law. You see, I was only a few meters away from you and Juan Quenum the night you made the poor man agree to kill Lazaro. I watched you pay him the blood money! Actually, I was waiting in the banana grove until it was dark enough to meet Carolina again in your launch —"

"You thieving Judas! I should have killed you when I had the chance!" Eduardo screamed while lunging for the rifle. But Francisco was ready and knocked him off balance.

Francisco worried for a moment that his red-faced captive was going to expire from heart failure before he could shoot him, sweating and panting as he was from anger and exhaustion. Francisco stepped back and patiently waited for Eduardo to catch his breath and get to his feet. "You'll be relieved to know that that night was the only time I had your daughter. Before that...when you about

218

killed me...we'd only talked. You might as well know that the baby she's expecting is probably mine. That's why she bought that monkey! What you did to us, to Carolina and me, that's the fourth reason.

"And the fifth reason is my father. After all the unhappiness you made me cause my folks —," Francisco angrily fought against the tears, "— the least I can do is put Papa's mind at rest and end his worry about what else you might be capable of! That's all I have to say to you. But keep walking! We're heading for that outcrop up ahead."

Francisco goaded Eduardo with the rifle to get as much distance out of him as possible until finally he collapsed to one knee and threw up his arms in despair.

"So this is it?" Francisco asked, more of himself than of his victim. "Do you remember what you called me the night you kicked me to the ground? You called me an uncivilized savage and a filthy pig. Well, Eduardo, Saturday's killing arrives sooner or later for every pig," he said matter-of-factly and facing the bowed head struck it with his rifle's butt. No sense risking the sound of the gun.

After shouldering the body, the rifle, and Eduardo's clothes, he continued on up the volcano until forced to rest. He sat down, put Eduardo's broken head in his lap, and dissolved in tears...mostly for Carolina, a lot for himself, and a little for Max. Then he threw away the rifle. Anyone killing another person should have to do it with his own hands; pulling a trigger makes it much too easy.

In March Francisco heard at last that Juan Quenum's body had been found half way up the volcano Santiago Atitlan. He learned from a Catarineco who showed up for coffee harvest at the small Valle Verde plantation where Francisco had found work. The news had reached Quenum's widow the middle of January, after his bones had been buried in Santiago's cemetery.

Francisco waited another full year before returning, until confident that he could face Carolina and, if necessary, lie in denying any involvement in her father's disappearance. The first of April Francisco went home, returning as he had come by way of Santa Catarina to learn what news he could. Diego told him that Julia had died, and then Eliseo, and then Mario in Patzicia only a few weeks apart. Julia had spent most of every week for a year with Rodolfo, only to catch pneumonia when caught in a rare summer rain and wind storm one evening while walking back to Santa Catarina. Immediately after her funeral, Marcos took off for the coast and had not been back since. As for Eliseo, he became depressed and showed little interest in anything after the new mayor arrived the first of January.

219

It was a mistake to yield to his wife's pleading to lease out their store. With nothing left to do he died within a month. His funeral was the largest that folks could remember...cemetery as full as on All Souls Day. To everyone's surprise, he had asked to be buried in a simple Indian grave with a wooden cross. As for poor Mario, he cut himself with his machete when gathering wood and the wound got too infected to cure even with medicine from the pharmacy.

After getting through that year of sadness and drinking, Rodolfo had been reasonably well of late, coming over weekly by launch to check out the Primavera holdings. With none of his blood relatives around anymore, Rodolfo usually would stop by to chat before returning home. Some of his depression was still there, to be sure, and Pancho finally told him only a month ago that the next harvest would have to be his last as foreman of the Primavera. But Pancho and Beatriz promised him the use of his hut for the remainder of his days.

About Eduardo's family Diego had learned very little, except that they had given up looking for Eduardo. "Nobody could make any sense whatsoever of his disappearance. The whole Ramirez family was at the Esperanza for several weeks. Max first confronted Rodolfo and Julia, learning only that you were on the coast, before he came storming over here to find Marcos. Marcos got scared and told him where he'd left you in Cerro del Oro. Good thing that you didn't know then that you'd end up at the Valle Verde plantation! If I were you, I'd stay down there some longer, but if you're set on spending time in these parts I sure wouldn't make my home with Rodolfo at the Primavera! My sister Maruca might welcome a cousin's company over here."

Francisco agreed to give that some thought, and heeded Diego's advice to skirt Panajachel and the Primavera in heading toward Solola for a look at the avalanche site. The cross marking Juan's grave was gone, and more of the dirt, rock and wood had been removed. But until yet another work crew was assigned to Panajachel he could relax in at least this regard. With a huge sigh of relief and with night descending, he returned to face Rodolfo.

For the next few weeks Francisco did construction work for Mariano up in San Andres above the lake, sleeping there as well and letting his beard grow out for what disguise that provided. Then, during Holy Week he took the risk of joining the Good Friday crowd gathering in anticipation of the procession. He came prepared to find Carolina there, hoping that he would at least get a glimpse of her and her baby if the Ramirez family was still in the habit of celebrating Easter in Panajachel rather than in Santiago Atitlan.

As he had hoped, Carolina had walked to town alone ahead of the family, to have a look at the carpet of flower petals that surely Eliseo's widow would have prepared in his memory. And, as at the previous year's Good Friday procession, she reasoned that — should ever Francisco reappear in Panajachel and endeavor to reconnect — it likely would be either at Easter or All Souls. To her not unpleasant surprise, therefore, she sensed even before looking up that the bearded fellow approaching to join her in the carpet's admiration was him. Expressionless, she motioned with her eyes for him to follow and with the baby headed toward the church. He found her sitting on the organ bench in the loft...absolutely beaming with eagerness to hand him his daughter. "Her name is Eva Francisca!"

The bright-eyed infant certainly was dark enough to be his. "So she *is* ours?" he gasped as he kissed first his daughter and then her radiantly beautiful mother.

"Well, isn't it obvious that she is! Just look at that nose of yours! Luckily she's a 'she' and not a 'he,' or the resemblance would be unmistakable!"

"But with the name 'Francisca,' surely everyone suspects?"

"Not likely, since Daniel chose it! Francisca was his grandmother's name, and I told him I had no objections whatsoever." She smiled, eyes dancing. "Daniel's family is pretty dark-skinned, and while Eva is darker yet, even Daniel has never said a thing. My mom and especially my grandmother raised their eyebrows at first, but Arcadia had prepared everybody to expect dark skin and all that hair, so convinced she is that that's the price anyone pays who is crazy enough to have a pet monkey when pregnant."

"So, for how much longer must I share with a monkey what little love you still have for me?"

"My house could be a monkey zoo, and I still would have as much love as you can handle!" She put her arms around father and daughter, eyes now overflowing with time running out. The procession would soon separate them for another interminable wait...this one had stretched into two years. Suddenly serious, she asked intently, "Francisco, why did you have me check on Juan Quenum? Do you think that he could have had something to do with Papa's disappearance?"

Relieved beyond all expectations with Carolina's devotion clearly as steadfast as his own, Francisco was just as ready as she for some serious talk. He quickly related what he had overheard in the banana grove, and why he thought the landslide wasn't an accident; it had been intended to kill Lazaro. He stopped short of revealing what Eliseo had learned about the intervention in assigning workers to that road crew. In fairness to Eduardo, it might have been the governor's doing. But he saw no reason not to feed Carolina's suspicion that Juan might have harbored hatred toward Eduardo. "Catarinecos thought from the outset that Juan wanted it to appear that he had been accidentally killed in that avalanche, so that he could get away from his wife. But I, too, have wondered if he wasn't just as interested in revenging the loss of his family's land to your grandfather and father. Eliseo told me that Juan and his family were still pretty bitter about that. And if Juan did accept money for killing Lazaro, then with Lazaro still alive and no proof that Juan wasn't still living as well, Juan might well have worried about Eduardo's wrath. He may have decided to confront Eduardo; why else would he have ended up over near the Esperanza?"

"That's what I think!" she said with relief. "But I couldn't get anyone to listen to me! All we know is what the hired man over there told us: that Juan wanted Papa to come to him...up there at the spring that supplied piped water to the plantation back before the earthquake. That's a long walk, especially at night, and Juan asked Papa to meet him there at 5:00. I think that Papa simply got lost. And we know that there have been several jaguar sightings that far down the volcano. Especially if Papa was injured, he would have been no match for a jaguar off by himself that way. He could have been carried enough farther up the volcano to never be found! But Max prefers to think that you were involved, now that he knows about Papa beating and threatening you."

Francisco wasn't sure how he would have responded had Carolina ventured to ask him Max's question. Fortunately the procession was rapidly approaching the church. Carolina said that she anticipated being able to get back to Panajachel for Good Fridays for some years to come, given the family's understanding of how sentimental she was over all those years of helping Uncle Eliseo with his carpets. So, if Francisco could also get back, using his father as the excuse for his remaining years, might they not have this organ loft rendezvous to look forward to a few years at least? She gave him a quick kiss on his cheek, grabbed Eva, and hurried down the enclosed spiral staircase on the loft's south side to join the procession entering the church.

Francisco waited a few minutes and descended the north staircase, continuing on to the front of the church to thank his patron namesake for this unexpected confirmation of his fathering Eva Francisca. As he skirted the central aisle procession to exit the church, he returned Carolina's parting kiss with a suggestion of his own when catching her eye. With her trace of a farewell smile, she turned away, but to his astonishment the woman standing near Carolina broke into a huge grin and *didn't* turn away. *Simona,* of all people! Carolina and Simona each standing there with a daughter, and neither knowing a thing about the other. In his excitement, he had forgotten to tell Carolina about Simona, but inadvertently, *because* of Carolina, he had just told Simona a whole lot more than he was prepared to. Simona started to move toward the door herself, but he didn't wait, exiting ahead of her and taking off on the run.

Of Simona he had seen very little since his return, and when they had met they had been unable to talk: first in the Panajachel market and then in the store when Simona was in line to have maize ground for tortillas in the town's first electric corn grinding machine. But her friendly smiles on both occasions were encouraging. She apparently hadn't gotten involved with anyone else. But that only made it harder, really. Unless he got away from Panajachel, sooner or later he would weaken and do something more foolish than inadvertently blowing her a kiss!

Two weeks following Easter Sunday, when rain clouds again began to gather on the coast, another road crew was appointed to work on the avalanche. Francisco's uneasiness increased daily as he took evening walks to monitor the progress made. Almost certainly the bones in Catarineco clothing would be found. Once it was known that the bones discovered across the lake and buried in Santiago Atitlan's cemetery could not possibly be Juan Quenum's, there would be new rumors about both deaths. Those bones would be exhumed and in all likelihood be proven to be Eduardo's. To stay in Panajachel until Juan's remains were uncovered was suicide. Even Carolina would then suspect that her brother was right!

When Simona next visited the store to have maize ground for tortillas, Francisco was waiting. He asked to walk her home. "I will be leaving Panajachel again soon, and I doubt that I'll ever come back — not for a long time anyway. I don't want to leave this way, without telling you good-bye and saying that I wish things had turned out differently with your mother. You said that love takes time, and I was hoping that we would have that time, to learn if it could grow between us. I would yet ask for you, but knowing how your mother feels, I don't suppose —"

Simona dropped her pan of maize as her hands went to her lips to stifle the gasp. Eyes a'sparkle with tears of joy, she blushed with a radiance that hushed Francisco. He didn't need to say more. "Oh, Francisco, I had given up a long time ago! The kiss you threw in the church brought the feelings rushing back, but with no word since I had pretty much given up again. You're right: my mother would never consent, and living together here in Panajachel would be too difficult. Just ask me, Francisco, and Laurita and I will join you wherever you are going!" Their first kiss was his proposal, and her arms wrapped around his neck her acceptance. "So, dear husband at long last, what produced such resolve now?"

Francisco lifted Laurita to include her in their embrace and replied, "I decided during that Good Friday procession that I'm ready to become a father!" With that, he bestowed on Laurita a kiss big enough for two daughters and on Simona as loving and grateful a smile as Francisco ever would bestow on a woman. For he sensed Carolina's embrace and blessing as well: "Marry a *natural*, my love!"

What remained also had been too long postponed: sharing with his father why Francisco, and now Simona and Laurita as well, had no choice but to abandon Panajachel and start a new life somewhere far away. It would be best that his father and all other Ajcojoms and their friends assume it was on the coast. With a heart heavy, but now more bearable with Simona's decision, Francisco set off to talk with his father.

———

That afternoon Francisco asked me to take a walk with him to the other side of the river to visit Eliseo's grave. On the way we talked about Simona. I wasn't surprised to hear that they had decided to elope, but I pleaded with him not to let that force him to leave Panajachel. "Who cares about the Cosmes? You can build a house over here near the Primavera and have no more to do with them than you want to!"

So Francisco decided to tell me more: about the real Juan Quenum's bones still awaiting discovery under the avalanche that had been intended for Lazaro. He explained why Eliseo and he had suspected Juan Quenum and Eduardo of plotting against Lazaro. He related the story of his first rendezvous with Carolina and of Eduardo's threat to fire me if Francisco returned to Panajachel before Carolina had married. I wept as the reason for Francisco's absence of two years became clear. "If only Elena could have known all of this," I sobbed, having to sit down beside the street to let all that sadness out. Francisco went to the tavern to get a cup of rum. We sipped it together until we had relaxed enough to continue.

Francisco was able finally to tell me the rest: the conversation he had overheard between Eduardo and Juan Quenum; why he had asked to work with Juan that week; how he had killed the poor fellow; what Eliseo had learned in Solola;

and finally the journey to the Esperanza. For some reason he didn't tell me then about Eva Francisca being his daughter. But probably just as well. A son had told a father as much as either could handle in one afternoon! Even the killing of Eduardo didn't finally sink in until we were at Eliseo's grave in the cemetery and he told me in more detail about spending the night with Julia and rowing across the lake with Marcos.

That was before he told me that he would be leaving with Simona yet that evening. Where they were going he wouldn't say for sure, for what protection that might provide me against Max's anger when the Ramirez family finally learned that Eduardo was dead. Since he had successfully eluded Max for so long on the South Coast, I assumed that was where they would go. He said that Simona wanted to meet me...that she would stop by with Laurita to visit at the Primavera before the two of them left by bus for Solola. Then he hurried off to walk to Solola himself, determined that no one from Panajachel would see him leaving town by bus. When they boarded the early bus north out of Solola in the early morning before Panajachel's first bus there of the day, they would not likely encounter any acquaintances from Panajachel. They simply would have disappeared.

I spent the rest of the afternoon walking, needing time to digest it all. I even walked up the Solola road as far as the avalanche, sitting down to rest against one of the boulders pushed to the side of the road. I wept while surveying the panorama of delta and the lake that I doubted my son ever would set eyes upon again. Somewhere beyond the ghostly volcanoes, shrouded in heavy clouds, lay the Esperanza plantation. I shuddered at the thought of climbing over such mountains and sleeping up there alone. Killing Juan Quenum was one thing, but what a frightening night before taking on Eduardo...I wished Francisco had spared me that disclosure. What, oh what, would I say to Max when Juan Quenum's bones were finally uncovered and the Ramirez family learned that it was Eduardo in the Santiago grave?

When I finally reached home, Simona and Laurita were sitting on the veranda. "We're early," Simona apologized, as we entered the house and I offered the only two chairs at the table. Laurita insisted on standing, at five years as tall as I was seated. Simona looked old beyond her years. Like Francisco, she hadn't had an easy life. And clearly she had become as independent a daughter as Francisco was a son, agreeing so readily to leave Panajachel for only God knew where!

For Simona's part, she welcomed this interlude with a new father-in-law whom she knew only by his remarkable reputation. She smiled and hesitantly broke the awkward silence: "If you are not too tired, Francisco suggested that I ask you how you got your name."

My eyebrow arched the way it does for all of us Ajcojoms when we are surprised, but I said nothing. I got up to collect cups, put some coffee on to heat, and retrieved a plate of sweet rolls from the cupboard before rejoining them. "Rodolfo Luis is a bit uncommon for a *natural,* I suppose. I was named for a priest who was killed trying to help Indians in the time of the *mandamientos.* You've heard about the *mandamientos?*" To my pleasant surprise, Simona knew that history very well. So I explained about the leaflet, the chain and crucifix, removing it from my neck to show them...first time I had taken it off in years, I realized. "My mother gave it to me when I was close to dying from a fall near Santa Catarina. I figure the priest's spirit saved my life, although as a kid I remember hearing arguments about whether my namesake wanted to keep me alive or take me off to be his star angel."

Remembering that Simona could read, I got up to fetch a box of keepsakes that Julia had brought with her when she came to live with me. "Since you know so much about the *mandamientos,* why don't you keep this leaflet that got Father Rodolfo Luis killed. My sister found it in my parents' things after my mother died...I had no idea that my mother had kept it all those years. Look here...at the bottom his name is written out, and if you look close you can still see the outline of a fish. When I was younger I dreamed a lot about a big fish. My father was convinced that I share the fish spirit of my namesake. So when I was about your age, Laurita, my grandfather gave this fish to me." I untied the wooden charm from the silver chain to give them a closer look. "Vicente used to carve wooden charms for me to sell during fiestas, but this one he carved for me to keep."

Silence settled in, as though Rodolfo had left the room. From the weight of heavy eyebrows his eyes slowly closed until not a muscle moved in the deeply wrinkled face. Laurita studied every line. The hair on his head and face was silvered, as much as the chain in his hand. Gnarled fingers were moving the links slowly through his hand, one by one, until he touched the cross and then the fish. His eyes opened, and he smiled at the rapt look on the face of his latest grandchild.

"I shall wear my crucifix until the day I die," he said "— but this fish charm from my grandfather should be passed on down to a granddaughter," and he tied the cord around her neck.

Laurita blushed, and her mother's arms drew the three close with a hug. Tears formed as she sorrowed over their impending departure: Laurita so needed Rodolfo's love after the difficult years with her own parents.

Remembering the other keepsake in the box, Rodolfo sorted through the papers and produced an envelope addressed to 'Chepe, my Sacristan.' "Chepe was my mother's father, who helped a priest here for many years. Father Sebastian was the last priest assigned to Panajachel before all the priests in Guatemala were asked to leave the country for a couple of decades. He wasn't replaced until Father Jacobo was assigned to this parish. Grandfather Chepe couldn't read very well, especially the kind of reading Father Sebastian apparently expected him to do. But he had the good sense to save this poem, another keepsake of my sister's that I didn't know we had until she gave me this box."

He unfolded the poem for Simona to read. "Francisco needs to keep and read this poem from time to time, especially 'The Psalm' part. Maybe it will give him the same comfort it has given me of late." Then Rodolfo settled back and listened to Simona, the first time he had heard Father Sebastian's poem read aloud:

'Ere The Day Is Moored to Eternity
The Dirge

Awaken, my children, and hark to the bell.
  When bestirred, then be stilled by this shrouded knell
    Tolled in lament by a yet wakeful bell.
A toll in the dark, your priest to depart —
  In mourning not one on the quay — as tolled on their way
    All faith, hope, and love now embark.
A priest's benediction, on this at least dwell...
  Ring out, rural bell, in one resonant swell
    Tolled benedicities in far-flung farewell.
Ah world, so weary, too deep have ye drawn
  Of draughts dissolving all dusk into dawn.
    Tolled blessing unheeded, a harsh requiem!

Alas, ye ungodly, at least don the guise!
  Clad this discordance! Dissembling lies
    Told the departing need fear no replies.
Declare no dissentions, no willful mistakes,
  Well learned this day's lessons — and yet, all too late,
    Told to a world no bell will awake...

The Psalm

A soft-whispered sigh wends its way through the night;
  The prayers of a pilgrim, his solace in flight,
    Tolled pleas for forgiveness petition the night.
Not yet ready to face what a new day might bring;
  Reliving this last, sunk in sorrow and shame —
    Told that the morn will be born with the stain —
One soul cries out in search of his grail:
  A winged entreaty that concord prevail
    Tolled out o'er the bay, a beseeching wail.
And 'ere the day is moored to eternity,
  It pauses to answer this pilgrim's plea —
    Tolled o'er the waves of a timeless sea:
'Eternity dwells in the close of each day,
  And forgives all the moment one soul kneels to pray.'
    Tolled peals of thanksgiving sweep down 'round the quay!
They sound, then are silent. The ensuing calm
  Reaches out to a soul deserving its balm.
    Tolled as a dirge, but redeemed as a psalm

About the Writing of Historical Fiction in Guatemala

To write historical novels set in the late 19th and 20th centuries in a country other than one's own is problematic enough; to do so with protagonists from the Mayan underbelly of Guatemalan society, and to endeavor to tell their stories when only an anthropological observer of their culture is fraught with risks. The reader deserves to hear an author's defense of such audacity.

I begin with the remarkable absence of literature about Mayas written by Mayas a century ago, this the result of policies denying public schooling and hence literacy to virtually all Indians in that era. The policies changed well into the 20th century, accompanied by establishment of a boarding school in Guatemala City for promising Mayan youth nominated from Indian communities. One such youth, Juan de Dios Rosales, of Panajachel went on to become the first foreign-trained Mayan cultural anthropologist and eventually a director of the government's *Instituto Indigenista de Guatemala*.

During his career Rosales assisted the first North American anthropologists to undertake multi-year career study of contemporary Mayan communities in Guatemala: Sol and Gertrude Tax (University of Chicago) and Ben and Lois Paul (Stanford University). The Taxes commenced such study in Panajachel from 1933-41, eventually training me — with the help of Juan de Dios Rosales — for my own field research that commenced in 1963.

Juan de Dios Rosales' data gathering and interpretation figure significantly in both novels. In this first book the successful petitioning by Panajachel elders of Guatemala's President Ubico for exemption from the Vagrancy Law of Ubico's administration was facilitated and documented by Rosales. And the massacre in Patzicia of the sequel novel, *The Rape of Hope*, similarly was documented in detail at the time by Rosales at the suggestion of Sol Tax. To my knowledge, there were no other Mayas anthropologically trained nor positioned by their career involvements to contribute so directly to the training and writing of non-Mayan scholars of that era. Would that Rosales had undertaken the writing of fiction himself. Now, in the 21st century, a host of Mayan writers — trained in Guatemala, Mexico, and the United States — write in Mayan languages and in Spanish, with several publishing outlets in both Guatemala and the United States

To my knowledge, the only documented accounts by Mayas of their lives at the turn of the 20th century are oral histories of several elderly Mayas in Panajachel that were recorded by Sol Tax in the late 1930s. One of these was published in *Currents* in *Anthroplogy: Essays in Honor of Sol Tax* (1979, Mouton). I similarly interviewed some fifty Mayas in the Lake Atitlan region commencing in the 1960s and continuing through the 1980s. A number of the Mayan characters, and especially the protagonists, in both novels are based upon one or more of those oral histories and interviews. By contrast, none of the Ladino characters nor foreign priests of *My Lake at the Center of the World* have any such referents. Any resemblance to prersons living or deceased is coincidental.

As for the events forming the stories told, some are true to the facts as I understand them, while others are totally of my imagination. For example, the village of San Antonio Palopo never, to my knowledge, experimented with a weekly market. And in some instances the time and place of events has changed. For example, the feuding between the two communities of San Antonio and Santa Catarina is based on comparable tensions that led to comparable violence at the opposite end of Lake Atitlan. The Judas Cave above Santa Catarina in the novel is actually above Panajachel.

Although all the Mayan and Ladino characters of *My Lake at the Center of the World* except are fictional, I have endeavored to remain true to the facts of an exiled clergy, laws guaranteeing plantation owners Indian labor, the resultant poverty and violence that defined their lives. The tale goes to the roots of the escalating violence in the subsequent half century that erupted finally in ethnocide against Mayas — recalled euphemistically as 'the recent unpleasantness' — in the story of *The Rape of Hope*. The opening chapter of this sequel novel is appended below.

Chapter One – 1940

On descending to his work site below the overflowing crest of fresh trash from the previous afternoon's dumping, Francisco noticed but gave little thought to how quiet it was for this early time of day. Only the occasional echo to his own chronic coughing from a fellow scavenger out of view, and fewer dogs snarling over the garbage up above. Not until he had filled his first bag of glass and tin cans for the day and had begun the precarious climb to higher ground did he realize that there also were no vultures overhead. In fact, he was surprisingly alone out here in the middle of nowhere...absent of even his wife's customary companionship. Nothing could be seen scavenging on either side of the ravine nor down the chasm of trash cascading out of sight into the mist of heat and noxious fumes hundreds of feet below. Perhaps the dumping above his and Simona's allotted scavenging area had moved since yesterday far enough across the leveled land-fill to take the army of vultures out of sight and hearing. But the more likely explanation for such eerie silence and empty sky was one of their own sufficiently near death to settle the buzzards in their patient vigil for its fresh remains.

There was yet another — ominous — possibility. Animal and bird instincts more experienced than his own could be warning that the gas build-up had reached a level too dangerous to risk scavenging for the time being. With no combustion fire for many months — none, in fact, since the Ajcojoms had made the Basurero dump their home eight months ago — the old-timers had been urging caution in venturing too far down the steep slope of compacted combustibles lest one of the dreaded fire balls make retreat impossible. The indicators were becoming worrisome: more vultures and dogs than usual dying of late, and more illness among the human scavengers as well. Indeed, Simona had been complaining of dizziness and nausea until finally yielding to his pleas to stay at home for a day in their shanty perched high on the rock ledge overlooking the vast, steaming wasteland. The air there was considerably easier to breathe.

To be sure, the behavior of veteran vultures was not to be ignored. And yet methane build-up was only one of the possible explanations for their temporarily abandoning the sky on any given morning. So how to proceed, given the blessing of such surprising reduction in the daily competition for edible scraps in the fresh garbage up above? He and Simona had opted most days of late to forego the food competition from neighbors and critters in the interest of collecting enough more saleable recyclables to permit buying store fare for a change. That was their one miserable advantage to having one less mouth to feed: they could afford to gamble on recyclables and not waste so much time looking for food. Even if this meant going without an occasional meal, as it did about every other day. But while Laurita had been alive, the risk for her of missing a meal had been too great in Simona's opinion.

Francisco had disagreed, but had deferred. After all, Laurita was Simona's daughter from her prior marriage. He suspected, however, that a desperate mother's insistence on regular meals for a sickening daughter — settling now and then for scraps of food dangerously spoiled — had only worsened Laurita's deadly diarrhea. Lime juice, generously applied, masked the foul taste enough to keep such scraps down, but Francisco was less convinced that the lime made their consumption any safer. Such an unfair dilemma for a mother...and yet it also was unfair to Francisco for her to rationalize that Laurita's death had had less to do with the food she had scavenged than with the infection from the rat's bite. Admittedly, it had been his responsibility to fill the cracks in their hut that permitted entrance to the vermin that on occasion found their way up the ledge. It hadn't been much of a worry while the rodent poison lasted, but the week they ran out and couldn't afford to buy more was when Laurita awakened them with her screams. They no more had had the money for taking her promptly to a curer or buying medicine than for the poison.

But arguing with Simona over the cause of Laurita's death solved nothing, and he had been grieving — he believed — fully as deeply as had his wife. The guilt just wouldn't go away. After all, he had delayed for much too long in asking her to marry him. And when finally he had done so, he had made their marriage subject to her willingness to elope and flee Panajachel and the lake region. She had abandoned her parents, and he had abandoned his father and siblings, none of whom had the slightest idea where they now might be. And look at where they were! The poorest excuse for a home that Guatemala had to offer the poorest of her poor: the capital's largest dump . The only difference between the human and non-human scavengers in the Basurero was who ate whom. Dogs and buzzards feasted not only on one another but upon the human corpses that had been

232

showing up of nights with greater frequency. Humans didn't eat each other — not yet anyway — nor seldom even the dead birds and dogs. Simona was thoroughly repulsed by neighbors who on occasion would eat a freshly dead vulture, asking how they could do so after watching on a daily basis the absolute filth that buzzards consumed. For his part, Francisco saw little difference between eating a scavenging chicken and a scavenging vulture. But this assuaged not at all his guilt over placing his wife in the position of having to make such unfair choices in her losing battle to keep a daughter alive. In effect he had asked Simona to gamble with a daughter's life in order to avoid — with the safe haven of the Basurero — the almost certain death for himself if remaining in Panajachel.

Max Ramirez, son of Eduardo and brother of Carolina who had given birth to Francisco's son, had vowed to kill Francisco in the same fashion that Francisco had managed to dispatch Eduardo. Francisco had done the killing from fear that the man would attempt yet again to wreak revenge upon the Ajcojom family for their role in getting Panajachel Indians exempted from forced labor on the Ramirez coffee plantations in the lake region. Max's obsession with hunting down Francisco was not to be denied. Accordingly, Francisco and Simona had done everything possible to conceal their whereabouts by subsisting initially, at least, in the city's redoubt offering the most anonymity: its dump. Within its confines, their poor excuse for a dwelling was part cave, part cardboard and tin enclosure in the shadow of a drab cement wall forming the perimeter of the adjacent 'City of the Living Dead,' the principal cemetery of the city. Such irony: the city's human dead residing side-by-side with those subsisting on the discarded waste of the city's living. It was more descriptively the Basurero that housed the living dead! But with Laurita's death, Francisco had vowed to Simona that they would find a less abominable place to live before the rains commenced again. Life as a scavenger in the Basurero was immeasurably more miserable during the six months of rain.

Despite this, some scavenger neighbors of the Ajcojoms were second-generation Basurero dwellers, with no anticipation — no desire, really — to leave the closely-knit community. And it was, indeed, a community: deeply caring of one another, as even Simona had been quick to admit. Neighbors could not have been more supportive during Laurita's losing struggle with life in such unhealthy surroundings. Every family there had sacrificed children to the Owner of the Basurero, the childless hag wandering the dump of nights whose foul-smelling breath could fell the healthiest of children who haplessly ventured forth too early or late of day.

The community was several decades old and well organized, with a leadership council that decided not only who lived and scavenged in the dump but where newcomers could freely scavenge for food and fuel for cooking and heating. Beyond these necessities, the rights to the saleable recyclables — principally clothing, furniture and repairable appliances, boards, cardboard, metal, glass and increasingly the new plastic containers — were also assigned to members. The Ajcojoms had been permitted to collect and sell during their initial six months only plastics, wood boards and cardboard, graduating recently to metal and glass. But everyone's dream — fed by oft-repeated stories of good luck — was to happen upon a valuable item that had been thrown out probably by mistake: jewelry, keepsakes, even money that had been stored away in something that then by accident had been discarded. The only way to leave the Basurero for a markedly more secure existence was luck such as this, or in happening upon someone's government-issued identity card with which to forge a new identity in a country where the government treated citizens as possessions essential to identify. For Francisco, a new identification card would be worth far more than any other valuable he could hope to find in the dump. Actually, identification cards did on occasion show up in the clothing of corpses — mostly murder victims. But with President Ubico's military intelligence most likely responsible for such disappearances, the risk of being found out if assuming any such identity was much too great. Even the use of his own identification card in seeking Guatemala City employment was too great a risk to take. After all, Max Ramirez was a graduate of the National Military Academy and now a career soldier with access to all the intelligence resources of General Ubico's army.

Ironically — sadly — it turned out to be Laurita's death that provided finally a ray of hope for securing his new identity card before the seasonal rains returned. For in death Laurita had moved only a stone's throw away. She had moved to an above-ground vault on the uppermost and least expensive row of burial crypts on the perimeter wall of the City of the Living Dead. With the intervention of Gabriel, one of the cemetery's caretakers whom Simona had gotten to know in the course of her periodic walks around the cemetery to escape the drudgery of the Basurero, a location had been secured for Laurita at the rear of the cemetery directly behind her parents' cave dwelling. Gabriel surreptitiously had removed and disposed of the remains from an ages-old crypt no longer endowed for perpetual care. And in so doing he also had promised Simona that — as long as he was living and employed at the cemetery — no annual payment would be required for the favor. With that decision to keep Laurita as close by as possible, Francisco had accustomed himself to Simona's even more frequent visits to the cemetery to replace the bouquet of flowers she endeavored to keep fresh below Laurita's new home. The cemetery's green grass and flowering bushes and trees, together with the countless bouquets of freshly cut flowers, had become her salvation: a heavenly denial of the dump's unrelenting reminder of hopelessness and decay.

Early on in the Ajcojom's sojourn in the Basurero, Simona had learned from Gabriel that a corpse occasionally was delivered without an accompanying relative but with the deceased's identification card still in his clothing. A lucrative business had evolved among the cemetery's cadre of caretakers of selling these cards to the likes of Francisco, if buyers had but the patience and resources to wait their turn.

Unbeknownst to Francisco, over these intervening months Gabriel had taken a liking to Simona that was not altogether unwelcome. Gabriel had offered to forgive the cost and to move Francisco's name ahead of others on the waiting list for new identity if Simona would but accept his making love to her in his guardian's shack as opportunity permitted. He never had married, she assumed in large part because of his large, unsightly goiter — the not-uncommon consequence of iodine deficiency in the diet of the poor. Simona since childhood also had endured a small goiter, barely noticeable but inclining her to sympathize with those similarly afflicted. While appreciating Gabriel's friendship, and especially his kindnesses to Laurita who usually had accompanied her on her cemetery outings, the idea of such intimacy with the man had repulsed Simona quite completely. But with Laurita's death and Simona's desperation to avoid the upcoming rainy season in the Basurero, she finally had agreed to Gabriel's offer. It might be the only way to get away from the dump. She had let him have her on a weekly basis for the past month.

"With this drizzle so early in the day, scavenging won't make much sense today," observed Simona nonchalantly. "— Isn't it about time for you to go with me again to visit our Laurita?" It had been a week since Gabriel's report that an identification card finally had appeared of a fellow with a Ladino name who was close to Francisco's age. More than likely the photo was old and faded enough to permit Francisco its successful use. Gabriel wanted to have a look at Francisco before turning it over to him, if Simona could persuade him to come to the cemetery.

Francisco reluctantly agreed, despite his growing distain for the cemetery's quarter-mile square of named avenues and streets lined with numbered domiciles housing generations of Guatemala's most visible families. As their owners had enjoyed in life, the dwellings often were multi-storied and fully furnished, segregated not only by wealth and social standing but by origin: a German avenue of neatly lined, identical domiciles standing at stiff attention; and an Asian neighborhood of individualistic, architecturally oriental homes of imposing grandeur. Massive mausoleums characterized families of Guatemala's government and military. The most naturalistic, grotto-like, of these huge tombs belonged to the family of 19th century President Rufino Barrios. Francisco had reminded Simona on their first walk around the cemetery that it was the death of Rufino Barrios in 1885, during an unsuccessful war to create a single nation of the small Central American countries, that had prompted Francisco's father's namesake, Father Rodolfo Luis Aragon de Leon, to expose to Indians the predatory intentions of Ladino coffee-growers. With his resultant martyrdom and his fellow foreign priests' expulsion soon thereafter from the country, the priest's worst fears had soon been realized: the land and labor of defenseless Indians inexorably had become Ladino property. Francisco's recurring anger whenever passing that grandiose mausoleum — en route to Laurita's nondescript and anonymous resting place at the rear of the cemetery — had become his excuse for so seldom accompanying Simona on her faithful weekly visits.

Francisco's father had bequeathed to Laurita, on the eve of Simona and Francisco's eloping to Guatemala City, a good-luck charm that Rodolfo Luis's grandfather had carved for him when he was almost exactly Laurita's age. It was a necklace likeness of the giant fish in Lake Atitlan that Rodolfo Luis regularly had encountered as a child when fishing — the fish that the family concluded must timelessly be the guardian spirit of first the martyred priest Father Rodolfo Luis Aragon de Leon, then of Rodolfo Luis Ajcojom, and who knows of whom else within the Ajcojom family. Would that circumstances had permitted the family to remain together at the lake where the fish's spirit obviously had chosen to remain. For it was painfully apparent to Francisco that in the city's Basurero their Laurita had received no blessing from his father's necklace charm.

Simona, however, over the course of her deepening relationship with Gabriel had come to see the events surrounding her daughter's death as providen-

236

tial beyond their human capacity to comprehend. Perhaps the guardianship bequeathed by Rodolfo Luis remained with them after all — but with Francisco, rather than with the daughter of Francisco's wife as Rodolfo Luis had intended. As a consequence of Laurita's death and Gabriel's assistance — despite the sacrifice of her shame — Francisco would now be blessed with a new identity for the challenges of life among Ladinos in the nation's frightening capital city. Or so she afterwards explained to her bewildered husband her impulsive kiss of gratitude to Gabriel for arranging the 'gift' of the identity card of one Jaime Andrade, a rather Indian-looking Ladino of about Francisco's age, born in Totonicapan in the far west of Guatemala.

"But I don't see much resemblance," complained Francisco back in their shack, "— Jaime has a pretty obvious scar down his cheek and a much more jutting chin."

"Well, I agree that you're a lot more handsome! But the photo is old and worn. You surely will get by if you grow a beard to hide the scar and your more retreating chin. Just be thankful that Jaime came from so far away, with no suggestion of ancestry around Lake Atitlan. I've never heard of the Andrade surname."

" I reckon that Jaime Andrade is as clearly a Ladino name as I could hope for. I'll give it a try anyway. We've got to get busy inventing our Totonicapan history, yours as well as Jaime's, memorizing the details to make sure that we tell everybody the same story once we move out of this place. And we should start getting used to your calling me Jaime. It seems to me that you can keep your name and same family history...no need for you to pass as a Ladina. But your roots should also be out west near Totonicapan."

"That's a relief. My challenge will be less calling you Jaime than getting used to making love with him, with all I've heard about the many ways that Ladinos do it! Can we start practicing as soon as we get home?"

Francisco gave her a rueful smile. "From the ease with which you kissed that fellow — on the lips no less! — I'd say you'll have no difficulty whatsoever with that."

With a twinge of remorse for all that her husband should never know, Simona gave him a forceful kiss and said no more. Actually, the cemetery's caretaker had turned out to be a gentle, albeit novice lover. She believed that he had meant it when he told her that he could very easily fall deeply in love with her. A more comely woman he could not imagine having had the privilege of knowing in this way — blemish free in all respects, and pleasantly plump in the right places with delightfully dimpled cheeks and even a neck that blushed when aroused! Had Gabriel ever suspected that she, also, suffered mildly from lack of iodine, he never had mentioned it. He had asked whether they might continue to see each other until Francisco found work elsewhere. She had said that she honestly didn't know, that it was too soon to know. As for Gabriel's plans, he had no expectation of ever changing jobs. Accordingly, if ever she needed help in any way after moving away from the Basurero, she would know where to find him. And not to worry about her daughter's care...Laurita never would be without flowers to look down upon as long as Gabriel remained alive.

With a tear in her eye, Simona had thanked him for this, saying that she hardly would be forgetting him. He was, after all, the only 'Gabriel' she had known and in his spirit worthy of an angel's name. This, despite his having taken advantage of her desperation during the darkest period of her life. He deserved to know that it had been difficult, but that she finally had forgiven him that. Her dignity deserved that she tell him so. The Basurero had reduced her to a shell of the woman she had considered herself to be back in Panajachel. But she would not let Guatemala City deprive her of her dignity.

Pronunication Guide for Kaqchikel

Consensus (more or less) only recently has been achieved among Mayas on the English letters to use in most closely approximating sounds used in the Mayan languages such as Kaqchikel. But since even in English some consonates have multiple pronunciations, depending on context, the following aids are offered to pronouncing the following words. The letter 'j' is pronounced 'ha' in the name Panajachel (Pa-na-ha-chel) and 'ho' in the word for shaman or curer, zajorin (za-ho-rin), and the final syllable of the surname Ajcojom. But the 'j' in the first syllable of the latter is pronounced 'ak': (Ak-ca-hom). There is a Mayan sound half way between ch and sh that usually is glossed in English as 'x,' as in Xingo (Shin-go), but in other contexts can be as accurately approximated by 'ch,' as in either Chocomil or Xocomil (wind).

If reading these novels aloud, inclusion of accent marks for both Spanish and Kaqchikel would help immeasurably in correct pronunciation, since Spanish generally accents next to last syllables while Mayan languages accent final syllables quite consistently. Use of accent marks would signal when these rules do not apply. But for ease of reading in English (unless also a reader/speaker of Spanish), I have judged accent marks to be more a nuisance than an aid.

Spanish Glossary

Alcalde.	Mayor of a municipality.
Alcaldia.	The civil officials of a municipality; also the building housing these officials.
Cafetal.	A grove of coffee trees.
Canicula.	The short dry period, usually late August between the almost daily rains of June and July and the even heavier precipitation of September into November.
Centavo.	A penny, one-hundredth of a peso.
Characotel.	Person believed to assume animal form periodically by virtue of having a spirit with an animal affiliation; also the animal itself.
Chicha.	A fermented drink made of brown sugar and a variety of Spanish plums.
Chichicaste.	A stinging nettle, sometimes planted in fencerows.
Cofradia.	A group of men (cofrade and several ranked mayordomos) and their wives, responsible for the care of and fiestas for a community-owned saint for a year; also the house or room where the saint is housed.
Comadre.	Term of respect (co-mother) used in addressing the godmother of one's child or the mother of one's godchild.
Comadrona.	Midwife.
Compadre.	Term of respect (co-father) used in addressing the godfather of one's child or the father of one's godchild. Also used in addressing spirits of the neighborhood.
Copal.	Pine resin incense.
Corte.	A wrap-around skirt.
Costumbre.	Literally, the custom; also any ritual performed by a curer or diviner (zahorin).
Gaban.	A brown woolen tunic worn formerly by men in Panajachel.
Huipil.	Handwoven blouse, sometimes with embroidery added.
Indio.	Literally 'Indian' but used by Ladinos — along with Indito — with derogatory and condescending connotations respectively. Indigena, the Spanish for 'indigenous person,' was the politically correct label for 'Indian' in governmental and academic parlance

throughout most of the 20th century, with Maya (noun)/Mayan (adjective) gaining in popularity among educated Mayas and Ladinos alike. However, 'Indian' continues to be the most common and neutral English translation for all Spanish terms referring to indigenous Guatemalans. For purposes of the novels, Indian is used interchangeably with Maya and natural.

Kaqchikel. One of the twenty-one Mayan languages/dialects spoken in Guatemala, and the one most common in the vicinity of Guatemala City.

Lengua. Literally 'tongue,' the term most frequently used by indigenous language speakers to refer to their own Mayan (i.e., 'natural') language.

Milpa. Cornfield, in which at least maize, pole beans, and squash typically are grown.

Natural. Literally a 'natural person,' used by Mayas to refer to themselves in the same way that lengua, 'natural language,' is the common referent to their native language.

Nixtamal. Ground corn mixed with water preparatory to making tortillas.

Patron. An employer, or benefactor; also used to refer to the community's principal saint.

Peso. A unit of old currency, equal to two U.S. cents by 1940.

Pulique. Ceremonial meat dish of pork, beef, or fowl in a sauce.

Regidor. Councilman; a ranked office in the alcaldia system.

Rodillera. A small, black and white checked woolen blanket worn by men, wrapped around the waist extending to the knees, and secured with a sash or belt.

Sacristan. An official of the church assisting the priest.

Secreto. Secret knowledge, such as a magical safeguard or cure, thought to be more efficacious if not widely known.

Taba. A game of heads and tails, using a bone.

Tablon. A raised narrow garden bed, separated from others by an irrigation ditch.

Totoposte. A large, toasted tortilla of corn and bean dough for multi-day consumption.

Traje. All native dress, as opposed to western dress used by Ladinos.

Tumpline.   A carrying apparatus of headband and attached rope supporting cargo.

Ulumina.   A species of fingerling fish caught in traps.

Zahorin.   A Maya (male) curer, diviner, or sorcerer; a shaman.

ROBERT E. HINSHAW

Robert Hinshaw is a native of Kansas, born in 1933.
He embarked upon doctoral study at the University
of Chicago in 1961 following a B.A. in philosophy at
Haverford College (Pennsylvania) and six years of teaching
and directing Olney Friends School (Ohio). In 1966 he
joined the department of Anthropology at the University
of Kansas, spending one year as visiting professor in
Guatemala's national University of San Carlos before
assuming the presidency of Wilmington College (Ohio)
1970-75. Thereafter he chaired anthropology departments
at Beloit College (Wisconsin) and the University of
Colorado-Denver before retiring from academe to write
in Colorado's mountains, on Guatemala's Lake Atitlán,
and at home in Kansas City, MO. His 2006 biography
of geographer Gilbert White led to membership in the
Society of Midland Authors.

Jacket design by Elisabeth Nord

Printed by James Printing, *Kansas City, Missouri, USA*

Published by